PELLEGRINO

Titles by Cait Logan

NIGHT FIRE
TAME THE FURY
WILD DAWN

DELILAH

CAIT LOGAN

J

JOVE BOOKS, NEW YORK

DELILAH

A Jove Book / published by arrangement with
the author

PRINTING HISTORY
Jove edition / March 1995

ISBN: 0-515-11565-7

A JOVE BOOK®
Jove Books are published by The Berkley Publishing Group,
200 Madison Avenue, New York, New York 10016.
JOVE and the "J" design are trademarks
belonging to Jove Publications, Inc.

PRINTED IN THE UNITED STATES OF AMERICA

10 9 8 7 6 5 4 3 2 1

Prologue

✦─◦◦◦─✦

WASHINGTON TERRITORY,
MARCH 1884

"We're wiped out," Delilah
Smith muttered to herself. She slashed her coat sleeve across
her face. Despite the cold day, her cheeks were damp with
sweat. Or was it tears?

She closed her eyes and remembered the sound of her rifle
bullets smashing into the dying cattle, easing their slow deaths.
She ran her coat sleeve across her face again and faced her
task. Her muscles screamed with pain as she bent to pull
and slash away the hide from the cow's thawing carcass. She
looked down the stand of trees, the bark peeled away by
her starving herd before they died in the fierce winter storm.
Thirty-seven more carcasses, mottled hides glistening with
melted snow, waited to be peeled of their hides. A stack of
twenty-three hides stood like a burial monument over her lost
dreams.

We've come so far, she thought desperately, her chest tight with pain. The wind swayed the mountain pines, echoing the whispers of the past that she barely kept at bay.

Somehow the past always came knocking when hard times were near. . . .

The hairs at the back of her neck tightened and she arched her neck to one side. The long braid she had tucked inside her coat shifted and the slight pain eased.

She'd inherited the Millennium gold mine, a worthless dugout hole. A year ago she'd sold the mine to buy livestock. Now she and her brother were squatters, keeping their land by never leaving it. In the middle of Indian land they had tended their cattle and minded their business; they prayed that Chief Joseph's surrender would keep peace.

A crack sliced into the harsh mountain air and Delilah paused. She instantly regretted her anger; it had torn the hide in her hands. Then, inhaling slowly, patiently, she began methodically slicing and pulling the mottled hide away from another carcass. It was Hope, a gentle strong cow, her markings showing her Spanish blood. She was one of the strong ones herded up from Yakima country. She'd swum the wide, powerful Columbia River, following the calf that had been ferried across. She'd had another fine calf in early summer and always nudged Delilah playfully. . . . "Hope, I am so sorry," Delilah whispered. Her thoughts slid along the wind and into the mountain's tall pine trees.

Flower's hide lay on the stack that would be sold to leather makers; the morning sun tinted the thawing blood to the shade of rubies. Traded from a rancher north of the Canadian border, the cow was mean enough to ford rivers, leading the herd into the jutting mountains with a toss of her horns. Flower had come across the high, dangerous Snoqualmie Pass in the Cascade Mountains, then Lady . . . Pokey. . . .

Delilah's hands were stiff. Blood from her palms soaked the cloth she had hastily wrapped around them before pulling on her gloves.

Her younger brother pried away another carcass from the frozen herd, taking care not to tear hides that could be traded. Delilah swallowed when Richard's gloved hand swept lovingly across the young bull's head. The calf was Richard's pet.

He had traded a prime beaver pelt for the sickly calf, then hand-fed and nurtured it until it romped across the mountain meadows.

The "cow-killer" winter had wiped out the herds of the cattlemen in the Okanogan country. Now everyone battled to salvage hides for leather makers. The chinook, a warm wind blowing up from the south, washed against Delilah's face and cooled her tears.

Richard looked up then, his face twisted with agony and fatigue. "Wipe your face . . . it's bloody from the hides," he said quietly, his voice unsteady in the wind.

"We're wiped out," she repeated hollowly, forcing herself to straighten as pain smashed into her muscles and bones and ripped through her heart. She lifted her face to the sun. At twenty-six she felt very old, as if she had lived forever.

Richard paused, his young face gaunt beneath the shadow of his hat. He bent to skin the carcass of his pet bull. "Wolves are circling. We'll have to stay the night."

"We'll take turns on lookout. Tallulah said she'd bring grub later." Delilah swallowed unsteadily, thinking of the older woman who was a lifetime friend. Tallulah's arthritis needed the dry warmth of the cabin, and her dimming eyesight prevented her from traveling without help.

He glanced up, attempting a grin that failed. "Just don't offer me beef for supper. I'll eat canned peaches. . . . Oh, damn. I just cut off the tip of my little finger!"

In the Smith cabin Tallulah stared at the candle's flame and thought of the dancers called the Hurdy Gurdy girls. She had traveled from Germany to San Francisco, then donned a Hurdy Gurdy costume and danced with gold miners.

Over twenty years ago they dressed in plumed headpieces and red dresses and danced with the miners. Tallulah mulled the tobacco tucked into her bottom lip, thinking of the rollicking dance—the best dancer was the man to hold a "Hurdy" girl in the air for the longest.

Canada's Barkerville. Rowdy, rich gold strikes, Chinese scurrying in their section of town. Then the Hurdy Gurdy girls and the music—they were dancers, she thought proudly, not soiled doves. They danced, working hard for their living. Tallulah closed her eyes, remembering Delilah's mother.

She arrived in the driving rain of a summer evening, sitting atop a pack mule and holding a seven-year-old girl in front of her. A brown-eyed, dusky-skinned ten-year-old boy sat behind her, his arms wrapped tightly around her waist.

They were shabby and dirty, but sitting on the mule with the summer rain glistening like a halo around them; it was a sight that Tallulah would remember forever. The woman was slight, beautiful, and terrified as the men gathered around her. A slender pale hand protectively pulled the dark shawl closer to her throat. The packer who had brought her had cracked his bullwhip above the heads of the men. . . . Tallulah breathed harshly, remembering the scene of almost twenty years ago.

As they watched the beautiful woman, wolfish leers split several of the men's dirty faces; however, most of the men were in awe, pressing nearer, taking off their hats, and worshipping her with their eyes. A white woman was precious and revered, yet without a protector, many would consider her "up for grabs." A man held up a fat poke, a leather-wrapped pouch, and another scowled darkly, punching him in the face. "Anyone can see she ain't that kind."

The girl gathered her baby tighter against her and spoke firmly to the boy. He huddled against her, trying to conceal his fear. The young woman had proud ways, a queenly lift to her chin.

In the shadows of the general store's porch, a pimp picked his teeth with a gold toothpick and eyed the woman like a cow on the auction block. A hard-eyed madam looked him up and down before she sashayed to another corner of the porch to call out to the mule packer.

Later Tallulah would wonder why she pushed through the men, cajoling, using her bulk to get near the girl. When Tallulah had lifted her arms, the woman eased her daughter down into them. The frail, frightened girl's solemn, wide blue eyes stared up at Tallulah and captured her heart.

A man had gently helped the woman down, treating her like a queen and bowing clumsily. She smiled in thanks and a wave of sighs escaped the lonely men. Then she turned and touched her son's leg, urging him down.

Haunting sky-blue eyes framed by black lashes dominated the pale oval of the woman's face. She looked younger than twenty, but a sadness clung to her like an old woman who had seen too much. "Someone stole my poke. My children are tired and hungry," she said quietly above the murmur of the men who were pressing close.

"I have a room," Tallulah had said in her best broken English. "You and the children are welcome. I am Tallulah."

She had omitted her family name from the old country. In San Francisco she had discovered it was better not to reveal too much of her life.

The boy shivered, his glossy straight black hair shining with rain; the woman rested her hand on his thin shoulder. She tested Tallulah's name, then said, "Call me Delilah. Delilah Smith. This is my son, Koby, and my daughter—Delilah. I named her after me so's everybody would know she's mine."

"One look at her eyes, and they will know," Tallulah had said quietly.

The woman smiled then, a true warmth that came from deep inside to warm Tallulah. "The room sounds good. My young'uns need a dry place."

The echo slid from the past—*"Call me Delilah."*

Tallulah sighed, her years weighing upon her bones. She'd met Delilah's mother in another land over twenty years before, and so it began. The older woman had seen the family ripped apart and the daughter struggle and survive; she'd brought the three of them—Richard, Tallulah, and herself—safely to a new, sprawling land.

Now a cow-killer winter threatened to separate the girl from her youngest brother. Delilah, the daughter, was to know more pain and Tallulah ached for her.

Chapter One

———◆———

                 "I don't want you to go," Delilah stated three days later. "We've cauterized your finger, but what if infection sets in?" Her throat tightened with fear. She placed her hand over her rapidly beating heart; her other hand clenched her tin drinking cup. "You go into Canada—up the Cariboo Trail, up to Barkerville—that's over six hundred miles north of here, and most of it is pure hell. If the cliffs and snow and Fraser River don't kill you, there are men along the way—"

    She shuddered, gripping Richard's unbandaged hand tightly. "Something bad will happen. I feel it."

    Richard's blue eyes darkened. "I was a kid four years ago when you brought Tallulah and me down from Barkerville. But I'm seventeen now and I'm a man. That means you can't make up my mind for me this time, Sis. I'm leaving before dawn," Richard stated tightly, pushing away the bowl of peaches he had been eating. He stared at the last beef-tallow candle. The rest of the tallow had been mixed with flour and whatever leaves they could scrape from under the snow to feed the starving cattle. "I'll never forget how the cows bellowed, standing out there in the night. . . . I couldn't shoot them, and when you did, I remember your face—like your dreams had died. Now the cows are gone, along with the last of our grubstake money."

He paused, held the bandage on his little finger, and looked at his sister. "I'll never forget it, Delilah. You did what I couldn't. You've always done more than what should be asked of you. Now we need money, and I know how to get it. Morton's gew-gaws—rings and nuggets—are rightly yours. . . . You married that bully. Now he's dead, and as his wife, that jewelry is yours. If the bag is still there under the old Morton house flooring near Barkerville, I'll bring it back. You said yourself that the jewels and nuggets would bring a pretty penny."

Delilah's cold, trembling fingers tightened, cradling her tin coffee cup. Her eyes moved to the cabin's shadows and anoth-er woman who was dressed like her in a man's work shirt, trousers, and boots. "Tallulah, say something."

"I would be wasting breath. Look at him, your brother. He is biting at the bit, wanting adventure. It's in his eyes. He will go." Tallulah, a tall blocky woman of sixty, sat down at the log cabin's rough-hewn table. She adjusted her bulk on the squeaking block with four legs that served as a chair. She dipped her fingers into a small snuff pot, tucked the tobacco inside her bottom lip, mulled it, and studied the two young people.

They bore their mother's aristocratic features and striking coloring—black glossy hair and brilliant blue eyes. Delilah was taller and leaner than her mother had been and, though the young woman denied it, she was just as striking—a haunting beauty with a smile that wasn't easily forgotten.

Tallulah stopped mulling the tobacco.

The girl seated at the table never smiled. She had survived, leaving a part of her heart in the past and the rest of it too scarred to feel.

Now her brother wanted to strike out, to prove his manhood, just as all young men wanted to do. Life was a cycle after all.

Delilah worried about her brother, just as Tallulah's mother had worried about her many years ago. Delilah would not heed the warnings when she swept out of Barkerville, determined to make a new life, nor would Richard. The boy was hungry for adventure. The young always were.

Tallulah heard a noise in the distance and looked at young Delilah's dark scowl over the candle's flame. She was stunning, with hair rich and raven, trapped tightly in a thick braid that swung to her waist. But while a smile had always lurked on her mother's lips, the girl's were tight and grim. Now she dressed in loose trousers and shirts, though once she'd worn drab dresses and petticoats.

At twenty-six young Delilah had already seen too much. She'd fought and survived the horror of three lifetimes. Tallulah had seen it all, and now the girl would lose once more.

Terror flickered through Delilah's eyes as they met Richard's. "Don't do this," Delilah whispered, the warm chinook wind howling around the small log cabin. "I've lost one brother up there. I can't go through that again. We can manage. We've always managed."

Delilah frowned at Tallulah and demanded, "If he won't listen to me, make him listen to you. Tell him to stay."

"She knows I'm going," Richard said firmly and rose to his feet. "I can be back by fall. You just hang on, Delilah." He bent to kiss her cold cheek. "Hang on and I'll be back."

She caught his rawboned wrist, her fingers digging in. "I'll come with you."

"You can't, Delilah," he whispered softly. "We've been squatting. If both of us leave, we'll lose everything."

"Then we'll get another place."

"Hell, it took everything and more to get what we have now." Richard's voice softened. "Look, Sis. I've talked to my friend Meryl. His dad was a bullwhacker, a freighter in the old days. Once he took packhorses up that old fur brigade trail—the Okanogan Trail north to the Cariboo Trail, across the Canadian border, and up into the gold fields. By taking an extra horse and traveling hard, I can be back before first snow. . . ."

Delilah's short nails clawed once at the rough table as she stared at the wall. A tremor moved across her lips before she tightened them. After a moment Richard patted her shoulder. "Reckon I've got a few things to do before tomorrow," he said. With a worried glance at Tallulah, he left the cabin.

Delilah stood facing the closed door and whispered, "We'll send him everything we can, Tallulah. There's the money from the hides. . . . He needs the buttons on his coat tightened, and that old buffalo robe is warm. There's dried berries and plenty of jerked beef . . . and he'll take our rifle, and his father's fancy little gun, and the horseshoe stickpin for luck."

She turned to look at the older woman, and their eyes exchanged the pain they both felt. Delilah reached for Richard's saddle and oil and placed them on the table. After a moment's hesitation, she began oiling the leather. "If he's going to be bullheaded, we may as well help him. Tallulah, start patching his clothes. We'll brew the last of the coffee tomorrow morning so he'll start off with a warm belly. First thing in the morning I'll melt the candle on some scraps of cloth so he'll have campfire makings. . . ."

The women worked quietly, each circling her thoughts while the fire crackled in the rock fireplace.

Tallulah patched the boy's clothing and thought of the girl's mother lying on her deathbed. Long strands of hair spread across the white pillowcase like an ebony river glistening in the lamplight. Deathly shadows lay upon her face as she whispered. Tallulah had bent nearer, holding the cold hands. . . . "Promise, Tallulah . . . my little girl . . . She's only eleven and she's frightened. She's angry with me for leaving her. . . . When it's time . . . when she'll understand . . . when she's a woman in love, give her my journals. . . . See that she marries a good man to protect her, and tell her to act like a queen . . . never forget that she is someone who is good and clean and sweet . . . that she must be strong for Richard . . . that Koby . . . how I love them all. . . . Tell them I love them. . . . I gave Delilah my name because that was all I had to give her. . . ."

The pale elegant fingers had tightened once before life had slipped away.

Koby. Tallulah drew the back of her hand across her damp lids, and tears dimmed her view. She pricked her finger and sucked it. Delilah had been only eight when Koby was taken by a crazed Russian miner wanting a strong son. She wouldn't eat for weeks, pining and hunting for her older brother.

Koby. Half Indian, half white, Koby was eleven when he was taken. The two Delilahs—mother and daughter—had watched every rider into town, stopped and stared at every black-haired boy. While the girl's heartbreaking sobs echoed through the small cabin, the mother's eyes were dry and bleak. Oh, she smiled when she worked with the Hurdys, dancing to the rip-roaring music and giving the men a bit of happiness—but her heart ached. . . .

Three children by three fathers, all loved deeply by their mother, who had fought, clawing for survival. . . . Delilah . . . Lady Delilah, the miners called her, because of her elegant manners and sweet, sad smile.

Tallulah watched Delilah's pale, grim face. Firelight skimmed a blue sheen along her midnight-black hair and caressed the eloquent, tight purse of her lips.

When it was time, when Delilah would understand her mother's hard life, the journals were waiting—*"I gave Delilah my name because that's all I had to give her. . . ."*

When Richard rode away the next morning, dawn spread a delicate pink over the melting snow. He turned once to wave before the tall pines swallowed him. The packhorse whinnied, and then the mountains were quiet.

Tallulah tucked Delilah's shawl around her as they stood, the chinook wind tugging at their skirts. "He's so young. He's just a boy," Delilah said finally, her face pale and taut.

"He has been a man for years. You've been so busy trying to keep body and soul together and taking care of us that you didn't notice. He's got his papa's old longarm and little gun and that lucky horseshoe stickpin. Come inside, Delilah," Tallulah murmured, wrapping her arm around the girl's thin shoulders.

"He's silly and young. He asked for a lock of my hair to carry with him. Of course I gave him one . . . it was little enough to do for someone flying off with half a brain. . . . Oh, leave me be," Delilah whispered softly, squaring her shoulders and staring at the snow-covered mountains. "Please."

"Liebling," Tallulah returned sadly, recognizing the girl's withdrawal as her memories swirled around her. "When you are ready, come inside where it is warm. Richard is doing what he must do."

Delilah fought the burning tears, the emotion wadding her throat. "Go ahead."

Richard . . . Richard . . . Oh, God, please keep him safe. . . . She hadn't cried in years; she wouldn't cry now. Delilah straightened her shoulders and gathered the woolen shawl closer to her. She nuzzled the cloth that had been her mother's. *Oh, Mama. Mama, what have I done? I never should have told him about the jewelry or the nuggets . . . never. . . . Oh, Mama . . . he's all I've got left of you. . . .*

That night Delilah lay with her fists pressed tightly against her side. She watched the firelight dancing on the wooden rafters and felt the cold fingers of the past wrap around her.

"Marry a good man, honey," her mother had pleaded on her deathbed. *"Marry a man with money so he can give you a proper home. . . . "* It was a familiar theme, one she had heard throughout her childhood.

"Act like a lady. Sit straight and always speak softly. Be pretty and sweet and marry a good man . . . one with breeding and a good family name."

So she had married Ezrah Morton. She had been so certain about him—

"You don't know who your father was. Your mother was a dirty whore, Delilah!" Ezrah screamed from the past. *"What did she use to barter her way all the way here . . . up from the Oregon Trail? There were men who swore they had her— an army of men . . . even an Indian 'cause she had a half-breed brat—Koby. So she was a lady now, eh? She danced— 'Terpsichorean Arts'—with the Hurdys, eh? Oh, right. The Hurdy Gurdys weren't tarts, were they? But your mother wasn't one of them because she was a dirty whore, eh?"* Delilah pushed away echoes of Ezrah's taunts, his rough handling. She'd tossed away his name and taken back Smith to wipe out memories of him.

Stories about her mother's wild life were embedded deep in her memory. As a child, the other children held her to the mud and with charcoal wrote *W* on her forehead, branding her as a child of a whore. Long after her mother's death, when Delilah began to bud, men watched her, wanting her and not concealing their desire. The kindly Mortons, Ezrah's parents, protected and loved her and Richard. It was naturally assumed that she should marry Ezrah.

But once they were married and his parents died, Ezrah could not spare her the tiniest kindness—

Her stomach contracted painfully. She pushed her fist against it and turned on her side to the cabin wall. She bit her lip and pulled the heavy quilt to her mouth to muffle a sob. Her family wouldn't hear her cry; they never did. *Koby . . . Where are you, Koby? Mama?*

She curled into a ball and forced her mind to go blank. She was skilled at that; experience had been a good teacher. She knew she had to sleep, just as she knew she had to survive.

Chapter
Two

At dusk Delilah jerked off her gloves as she passed the familiar sight of a miner's pack hanging outside the cabin door. High-grade silver had been discovered the year before on Ruby Mountain and Peacock Hill, and a mining district was created. Miners were flooding into the country by the hundreds. Small, wild boomtowns had sprung up, and money flowed like a silver river through the hands of gamblers and shopkeepers.

Delilah had seen enough of boomtowns in her life, but she loved the mountains and the lush meadows. When the silver rush died, the land would still be there, filled with sage and pine. She was twenty-nine now, and all she wanted was her brother, a measure of peace, and enough money to care for her loved ones.

She'd claimed her "four forties"—one hundred and sixty acres of homestead land—the year before. Stripling fruit trees from Okanogan Smith's farm lay in rows a small distance from the house.

Hiram "Okanogan" Smith had left his mark on the new land, bringing the first fruit trees, cattle, and starting the hard-rock mining business. Delilah liked having her trees descended from the stock of the legendary, colorful pioneer, rooting them in her soil.

Delilah looked at the mountain shadowing her cabin. When she could afford wood from the sawmill, and the labor, she'd build a water flume from a high rocky ridge down to her orchard.

Delilah stood still, caught in the chilly late afternoon. Mountain shadows slid over the pines and tinted the remaining snow blue. This was her home . . . hers and Richard's and Tallulah's. Artissima Parker, a southern woman hit by hard times and staying with them now, would be moving on when it was time.

Delilah inhaled the sweet, pine-scented air. She'd built her pride from nothing and a few salted hides. She'd put in grueling days laboring with sagebrush, stumps, rocks, and livestock. After dark she'd worked with pencil and paper to make every penny count. Working in the Mortons' store, she had developed a skill that she used now—calculating. Somehow she could look at a column of figures and the answer jumped out at her. She'd calculated hours and days to barter and buy her herd and every improvement on the homestead. She knew values and losses, and she did not intend to lose. Ever.

Just last night she had added another small medicine jar of coins and nuggets under the cabin's flooring. The "hard time" money stayed hidden; she didn't want another moneyless winter like the one that had stripped them three years ago.

Miners passed Delilah's ranch, and for a fee they could feed their stock, take a bath, and spend the night in a clean bed. Though the men slept in a lean-to against the cabin, they enjoyed meals with the women. Tallulah washed clothes, dried them over the new cookstove, and mended. Artissima Parker's white bread and jams brought a fancy price; then there was jerked beef and cold coffee to send the men into the mines.

Miners stopped to watch blond, brown-eyed Artissima bake cakes on the stove they had hauled in in pieces. Her skirts swishing around the cabin, her songs and the wooden spoon beating batter reminded them of home.

Delilah listened to the miner's rumble inside the cabin and Artissima's soft lilting accent. Artissima Parker could charm the lowest "scum of mankind," and if she couldn't, she could beat him at cards. A pure lady of the South, Artissima had been stranded on the homestead, but not beaten. She'd taken one look at Delilah's barren cabin and said, "Lawsy me. You'd never know two women lived here—'course I know you're tangling with the land, trying to cut out a homestead, and there's no time for the gentler arts."

She'd scanned the cabin. "You need me to take care of you, honey. . . . What, no stove? Why, a lady always needs a proper stove."

Artissima had informed them that she would be staying for a few days and would pay her bed and board. After a week she admitted that the only way she could pay was with "Housewifery, of which I am proud to say, I do exceptionally well."

Delilah opened the cabin door and was immediately surrounded by the welcoming scents of dinner. Tallulah's broad smile warmed her as Delilah hung her hat on the peg and tucked her gloves into her coat pocket.

"Artissima, you've been with us a year, and every lovesick man in the territory knows where he can come to get his letters written and read," Delilah said when the grinning, outgoing miner closed the door behind him.

Artissima held up the coin and grinned. "Eee-yah!" she crowed. "I just love Yankee money. They just love my little sweetheart letter business. Poor souls. Some of them can't write, you know."

"Not everyone had time for schooling," Delilah reminded her, then wished she'd hadn't spoken so sharply.

Artissima smoothed the awkward moment, saying softly, "I have been very lucky in my fortunes. You just rest, honey. We've got a nice dinner waiting for you."

The two women faced each other, and something passed between them. They were sisters of bad fortune. Each had fought grimly to survive.

"You're right, Artissima. I am too tired. I apologize," Delilah said, stunned by the other woman's quick hug.

"Shush now. I'm a chatterbox and I know it."

"Mmm, maybe . . ." Delilah returned teasingly and Artissima grinned.

"If you don't watch out, girl, you'll let go and smile one day. Reckon you'd blind us all if you did."

"You shush now," Delilah tossed back, her face warming while Tallulah chuckled.

Artissima's smile slid away and she stroked a strand of Delilah's hair away from her temple. "Whoever punished you for being a beautiful woman should be horsewhipped, then tarred and feathered. I know the look. I've seen it in the wealthiest to the poorest families. It's a plain, dowdy look—hair pulled straight back until your eyes are almost squinty and loose, ugly clothes. I'll bet if you put on a dress, you'd have the beaus hopping around here."

Delilah quickly turned away from Artissima's close study and glanced at the empty shelf used for mail, praying for a letter from Richard. They weren't letters really, because Richard couldn't write. But the envelopes were marked with a big *D*, and the papers were filled with drawings and finished with a heart and an *R* that meant he was safe.

Delilah bit her lip, wishing desperately for a letter. She met Tallulah's worried gaze. "It's been over two years since we've heard from Richard."

"The boy will write," Tallulah said. "He is safe, *Liebling*. Sometimes boys forget when they see a woman. . . . He will write soon."

Delilah stared out of the window to the rough road, then to the mountains. "I want him to come home."

"He'll be home soon. You'll see. All he has to do is follow the beautiful letters Artissima writes for men. When she reads their sweetheart's letters to them, they wish for her and not their sweethearts, eh?" Tallulah referred to the river of men who passed each other as they traveled from the mining camps along the Cariboo Trail. They shared their lives around camp-fires and mile-houses and gossip traveled more quickly than newspapers. The men's lives were intertwined and Artissima's love-letter business was becoming famous. Several miners had

once you put this on, the beaus will hover around. I'm knitting you a cap to match."

When Delilah looked at her, Artissima grinned and said, "Lordy, girl, you don't say much, but your eyes are pure blue fire. Why, some day your fair love will come here and sweep you away from us"—she placed her hand on her bosom—"and I, lately of the South, will remain a spinster and a businesswoman till my dying day."

"Artissima, are you finished?" Delilah asked softly.

Artissima grinned, winked, and lifted another coin to the lantern light. "Corn pone tonight, Delilah. With sweet butter and buttermilk from Pansy."

The blond sausage curls at the back of her head bounced when she shook her head, studying the jar. "My, my. Doesn't money have a pretty little old shine to it. So romantic. Such a rich shade of gold. By the time next year comes, I'll have enough to buy me a house. A big house with pillars in the front, just like my daddy's house on the plantation. The South will rise again." She finished with a dramatic wave of her hand.

She hugged the jar to her starched blouse for a moment, then lifted it away to smooth the pristine material. "When Christmas comes I'm gonna wrap those big white pillars in green branches, just swirling them up to the top of the porch. I want a porch—a big one for rockers, so's the gentleman who will come calling for me can sit in the shade and sip his lemonade. 'Course I just want him for appearance's sake, you know. Like a pet."

She winked at Tallulah, who was shaking her head and muttering as she cleaned the rabbit and birds. "While he extols my heavenly beauty, of course. Delilah, honey, you just wait. Your Prince Charming is coming, and he'll tease a pretty smile out of you yet."

Delilah lifted one slim, mocking black brow. "I thought you planned to remain a spinster until your dying day. I'm a widow, Artissima. I'm twenty-nine and not a young girl waiting for a magical kiss and for dreams to come true."

"I am. I'm waiting for my Prince Charming. He'll be a gentleman through and through. A courtly man with tender words and endearing little gallant kisses on my hand. And he'll have a bankroll that would choke a horse."

Artissima playfully jerked Delilah's waist-long braid. "You, you poor thing. You'll have to practice kissing the back of your hand before you can return a gentleman's proper kiss."

Her eyes lit up and she bent to take Delilah's hand and kissed the back gallantly. She frowned, dropping Delilah's hand and wrinkling her nose. "Honey, you smell of horse and leather," she stated flatly. "No man worth his salt will want to do much kissing of that hand."

Chapter Three

———————·❦·———————

Simon Oakes stared at the body, half covered by snow, and lying on the ice covering the small lake. He slowly drew his North West Mounted Police uniform gauntlets from his trembling hands, then tucked them in his belt. Sunlight caught in the frozen blood on the lake, the color as scarlet as his tunic. The March wind sent a flurry of snow against the body. Simon's lungs hurt, and he realized absently that he had not been breathing. His body was icy, his heartbeat paining his chest. . . . *Rand . . . oh, Rand, no . . . no . . .*

Simon slowly crouched to touch his dead brother's cold, sodden hair. Rand's wife and children would not be seeing him again.

The portly Irish constable crouched beside Rand's body. "The lake's ice is thawing. We'd better watch our step now, Sergeant. You recognize the deceased as your brother?"

Simon nodded. "Randall Angus Oakes. Married, thirty-nine,

father of three daughters and one infant son. His wife was worried when she didn't hear from him last Christmas. She summoned me at Fort Macleod, and I left immediately. Rand was building a cabin, and they were to join him this spring . . . after his latest baby was strong enough to make the trip. It's March now. They would be on their way."

The constable reached beneath Rand's buffalo-hide coat and worked the blood and ice until a cigarette butt came free. "My brother didn't smoke," Simon said. "Nor his partner."

"From the damage done to the body, sir—"

Simon glanced at the other man sprawled on the ice; his skull was crushed. "It happened before Christmas." He nodded to the small log cabin nestled in the pines near the lake. "They had decorated a tree in the cabin."

The constable inhaled, scanning the lake's ice and snow. "They were ice fishing. The line is still in his partner's hand. There's only one cigarette near him, while this chap—your brother—has several all around him. The tobacco is a fancy blend . . . fancy paper, too, what's left of it. The bodies are in remarkable shape. Must have been a blizzard immediately after their death . . . no animal markings around. There's no wounds on your brother. What do you suppose did him in?"

Simon eased away the weathered buffalo hide from the ice. "This."

The small gaping wound lay open to the bright sunshine. Simon pointed to icy beads of ruby-red blood. "A shot in his upper thigh. Small caliber and not serious if tended. But his hands were tied. He crawled a bit. Then he died."

The constable stared at Simon, then down at the cigarettes. He looked back at Simon. "The cigarettes were under the body. . . . The bastard shot him, ate his food, kept warm in his cabin, and watched him die."

Simon unsheathed his knife and eased the point under the bullet in Rand's wound. The lead fell to the ice, rolled a foot away, and lay rocking, gleaming in the bright sunlight.

The constable picked it up and studied it. "The lead is marked. I've seen these two markings before"—he used a pencil to point to small grooves in the lead—"in crimes done by one Mordacai Wells."

Fifteen miles north of the Washington Territory border, the manager of the way station leaned back against the barn's stall, peering through his pipe smoke to Simon. "You're a North West Mountie, eh?"

"I am on special assignment," Simon returned, taking off his buffalo-hide robe and tossing it across the stall boards. The special duty was his own: he had taken leave to find his brother's killer. A killer-youth and his gang had gone on a rampage in the vicinity and were seen by an Indian near Rand's cabin at Christmas.

Simon had approached a commissioner from the force who was on a tour in British Columbia and received special permission immediately. The commissioner had thoughtfully rolled the small murderous slug with his finger, then slashed his name across Simon's leave-of-absence papers. "Like you, Rand distinguished himself in the Riel Rebellion. He was a credit to the force. Take your leave, Simon. Keep in touch and find the bloody coward who killed a fine man, your brother. I will personally see that wages are paid to you in advance and a sum is added to finance your needs. I'm certain the force would want to contribute to the capture of Rand's murderer. The Blackfoot call the force *a-in-a-ka-quan,* or catchers, for good reason. Do the job and dig that murderer out . . . and my sympathy on the loss of Rand. I very much liked him."

While Simon had special papers to work within Canada, he was ordered to place his uniform aside if his search took him into United States territory. He turned to the manager of the roadhouse. "Have you heard about Mordacai Wells? Black hair, tall, and slender? Acts as though he's got some breeding? Around twenty?"

"Let me think on it. My missus takes to young boys like they were her own. If one passed through like your man, my Maggie will know. You'll be staying the night. This is the finest mile house along the Cariboo Trail. Of course, we don't do the business we did back twenty-five or so years, during the Cariboo Gold Rush. . . . Put up a tent and started serving food to miners. They slept in another tent. Now we've got this fine log establishment. That will be two dollars for the bed and meal. The bed might be a little short for a chap of your size—"

He scanned Simon's six-foot-four height. "And might be a bit narrow at the shoulder. But the feather tick is warm and clean, and the rest of the lodgers seem clean and well behaved. My wife's a fine cook, and I've got horses for trade if you want. . . . This one's played out."

He glanced at the covered holster, then at Simon's face. "I'd say, sir, that whoever this Mordacai Wells is, if he's the chap you want—he won't be happy to see you. You're big enough to take on a bear, eh?"

Simon took the good-natured tease easily, as he had been doing since he was a gangling teenager. "Right now I could eat one. You might inform your wife that I've been eating nothing but jerked meat and bannock bread crumbs for two days. I intend to eat my way through whatever she's got in the house . . . starting with a gallon of hot tea."

The man laughed outright. "My Maggie likes good eaters. She'll send you on your way with plenty of food. You're married, eh?"

"Couldn't find a woman who could keep me fed," Simon shot back easily and began stripping his saddle away from his horse. The gelding had been issued to Simon two years earlier; the sturdy horse had seen him through the métis' Riel Rebellion. Of English or French and Indian blood, the métis were discontent with authority and had set up a rebel government. Simon's older brother, Rand, had stayed with the Mounties through the bloody rebellion, then, after a ball shattered his shoulder, he left to ready a homestead for his family. "We're going to raise cattle and gardens and populate the countryside with wild Oakes brats," Rand had said with a big grin.

While the way station owner shoveled hay to his livestock, Simon glanced impatiently to the flakes of snow fluttering like small lace doilies. He jerked a pitchfork from its rack and began working beside the man; he needed the movement after hours in the saddle.

"You're from English stock? The name Oakes is usually English, eh?" the man asked. "Or French? I hear a bit of a Frenchie in your talk."

"I'll watch that. It creeps out when I'm tired," Simon said, thinking of his five brothers and sisters speaking in rapid French. Suzette used her hands too much and giggled wildly; Victoria acted like the queen for whom she had been named. Rand's booming laughter had drowned out Thane's and Vance's deep voices. . . . The Oakes family shared English and French blood, dark green eyes, and waving dark brown hair that tended to lighten with sun. Their mother and father called them "The Ruffians" and treated each one to a very special love. Echoes of their giggles and laughter wrapped around him. . . .

His brother's life had been ruthlessly taken by Wells. Rand's grave was covered with snow now, overlooking the sheer cliffs of the Fraser River. His grieving widow and four children had never been able to make the trip from Montreal; the farm they had planned would never be. . . .

Wrapped in the wanted poster for Wells, the bullet found in Rand's leg rested in the scarlet pocket of Simon's uniform. The distinctive marks on it resembled ones used in two other murders and bloody robberies. Two long scratches in the lead defined scarring of the gun barrel, two small burrs that dug into the bullet as it passed through the barrel; the small caliber was commonly used for derringers. Witnesses usually noted a man with black hair, a cold-blooded well-dressed youth with a stickpin shaped like a horseshoe. Every witness had noted a four-barreled Sharps derringer with pearl handles and a design etched in silver.

That night Simon lay in the small bed framed by boards. Six other men, all miners traveling southward to mine silver in Washington Territory lay in the other beds and on the floor.

The mile-house manager's wife did remember a well-behaved youth matching Wells's description. He'd passed through almost three years ago wearing a lucky horseshoe stickpin on his worn clothing. He was proud of his father's little derringer with its fancy pearl handles and etched, silver barrel.

The boy had been lonely, talking about his sister and their ranch near the Similkameen River. Maggie couldn't remember the boy's name exactly—"There were so many young lads off to seek their fortunes. His last name was short and common, I do remember that. Smith, I think it was." She remembered almost everything the boy had said: He'd mentioned mining and orchards. Maggie had heard of pioneer Okanogan Smith's apple orchards. The boy had said the ranch was south of the Canadian border on the old Moses reservation, not too far from the Okanogan River. It was south of Hiram Smith's— Okanogan Smith's—orchards, and there was silver mining in the area. Earlier there had been gold mining at Rich Bar. ". . . He loved his sister, that boy did. Said she had pretty blue eyes the shade of his," Maggie had finished.

She had frowned, then lifted a chipped jar from her shelves. "He and another lad shot cans on a wager. We save the balls embedded in that old tree, so that one day we can look back at all the lads that have passed through and eaten my apple pies. My man said the boy's gun had a flaw in the barrel that marked the lead as it passed through. He showed me the gun. It was pretty, so small, like something a woman would carry."

Maggie had dumped the lead balls on a folded towel and prowled through them with a flour-dusted fingertip. "Ah, there it is. The lad with the blue eyes and the sister shot this one."

Simon looked at the big, evenly planed logs of the house. He'd been following Wells for eight months and the trail was cold. Smith could have changed his name; however, the stickpin shaped like a horseshoe was unique, and the marks on the bullets were a match. Wells and Smith were the same man. With the provincial police and the word of a Mountie leaving his normal assignment to hunt the murderer of his brother, Wells had gone underground. But Simon was certain he'd surface one day like a viperous snake coming out of a hole. He could turn up anywhere, possibly near a sister whom he loved.

Simon shifted uncomfortably on the bed, then lowered his toe to nudge a sleeping boy on the floor. "Trade you."

"But, sir, you are a Mountie," the boy whispered back in

awe. "You should have a proper bed at your age."

Simon thought of the frozen prairie ground he had shared with Rand during the Rebellion. . . . At thirty-five he'd picked up his share of wounds. A Blood brave's blade had left a deep, ugly scar that ran from Simon's right breast across his belly to his thigh. It ached as did every other wound he'd gotten in eight years of service to the Queen. Eugenia couldn't bear the thin wages, the isolation and solitude she would endure as his wife, nor his "bloody gruesome scars."

Eugenia Waite—they'd been engaged for four years when he enlisted in the Queen's service. The day he announced he'd enlisted, she arranged to have his unborn baby die rather than marry him. She'd had blue eyes, too, and she didn't want "savage little, unruly Oakes brats underfoot."

Using an African woman's teas, Eugenia had aborted the tiny mass of blood and tissue that would have been his son.

That was eight years ago.

He hadn't loved Eugenia, but he had wanted his child. The loss left an ache. He wanted children and a good marriage with laughter. Simon settled on his side.

Rand's face floated briefly behind Simon's lids; Rand's loud guffaws echoed through time. . . . Rand's happy marriage had caused Simon to want children and a home and a sweet, loving wife. Years weighted Simon—he wanted a wife and children warming his heart—then he pushed away the emptiness. "If I stay here the night, you'll be straightening me in the morning. Old bones, you know."

"Aye," the boy whispered knowingly. "The bed is an ill fit. You're a big chap."

Simon tugged his bedding down to the floor and the youth settled his blankets into the bed. "Thank you, sir."

Placing his arm behind his head, Simon looked to the window and watched the snow fall. He smiled, wishing briefly for Amelia's warm soft body cuddled with his under heavy blankets. A loving woman, Amelia would be the perfect wife; her round body was made for bearing children and she knew farming. They could make a good marriage after he found Rand's murderer and brought him to justice. He'd been saving for years, wanting a farm and a wife to share it. Amelia had the same needs. He wanted a family just as large and wild as his parents' brood. He gripped the small bag under his pillow, which contained the funds he'd withdrawn from the bank.

Amelia was Rand's friend and understood Simon's need to find his killer. Her telegraph to him was simple. *Take care. Your Amelia.*

Simon pushed away thoughts of Amelia's welcoming, lush body and her bubbling laughter and the children he wanted romping around him. The packer with forty-five mules snored loudly. In the morning he would be headed south, heading off the old Cariboo Trail and picking up the Okanogan Trail into American land. With the mules breaking snow ahead of him, Simon would travel faster and more easily. He turned on his side, easing the pain from the puckering new scar, and wondered about Wells's sister, the woman with blue eyes.

Miners knew about women with striking eyes. They became legends from camp to camp. The trail would be easy to follow. If Wells was so closely attached to his sister, eventually he would return to her.

Once Simon found the woman with the striking blue eyes, he would wait. . . .

The métis stood in the snow on the ridge overlooking Delilah Smith's ranch. He patted the mottled rump of his Appaloosa gelding and pushed back his heavy coat to rest his left hand on the worn butt of his Colt forty-five.

Smoke rose from the cabin's chimney up into the cold November dusk. The métis lifted his head to the wind, catching the scent of white woman's cooking.

His eyes narrowed, following the blocky body of a big woman moving to the clothesline strung between two posts. She moved slowly, age weighting her bones.

Placing his slender fingers over the gelding's muzzle, the métis whispered gently, "Lasway, hush." The French-Canadian word for silk described the Appaloosa's strong stride. The métis's Blackfoot cousins had insisted that he take the horse before he began his journey.

He listened to the twigs crunch and, without moving his head, traced the deer herd moving down the mountain. The big buck turned and stared at the man. "Go, safely, my brothers," the métis whispered in the Blackfoot language that was still new to his tongue. The Sun Dance scars on his chest had barely healed before he began his quest.

He was tired in his heart; he ached for his lost childhood, the loving mother who fought for her half-blood son, and the little sister with big blue eyes. He ached for Snow Bird and his two small sons taken by a white man's fever.

He had found his father's people after years of searching. Now he wanted to finish the search—

He smoothed the small notch in his right earlobe as he thought about the woman with the fabled blue eyes—Delilah Smith was his sister. "I am Koby Smith," he whispered to Lasway, letting the name settle on his tongue. It tasted unfamiliar. "Koby."

He closed his eyes and let the sounds of the swaying pine branches overhead take him back to another time.

His mother's eyes were vivid blue and loving; her kiss against his cheek felt like the brush of a dove's wing—"Take care of Delilah, Koby. I love you both . . . love you . . ."

Had Lady Delilah loved him, a half-blood child? His mother had not searched for him. He'd waited in the dark cellar of the mad Russian miner's shack, waited for a mother who tossed away her half-breed son easily. . . . No one came to find him. . . .

Perhaps too much time had passed; perhaps it would be better not to meet the blue-eyed woman—perhaps the past should stay silent and cold.

Lasway whinnied to the horses and mules feeding near the cabin, setting off a round of barking from dogs. Koby scanned the animals and recognized them as sled dogs. They were strong now, comfortable with the snow that had begun falling. A long old-fashioned sled lay on top of the woodpile, and a grizzled, stocky man chopped wood nearby.

Koby swung up into his saddle. "It is time. I must know that my little sister is happy and safe. Then the circle will be complete."

Artissima placed the hot pan of light soda biscuits on the table and stood listening. She waited for the second knock and looked at Delilah, who stood with her pistol leveled at the door. "Who is it?"

"I need food and a bed," the soft deep male voice returned.

"You're late, mister. We like guests to turn up before supper so we'll know how much to cook," Artissima said, unlatching the door and swinging it wide. She stood aside, allowing Delilah a clear shot if the stranger was dangerous.

The half-blood filled the doorway. A pistol was strapped low on his left thigh, and he held his black hat in his hands. "Ma'am," he said in a velvety-smooth voice that lifted the hairs on the back of Artissima's nape. His long straight lashes caught the kerosene lantern's light as he stared past Artissima to Delilah. He looked at her steadily. "Ma'am."

"Can you pay for your supper and lodging?" Artissima asked while the man continued to stare at Delilah. When he didn't answer and Delilah lowered the pistol, Artissima prodded sharply, "Well? Cat got your tongue, sir? I asked you if you can pay. Coin or nugget . . . we'll take barter, too. We're needing ranch work done."

He nodded and Artissima shook her head. "Go feed your animal, and we'll have hot water for you to wash out in the lean-to."

His black eyes slowly slid away from Delilah's puzzled ones to pin Artissima. She caught a wave of male arrogance and impatience, and it set her temper flying. She'd had a lifetime of men looking down their noses at her. "Delilah, perhaps he should find other lodging. . . . From the looks of his six-shooter, he's ventilated a few gentlemen. We don't need to shelter his kind."

The métis's black eyes narrowed slowly, stroking Artissima's face. They moved slowly downward, over her neat white blouse and skirts as though comparing her stylish, starched clothing to Tallulah's black dress and Delilah's worn brown blouse and trousers. Then the steady gaze lifted to her face. She was flushed from the oven and the anger that always leaped when arrogant men reminded her of the boundaries of her sex.

"Woman, I can pay," he said in that soft, darkly rich voice. The dangerous, deep purr barely sounded above the wind.

"Put your animal in the corral and feed him," Delilah interrupted, lowering her pistol and shoving it back into the holster hanging from a wall peg. "He looks tired. We'll heat a bucket of water for washing in the lean-to before you come to supper. You'll be bunking there. Bring any clothes you want washed and mended with you."

The man's eyes went past Delilah to Tallulah. His mouth tightened and he frowned slightly as if trying to remember something. Then he nodded, turned, and walked into the shadows.

"Well!" Artissima exclaimed, slamming the door behind him.

Later, Delilah studied the half-blood while they ate. He returned the stare, holding her eyes as if looking deep into her soul.

Tallulah also studied the man, her frown puzzled. There was tenderness in the man's black eyes when he looked at Tallulah. His hard lips softened, the curve almost beautiful. "Tallulah," he repeated slowly, softly, then looked into the lantern's flame. "Smith. It is a good name. That is my name— Smith."

"Just Smith?" Artissima threw back instantly.

He leveled a cool look at her. His black hair caught the light in blue glints. Cut short, it was well brushed and curling at his nape. Over his butternut-colored trousers, he wore clean, soft buckskin leggings and moccasins; his homespun dark red shirt was neatly buttoned. "Smith," he said slowly, firmly, as if tasting the name.

"Good name. So's Moose," Moose McCord rumbled.

Artissima inhaled impatiently and watched the four other people at the table. The man didn't offer his first name, nor did Delilah ask it. Though he didn't speak, his manners were impeccable. He handled the fork and knife slowly, as if trying to remember the shape and feel; he didn't stuff the cloth napkin into his collar as most of the men did, but placed it over his lap. When eating Artissima's fried dried-apple pie, he closed his eyes briefly, as if turning inside to the shadows within him.

When his eyes opened, they found and locked with Delilah's.

Her face softened. "You come to breakfast with Moose in the morning, Mr. Smith."

Later the three women sat at the table, as they did each night. Delilah tried to work with her columns of figures, while Tallulah patched the stranger's shirts and Artissima's knitting needles flashed, fashioning a man's stocking. "I want to know what's happening. Who is that man, other than a no-talking, arrogant, too-tall man who moves like a cat. Can't stand a man who doesn't talk. You can't tell what he's thinking until it's too late," Artissima stated, ripping away an incorrect stitch. "You two are acting like you've seen a ghost."

"He could be someone we used to know," Delilah whispered, closing her eyes. She held Tallulah's hand. "Oh, Tallulah, do you think it's possible?"

Artissima threw down her knitting on the table. She stood and placed her hands on her waist. "What is it? I demand to know what is causing you to act this way."

Delilah placed her arms around herself and rocked slowly on the chair, tears shimmering in her eyes and dripping down her pale cheeks. Tallulah's rough hand closed on Delilah's shoulder as she rocked.

Instantly concerned for her friends, Artissima knelt between them and placed her arms around them. Delilah rarely gave way to emotion, and now she was trembling. Artissima hugged her and smoothed her single, long braid. "Honey, don't cry. . . ."

"Oh, Koby . . . Koby . . . Mama said my brother had a nick in his right earlobe. A miner was showing off how well he could throw a knife . . . a half-breed boy seemed just the target. . . . Tallulah, he holds his head so proudly, just like Mama told us to do. His mouth has that uplifting curve at the corners, just like Richard's. Oh, Tallulah, Smith looks like Richard."

"*Liebling*, it might not be him," Tallulah warned unsteadily, drying her eyes with her big apron.

Let him be Koby, Delilah thought desperately the next night after supper. She cleared her throat. "Mr. Smith, I . . .

thank you for helping herd that wild horse back into the corral. Phantom hasn't made up his mind if he wants to stay with us."

"The wild horses call him to come to them." The man watched Tallulah mutter a curse in German as she missed a stitch and pulled it free. The lines beside his eyes crinkled slightly, his dark eyes warming. "Tallulah," he said quietly, as if tasting more than her name on his lips.

"My little sweet potato, don't worry about it," Moose cooed in his rumbling voice.

Tallulah's indignant expression rounded on him, and she hissed something dark and fierce in German. Artissima muffled her laughter behind her hand and rose to pour coffee. Tallulah stood. "You sit there, all of you. I wish to do the dishes by myself."

"I'll help, my dove," Moose offered.

"You . . . you take yourself away, you bad man," Tallulah muttered.

"He's been exiled for ungallant actions," Artissima stated primly and began clearing away the table. She carefully avoided coming near the younger man.

"Mr. Smith . . . would you mind telling me how you came to be missing that bit on your right earlobe?" Delilah asked slowly, carefully. Her heart beat wildly in her chest. *Please, let it be Koby . . . please . . .*

"A half-blood child does not have an easy time."

Despite his dark coloring, he looked like an older, harder, more weary version of Richard. Delilah gripped the napkin in her lap with one hand and placed her other over the rapidly beating pulse in her throat.

Koby had laughed and grinned and pulled her braids. He'd kissed away her tears when no one was watching. He'd gotten a spanking for frightening her with a big spider. He'd fought bullies bigger than himself to protect her. She'd idolized—loved him desperately.

"Are you Koby Smith?" Delilah's unsteady demand echoed loudly around the cabin.

Tallulah and Artissima placed aside the dishes. Each placed her hand on Delilah's shoulders and stood behind her. Tallulah prayed softly in German, and Artissima snapped, "You answer the lady, mister."

The métis's eyes locked with Delilah's. Then he said slowly, "You have our mother's eyes and her beauty."

"Lordy me!" Artissima exclaimed as the man slowly stood and paused, his hand on the door.

"Koby, you will not leave," Delilah ordered in a soft, trembling whisper.

He nodded once, his knuckles showing palely beneath the dark skin as he gripped the door. "We will talk. The wolves are near. . . . They took a calf last night."

"I'm coming with you . . . Koby," Delilah said, jerking on her coat. She took her gun belt from the peg and the rifle propped against the door and stood, looking up at him. "Koby," she whispered with a tremulous smile.

Artissima inhaled sharply. "Will you look at that? Delilah smiled . . . or just about."

Tallulah began crying and muttering into her apron, and Koby shook his head. "My little sister has not changed. She always followed me. I called her Me Too."

Two days later Artissima plopped a plate of fried chicken on the dinner table. "You two beat all," she muttered, seating her skirts in a huff. "So far as I can see, you're two peas out of the same pod. You're brother and sister and you haven't seen each other in a coon's age. . . . You pack up the first night and go wolf hunting. The two of you bring back five big pelts and go on like nothing happened . . . and *you're not talking.* You could be two strangers! There's things to be said . . . like what happened to each of you—"

She met Delilah's amused eyes. "Lordy. I am purely exasperated with the two of you. You both keep things to yourself."

"Things you might want to know, Artissima?" Delilah asked gently, teasingly.

Artissima inhaled, lifting the starched pleats on her blouse. "The both of you are enough to make a sane person go mad. You look at each other and you say things that I don't understand. Now how's a body going to help you two get together when I don't know what's happening?"

"When it is time, we will talk," Koby said quietly.

"I should hope so," Artissima flung back. She lifted her eyebrows and pointed her fork at Koby. "Listen, you. I won't take any back talk from you. You just turn up . . . all of a sudden Delilah here lets go of a smile once in a while, and everything is just peachy—"

Koby stared at her without expression, and Artissima simmered, waiting for an answer. "Well? What do you have to say for yourself?"

He turned to Delilah slowly. "Little Sister, your friend is a chattering magpie."

"Chattering? Well, I never—" Artissima stopped in midsentence because Delilah had begun laughing.

Tallulah's laughter blended with Moose's guffaws. Artissima looked from Delilah, who was wiping tears away from her face, to Moose, to Tallulah. She looked at Koby icily. "You do not amuse me, sir. All I can say is, if you're going to stay here, you might as well try to raise the doorframe. We can't spend time patching you up if you forget to stoop when you come in the house."

She paused, lifted her chin, and continued, "You are staying for Christmas dinner, hear?"

Chapter Four

The late January wind sliced through Simon's layers of clothing. Ice clung to his beard and the thick buffalo cloak. Sleet and snow stung his face. His stallion was tired now, and the wolves' yellow eyes gleamed in the eerie half-light before night. The wolf pack moved in unison, like a large, hungry animal, cunning and waiting to feed. . . . The leader was bold now, showing the pack his bravado, and the lesser animals were sliding through the trees, circling, waiting to sink their fangs into Tahmahnawis's powerful back legs, hamstringing him. The stallion's front hooves struck out at the leader of the wolf pack and sent him rolling across the deep crust of snow.

Simon clung to the saddle with one hand and fired his carbine into the mass of yellow eyes. The replacement for Simon's tired gelding, the big Hambletonian-cayuse stallion, had been bred for size and stamina, and he had proved his worth. They fought desperately now, the man and the great horse, caught in the swirling mist of snow and sleet. Simon talked to the horse and himself, fighting the weakness caused by the burning slash of a bullet across his shoulder. Blood soaked his woolen clothing, and the scent drew the wolves.

"Tahmahnawis, come on . . . come on, Magic—" Simon used the Chinook jargon name for the stallion he had purchased when his horse was too tired to go on. "Just a little farther, eh? Come on, boy . . ."

The snow and sleet had begun when he was past the halfway mark to the Smith cabin, and he'd decided to go on.

Two thieves lay dead on the snow-covered wagon road behind him. Simon squeezed off another shot into the pack, and a loud yelp cut the crisp, freezing air. The men had cut a tree, crashing it across the wagon road that was already deep with snow. Their first shot had burned a furrow across Simon's shoulder. His shots found them before they fired again, and the two men lay dead in the snow.

"Bloody hell!" Simon ground out when the leader of the pack returned, fangs bared. Simon was tired and weak; worn by breaking snow and fighting the wolves, Tahmahnawis's great strength was fading—

The Smith woman with the blue eyes and the glossy black hair was easy to find; the miners spoke her name with a dreamy sigh. "She Walks Alone is her name," the old Omak Indian had said when Simon stopped by his shack.

At the mining town along the river a man had peered out of his shack, and steam rose from his mouth as he called the Smith woman "a loner . . . too quiet. She might be twenty or forty—hard to tell, the way she wears her hair all tied back and those loose mud-brown clothes. Got eyes that haunt a man when he's waiting out the winter."

Another man had said, "Sure, I know the Smith boy. He's lively to the woman's quiet ways. She reminds me of a shadow in a way . . . doing her business quiet-like and leaving fast as she can. Good with numbers. Real pretty woman. Won't have anything to do with the local boys."

What was Delilah Smith doing now? Simon thought absently, then jerked himself upright in the saddle. The loss of blood was making him weak, his thoughts wandering—Tahmahnawis squealed as fangs sank into his legs, and he went down, plunging Simon into the deep snow.

The wolves were quiet now, circling in the bluish snow as the sleet beat down on Simon. Gripping his carbine, he worked his way through the deep snow to a tree and climbed slowly, painfully upward. Simon settled his back against the tree and shot the ten wolves around the fallen, bloody stallion. Then, taking careful aim, Simon ended Tahmahnawis's agony. "Sorry, boy," he whispered, then leaned his head back against the tree to stop the dizziness. He took the flask from his pocket and poured the whiskey over his handkerchief, easing it into his shirt and over the wound. Simon held his breath as the alcohol burned, then tipped the flask to take a sip. "Sorry, Tahmahnawis," he repeated.

Closing his eyes, Simon settled back against the tree as the night and the snow began to fall—

Rand laughed at him, the echoes keeping Simon propped against the tree when he'd begun to slide into the snow. . . . *"So you've never told a woman you love her, Simon? Ah, now. You've not had reason to, then. The woman who takes you on would have to be a lass of great courage. . . . Someday one such fine lass will come along, and then, then, my fine arrogant brother, you'll tell her you love her . . . because that's what is in your heart. . . . You'll see her and you'll know, just as I did with my Pam. . . . 'I love you,' you'll say . . . 'I love you. . . . ' "*

Delilah stood against the cabin, which shielded her from the bitter January wind. In the light before dawn the wagon road wound through the trees to the cabin. Moose's dogs snuggled down in their snowy beds, protected slightly by the shabby lean-to near their pen. The leader, Baby Boy, looked at her with white eyes, then stuck his nose into the curl of his furry body.

Moose mourned the loss of his big dog teams and babied his last six dogs with a winter gruel of frozen blood and bones. Each day Artissima baked a huge pan of corn bread for the dogs, and Moose mixed it with deer he had "cached" for the winter. On occasion Moose's crony, Rat, would drive his team to the cabin, and the two would spend days reliving dogsledding—"dog-punching"—in the North country.

The cold air started to freeze Delilah's nostrils closed, and she tugged the shawl that Artissima had knitted her for Christmas over her face. She stared at the empty road, praying for her brother. "Richard, where are you?" she whispered. "Richard, come home. . . ."

She ached for Richard. Though she was only nine years older than her brother, she had soothed his colic and his baby ills. She'd lost so much of Koby; she couldn't bear to lose years of Richard's life, too. Was he alive?

She shook aside the thought and concentrated on the road, a pale blue ribbon winding along the shadowy mountain. The snow was too deep now for travelers, and the stock kept close to the ranchyard. The cattle and horses had pawed through the first snow and eaten the bunchgrass. Locked in a white prison, they survived with the hay Delilah had stored. Koby and Moose had moved into the cabin now, their cots separated from the main room by a hanging blanket.

Koby had worked with Moose, cutting timber for a large, crude shed to protect the stock from winter. Much to Moose's relief, the younger man kept the heavy snow, which could crush a building, from the roofs of the cabin and shed.

Beneath the folds of the shawl, Delilah's lips curved as she thought about Artissima and Koby. Artissima prowled the cabin, bristling when Koby was near. Koby was quiet and relaxed, which caused Artissima to steam. When Koby and Moose calmly discussed the miners who had gone berserk in their wintery solitude and killed each other, Artissima had ignited and thrown a pan of fluffy biscuits at them. Koby had stared at her, but Delilah noted a telltale crinkling at the corner of his eyes. When she leveled a barrage of heated statements about keeping secrets, Koby handed her a small doll fashioned from leather. Her lips had snapped shut; she thanked him quietly and announced that she was making her famous fried dried-apple pies. Artissima had forced and prodded Moose into showing her how to run the dogs over the pasture's frozen snow. But because she actually wanted to ride, tucked in a warm nest, and dream about when she was a little girl riding in a fancy fringed wagon, Delilah became the driver. Artissima had brightened Delilah's life and worked to earn her place; it was a small matter, and Artissima's delighted expression warranted the effort.

Delilah enjoyed the hissing of the runners, the straining of the dogs, anything but the cold silence of night and the echoes of the past—

Koby slid from the shadows, wearing a blanket around his light shirt. He leaned back against the wall beside her, and they stared at the winding road buried beneath a solid five feet of snow. Delilah shared many silent moments with Koby now, and in the silence they were close.

"It is a good time . . . before the rest wake."

"Yes," she answered, sensing that Koby had followed her for a reason. The silence and the cold mist closed around them. From the past curled a sense of safety that she had known when Koby was near.

He spoke slowly, as though the memories caused him pain. "I had a woman and two small sons. I trapped and fished, took white men hunting for game. Life was good." Koby paused, and after a long time, he said, "Snow Bird, my woman—my wife—liked Christmas giving."

Delilah stopped breathing. Koby had not spoken of his life, nor had she asked.

"My sons were strong. But the fever took them and Snow Bird. I burned the cabin. Once our mother said I was Blackfoot, so I went to seek my father's people . . . to learn why my blood is mixed. It is an old story. My father was hunting. From buffalo hunters he stole a sick white girl with sky-blue eyes and sleek black hair. After they had spent the winter together, whites found them and killed him."

"Does the story give you peace?" Delilah asked, watching Koby's rigid expression.

"No," he said after a long pause. "After I was taken, Mother never searched for me. She told me to keep this—" He lifted a voyager's worn medallion from the leather thong around his neck. "It was my father's, and that is how they knew I was his son. She said to wear it, and I would always be found. But I wasn't. Yuri told me that she sold me to him . . . that she did not want to see me again. She could have found me easily."

Delilah touched his face. Her mother had not mentioned Koby's name from the time he disappeared. "Koby, Mama asked for you when she was dying."

"A bastard métis? You think she wanted me hanging on her skirts?" Koby asked bitterly. "You think I don't remember the men looking at her—Lady Delilah? I was her shame."

"If you were her shame, so was I. I don't know who my father was, and she never married Richard's father."

He pressed his lips together. "It is done."

The frozen sap in a pine cracked suddenly, the sound exploding like a shot, and Delilah swallowed, emotion tightening her throat. She remembered the men in the mining fields too well. They had looked at her slyly with an expectancy as she grew older. Lady Delilah's legacy of beauty was a nightmare of survival. The Mortons had been kind, giving them a warm dry room at the back of the store for a time. "I remember Richard's father. Ben was a good man. A cowboy driving cattle up from the Yakima. He was good to us. They were to be married. He had a mine called the Millennium, and he planned to work it and become a millionaire. We were going to move, but then he died."

Richard's father had left a deed to Delilah Smith—the claim to the Millennium mine—

"You look like Richard."

Koby nodded slowly and looked at the mist swirling around them. "More snow today. . . . I would like to meet Richard."

Delilah closed her eyes and prayed. She began rocking back and forth gently, hugging herself. Three lives so closely twined by their mother's blood, two brothers who had never met— "You will. He'll come back any day now."

Koby brushed away a gleaming black strand from her forehead. "You look like her," he said gently. "But there is a closed door inside you. You have had a hard life, but something inside cuts you and makes you bleed. I think . . ." he whispered slowly, "that your husband was not a good man."

She inhaled sharply, sucking the frozen air into her lungs. "No . . . he wasn't. While his parents were alive and before we married, he seemed—Mother wanted me to marry a man from a good family, a family with good background and money. I liked—no, *loved* Mrs. Morton, and Mr. Morton was like the father I never knew. I married Ezrah thinking that our marriage would be as perfect as his parents'. I was leaving him when he . . . when he had an accident and died."

Her brother nodded. "So the bud never became a woman."

She looked at him sharply, tracing the high cheekbones that matched hers. "What do you mean?"

Koby shrugged. "When it is time, you will know."

"*Koby, don't you leave me,*" Delilah whispered sharply, terror flying within her as she clutched his arm.

His hand covered hers. "No."

They stood side by side against the cabin. "She gave us each other," Koby said finally.

"Yes, and Richard. Oh, I miss him, Koby . . . like a piece of my heart. Wait until you meet him—he's tall and strong and a little awkward. He's got blue eyes and black hair like mine. . . . And he laughs . . . and he's kind and . . ."

With her shawl Delilah wiped away the tear that was freezing to her eyelashes. "I was Mama's midwife—a scared, nine-year-old girl. Tallulah was working—cooking for a boardinghouse of men—when Mama's time came. I couldn't leave her . . . there was no one around. . . . Richard took a long time in coming. Something went wrong . . . she just stopped trying. . . ." Delilah swallowed away the dry emotion tightening her throat, and Koby's large warm hand lifted to squeeze her shoulder. "She just stopped trying, Koby. She said she was tired when Richard finally came. It took her two years to slide away. We buried her beside Ben. Tallulah and I raised Richard as best we could. People helped along the way."

The Mortons had been kind, and Delilah had desperately wanted to repay them and be a member of their family. She'd wanted to please them and had married Ezrah when she was eighteen. Three years of marriage to him provided safety for Richard and Tallulah, but Delilah had paid behind their bedroom door.

Wrapped in their thoughts, Koby and Delilah stood listening to the pine boughs crack with the heavy weight of snow.

The cabin door slammed, and Koby closed his eyes. "*She* has found us," he muttered.

"Shhh. Artissima isn't quite certain about you."

"You are her chick. She fears I will hurt you."

"Shhh. Be nice," Delilah whispered, enjoying Koby's doomed, dark expression.

"There you are," Artissima said briskly as she rounded the cabin's corner. She looking from Delilah to Koby and back, then picked her way across the wide plank covering the snow to them. "My, isn't this nice? A little chat before dawn and before the rest of our little family wakes?"

Artissima stepped between Koby and Delilah and gathered the blanket around her shoulders. She scanned the snow-covered road. "What are we looking for?" she whispered.

A shot cracked twice. In a moment it cracked two more times, rapid fire.

"That," Koby said darkly, edging away from Artissima. "We're looking for that," he said, though the shots were the first they had heard.

Artissima craned her neck, looking into the darkness. "Horse feathers. That's downright foolish. Koby, you can't *see* a sound."

Koby groaned and Delilah found herself smiling beneath her shawl.

Two more shots sounded, and Koby stood away from the cabin, his body straight as he listened intently.

Delilah touched his arm. "Koby, someone's in trouble. Oh, I hope it isn't Richard. . . . I mean I hope he's coming, but not in trouble."

Koby scanned the swirling mist, then the mountains looming in the ghostlike shadows. "We must find him soon. The snow will keep falling and the temperature is dropping."

Delilah tested the heavy crust over the snow with her boot. "It will take too long to break through this. The sled could take me partway—"

"You?" Artissima asked.

"Not you. Me," Koby stated flatly.

Artissima rounded on him. "Why you?"

He shrugged. "A man is bigger and stronger."

She angled her chin upward, then smiled tightly. "But, Koby, dear . . . look . . ."

Then she stepped off onto the thick crust and stood upright. She bounced, testing her weight on the crust. "Well, lookee here, Koby. Maybe big and strong . . . being a man and all . . . isn't what is needed. Moose said his old sled is light and the seven-foot length spreads out the weight."

Koby scowled at Artissima. "A dogsled cannot move through the trees on the mountain."

"Snowshoes," Artissima shot back. "Big ugly snowshoes. Delilah and I had fun playing with them last winter, didn't we, Delilah? Wasn't anything else to do but play in the snow. Lord knows, there was plenty of it."

"Koby, give up," Delilah said softly, smiling at her brother's frustration.

Delilah stepped onto the snow and carefully tested it by walking around. Layers of ice over snow supported her. Koby placed his boot onto the crust, and it crumbled beneath him. He shook his head. "No. I will use the big draft horse to break a trail. I could use the snowshoes—"

Fifteen minutes later Artissima tucked a jar of hot coffee into the layers of blankets and furs on the sled. Koby placed several heated rocks into the blankets, and Artissima said in a huff, "That Koby is just like you . . . stubborn as mules the both of you. No talking, stubborn mules. . . . Now the both of you don't think that I can—Oh, why I bother, I don't know."

Delilah stood on the back runners and concentrated on the dogs, who were eager to run. She listened for the shots that had sounded every fifteen minutes. The canyon echoes made it difficult to tell how far away the shots were fired. "You can't come, Artissima, because of the weight."

Artissima stared at her. "What? Are you sayin' I'm fat?"

"My sister says you are rounded and softer than she is. There may be more weight when she comes back," Koby said slowly as he tucked his pistol into the sled. He met Delilah's eyes and pointed to it. "You are foolish."

"Oh, land's sakes. I'm round and soft and Delilah is foolish. My, my, Koby. I just bet you delight the ladies," Artissima muttered.

"Upon occasion. It has been a long time since I lay with a woman," Koby returned easily, not taking his eyes from

Delilah's. While Artissima blinked, her cheeks flushed and her lips moved soundlessly, Koby said to Delilah, "This is not wise. I can travel on snowshoes."

She touched his cheek with her glove. "But not as fast. The temperature is dropping. Whoever is firing those shots may not have time to wait."

When Koby frowned down at her, Delilah wrapped her arms around him and held him tight. "I'm strong, Koby. It could be Richard out there, but whoever it is, he needs help soon."

Koby wrapped his arms around her and slowly gathered her to him. "Whoever fired those shots is not too far away. You have an hour. Fire one shot when you get there and another when you begin to come back."

Artissima inhaled sharply. "You two are making me cry. *Now* you decide to hug! I've been waiting for two months for this."

"Maybe when you don't tell us what to do, we do it," Koby returned.

On impulse Delilah reached out and snared Artissima close to them. Koby looked stunned for a heartbeat, then he scowled at the women and stepped back, folding his arms over his chest. "Go."

Delilah held her breath and carefully eased each foot on top of the runners. The old-fashioned birch sled creaked, and the six dogs, harnessed in single file, listened to Moose's crooning. He looked at Delilah, and when she nodded, Moose patted Baby Boy and released the harness lines. "Go! Show this gang of unbelievers how you can run, boys!"

The sled hissed smoothly over the snow, the dogs running quietly, their paws encased in booties to protect them from the sharp ice. The pines sheltering the road were heavy with ice and snow, boughs bending and breaking. The dogs were getting stronger, their primitive instincts sharpening. "Richard, please be safe . . . please let it be you," she whispered urgently beneath the shawl covering everything but her eyes.

She stopped once to pull fallen branches from the road, then suddenly—thirty minutes after she'd left the cabin—she saw the dead wolves and the horse, snow almost covering them.

The dogs were nervous, catching the scent of blood and quarreling in their harnesses. Delilah followed Moose's instructions and wrapped the lines around a small tree. She spoke firmly to the dogs, then moved quickly, carefully, across the snow, following the path of broken snow to a tree.

Oh, Richard—please let it be you. Please be alive, she thought desperately.

"Richard . . . ?" she called softly. Braced against the tree and wrapped in a buffalo cape, the big man straddled a limb that was seven feet above the top layer of the snow. A drop of blood hit the new snow at Delilah's boots.

"*Kwan. Kwan*, Baby Boy," she said harshly, using the Chinook word for "quiet." The dogs stopped snarling, and Baby Boy's white eyes blinked at her almost innocently. "*Kwan*," she said firmly. Delilah climbed up the few limbs to the man and brushed away the snow clinging to his face.

"Oh, Richard—please . . ." She closed her eyes as her heart tore gently. The tangled dark hair was wavy—the man wasn't Richard.

His lashes stirred and, fighting the impatience in her voice, she whispered, "You're safe now. Come with me and you'll be warm." Her mind echoed, *Richard, where are you?*

"You're late and you're a woman," he grumbled in a deep, raw, and disappointed tone. "Can't . . . move . . ."

Delilah stripped away her glove and placed her hand along his jaw, making him face her. The shape of his jaw was unforgiving in her hand, and a trickle of uneasiness washed over her as she sensed that this man was powerful. He was so pale, his closed lashes struggling to open the ice covering them. She brushed away the snow resting on his rugged, jutting cheekbones. "Of course you can. You'll do what you have to do to survive."

" . . . Cold . . ."

"Shhh . . . save your strength. . . . You have to come with me. . . ." Would he die? Because he looked so pale, so alone and near death, Delilah moved his face, taking it into the warm curve of her throat and letting him rest against her.

He breathed quietly, slowly, his frozen lashes stirring against her skin. "I'm weak as a wee baby," he muttered slowly, and the sharp smell of alcohol rose in the air.

"Come on . . . slowly," Delilah whispered. *He's a fool out on an adventure; a drunk who wasted a good horse's life,* she thought darkly. Whoever he was, he was heavy and solid, and his words were lashed by a slight accent. An adventure seeker, not bound by common sense. She'd seen hundreds of them in her life. "I'll help you down. Let me put your foot on the limb. . . ."

"Do the men in this country send beautiful women to do their dirty work? Where's the cavalry?" he grumbled. After a heartbeat his lips stirred against her throat in a small smile. "Miss, I'm a big ox of a man. . . . Don't worry . . . I'll get us to safety."

With tremendous effort, he pushed free of Delilah and leaned against the tree. Then he leaped into the snow, taking his carbine with him. Delilah scrambled down the tree and began digging away the snow to the man. One green eye opened to greet her. "What . . . took . . . so long? Where are the men?"

"Men?"

"Damned petunias they have here for men, when they send a woman on a rescue."

Delilah frowned. The twinkle in the man's eye surprised her. She recognized the man's teasing tone, and she wasn't in a mood to be teased, nor banter with a man who didn't have sense enough to do his drinking where he was safe. If the stranger had any sense, he wouldn't waste time. She pressed her lips together and grimly began pitting her strength against his weight. Unable to move him, she knelt beside him. "Mister, you have to help me."

"Simon Oakes . . . at . . . your . . . service. . . ." he whispered, managing to stand unsteadily in the hole he had broken through the snow. "Don't . . . worry. You're safe with me," he said unevenly.

Standing on the snow's crust next to him, Delilah wiped the snow and sleet away from her face. The mountain of a wounded drunk now stood deep in the snow. His beard, the slouch hat covering his head, and his buffalo robe were coated with ice; he was standing unsteadily and looking at her

boots, and *he thought he was rescuing her*! She shook her head
and tried desperately to remember Moose's instructions—she
reached into her pocket for the small metal flask and the candy.
"Mister, I have a dogsled. We have to get you on it."

"Yes." His bloody glove shackled her ankle. Delilah allowed
the trespass; she was his anchor to life.

"Open," she ordered, bending and pushing a small piece of
Artissima's chocolate candy next to his lips. When he took it,
she lay the flask against his lips. "Open. Drink."

"I'll not be fed like a wee baby." The words were slow and
resentful, wrapped in steam and in a stiff accent.

Delilah pushed another piece of chocolate through his cold
lips. "Shut up. Do as I say."

"Good candy," he managed in an uneven, conversation-
al tone. Delilah closed her eyes. A drunk who appreciated
Artissima's candy wasn't what she needed with a blizzard
approaching and five feet of snow already on the ground.

She worked quickly, pulling, coaxing, easing the big man
into the sled and covering him with blankets and a dry buffalo
robe. He reeked of whiskey and when she tried to lift his shirt,
he groaned—the cloth had stuck to the wound.

While she moved quickly, placing the heated stones at his
feet and helping him drink the lukewarm coffee, he tried to
talk. Simon Oakes was trying to comfort her in her time of
need. "Good," he said wearily, then opened both dark green
eyes. "Tired. You have blue eyes. . . . A brave, strong lass . . .
Let the dogs have their head . . . they'll take you home. Don't
worry. I'll take care of you. Oh, by the way, I love you."

Delilah stared at him and frowned. No man other than her
brothers had ever said he loved her. The stranger was barely
conscious—he thought he was saying "I love you" to his
sweetheart. Delilah inhaled, then ran to the horse and quickly
unstrapped the stranger's saddlebags and bedroll, placing them
on his feet. "We have to hurry. A blizzard is coming."

"Shush, woman. I'll take care of you," he murmured before
he passed out.

Moose and Koby held the stranger while Artissima sewed
his wound with silk thread. "Learned this when I was girl. The

war didn't leave a body time to faint before they were tossing another under my needle. I always regretted not being able to have a fit of the vapors."

"You are a strong woman," Koby murmured gently.

Artissima patted away the fresh blood welling from her stitches. "Had to be. Wasn't time to be anything else. Look there," she murmured, pointing the needle to another scar. "Whoever stitched that wasn't a lady who had to sew her own clothes."

"Did it myself," the injured man muttered in a disgusted tone. "Right good job."

Then the men washed the man's body gently, silently noting a slashing scar that ran from his shoulder to his thigh. "Knife," Koby noted.

"A big slug has been dug out here," Moose added quietly. "Another here. The man has been in a fight or two."

The man called Simon had never let go of Delilah's hand; rather his fingers had locked to her wrist as he floated in and out of reality. She resented his hold on her, as if nothing would free her from him. She hadn't been touched, shackled by a man's grasp since Ezrah. Though she resisted showing it in her expression, the memory frightened her. When Simon's lean brown fingers had first wrapped around her wrist, she had been startled and jerked away.

Simon had thrashed feverishly against Koby and Moose, his hand seeking hers. Artissima had nodded grimly to Delilah. She knew he needed her, his anchor on life, and had allowed him to hold her wrist, his thumb smoothing the fine skin, testing her pulse, caressing. . . . The tight, possessive hold reminded her of shadows that waited, causing her stomach to roll and her hands to dampen. . . .

Koby glanced at her, then frowned and placed his hand on her shoulder for a brief instant. "You do well, Little Sister."

There were three women in the cabin, Simon decided sleepily. An older one with a heavy German accent was called Tallulah; a younger one named Artissima had a southern states accent; and then, the one they called Delilah.

Delilah . . . Delilah . . . The name circled his brain, dancing through it with images of a woman's haunting eyes filling her pale face. *"I love you. . . . "* Of course he did. He'd love any woman who would risk her life to save him. Rand had slid into Simon's mind, teasing him that night as he tried not to slide from the tree. . . . *"A lass of great courage . . . 'I love you.' "*

Rand . . . Rand . . .

This woman's skin burned his mouth, her scent exotic and lingering . . . soft, hot skin. . . . Her blood pulsing beneath his lips . . . warm . . . hot . . . sweet . . . brave . . .

Delirious fool, of course you love her. You'd love a man as well if he pulled you from death—

Loving a man . . . he'd loved Rand, his brother. . . . Rand was dead.

The wolves . . . Tahmahnawis's blood on the bluish snow . . . so cold . . . another drink of whiskey, its warmth seeping through him momentarily . . . his shoulder fire-hot . . .

A pad of something cool and sweet-smelling lay on his bare shoulder. . . . Flannel sheets lay under him—a feather-tick pad rustled as he moved. The scent of baking and stew layered the darkness; dishes clattered, a door closed and the roof creaked. . . . Simon lay listening to the men's voices. Moose was an older man with a harsh, loud voice who told stories at every turn. Then there was a younger man who spoke little—Koby.

They were a family who cared for one another.

Delilah spoke little, even when teased by Artissima.

Delilah, the woman with the blue eyes. Simon closed his eyes and saw her again, peering at him. She'd given him the warmth that she'd had, the sweet curve of her throat, and he'd clung to that memory through the haze of fever and pain.

Simon opened his eyes, staring at the flickering firelight on the timbers overhead.

He owed his life to the woman with vivid blue eyes, haunting eyes, and long, silky black hair with a perfume he would remember when he was a hundred. Simon smiled grimly. She'd been impatient with him for some reason, her body, slender and strong, pushing him onto the sled. . . . Her terse orders had cut through his need to sleep. She'd whisked him away from death and sat with him while the others slept.

Richard, she had called, her voice soft in his hazy mind. Desperation ran through her tone.

Delilah was Richard Smith's sister, the woman he had come to find.

Rand . . . murdered, his blood frozen to the ice . . .

Delilah loved her brother enough to throw herself into an upcoming blizzard.

"Rose-hips and lemon-peel tea," Artissima was saying firmly. "You are not going to put Delilah's big orphan in a sweat house and steam him like a clam."

"He is a man, not an orphan," Koby said in a dark, growling tone, before Simon slept. "The steam will sweat away his fever."

It was night now. Fire crackled in wood, the wind howled . . . Moose snored, and the roof creaked. Shadows and fever stalked him. A woman in a woolen shawl leaned close to Simon. Her heat slid over him . . . so warm. Folds of flannel brushed his hand as it lay over the quilt. Simon breathed quietly. . . . She'd gotten up from bed to come see to him while the others slept. . . . Cool hands smoothed his face, and dark blue eyes leaned over his. They were tender and warm, fringed with black lashes. He stirred, wanting to tell her he loved her again.

Oh, God, he needed to tell her. "Shhh. Simon, I knew you were awake . . . the cot has been creaking. You're worried, aren't you? You're safe now. . . . Simon, your fingers and your toes are safe. . . ." Cool fingers wiggled his nose lightly, playfully. "See, Simon . . . you have your nose." She tugged at one earlobe and the other. "You have both ears. No frostbite, Simon. No wonder, you had enough alcohol in you. Shame on you. Your Amelia should take you in hand."

So the little devil had a sense of humor, tormenting him on his deathbed, did she?

She eased aside the quilts and one at a time cradled his stocking-covered feet, smoothing them gently. "See, Simon, you have feeling in your feet." She slowly slid a finger over each arch and repeated the small torment. His toes curled instantly. "See? Toes that work."

She liked to play, did she? Tormenting her captives while they lay helpless? Or search their clothing—that was the only way she could know about Amelia, by reading the telegram tucked in his pocket.

She replaced the quilt, tucked it around his feet, and took his right hand, holding it in firm, slender fingers. "See? This hand is good and the other—"

With great effort Simon eased his left hand farther away from her, and she leaned across him to capture it. Her hair swept across his face, and he inhaled the exotic scent, savoring the silky strands as they clung to his cheek. He turned slightly, his face resting in the warm feminine scents of her skirt. He nuzzled the softness of her stomach and wished that she would lay with him.

She'd come from the night, warm and scented and alive. She'd known somehow that he needed comforting, the gentle teasing. . . . She'd known that the fear of an icy death still clung to him . . . and she'd come to him.

Who was this strong, brave, quiet woman? Not her name, but who was she?

What man could call himself a man and let his woman fly into a blizzard to pluck a man almost twice her size from death?

Who had held her close?

Who had made those soulful, haunted eyes darken with sensual hunger and gleam with delight?

Who had wrapped that long silky hair around him and supped upon her body until she clasped him tightly?

She took his hand, and Simon's fingers curled around hers. She held his hand, and Simon found his body stirring, hardening—He damned the draining weakness as she tugged away from his light grasp. She smoothed back the wave that slid across his brow and rested her hand on his head. "Shhh, now. Go to sleep, Simon. Rest. . . . You're fine. . . . Just rest now . . . rest . . ."

"Delilah, no need to thank me," he managed to whisper, then he dozed, satisfied with the sound of her outraged gasp. The little witch liked to tease poor, ill men, did she? She needed a bit of it in return.

"Go to sleep," she whispered after a time, her hand stroking his hair. Simon concentrated on the soothing fingers and allowed himself to drift to her whisper . . . "Sleep." Then she tugged the quilt up to him and tucked him in like a baby.

Simon smiled and nestled against the flannel sheeting. *Fine Queen's Mountie, you are, Simon Oakes . . . tucked into bed and put to sleep like a wee baby.*

Chapter
Five

"I want my clothes," Simon
demanded the next morning when Delilah brought the nourishing cup of hot barley-and-beef broth to his cot.

"First you'll eat," she returned tartly as he lay looking at her
from his cot. The bandage across his shoulder gleamed white
in the shadowy light of morning. A wild mane of tangled, crisp
dark brown hair lay across the flannel sheeting. It swirled and
flowed into a new heavy, dark red beard. The beard flowed
into a matte of black hair covering his chest, the white bandage
startling against his dark skin—Artissima had insisted Simon's
chest be wrapped to safely hold her stitches.

Simon had slept through the morning, and when the others
were certain he was safe, they set off to salvage his saddle and
the wolf pelts. Artissima had refused to be left behind, and
Tallulah wanted the outing. The men had grumbled, but in the
end had grimly issued a long list of orders, allowing the women
the sled while they used giant snowshoes. Delilah was to rest.

Simon filled the cot Koby had vacated. The newcomer was a tall, broad wedge of a man lying beneath the quilt. A man who thought he could rescue her even while he sank into unconsciousness.

He watched her now with those peculiar green eyes, and the dim light in the cabin caught the fiery-red tints in his beard. "You're a tyrant, Delilah Smith. But a beautiful one," he said slowly, his eyes flowing over the braids on top of her head, sweeping down the length of her throat, and lingering on the loose brown blouse and trousers. "You were so strong and determined to have your way with me—"

He grinned when she scowled down at him. He reminded her of Richard when he knew he was in trouble and was trying his best to get his way. "You'll help me sit up, won't you?"

"No." She wasn't in the mood for teasing or personal flattery.

Simon's eyes narrowed slowly, dangerously, then he said very precisely, "Artissima would scalp me if I tore open her fancy stitches. Of course, the damage wouldn't be my fault. It would be yours." He gritted his teeth and pushed slow, straining against his weakness to sit up. Delilah pushed his bare shoulder back down. Simon's hand immediately locked over her wrist, keeping her palm flat on his shoulder. It was solid, heavily padded, and feverishly warm.

His eyes darkened, his mouth grim beneath his beard. "Thank you, Delilah. Thank you for my life," he said quietly as he lifted her palm to his lips and kissed it. Then he turned her hand and kissed the back before allowing her to pull away.

The warmth of his mouth lingered against her skin, and she brushed it against her trousers. "You were drinking and foolish and you cost the life of a good animal," she said, nettled by his dark, quiet look. "Who are you and what were you doing, crossing the mountain with a blizzard starting to break? Never mind, I know your type."

"Do you?" The deep voice was too soft, too smooth. Then he closed his eyes and pushed himself to sit against the cabin wall, his face pale. "You could adjust a pillow behind my back," he suggested between the tight line of his lips.

"From the way you charmed Artissima and Tallulah, you're obviously a ladies' man and you've been pampered. Dear Amelia may coddle you, but don't expect it from me."

"You've picked my pockets and read my telegram. Very well," he said grimly before struggling to sit up. He paled, his face damp with sweat, the cords on his throat standing out in relief. A tiny red stain appeared on his injured arm.

"Don't." Delilah shrugged, balanced the cup in one hand, and tugged his pillow behind him. She sat on the edge of the cot and placed a spoonful of the broth into his mouth.

"Fop that I am, I can pay for my keep," he said flatly, emerald eyes lashing at her. "That's what you do here, isn't it? Offer room and board for payment? I have payment."

Though she didn't lift her eyes, she sensed him studying her carefully. He wouldn't find her annoyance. She'd learned long ago to keep her expressions under control. "Yes, you'll pay."

He closed his lips when she lifted the next spoonful, then he said doggedly, "When I'm fit, I'll help out around the place."

She shrugged and continued feeding him. She wasn't used to serving men in their beds, and the action nettled. "No need. You'll be on your way as soon as you can."

"Will I?" Delilah didn't like the challenging edge to his voice. She dabbed his lips with a napkin and frowned at his close scrutiny. "Did I really tell you I loved you?"

"You nearly died. Men say strange things at times like that. You were probably thinking of 'Your Amelia.' " Delilah crossed her arms and stared at him coldly.

Simon closed his eyes. A little of Amelia's friendly chatter would suit him now. "Yes. Would you shave me now, please?"

When she hesitated and stood, Simon frowned at her impatiently as if she were dense. "It's customary, isn't it? To shave a sick man?"

Delilah turned and placed the cup on the table. She ran her hands down her trousers, smoothing them. It would be hours before the others returned. "You can wait."

"Ah. But I can't. I want a shave now." Then he threw back the quilt and placed his feet on the floor. Bracing his hand on the wall, he eased upright and stood unsteadily. The midday sun caught on his chest, tangling with the crisp black hair. The sunlight stroked the veeing line of hair to the sagging waist of his pajama bottoms. "There. Now to get my saddlebags and pour a basin of hot water."

Delilah frowned at him. He wouldn't make one step away from the wall without collapsing. The striped pajama bottoms matched the top, which they had found in a small valise with a dress shirt and a suit. Simon had refused to wear the top. The flannel pajamas had stunned Moose, and Koby had grinned. Artissima was certain that the rescued man was a "man of quality" despite his battle scars. Delilah watched Simon waver, and the knot of the pajamas began to slip. . . . His hips were very white where his tan stopped. . . . She closed her eyes, then opened them to Simon's pale face. "Sit down."

"Will you shave me, miss? Or will I do it myself?" he asked too precisely, his hand locking to the logs, bracing him.

Delilah tightened her lips. Whoever he was, Simon was used to getting his way. In another moment he'd be lying on the floor, and she'd have a fine time getting him back into the cot. "Fine."

"I don't want a trim. I want a shave. Do you know how?" he demanded. "Artissima does the cooking and Tallulah cleans. What do you know how to do?"

"Sit!" Delilah was surprised that she had almost yelled. She had fought below-zero temperature to pluck him to safety, and now he issued demands and challenged her?

She forced herself to inhale quietly. She didn't have to explain anything to him.

He smiled tightly and eased himself down to the cot. He sat back against the pillow and raised his legs slowly up on the cot. While she dug into his saddlebags, jerked the straight razor and a fancy bristle brush and soap mug from it, Simon sighed tiredly. "Good girl. I knew I could count on you."

Minutes later Delilah began briskly rubbing the soap brush over Simon's heavy beard. "You could have waited," she muttered. He closed his eyes while she stroked away the dark red beard.

She reached one arm around his head to pull the skin tight on his jaw and slowly pulled the razor upward. His skin was too warm, rough beneath her fingers. White lines radiated from his eyes, and the tips of his lashes were bleached from the sun. There was a small scar next to his temple running into his hair. She brushed back a strand and found it crisp and clinging to her fingers.

Simon's jaw was square and firm as she angled it upward to slide the razor up on his throat. She remembered the solid feel of that jaw from the rescue and her thoughts that once this man locked his mind to having his way, only the devil could stop him. Or an angel.

She wiped the blade on the towel around his throat, and her fingers brushed the warm, rough hair on his chest. Delilah jerked her fingers away and continued methodically.

"Fourteen strokes. Good girl," he murmured before she placed the steamy towel over his face.

"Perfect," he whispered when she lightly soaped and shaved away the last of his beard. "A little short in front of my ears, but not too bad."

Delilah inhaled, then briskly patted away the remaining soap with the hot towel. Since Ezrah's exacting demands, she wasn't used to waiting on men, much less touching and coddling a man who demanded shaving when it wasn't necessary. She didn't need or want his comments on her skills. She dropped the warm towel over his face and frowned at him darkly before jerking it away. Simon lay back and acted as though he had been shaved by legions of women. Very likely his Amelia treated him like a king.

She swished the razor's straight edge in the bowl and watched the dark red stubble float away in the soap. Ben, Richard's father, had a dark red beard, and she'd watched her mother shave him.

Richard, where are you? Oh, please, please be safe.

Delilah's fingers tightened on the razor's handle. She had learned from her mother how to shave men's beards. Delilah stirred the dark stubble and watched it swirl in the soapy water. Her mother had known how to tend men; she'd had three children from three fathers and had never married. Delilah's hand trembled when she dabbed away the remaining lather on Simon's jaw.

"According to my mother, a gentleman should always appear his best when in the presence of a beautiful lady," he returned in a matter-of-fact tone before he fainted. It was then that she noticed his hand had curled around hers.

His palm was squarish, big and warm and calloused.

The grip of his fingers and thumb was firm and frightening.

Six days later, Simon poured batter onto the griddle. "It's very important, Artissima, to blot the restored dried huckleberries and to roll them in flour before adding them to the batter. Just as important as it is to sear a good roast, trapping the juices inside before cooking it slowly. A splash of good wine and a good *bouquet garni* of parsley, thyme, marjoram, summer savory . . . and oh, maybe a bay leaf."

He tested the griddle cakes, lifting the edges with his spatula. He waved it like a musician's baton while he studied the griddle cakes. "So you froze butter? With honey?" he asked in the tone of a man who had just discovered sunshine.

"Of course. The huckleberry syrup is ready when you are, Simon," Artissima answered happily. "Drying the berries on the roof and under muslin to keep the flies away now all seems worthwhile. I've thought of a way to extend the lovely tin of tea you brought. We'll forage twigs and leaves from the berry bushes, dry them out, and add them to your wonderful tea."

Simon flipped a griddle cake high into the air and neatly caught it on the spatula, easing it into a warming plate. "Artissima, do you realize the great risk? The flavors you'd be blending? You know I don't agree with your chicory and coffee recipe."

Seated at the breakfast table, Delilah inhaled and tried to dismiss Simon and Artissima's ongoing debate about adding chicory to coffee beans, then the value of adding an eggshell or cinnamon to freshly brewed coffee. Koby stared at Delilah, his expression impassive. Then he tugged the notch in his ear, a sign that he was deep in thought. Moose scooped up the small pitcher of heated huckleberry syrup, scowled down into it, and announced, "There's no reason to eat this when there's meat and potatoes at hand."

Moose leaned closer to Koby and Delilah and whispered, "He had a tin of tea in his saddlebags. Tea . . . for a man. Funny—a man cooking these fancy foods, isn't it? I mean, making cakes and wishing his arm was good enough to knead bread. It's unnatural for a man to do dishes and cut cookies. How did he get those scars? In the kitchen?"

Tallulah slapped him lightly on the arm. "Hush. He's a good, sweet man. He talks different and comes from Canada. Maybe all the young men cook like that up there now."

Moose lifted his bushy eyebrows. "Men? Men cook real grub—meat and potatoes."

Koby snorted and Delilah closed her account book. She stood and placed it on a shelf. She'd had her fill of Simon Oakes and had stayed away from him. He delighted Artissima, who welcomed him like a long-lost friend. They shared a love of cooking and discussed current fashions and mourned the lack of plays and books. Simon had made himself comfortable and cooked most of the meals with Artissima hovering nearby, giving suggestions and making notes in her cookbook that she hoped to publish one day.

Koby's eyes slid to Simon's embroidered suspenders and closed briefly, as if willing them away. He stared stoically at the huckleberry griddle cakes, which Simon had just placed on the table. Artissima and Tallulah beamed when Simon helped them into their chairs. He looked at Delilah. "Come along, like a good girl," he said, too patiently.

Koby's eyes lit up, and Delilah wanted to scream. The freezing winds had made it impossible to stay away from Simon's grasp for long. He seemed to take every opportunity to be near her. She didn't like his size, nor the way he maneuvered her within her own home. With Simon's height and shoulders barring her, she was forced to step around him. Taking a deep breath, she smoothed her trousers and walked slowly to the table where he waited, his hands on the back of her chair.

She knew those hands. They were strong and unrelenting when he'd wanted to hold her wrist. She flicked him a dark look, then sat. In a skilled, gentlemanly movement, Simon eased her chair closer to the table and sat beside her. She met the cool, satisfied stare he sent her way. "Delilah," he murmured smoothly in a deep, intimate tone that raised the hairs on the nape of her neck.

That afternoon Koby studied the man who was watching Delilah pitch hay to the stock. "She likes to feed the cattle," Koby said when Simon turned to him. "She works too hard to see that they have hay. She wants to do it herself. She has trusted few people in her life."

"Tallulah said Delilah's first herd starved," Simon returned, stuffing the kindling he had chopped into a bucket. He ran his thumb over the blade of the hatchet and thrust it in with the firewood. "I'll sharpen the blade tonight."

Koby nodded, turning fully to him and placing the snow shovel against the cabin. The tall men looked steadily at each other. "You want my sister."

"Yes." Simon did not deny his needs. Delilah's graceful movements stirred him sensually. Living together had heightened his need. In those few days he knew he wanted Delilah more than he'd wanted any other woman. He noted a fine anger brewing within himself. He'd set his mind to getting a wife once Rand's murderer was brought to justice—Delilah wasn't wife material. If ever a woman threw bristling, cold spikes at a man, it was Delilah.

Then there was the curiosity—how would she look flushed from lovemaking? She knew how to control her emotions, shield them. Simon wanted to rip away that careful, cool mask and find the woman who challenged and excited him.

He jammed his hands inside his pockets, frowning at the woman who stood staring at the wagon road as if waiting for something, someone. There was no reason why he should want her.

Dressed in men's trousers, a too large coat, a sky-blue knitted cap, and her shawl, Delilah looked small and vulnerable in the midst of snow and looming pine trees.

She wore loose shirts and trousers in dull colors. She pulled her hair back and braided it tightly. She was scrawny, lean-hipped and leggy as a half-grown boy.

He thought of womanly breasts and white, plump, hot thighs. He closed his eyes and promised himself that when Richard was brought to justice, he would find Amelia and drag her before the altar. From the plump look of her, their first child would be born nine months after the wedding. He intended to spend a week pleasing her, expending whatever energy necessary to remove the insane and insistent urge to bed Delilah.

Simon frowned as he studied Delilah's lonely, vulnerable stance and closed his eyes, shutting her away from him.

Koby shifted slowly, and Simon's eyes dropped to the six-shooter tied low on Koby's thigh. "You are a hunter. What are you hunting?"

"I'm hunting my brother's killer, and the trail is cold. I haven't had a home in a long time. So I'm resting for a time, enjoying myself. . . ." He wasn't leaving until Richard Smith arrived. The brother and sister were too close—he would come to her. Delilah saved Simon's life; it wouldn't be easy to take her younger brother away, to make him stand trial for murders and robberies. Koby was a shootist, and from the way he wore his Colt pistol and the .44-.40–caliber twin bandolier hanging in the cabin that fit either his pistol or his rifle, he was probably very deadly. He would protect Delilah.

If he took her younger brother prisoner, she would fight him every inch. Simon's lips pressed together. There were other things that he wanted Delilah to do to him and things he wanted to do to her.

It had been a good long time since he'd been with a woman. His need was predictable and too sharp. Delilah was a woman of mystery; it clung to her like a cloak and the perfume that was her body's scent.

He thought of Delilah's lean body. Tangling with her could leave him with bruises and frostbite.

Simon remembered pressing his face into her body when she leaned over him that first night. The warm fragrance had haunted him since.

"I understand when a man—a hunter who is badly tired—wants to rest . . . wants a warm home in the winter. I do not understand cooking fancy cakes and wrapping beef roast in pie dough with flower patterns or pouring sauces on everything,"

Koby stated flatly. "A man cooks to live, not to play."

Simon shrugged, watching Delilah move toward the snow-covered wagon road and scan it. "She's longing for your brother, Richard. It's eating at her. She's keeping other emotions to herself as well. She won't be happy until she has found her answers."

"I know this."

Delilah didn't like being near him, Simon thought, remembering how she edged away and around him. There was a disdaining impatience when she turned to find him too close, a quiet, controlled anger that he longed to fuel.

He couldn't push her now. He wanted to be near her when Richard arrived.

He remembered her eyes when he had been very ill—they were soft and warm and haunting.

"You and Delilah have the same proud manner. You speak very little and yet you have deep feeling for each other. Your mother must have been a wonderful woman."

Koby was quiet too long, then he said, "She was a woman who liked to laugh."

Simon sensed intense, dark emotions. "Delilah doesn't smile easily. That same stillness is in you."

Koby shrugged and looked at the cattle. He smoothed his right earlobe. "I watch you with your fancy merino wool undershirt and suspenders and flannel . . . pajamas. You have different ways, but you are a good man. You talk with the dogs and the cattle. . . . You feel one with the wind and the earth, and your spirit is clean and strong. You grieved for your horse in a quiet, deep way. You give Moose and Tallulah a warmth I cannot. You will not hurt my sister, Simon Oakes," he said knowingly.

Simon inhaled the freezing air. Koby rarely spoke more than a few words, but his thoughts ran deep. "No . . . I won't hurt her." He met Koby's eyes evenly. "But I want her."

After a pause Koby nodded. "She chooses her life. You see more than her face. You see inside. How she has fought for her life, how she has kept Tallulah safe. Delilah has raised my brother Richard. This was not easy for a woman alone. She has paid prices. You see she gives Moose a home and makes him feel like he is working for his pay when he cannot. She sees that his dogs are fed when they are costly to keep."

"Yes, I see a little inside Delilah and I want her," Simon repeated slowly. Koby and Delilah cared deeply about those around them, and Delilah clearly loved Richard.

Could Richard share this tender blood and kill ruthlessly? Koby and Delilah hated whiskey traders; their product was generally a blend of everything but genuine liquor—for Indian trade goods. Yet Mordacai Wells was a known whiskey trader.

Simon inhaled the freezing air; it knifed into his lungs. Mordacai Wells slaughtered deer to practice his marksmanship; Richard Smith had nursed an orphaned fawn back to health, according to his sister. He'd mended a hawk's wing and nursed a foal into life when the mare had died. The boy had fought two drunken white men abusing an Indian woman. While Wells was described as an emotionless killer, Richard Smith laughed easily and played boyish pranks that hurt no one. Could he have changed in three years?

Simon looked at Delilah. As a woman, she fascinated him. So fiercely independent, hoarding her secrets in her silence, Delilah loved the people around her. It was in every touch, every look.

Simon wanted those thoughts, those touches and caring looks. He pressed his lips together. She was the sister, the protective older sister, of a man he had sworn to arrest and bring to trial. Little could come of seeking Delilah out as a woman.

She barely acknowledged his presence now.

After Richard was in custody, she'd hate his accuser.

Simon frowned at Delilah's lonely body silhouetted against the vast, blinding snow. He wanted to peel away her defenses, find the woman who loved so deeply that she'd risk everything for her loved ones.

There was that, and the damnable need to kiss her.

Simon had an idea that one kiss from Delilah wouldn't be enough. Not nearly enough.

He wanted to penetrate that cool, quiet grace and stir the woman beneath. If ever a woman needed stirring, Delilah did, and Simon found a smile curling on his lips. Stirring Delilah to a froth was an exciting idea. She thought him to be an adventurer and a drunk, her eyes flicking contempt at him when he deliberately blocked her path in the small confines of the cabin.

He really couldn't help teasing her. She responded wonderfully. Not in a wild temper, but rather a steaming heat that excited and delighted Simon. When he told her that she didn't need to hide the liquor he had just found, Delilah had steamed beautifully.

Koby smiled slightly as Simon took a step toward Delilah. "Since you are hunting, be careful. Your prey has a dark temper. The rest do not know this, but she does. Maybe she will add more scars to your pelt, Man With a Red Beard."

"Delilah is a woman of conscience. She'll sew them up."

Koby grinned, shook his head, and began shoveling snow. He looked up when Delilah shrieked. Simon had just pelted her with a snowball.

Delilah stared at Simon, who grinned broadly. "What do you think you're doing?" she asked tightly as she brushed the snow from her shoulder.

Simon bent and began forming another snowball. "The snow is just right."

"For what?"

She shouldn't have asked. The second snowball hit her stomach. She scowled at him and swept away the snow with a flick of her glove.

"Well, come on. Make a snowball and do your best."

"I've never thrown snowballs in my life." She hadn't had time to play in her lifetime, nor had she regretted it. Until now. Right now she'd play snowballs with Richard until eternity froze over.

"Time to start." Simon's challenge interrupted her thoughts of Richard and her regrets. The third snowball hit her shoulder, and he said, "You're behind. Look, I'll stand here. Won't say a word and you can hit me anywhere. Right in the face if you want. I'll close my eyes and I won't move." He stood, legs apart in the narrow channel through the snow that was piled high on either side.

"You're acting like a child. I don't have time for games," Delilah snapped, and began to walk back to the cabin. "Nor fine-feathered vagrants."

She'd had enough of Simon. He'd moved into her life and turned it upside down with cooking, afternoon teas, and card games. He read Artissima's poetry books aloud and delighted Tallulah with his flourishes of gallantry—she'd blushed when he bowed deep to her. Now he stood in the path blocking Delilah's return to the cabin. The deep snow prevented her from going around him easily. He loomed over her. "I am not a vagrant. I am paying for my keep."

"Step aside." Delilah faced him. He was angry, his jaw locking into an arrogant angle. Well, so was she.

She lifted her chin and resented the distance between her face and his. "I said, stand aside." She didn't like the sound of her raised voice, nor the scowl on her face. With effort, her fists tightening, she forced her expression to cool into one of bland indifference. "I'm considering asking you to leave."

"What? You want to lose the money for my keep? Then there's the matter of your gentle heart, Delilah. You plucked me from death. According to some Indian customs, you are responsible for me now. You wouldn't turn away a man needing shelter in the very deepest winter, would you?"

"I don't play or tease, Simon. I'm not like Artissima and Tallulah and whatever long list of women who have pampered you in the past . . . and I'm not 'Your Amelia,' " she warned, anger trembling around her. "Out of my way."

He tilted his head, and the sunlight slid along the snow to tangle in the reddish tints. "I'd have to back up, Delilah. I'm not a man to do that lightly."

Then, in the next instant, Simon bent and lifted her easily. His face was close to hers, his expression dangerous. Before she recovered fully, Simon pivoted and placed her on the other side of the snow path. He gently dusted away the snow clinging to her cheek with cold, hard fingers. "There. There. Please don't ignite, little Delilah. Just say 'Thank you, Simon' very nicely."

Delilah took a breath, placed her hands on his stomach, and pushed. Instantly Simon locked his hands onto her wrists and

took her back with him into the deep bank of snow, turning
his body as they fell.

She landed beneath him, her wrists still caught in his hands.
Simon stared at her, his eyes darkening. "Get up—" she whis-
pered fiercely, and stopped as his lips brushed hers lightly.
They lingered and heated, and Delilah held her breath as
Simon's lids closed, sunlight dancing across his lashes.

Their breath swirled into the cold air, mingling, curling, and
enclosing them. Delilah caught the dark hunger Simon quickly
shielded.

She stiffened, her heart ricocheting against her chest, pounding wildly. She hadn't lain beneath a man in an eternity,
yet all the ugly past came back, circling her in the blinding
sunlight and the cold snow. She had lain still then, too, while
Ezrah tried to prove his virility and failed. He'd railed at her
later: "Everyone knows about your mother and her half-breed
son. You don't even know who your father is. Then she
bore another bastard, Richard. You have her name, but you
can't please a man in bed. . . . You're stupid and cold, not a
woman. . . ."

The legacy that was her mother's gift would always come
back. She felt nauseated now, sweating despite the freezing temperatures. She began trembling and hated herself for revealing
her weakness.

When she opened her eyes, Simon's frown was tender and
concerned. He tugged the woolen cap she had been wearing
down over her ears. "Shhh . . . Quit squirming. Can't you see
I'm trying to get up and you are too heavy?"

She blinked, shivering in her emotions. Simon Oakes probably outweighed her by almost a hundred pounds of solid
muscle. "What?"

"You're squashing me, lass. I'm a dainty thing," he whispered, watching her closely. Then, holding her gently, he rolled
carefully to his back. He lay beneath her, solid and warm, his
arms at his sides. He was teasing her, and she didn't understand
any of it.

The air stilled as she looked down at him, tears burning at
the back of her lids. "Shhh," Simon whispered gently. "Up
you go. Good girl."

That night, while the others slept, Delilah dressed quickly and eased from the cabin. She wanted to be alone with her thoughts and her desperate longing for Richard.

As a boy, Richard had pelted her with snowballs and demanded that she build snow forts. He had sulked when she had worked rather than played. Simon's play had brought her need for Richard instantly surging to life, and she regretted not playing with her little brother.

She should have taken time to play with Richard. Echoes of his *Play with me* swirled through the shadows. Play? There had barely been time to survive—

Was he safe?

Why had his letters, no more than little pictures on paper, stopped?

Was Richard alive?

She had to find him.

Chapter Six

The last week of February
Delilah closed the door to the barn. She needed privacy. The small cabin left little room to escape Simon—his poetry readings, his cooking, and his easy, polished manners with Tallulah and Artissima. His gallant flourishes seemed even broader when he applied them to Delilah, his eyes teasing her.

Teasing. Simon was an overgrown, self-indulgent boy who knew how to charm men and women. Delilah frowned. He wasn't charming her. She hadn't had experience with charmers, but Simon was one. It poured out of him like melted butter. He was a ladies' man for certain and seemed to delight in tormenting her with it.

Simon's embroidered suspenders were the mark of a dandy.

His stories were that of an adventurer with no roots.

He'd arrived drunk and had caused the death of a horse.

Simon had been encamped in the cabin for a full month, filling it with his huge body and a subtle masculine scent

she would recognize in a crowd. She resented the ease with
which he fit into her family, apparently used to idling away
the long hours of winter's enclosure. She doubted that he
was hunting his brother's murderer; a man like Simon moved
slowly, elegantly.

Especially when he tormented her—he hesitated just a second before he stepped out of her way, and his green eyes
lighted when he suspected he'd nettled her. He acted like a
huge boy at times, like when he'd danced around the cabin
with Tallulah.

Like flicking a small bit of flour in Artissima's face.

Delilah frowned. . . . Like asking her to practice birdcalls
and placing his hand on either side of her cheeks. "Pucker
and blow," he had ordered before she'd jerked away. There
was just that slight caress of his thumb along her jawline—

*"You're squashing me. . . . I'm a dainty thing. . . . Shhh. Up
you go. . . . Good girl. . . . "*

Simon Oakes was about as dainty as a playful grizzly.

Filled with scents of hay and animals, her private place was
a snug escape after the others slept. Two favorite milk cows
shared the looming shadows with the horses. The cattle herd
was not far, resting in a small valley protected from wind and
returning to the ranch to feed. Delilah leaned her head against
Lasway's warm throat and hugged him closely. Accustomed
to treats, the Appaloosa snorted and nuzzled her pocket. She
fed him a small carrot from the root cellar and patted Kloshe's
forehead. Kloshe was a strong little cayuse mare, and because
she was gentle, Delilah had given her the Chinook name for
"pleasant." The other horses circled Delilah, and she gave them
each a precious bit of carrot.

"Richard, where are you?" she asked the moon peeking
through a crack in the logs. She wrapped her shawl more
closely around her chest, rocked herself, and thought of her
lost brother. "Richard?"

Koby's face was the dark mirror of Richard's angular young
one. While Koby's expression was either impassive or guard-
ed, her younger brother's emotions were easily read. Richard
had delighted in pelting her with snowballs just as Simon had
last week.

He'd watched her since they'd fallen in the snow, the curious lick of green eyes finding her when she was deepest in thought. Delilah covered her damp eyes with her hands and breathed slowly.

Simon had kissed her . . . a warm brush of his mouth against hers . . . and she'd panicked, pushing against the solid width of his shoulders. Was the pain shifting quickly across his face from his healing wound or from something else?

Delilah ran her fingertips slowly across her lips and frowned. Simon Oakes's lips had seemed . . . sweet. So had Ezrah's . . . at first; they had changed after their marriage.

She'd forgiven Ezrah many things, such as his lack of courtesy. In a time when people lived in a bold new country, Ezrah had seemed no different from other men. Simon seemed all too different.

Simon Oakes was a match for Artissima's fancy manners. He pulled out chairs, seating the ladies properly at the table, and tonight had offered to polish Delilah's boots, saying that they were cracked and needing oiling. Simon's boots were black and gleaming—a vanity a workman would not have time to maintain. Delilah raised her leg and studied the butternut trousers tucked into her high laced boot. She oiled her own boots just fine.

And, no, she didn't want her hair braided and swirled as intricately as Simon had fixed Artissima's. She refused to fall before Simon's pampering, as had Tallulah and Artissima.

Delilah closed her eyes and remembered Simon's big, dark hands fashioning a dainty doily with a crochet hook he had extracted from the sewing kit in his saddlebags. She shook her head.

Koby, Moose, and Simon lingered over repairing leather reins and sharpening knives. They discussed salmon oil and dressing a bear, tanning hides with brains and stretching them. There was knife sharpening and gun cleaning and cards. Simon had repaired Artissima's beloved "lately of the South" ruffled parasol; he delighted Moose with chilling readings of Edgar Allan Poe. Tallulah was clearly besotted when Simon concocted a special soap and a soothing oil for her chapped skin.

When he wasn't endearing himself to everyone but Delilah, Simon read Artissima's precious novels. They discussed *Moby Dick* so intensely that Moose began telling whaling stories that lasted for days.

When Simon learned that Koby had smoked salmon on hand, he prepared a Russian soup of salmon, salt pork, tomatoes, dried onions, and potatoes. An old miner, Moose remembered the recipe and was delighted. This led to a debate on *Kwass,* a home-brewed malt liquor that Moose insisted had no equal, and Simon baked a *perok,* a Russian salmon pie.

He tucked Tallulah's huge apron around his chest and kneaded and rolled pie dough with concentrated relish—as if he were creating art. A big man, Simon moved easily in the small space. When he and Koby returned with rabbits and birds, Simon couldn't wait to start cooking.

He stuffed and roasted birds. He made gravies and stews. He hummed happily while he basted and kneaded. No doubt his beloved Amelia liked him fussing in the kitchen.

Just who Delilah needed—a pajama-wearing dandy, an adventurer and a drunk who loved to cook. Poor Amelia was waiting for him, and he dallied day by day. Delilah inhaled sharply, then flicked her large shawl open and spread it upon the haystack. She eased down into the hay, keeping her hair on the shawl.

The cabin was crowded, and at times tempers flew, soothed by Koby and Simon. This was her time, a quiet space in the night, when she could be alone with her thoughts. She wrapped the shawl around her and lay there, listening to the barn creak. The cows and horses stirred and settled as the barn door creaked slightly and Baby Boy padded to her, his eyes white in the moonlight. Delilah didn't move, but stretched out a hand to pet the sled dog. "So you've escaped the pen again, have you? Come here," she murmured, tugging him close and settling back into the hay.

She nuzzled Baby Boy's warm coat. She had Koby and her dear friends and the horses. There was little Amoteh—"Strawberry" in the Chinook language; Boston; Magnolia; and Lamontay, the "mountain." Lamontay, a big draft horse, whinnied when Phantom came out of the shadows.

The stallion's pale hide caught the faint light. He was a big, strong, mixed Hambletonian breed who had appeared to claim Kloshe back into his wild herd. He'd stayed close since Christmas, returning with a fresh bullet wound skimmed across his rump. No one had attempted to ride him, though Koby had plans to begin breaking the stallion in the spring.

Baby Boy shifted comfortably and nestled down in the hay with her. She rocked him gently, her friend in the night, and closed her eyes.

From the shadows Simon eased the barn door slowly closed.

The moonlight lay on Delilah's pale face, gleaming in the long hair spread around her head. She was sleeping now and vulnerable.

Simon's hand closed into a fist. He wanted to hold her, to shelter her for a time, just as she cared for Tallulah's approaching blindness and Moose's worsening arthritis. She'd given Artissima the protection a single woman needed in a savage land, a home to tend and a quiet, enduring friendship.

When Delilah lay beneath him in the snow, their steamy breath mingling between them, her eyes had widened for just a heartbeat, fear racing through them. She'd been startled like a doe caught before a hunter's rifle. A tremor had run down her body, and her face had paled instantly. Some fool had frightened Delilah badly—

She had saved Simon's life, risking her own, and she'd fiercely protect the young brother he had come to take. Simon had learned that she'd battled nature and lack of money and men who wanted to marry her for her ranch. Simon watched the dark fringe of her lashes and the soft, gentle curve of her mouth. Passions ran deep in Delilah, and she covered them well.

There was just that flounce of anger when he came too near, that flash of blue fire in her eyes before she quickly shielded her emotions.

Delilah snuggled on the hay. When she settled with a sigh, Simon realized he had been holding his breath. Baby Boy's white eyes watched Simon move through the shadows and crouch beside her. He studied the soft curve of her cheek, the shadows playing around her eyes, the sweep of silvery moonlight across her lashes. Her hand lay curled near her face and Simon wanted to press a kiss into the very center of it. A black silky strand crossed her cheek and Simon eased it away from her mouth.

She stirred, and before Simon could move back into the shadows, Delilah's lashes fluttered once, then her eyes opened.

They stared at each other. "What do you want?" she asked unevenly, her face tight and pale in the moonlight. She sat up and angrily whisked the long hair away from her face with a sweep of her hand.

"Why are you afraid of me?" Simon asked, realizing suddenly how much this woman captivated him. Flushed from sleep, looking disheveled and cuddly, he wanted to hold her and tell her that everything would be all right.

His stomach clenched. Everything wouldn't be fine—he was after her brother, a brother she had raised and protected for a lifetime. Her instincts to protect Richard would be as fierce as a mother's. The muscles in Simon's jaw contracted; Rand's killer would be brought to justice.

"I'm not afraid of you."

"Would you stay and talk with me?" he asked gently. In his time at the cabin, Delilah had not spoken freely to him.

Her eyes flicked at him warily, then away into the shadows. "There's no reason. There is nothing to say."

He settled on the hay, a distance away from her, and Baby Boy came nuzzling his hand, wanting a petting. Simon stroked the black fur thoughtfully. "That day when I threw a snowball at you—when I fell on you—you were frightened."

She impatiently flicked a piece of hay away from her cheek. It fluttered to her breast, lifting and falling with each breath. "No, I wasn't. I'm going into the house."

"Yes. I knew you wouldn't stay. I knew you'd run from me." Simon tossed the verbal bone at her and watched her chew on his challenge.

She hesitated, lifted her head, and looked at him coolly. She wrapped the shawl around her. "What do you want to talk about?"

He lay back in the hay and folded his hands over his stomach. "I'm waiting."

"Well?" she prodded impatiently. "Talk."

"You talk."

They sat in the silence. "All right," Simon said slowly. "You don't like me, do you?"

"I don't have to."

"Have I embarrassed you? Made you uncomfortable in some way?"

"You're a drifter, Simon," she said slowly. "Amelia is waiting for you, and you don't seem bothered to be away from her. She's probably worried. You've spent time with women—your ways are easy, like opening doors and pulling out chairs to seat us. I especially don't like that bit of refinement. If you're a married man, you don't act it."

Simon smiled. He irritated Delilah, which was better than indifference. Disturbing Delilah, dragging her out of her quiet control, was exciting. "I've never married. Are you saying that I might—just perhaps—make my living from women? Why, Delilah, you compliment me."

She shot him a frown. "No cowman would have taken a horse out with a blizzard hanging overhead and waiting to let go."

He shrugged. This woman knew where to place her barbs. "True."

Delilah eased to stand. She faced him squarely, her legs slightly apart. "You're a drifter and a dandy—a ladies' man, Simon. No doubt some women appreciate your easy ways. I don't. You're used to whiling away time—reading and playing. I've got no use for drifters, dandies, or drunks," she said, reminding him of his condition when she had rescued him.

"I will marry," Simon stated, defending himself. Delilah was the only woman who had ever questioned his honor or caused a dire need to toss her on the hay and show her ways to while away time that were more enjoyable than reading and playing. "And beget children. As it happens, when I find the right woman, I'm marrying her on the spot."

He'd decided to marry before Rand's death. Somehow, seeing his brother lifeless had reached into Simon's gut and

twisted some infinite knot of want to create a child, to foster
a life and nourish it and love the woman who shared that life.
He'd always wanted a family and love like his parents and his
brothers and sisters, but Rand's death threw Simon's empty life
and dreams at his feet. Delilah's low opinion of him scraped
his past life and left him raw.

She took a deep breath and shrugged. "Fine. Marry when
you want. Beget all the children you want. You have money
for your keep, and the snow is too deep for you to move on.
So you're staying for a time. You'll move on when you can. I
don't believe that story about finding your brother's murderer.
But it makes a nice tale."

"Why, Delilah, that's the most you've said to me for an entire
month. I didn't know you cared," Simon pressed, delighted
when vivid anger shot into her face. Delilah wasn't the calm,
cool woman she played, and knowing that he could delve into
her emotions, stirring them, delighted Simon.

He studied her squared shoulders, her fists pressed into her
shawl. She reminded him of lightning zigzagging against a
dark thunderous sky.

Her eyes narrowed dangerously, like twin silver blades cutting at him. "I know about men like you. I've seen them all
my life. Maybe not so grand, decorated with embroidered
suspenders or black, shiny boots. I've known hardworking
men—miners, cowmen, farmers, and wolfers. They get what
they want, and they pass on. You will, too. Like leaves blowing
away in the wind."

She was trembling, forcing her head high, her knuckles
white on the dark shawl. Her control was thin now, and Simon
pricked at it, foraging for answers. "So you've had to fight to
survive. Who hasn't?"

He was challenging her, pushing, invading what she wanted
to hoard away, and he knew it. He wanted to rip away the cool
mask she gave to others and leave nothing but truth between
them. Over her shoulder, Delilah stared at him through the
shadows. "I doubt you know what I'm talking about."

"No, I don't. Because you haven't told me, have you?" He
lay back in the hay, his fingers locked tightly behind his head.
A shaft of moonlight coming through the old roof caught on

Delilah's white face. She turned suddenly, the silky, long black hair flying out exotically before it settled around her shoulders, spilling down over her breasts.

"I don't have to explain anything, but I'll tell you," she whispered in a low harsh voice, pushing the back of her hand impatiently across her face. Simon heard the loud sound of his heartbeat. Or was it hers?

She lifted her face to the moonlight and tears shimmered on her lashes. "My mother's inheritance to me was her shame. I wear her name, Delilah, and I've paid for everything she ever did. It didn't matter how hard I tried . . . how hard I worked . . . what she was . . . what people thought she was—they said I was cut from her mold."

The tears were trailing down her cheeks now, silvery trails glistening and slipping to her chest like tiny diamonds threaded onto a silken string. Her hand drew slowly into a fist, then rose to press against her throat. She was rocking on her heels now, the pieces of her life tearing at her, pulling away heart and nerves and skin. ". . . I was horrible to her. . . ."

The thin whisper echoed throughout the shadowy barn as Delilah slid to her knees. Her shoulders hunched, and she curled into a ball as if protecting herself from blows. Simon sat up slowly. Little kept him from picking her up and holding her close. He held his breath for a heartbeat. He'd seen men and women who had controlled the monsters within themselves, and who faced fears and the past. Tearing of the heart was as painful as wounding of the body. If he pushed her too much . . . "Koby says you look like her," he said gently.

"Yes." The word was a desperate sob hurled into the shadows. Delilah's body curled tighter, her hair spilling around her and catching the silvery moonlight as she rocked herself. "I yelled at her. . . . Oh, she was so sick, so frail, and still beautiful, with a smile that—We were living on nothing. Richard needed food. . . . Tallulah was working so hard, and I . . . I hated my mother for what she'd done—"

What was she doing? Delilah asked herself desperately as she brushed away the tears flowing hotly down her cheeks.

Here she was, sharing the deepest part of her pain with a drift-er—a fancy-suspender-wearing drifter, she corrected. Then Simon was drawing her to her feet and wrapping her in his arms. He rocked her gently and Delilah reached out and clung to him as though he were the last strong tree preventing her from falling into a cold, endless abyss. She should step away, if only she didn't feel so safe.

She inhaled Simon's scent, singling it away from the rest, and fought the dark quiver of warmth circling her. She didn't want to recognize the painful needs swirling within her, beating at her. Her senses tingled, heated, and glowed as Simon's open hands stroked her back and smoothed her hips.

Delilah stood very still within his arms, aware that the vein in his throat pounded heavily against her face. Whatever was happening to her, shouldn't be—not with this man, this drifter, this ladies' man with the embroidered suspenders and the fancy recipes. His uneven breath stirred the tendrils clinging to her temple. She sensed him struggling as a great tremor ran through him and his arms tightened. She fought the urge to arch against him and lock him to her. She couldn't move away any more than she could stop breathing.

"Well," he said finally, in a quiet explosion of breath, as if the word answered everything. "Delilah, when a loved one leaves, it's natural to be angry for a time."

Then he reached down to lift her chin. His kiss was so slow she could have moved away. So gentle she ached for more. So seeking, she wanted to arch up into him and hold on until the world drifted away—Delilah floated beneath the soft, warm brush of his mouth, again and again—

Then a horse nickered, throwing her back into the cold airy barn and against a man whom she held in contempt.

"You know just the right things to say, don't you, Mr. Fancy Manners?" she shot back, stepping away. She trembled and wished Simon back to that tree limb in the blizzard. This time she'd leave him there. Whatever he caused her to feel wasn't what she wanted, and anger shot through her like a hot branding iron. How dare he step inside her life? How dare he hold her so gently? How dare he kiss her, stirring something so dark and sinful she didn't want to acknowledge?

Delilah battled her past and the unnerving, recent brush of Simon's lips. He loomed in the shadows over her as if nothing could dislodge him. "Natural? Nothing was natural," she said flatly, fiercely. "Don't you understand? She gave up after Richard was born. She said she was so tired. I saw her leave life—leave us when we needed her, and I—"

"You were a child." Simon reached out a hand and smoothed away a sleek strand from her cheek. Her hand lashed out at him. She was shaking, tears streaming down her cheeks.

The layers of control were bursting now, coming apart, seam by seam. "We lived on charity and scraps ever since I could remember. 'Marry a good man,' she said. I did, or thought I did—I won't marry again."

"You will, Delilah. You'll change your mind," Simon murmured as if he was as certain of that fact as he was certain of dawn.

"No." Delilah wrapped her shawl and her control tightly around her. "That's enough. Far too much. I don't believe I can forgive you for this, Mr. Oakes," she stated unevenly. Then she was gone.

Simon watched her stride into the house and close the door.

"Ah, Baby Boy," he whispered, rising to close the barn door. "There are scars and there are scars. Our Miss Delilah is fighting desperately to conceal her emotions, and she's angry now with me. But we've seen through the door, haven't we?"

Delilah's lips were soft as down, a tremor of hunger simmering just beneath that sweet taste. She might hide in loose shirts and pants and cool control, but he'd seen through to the lightning and the fire.

He sank into the hay, and the running dog curled close, his eyes pale in the moonlight. Simon stroked the dog's lush fur and thought about Delilah fighting him and her past.

Richard would come back to his sister. The bond was deep.

From the target near the house—a tin can nailed to a pine tree—Simon had dug out a slug with the same rifling marks as the one that killed Rand. He could get a conviction on that alone. The deep blue eyes and the horseshoe stickpin added to the convincing list.

The puzzle fit; all Simon had to do was to wait. He'd waited two months, and the suspect wouldn't be traveling far in the deep snow.

March swept by, melting the snow in the low valleys, and Delilah avoided Simon. He nestled in the bosom of her home as if he would never leave and delighted Artissima by crocheting small doilies. He had won Tallulah's heart already, but the gift of a small magnifying glass endeared him even more.

The first week of April, Delilah fought the fever from her lingering cold and chose the seeds that she wished to purchase from the general store. At her side, Artissima made lists of the necessities in her slanted, elegant script. Delilah glanced at Simon's big, dark hands deftly working the slender crochet hook and shook her head. Whatever he was fashioning was long, exquisitely delicate, and draped down across one knee. The silver hook flashed as he advised Tallulah how to sugar-starch the ruffled doily he had just completed.

Delilah closed her eyes, sniffed, and wished him away to Amelia, where he could begin begetting. Delilah's headache worsened when Artissima and Simon debated on various cures for her fever. When Simon suggested that she add whiskey to the tea they made her drink, she glowered at him.

He had smiled back blandly as if everything in the world was perfect.

Delilah regretted her dark frown at him. It only made her head hurt worse, and the loss of control irritated her.

"You know, I get hungry for jellied moose nose every once in a while," Moose grumbled conversationally as he rocked by the fire, a blanket across his knees. "That and a broiled caribou head would hit the spot now."

Simon chuckled and the low, rumbling sound traveled along Delilah's tight nerves. ". . . Four pounds of beans . . . one of carrots," she finished. "Has Koby come back from checking on the cattle? I should have gone with him."

"No, you shouldn't have gone. You've got a spring cold, honey," Artissima returned, neatly folding her list and placing it on her business shelf. "Simon, poor Delilah looks miserable."

"Chicken broth," Simon returned, placing aside his crocheting on the table and studying Delilah closely. "A good chicken broth with onions would do wonders for her. Green onions and garlic with red pepper. Perhaps a good egg drop soup."

He glanced at the double columns of numbers in front of her. "That looks like a code," he said, studying Delilah's figures more carefully. He picked up the paper and concentrated on it. "It is a code. An intricate one. Delilah, you use numbers for store goods."

Delilah grabbed the list away. Simon poked into everything; no portion of her life seemed safe from his prying.

"She does?" Artissima asked, taking the paper and holding it to the light. "Why, land's sakes, honey. These are just the numbers you gave me for pounds of bean seed and carrot. Look at that. The slash under the numbers means half—yes, you told me four of beans and one of carrot seed. Then look at this, you've added up the cost." Artissima stared at Delilah blankly.

Delilah didn't want to share her past or how she used the code to keep inventory and clerk at the Mortons' store. Numbers had always come very easily to her, and it was a secret she hoarded with the rest. She braced her elbows on the table and placed her hands on her head, trying to contain the throbbing headache. "I want Koby," she muttered, fidgeting with a tendril that was pulled too tightly at the back of her nape.

Koby would rescue her from Simon's eternal prying.

"She braids her hair too tight," Simon murmured, deftly undoing the plaits and smoothing her hair before she could stop him. Delilah pushed back the rippling mass and glared up at him.

Since she was never ill—nor could afford to be—she blamed Simon for her feverish cold. She'd begun to think of him as an immense, immaculately mannered bad-luck omen. She'd gone an entire lifetime without anyone recognizing her skills for summing, and he'd ripped away that secret in a space of one breath.

"He'll be back lickety-split," Artissima said soothingly.

Delilah stood and braced her hands on the table. "It's getting late. I'm going after him."

"No, you're not," Simon said quietly, firmly, before he pulled her onto his lap and held her head against his shoulder with one big hand. He pressed a handkerchief against her nose and ordered, "Blow."

She glared at him, trying to fit words through her lips to properly scald him. "There, there . . ." Simon crooned to her disbelief. She hadn't been cuddled and rocked and comforted since she was a baby. Simon drew her against him and tucked his chin over her head. It was like being wrapped in a warm, living chair.

His other hand stroked her back and hair, and he cradled her against him as easily as a child. Delilah closed her burning lids and pushed against him feebly. Whatever soft living Simon had done, his body was muscular. She didn't believe the image of herself—a grown woman—perched on Simon's knee.

She sensed Artissima, Tallulah, and Moose hovering nearby, and then Simon began to rock her gently. "Shhh, little Delilah . . . shhh . . ."

"I'm not your darling Amelia," she muttered and wondered how many times Simon had cuddled Amelia on his lap. The thought plopped into her fever like cold spit.

He chuckled and gathered her closer. "Amelia is a soft little thing. Not at all like you."

"Huh. That means big hips and an enormous bosom," Delilah muttered darkly. Simon's burst of laughter caused her headache to feel as if it had added another heavy brick. "You'll have to give up womanizing when you marry, Simon. It won't do," she added darkly.

"I will. I intend to womanize my wife and make the bed creak for a full week after the wedding," he said coarsely, a sudden tenseness humming around his body.

Despite her fever, Delilah's body started aching and her breasts swelled against Simon's hard chest. She blinked with the sinful thought that she wanted to press her naked breasts against his hairy, hard chest.

Delilah scrunched her eyelids shut. The fever had caught her, unbalanced her mind.

Artissima wrapped a blanket around Delilah, who pushed it away and tried to rise. Her head throbbed and Simon gradually eased her down onto his lap. The rocking and soothing stroking on her back continued, and Delilah closed her eyes. Why was he doing this? she wondered distantly.

She was safe.

His arms were strong, his hands soothing.

She could rest, and she was safe, if only for a moment. At least until the sinful thoughts came back. Because she certainly wasn't having Simon Oakes served up to her on a creaking bed.

Delilah shuddered. There was Amelia waiting, with her soft bosom and big hips.

"I'm not a child," Delilah heard herself murmur as Simon's big hand cradled her head against his shoulder and his fingers smoothed slow circles on her temple.

"She didn't sleep last night or for the past week. She's been working outside and fighting her cold," Artissima was saying. "You keep rocking her, Simon."

Delilah listened to the heavy thud of Simon's heart beneath her cheek.

She was safe. Amelia would have to wait.

Simon's chair began creaking as he rocked; Artissima and Tallulah spoke quietly and began the evening meal. Simon held one of her hands, sliding his larger fingers between hers. Silly, she thought. A silly thing to do, holding hands. Somehow it made her feel better. Then Simon whispered against her temple, "Koby is safe. He won't leave you, my dear Delilah. Your Koby will be back. . . ."

She awoke to Koby's black, concerned eyes staring at her, his big hand cold on her flushed cheek. He was crouching in front of her as she lay on Simon's lap. "Little Sister," he said, smiling tenderly. "So you are a baby now?" he asked softly, his eyes teasing her as she pushed away the blanket covering her and sat up.

Her hair slid coolly along her cheek. She looked into Simon's dark green eyes and blinked.

There was hunger in Simon's look, his body taut beneath hers. His gaze drifted to her lips and lingered.

She thought of the bouncing, creaking bed. She thought of Simon's heavy body lying on hers. She thought of Simon taking her small breast in his hand and comparing it to Amelia's giant udders. She knew Amelia was soft and round, because men wanted well-stuffed women. From the hot look Simon was giving her and the tension humming through him, he truly needed Amelia. Delilah could almost hear the bed creak—

Simon shifted slightly, and Delilah looked at Koby blankly. Koby was grinning widely, a flash of white teeth against his dark face. "Ah . . . if you would kindly take your baby sister. . . ." Simon invited Koby in a deep, uneven tone. "She's squashing me."

Koby's eyebrows lifted and he chuckled as Simon stood upright with Delilah in his arms. "Here," he said in a raw tone, easing her into Koby's arms and striding out the door. "I've got to check on the stock."

Koby laughed outright.

Chapter
Seven

The next morning Delilah pushed back the bowl of cooked cracked wheat. The warm chinook wind howled around the corners of the cabin, and snow slid from the roof. She gathered the blanket Tallulah had wrapped around her shoulders closer in one tight fist and leaned toward her brother. "Koby, what do you mean, 'Richard is running from the law'?"

Koby shook his head. "It has to be Richard. The description matches, even if the man's name is Mordacai Wells. Same age, same height, black hair, and blue eyes. The rifling from the gun barrel is marked. There are twin burrs in the barrel, marking the bullets—"

"What do you mean?"

"The constables have the slugs from the bodies—there were murders—and from the robberies. Witnesses identified that fancy gun of Richard's—pearl handle and etched silver. The rifling marks match exactly, and Wells sports a horseshoe stickpin."

Delilah's hand went to her throat, her body suddenly cold despite the warmth of the blanket. She gripped Koby's hand with her free one. "Koby. Oh, Koby. It isn't Richard. I know it."

Koby's fingers curled around hers. "Wells is missing the tip of his little finger, left hand."

"I don't believe it . . . not a word, Koby. You say they saw him in the Quesnelmouth-Barkerville area. That's almost six hundred miles north of here in Canada. Who told you?"

Her brother shrugged. "Miners' stories flow like the wind. Even now they are whispering that it is Richard using a false name."

Artissima rested her hand on Delilah's shoulder. Tallulah and Moose quietly drank their morning coffee. Simon lounged against the wall, bracing his shoulder against it, and studied the shine on the toe of his boot. The fire crackled in the stove.

Delilah met Koby's dark eyes. "I'm going after him," she said, her knuckles showing whitely beneath her skin.

"No, you're not," Artissima stated firmly. "Koby, tell her that she's not going."

Koby studied Delilah's pale hand wrapped tightly around his dark one. Delilah would go. He read it in the tears brimming from her eyes, in the set of her body. "It isn't wise. I will go."

"I'm going," she whispered desperately, and Koby nodded slowly.

"No," Artissima snapped. "No, you aren't. I won't hear of it. Koby can go."

Delilah turned to look up at her. The look held and darkened. "You'll be fine," she said quietly. "Koby can take care of the ranch."

She glanced at Tallulah and Moose, who suddenly looked very old. They needed help and protection. "Koby is staying."

"You're not going alone," her brother said quietly. He looked at Simon, who was flipping carelessly through a cookbook. "I'll come with you. Simon, will you manage while we're gone?"

"Me?" Simon's eyebrows lifted. "Manage a ranch? I wouldn't actually have to plow or anything, would I? What

if one of the cows needs help at calving time? . . . Ah, here it
is, Artissima, 'How to Pickle Pigeons.' "

Delilah closed her eyes. She breathed deeply once and
prayed for Amelia to rescue Simon. Once he was busy with
his begetting, he wouldn't have time to interfere with other
people's lives. "Koby, I don't want to lose everything. We've
worked too hard. Simon is a drifter . . . a dandy. He's not a
cowman. He's probably never pulled a calf from a cow in his
life. We can't count on him. You're staying."

She took a deep breath and finished with the most damning
evidence against Simon: "He wears pajamas and embroidered
suspenders, Koby. He crochets."

"I may not be suited to ranching, dear Delilah," Simon said
smoothly. "But you might need a traveling companion, and
don't forget—I am an adventurer, looking for new worlds. I am
at your service, and I am indebted to you for my life. Perhaps
along the way, I'll hear word of my brother's murderer." With
that he bowed deeply, cookbook in hand.

Delilah counted to ten. The anger and frustration circling
her erupted. She slashed out her hand, dismissing the idea,
and used one of Artissima's favorite phrases: "In a pig's eye
you are. Your boots might get dirty. You'd be about as handy
as a wart on the backside of a snake. I don't need a cook, and
I can't baby you."

Simon smiled coolly. "My dear. One never knows the uses
of a wart on the backside of a snake. It could prove to be quite
handy."

Delilah closed her eyes again and was surprised to hear
her quiet groan of frustration. She thought she heard Simon
chuckle.

The next afternoon Delilah came back from the barn and met
Koby and Simon. "I've decided," Koby said quietly, watching
her, "that I will go."

Delilah gripped the bridle she was bringing into the house
to oil before the trip. She turned to him.

Koby's long legs locked at the knee as if expecting an argument, and he nodded solemnly. "You are a woman. When you
brought Tallulah and Richard down from the gold fields, you
had their protection. It is too dangerous for a woman to travel

alone. The Similkameen silver and the Cariboo gold fields are filled with danger. Death from natural causes is not common. You know some safety here. I will go."

"You don't know the people that Richard is likely to contact—I do," she returned, her fingers tightening on the leather. "Richard was afraid of the steamboats. He's deathly afraid of water. Coming down, we took one short trip and the rest on land. He'll be traveling overland, taking the route along Okanogan Lake, Kamloops, and Cache Creek, then the Cariboo wagon road up to Quesnelmouth, then on to Barkerville."

"You give me a map and tell me who Richard is likely to see, and I will find them."

Delilah looked away from Koby's set expression; he looked too much like Richard declaring his rights as a man, determined to take care of her. "Koby, some of them will not respond to you. They won't help you."

His head went back with the same pride as Richard and herself. "Because I am a half-blood."

She didn't want to hurt him. She touched his arm. " . . . And because you know how to use a gun. You wear it like an extra limb, Koby. If Richard is hiding, he doesn't know you. He does know and trust me without question. Don't you see? It has to be me."

Koby's face darkened; his lips tightened. "A woman can't defend herself."

Delilah thought of the times she had defended herself and her family. She thought of the drunken man on the Fraser steamboat, pressing her against the railing. Trying to protect her, Richard had crumbled from the man's backhand blow. Delilah rarely used the skills that Meizhen had taught her, but in her anger she had struck out at the man, sending a blow into his stomach and knocking him to the plank flooring.

Meizhen, a Chinese girl who was Delilah's only childhood friend, had several brothers in the Tong brotherhood. Meizhen, whose name meant "beautiful pearl," was small, agile and was ashamed that she could best any of her four brothers. She had learned to defend herself, and she had taught Delilah in quick sessions in the Barkerville alleys.

". . . A woman is helpless. . . . any woman, Delilah. It's too dangerous," Koby was saying with rare emotion.

"I don't want to argue," Delilah said quietly. She looked at Simon, who was flicking hay from his coat sleeve. His careless arrogance perturbed her. He seemed to bring out her moods, her temper, and she resented letting her past slide beneath his nose, opening her wounds to him. "Is that what you think, too?" she asked Simon carefully. "That I'm helpless? That I need you to defend me if Koby *allows* me to hunt for Richard? Remember, Simon—you owe me."

"I remain in your debt. Yes, Koby. Delilah is calling in my debt. Would you please allow her to make the trip?" Simon returned gravely, but Delilah saw his eyes twinkling.

She had had enough of Ezrah's *"I won't* allow *you, Delilah."*

The two men loomed over her, reminding her of how many of Ezrah's "allows" she had accommodated in the three-year marriage. She knew who Richard would be contacting better than Koby. "So the both of you put your heads together and decided that poor little Delilah can't manage the hardships of the Cariboo. Is that right?"

She turned to Koby. No one was keeping her from finding Richard, not even Koby. "Is that right?" she repeated the demand.

"Yes. It is so," he said firmly.

"Let me have your gun," she said, tossing the bridle to Simon.

Koby slowly, reluctantly, drew his revolver from its tooled holster. Delilah scowled up at him. She had no time for playing. "Give it to me, Koby. I won't hurt it."

He hesitated. "The trigger has been filed."

"So it has a hair trigger. Anything else?" she asked, taking it and hefting the weight experimentally. She pointed it toward the ground and looked down the sight to Simon's well-polished boot toe. He moved it away.

"Delilah . . ." Simon's deep voice warned her.

Delilah lifted the pistol, carefully placed her finger on the trigger, and scanned the woods for a four-inch barren tree branch. "Who do you think fed this outfit and kept deer and rabbits on the table?" she asked tightly. She frowned up at

Simon. "We had a few skillets of snake meat, too, when times were tough. I'll bet you can't find fried rattlesnake in Amelia's cookbooks."

She didn't know why Amelia came to mind, she just popped into Delilah's frustration and wiggled her soft breasts and round hips on Simon's creaking bed. Simon needed to realize that not all women were soft and cuddly, just waiting for a man to take care of them . . . to stake them out and make the bed creak and beget children in their lush hips.

She was angry now, faced with two oversize men blocking out the sunlight and telling her what she could do. "See that branch separate from the rest?"

The branch fell just as the shot echoed in the small valley. She briskly handed the revolver back to Koby, who shook his head. "It is not enough."

"Fine," Delilah said, resenting his arrogance though she knew he wanted to protect her. If he needed a demonstration, she would oblige. "Remove your weapons, Koby, and prepare to defend yourself."

Simon chuckled and Koby stared at her. "This is not funny, Little Sister."

"Ah . . . perhaps I could be of service. You could demonstrate your skills on me," Simon offered as he stood at Koby's side.

Delilah looked up the distance to Simon's cheerful grin and regretted the temper he could arouse in her. "I don't want to hurt you," she said between her teeth.

"A little sweet thing like you? I'll take my chances."

Koby's broad grin added to Simon's challenge. Delilah took one look at the two amused, grinning males and inhaled slowly. "Fine," she repeated before she moved quickly, stepping close to Simon and turning as she grasped his arm. He was heavier than she thought, more fit, but she bent and flipped Simon at Koby's feet.

Simon sprawled in the mud and snow with a satisfactory thud. There was one short, fierce curse in French, and then he glowered up at her.

She wondered briefly why she hadn't thrown him when he was kissing her that night in the barn.

Delilah allowed herself a tight smile even though besting Simon did wonders for her dark mood. She barely withheld a grin as she took the bridle from him. He looked stunned and a little outraged.

Koby frowned down at her. "It is not enough," he persisted.

"Fine," she repeated once more, then she hooked her leg behind Koby's and pushed him on top of Simon.

The two large men scrambled to their feet and swept away the mud and snow clinging to them. "Are we done?" Delilah asked before she entered the house.

That night after supper Artissima tossed out, "Koby, I declare, you are just as dark and gloomy as that old war. A body can't tell what you're thinking most of the time, but you sure have a burr under your saddle."

Koby flicked an arrogant, nettled look at Artissima, then looked at Delilah. "You will tell me where you learned this. You have had to defend yourself from men . . . the man who harmed you, haven't you? This man you married?"

When she didn't answer, Koby left the house. His expression was cold fury.

Simon ran his hand across his jaw, his expression dark. "I'm going," she said flatly, daring him to challenge her. Simon lifted his spread hands in a sign of surrender, then followed Koby out the door.

Delilah placed her hands on her hips and stared at the closed door. Then she closed her eyes, a gesture of frustration that was becoming a habit around Simon, and promised herself that tonight she wouldn't dream about that unnerving sweet kiss in the barn.

"Coffee," Delilah said, glaring over the campfire at Simon ten days later.

"Tea," he returned grimly while frying chopped bacon in a deep pot. He stirred it with a wooden spoon, sniffed, and threw in a handful of dried onions. "You're done in. It will soothe you before sleeping."

Delilah crouched by the campfire and scooped clean snow into the cooking pot. She'd been riding hard, pushing Phantom to his limits, and Simon had followed on Lasway. He'd been there, big and unstoppable every time she looked over her shoulder. They had followed the old Hudson's Bay trading route and camped near the upper Okanagan Lake in British Columbia, Canada.

She crossed her arms, placed her cold hands beneath her armpits, and stared at the fire. Koby, Artissima, Tallulah, and Moose had all tried to stop her. Koby had never wavered from having Simon travel with her. She had agreed in the end because she believed she could either outdistance Simon or make life so difficult for him, he would soon be shed. She didn't understand Koby's trust in a man he barely knew. "Don't hum," she ordered absently.

"Hmm?" Simon frowned as he concentrated on dicing peeled potatoes into the bacon-and-onion mixture.

"You hum while you cook, Simon," Delilah noted stiffly. "Don't."

She refused to mention how much his thorough, neat behavior annoyed her. Everything had to suit him before he began traveling or before he settled down for the night. He polished pots and his carbine with equal, thorough attention. She suspected that Simon did everything that mattered to him in a manner dedicated to complete success. She reluctantly admitted they shared absolute dedication to goals. However, her goal was to remove Simon from her. To strip him from her like excess lint from a black hat.

Delilah frowned; she couldn't overlook one fact—she trusted him not to harm her. After all, his head was occupied with Amelia.

Simon caused Delilah uneasiness. She hadn't thought about kissing before Simon fell with her in the snow. Now she realized that perhaps she had missed another portion of her life, one that was too late to correct. She kicked a branch protruding from the three feet of snow.

"Ah. Someone is in a bad mood," he returned lightly with a sympathetic smile as he crouched by the cookfire. Then he lifted his wooden spoon and sniffed appreciatively at the potato soup he was cooking.

He was dressed in his thick wool-lined cloth coat, a coat that was much warmer than her own worn coat. His brown trousers were tucked into the shiny tops of his boots. Delilah knew that Simon would polish away the mud from his boots before settling down for the night. In the morning he would shave in exactly fourteen strokes. She'd counted for the last two mornings. Then he'd lather again and trim away what he'd missed. He was cheerful in the morning after his first cup of coffee, though he would rather have tea. Simon was very predictable, precise, and irritating.

"Do you know how much time we lose setting up camp each night and cooking hot meals?" she demanded, anger rising in her. Simon had let her best him; his body had tensed instantly when she'd moved against him, then he had relaxed and allowed her to throw him. That knowledge had fueled her anger for days, and Delilah pushed it down. She picked up a stick from the fire and watched the blazing tip. "When you leave, remember that Lasway is my brother's horse. I believe they hang horse thieves."

Simon leveled green eyes at her. It was a cool, assessing stare that rankled Delilah's uncertain mood. "I owe you my life, Delilah. I am obliged to stay with you and offer you my protection."

"My brother could be here instead of you. Instead I found a drunken, pampered adventurer who had cost a good horse its life."

"My hero—excuse me, my heroine!" Simon exclaimed, placing his hand over his heart dramatically. He held Delilah's eyes. "I regret losing Magic. He was a fine horse."

"That's something at least. I can move faster without you," she said, lowering the blazing stick into the fire. Last night Simon had slept beside her in the lean-to they had fashioned from branches and a tarp over the snow. It was a practical arrangement, though Delilah didn't like to admit it. She had awakened to his hand stroking her hair. He'd been sleeping, snoring slightly, and smoothing her hair as if she were a favored pet. When she'd pushed his hand away, there had been just that bit of resistance—as if he kept what he wanted. She had maneuvered around in the lean-to, lying a distance away from Simon's feet. She awoke to Simon's hand shackling her ankle. His thumb had burrowed beneath her trousers and her stocking and was caressing her foot. Delilah did not look forward to sleeping within Simon's reach again. "Koby's notion that a woman shouldn't be alone on the trail is outdated. Consider yourself let go. Leave the horse."

Simon arched one dark brown brow and dropped a scoop of tea leaves into the water pot. "I'll see you through this challenge. I'm afraid you're stuck with me—I'm in your debt, remember? I owe you my life. You'd feel better if we stopped at a farmhouse where you could freshen up. Take a bath, wash your hair, that sort of woman thing. A good steaming bath would take care of your congestion. The horses and the mule could use a warm barn and plenty of grain."

He placed the lid on the water pot. "You know about horses, don't you, Delilah? No one knew Phantom would let you ride him until you swung your saddle on him. You like to keep your secrets, putting everyone outside what you think is best. You've never had to share burdens with anyone, have you? You've simply put one foot in front of the other, doing as you see fit, when you see fit. Did you stop to think that Koby might have shot Phantom if he'd tossed you? Or how Moose and Tallulah would have mourned if Phantom snapped your precious neck?"

His deep voice thrust at her. "Did it occur to you that people want to take care of you? That you take more than you give when you don't allow them to help you?"

"I'm not one for talking. I knew Phantom would let me ride him or I wouldn't have mounted him. This isn't a leisurely stroll, Simon," she said flatly. "Richard could need me right now. I intend to make good time. Just asking questions—if anybody has seen him—is taking too much time."

Simon lifted another eyebrow. "You won't do him any good if you die of pneumonia, will you?"

Delilah stood and looked down at him. Even with the money she had borrowed from Artissima, she didn't have enough to stay at the way stations. While Simon might be used to women tending and pampering him, Delilah was not supporting him. "I won't pay for your keep. You could leave and have Amelia's bed creaking before too long."

A muscle ticked in Simon's jaw, though he casually ignored her. He stirred the boiling soup, dropped a bay leaf into it, and inhaled appreciatively. He plopped an elk steak he had purchased from passing Okanogan Indians into a skillet. While the meat sizzled, he said, "Dinner will be ready shortly. Drink your tea."

Delilah closed her eyes. She never lost her temper. She planned how she would handle situations. She could be just as methodical as Simon, and now he was in her way.

Simon tested her control. She sniffed and Simon looked up. He had shaved in the morning—a meticulous process in which he later folded his supplies and tidied them away—and now his red beard had begun to darken his jaw. "Your nose is running and you're sniffing, Delilah. Go on now, wrap up and rest. I'll bring your tea to you, and you can relax while I finish preparing our meal."

She closed her eyes, then opened them with the suspicious thought that Simon was pampering her.

She had never been pampered in her life. Delilah closed her eyes again and took a deep, steadying breath. While Simon watched her curiously—like a cat watching a field mouse he had in his paws—she would not vent her frustration. She would wait until she was better in control, and then she would sever Simon from her. She walked to the lean-to and slid into it; facing the fire, she leaned her back against the saddles and covered herself with the heavy quilt Tallulah had insisted she pack.

She stared at Simon, who was concentrating, sifting a small amount of salt through his fingers into the skillet. He looked like a man who would enjoy begetting.

He lifted the lid to the soup, stirred it, and lifted the wooden spoon up to his nose. He lingered over the scent—a habit that annoyed Delilah. He also folded and rolled everything neatly away, his large hands skilled and swift as he packed. Of course he would be skilled at traveling. He was an adventurer. She didn't believe he really felt obligated to her or was hunting for word of his brother's so-called murderer. It simply suited his needs to leave the ranch at the same time.

Delilah glanced at the heavy knitted stockings that Simon had meticulously washed and hung to dry over the fire. He seemed comfortable scrubbing his clothing in the bucket of melted snow water. His brisk, precise movements marked everything he did.

She had opened the darkness of her heart to this man and had immediately regretted it. "You taste food with your mouth, not your nose," she muttered aloud and settled back again.

The bulky saddlebags slid down against her, and Delilah rested her arm on them. Then she remembered the journals that were her mother's, the books that Tallulah had insisted she take with her. Tallulah had come running from the house carrying the books just as she mounted Phantom to leave. Until that time Delilah had not known her mother's journals existed. Tallulah had explained that she had promised she would keep them safe until the time was right. Tallulah thought that now was the right time for Delilah to read her mother's journals. Sliding the three fat, worn black books into her lap, Delilah smoothed them with her hands. She opened one and studied the neat script flowing across the pages.

She couldn't read.

Tears came to her eyes as she smoothed the pages with her fingertips. There had been no time to play or to go to school. When her mother lay dying, she had begged to teach Delilah.

A tear dropped to the black ink and blurred it instantly. Taking care, Delilah carefully blotted the damp place with the hem of the quilt.

She had been too busy surviving—taking care of Richard and her mother, keeping the stove going, running errands for the Mortons and millions of other tasks—to keep them warm and fed while Tallulah worked for wages.

Tallulah. Poor dear Tallulah. How she had worked—doing housework, cooking, mending, anything that would glean a few coins to help them. Though Chinese labor was available for laundry and cleaning, many people distrusted them and had offered Tallulah work.

As a child, Delilah already knew fatigue and fear. She'd known it from birth. She'd known as a small child that there were classes of people, a difference in the races, and in the children who played along the streets.

People tried to help. There was kind Mr. McPherson, and Janet Crabtree with too many children already. Delilah had hated the pity worse than the fear. Pity drained her pride and she didn't have enough to spare one bit.

Delilah ran her coat sleeve across her damp eyes. She'd been so cruel to her mother, slashing at her through the pain they both shared.

As a child, she'd been angry, so very angry with her mother. *"I don't even know who my father is. You didn't even try to find Koby . . . then Richard—Oh, Mama, you're not even trying to live—what will we do?"*

Through her tears the neat black script looked blurred. Page after page of it spread across the book, then the other two. Delilah concentrated, fighting the rage within her. She clasped the three books against her, held them tightly, bent her head, and let the tears come.

Ezrah was there, lurking in the past. *"Sure, you can do sums. Put a line of numbers in front of you and you can add. But my wife can't read, can she? You can't even read, Delilah. But then book learning isn't what your mother raised you to do, is it? No, you're not going to ask the schoolteacher to help you, Delilah. I don't want anyone to know that you're stupid. Stupid and deficient as a wife."*

Delilah rocked herself, the journals cradled tightly against her.

She hadn't wanted to take the journals. Then Tallulah's eyes, tears flowing freely, and Koby's black worried ones had caught her heart. Delilah wrapped her fingers tightly over the books that shared her mother's thoughts.

Did she really want to remember her mother? Or was the pain better trapped beyond the years?

Delilah rubbed her face on the knees she had drawn upward. There was too much pain behind her. Dare she risk looking into the past?

She buried her face in her knees, then wrapped her arms around her knees and rocked, the books digging into her stomach. *Mama . . . Mama . . .*

Simon stood over Delilah as she slept in a sitting position, her head resting against a stripling. She looked so small and vulnerable, her long braid curling around her white throat, and her body curled beneath the thick, worn quilt. He crouched beside her, balancing on the balls of his feet and studying her. Her hands held the journals tightly. He eased the open one away from her and noted that it was upside down.

Simon had known for a time that Delilah couldn't read, but that she was experienced in concealing it. Delilah was a valiant woman, struggling against tremendous odds, protecting and caring for those she held dear. His fingertip stroked back a tendril that lay at her temple. He wondered how many people had soothed and comforted her. Who stood with her in her fears?

He frowned. Delilah fascinated him, and he longed for the woman she so carefully concealed to emerge. His frown deepened because nothing could come of a relationship between them; Delilah was committed to defend a murderer that Simon must bring to justice. Or was Richard guilty? How could Koby and Delilah have a brother who was a cold-blooded killer?

Richard did not fit the picture of a man who smoked while another's blood spread onto the lake's ice.

Richard would meet his justice one way or another, Simon had decided. His fingertip stroked the thick braid, warm from Delilah's body, and instantly her eyes opened.

The dark blue stare held his for a heartbeat as she awoke. "Supper?" she asked in a low husky tone that stirred Simon immediately. It was the sound of a woman awakening. Awakening or emerging from a passionate encounter.

He cleared his throat and stood. "Supper. Stay where you are. I'll bring it to you."

She threw back the quilt, and Simon bent to press his hand against her shoulder. "You stay put," he ordered.

Fine thing, Simon Oakes, he thought as he brought their meals to the lean-to. *You want to make love to her, and she's the only person that can lead you to Rand's murderer. You barely kept yourself from crawling into her pallet with her. You're so hard now you can barely walk.*

The knowledge that his body needed Delilah's desperately didn't surprise him. He was too aware of every scent, every graceful movement of her hands and body, the warm line of her throat. Delilah was wearing trousers for the trip, and Simon's gaze was drawn to her hips and thighs when she mounted or dismounted. This morning he'd awakened in a sweat, and the dream of Delilah's white soft thighs flew into the freezing air. She didn't fit the picture of the laughing, warm woman who suited Simon's notion of a lover, of a friend and a wife and the mother of the hoard of children he wanted desperately.

Simon handed Delilah's plate and cup to her and sat on a nearby log to eat his meal. He shielded a smile. Delilah ate ravenously, digging into the braised steak and potatoes and taking a second helping of potato soup. When she was finished, she looked at him resentfully. "Yes, it was good. Thank you, Simon," she said very properly, as though the compliment had been dragged out of her.

"You're very welcome," he returned smoothly and noted the warm flush on her cheeks and the drowsy look in her eyes. "Why don't you just lie down and I'll clean up?"

"What are you trying to prove, Simon?" she asked tautly.

"That you need me, dear heart," Simon returned easily as he took her plate and cup away.

"That will be the day," she muttered darkly, scowling up at him. She gripped the quilt in her fists and sniffed. Her dark blue eyes challenged him to mention her weakness. "You're not endearing yourself to me, Simon Oakes," she stated when he began to wash dishes. "And you don't owe me anything."

Simon inhaled and placed a bucket filled with snow on a flat rock near the fire, readying for the morning. Early this morning Delilah had eased from the lean-to, careful not to disturb him. While he watched, she'd built up the fire, checked on the two horses and the pack mule, and returned to the fire. In the darkness before dawn, Delilah had unbraided her hair and spread it around her shoulders, brushing it thoughtfully as she looked into the flames.

At that moment Simon's desire rose so savagely that he wanted to carry her back to the pallet. He wanted to bury himself in that taut, sleek body, catch her slight breasts in his palms and fill her with tenderness and himself, pushing away the man who had hurt her so badly that she'd had to defend herself from him.

Now he watched her enter a small stand of trees and return to check on the animals. She leaned against Lasway, and Phantom came to stand on her other side. The horses nuzzled her, the firelight catching the steam rising from their nostrils. She hugged them, one at a time, petting and talking quietly to them.

Simon studied the fire, then added wood to it slowly. Richard waited ahead of them, and Delilah would protect her younger brother. She would hate the man who arrested or killed him.

Delilah carefully stepped into the pallet and sat to take off her boots. They were worn and shabby, just as her coat. She'd spared money for the others' needs, but not her own. Her coat irked Simon; it was threadbare while his own was lined and much warmer. The shawl, sweater, gloves, and stockings that Artissima had knitted for her had given her warmth. Simon doubted that Delilah's shabby bag contained a proper dress or a pretty ribbon.

Simon carefully placed a cup of oil on the stump. By using a braided length of cloth that served as a wick, he had created a lamp. "Watch it," he said quietly as he sat and drew off his boots.

Delilah had never looked more lovely, dressed in her shabby coat and trousers and covered with the quilt. The light caught in her braids and warmed her face as she sat, holding a journal upside down. Simon drew off and polished his boots quickly, then placed them neatly to one corner. He lifted his crocheting to the light, studying it. "So what are you reading tonight?" he asked casually.

She looked over the top of the journal. "Tell me, Simon. The first night we camped on the trail, you were determined to sleep near the fire. It snowed and I had little option but to invite you into the lean-to. Now you have installed yourself comfortably at my side. Do you know how annoying that is? To be squatted upon? Especially by a man I don't want near me? How do I know that you won't take everything and run off while I'm sleeping?"

He counted the stitches and proceeded to crochet. He needed the concentration. There was just enough outrage and indignation in her voice to make an interesting brawl. Right now a good out-and-out with Delilah might clear the air. At times Delilah caused him to forget that he was a thirty-six-year-old man instead of a boy taunting his first girl. "I promised Koby and I always pay my debts. As I said, I owe you my life."

"Humph. I doubt a man like you keeps too many promises." Delilah returned to her upside-down reading.

"What are you reading?" he asked casually as she concentrated on the journals. He let her thrust at his honor slide away into the pines; he intended to keep his promises to himself where Delilah was concerned.

Delilah shrugged. "My mother's journals."

"Would you want me to read them to you?" he pressed. "You could rest while I read—"

Delilah snapped the journal shut and jammed it into her saddlebags. "Of course not."

"Then I could teach you how to crochet."

The look she flung him was of pure disgust, and Simon pushed down the chuckle rising in him.

Simon continued to crochet, and Delilah pulled the quilt over her, turning on her side to watch the fire and the night. Wolves and coyotes howled, the eerie sound floating on the still freezing air. "They sound so horribly lonely," Delilah whispered drowsily.

"We'll find your brother, Delilah," Simon returned gently. But she was already asleep, burrowed deep in the blankets. Simon placed his hand on her shoulder and left it there.

Chapter Eight

‹✦›

At five o'clock the next morning
Delilah saddled Phantom, checked her cinch, and swung up
into her saddle. She reached behind her to check the security
of the pack. It was small and light, chosen carefully from the
camping gear Simon packed and unpacked every night. Her
mother's journals were tucked in the saddlebags.

Awakening to Simon's rough face tucked in the curve of her
throat had frightened her at first. He lay sprawled against her
backside, blocking the entrance of the lean-to. With the heavy
canvas tarp at his back and the thick boughs on the other side
of her, she'd slept warm throughout the night.

Delilah scanned the dark pine forest which surrounded
them, and frowned. She was getting used to him. She'd found
herself enjoying his tales of his lively brothers and sisters, of
their parents, still in love after sixty years of marriage. His
father treated Simon's mother as though she were his best
girl, his bride. Simon wanted a marriage just as strong. "I

won't settle for less," he had said firmly. "I am a thorough man. Once I set my mind on a course, I usually get what I want."

While he dreamed of begetting children on Amelia, Delilah had no time for delusions.

Simon ached for a brother who had been murdered. It was in his eyes each time he spoke about Rand. Delilah eased Phantom away from camp, winding around the pine trees that separated them from the wagon road. She knew what it was to lose a brother.

"Hey!" Simon's shout echoed through the freezing air. "Bloody hell!" He loped toward her, dressed in his red union suit buttoned to the neck and his polished black boots.

Delilah turned in the saddle and waited for him. He was the only person she'd bared her heart to, and she resented opening herself to him.

He leaped over a log and continued loping toward her, passing through the tree shadows and the bluish-tinged snow. His long legs cleared another log and Delilah frowned. She just resented him.

"Running off, were you?" Simon said between his teeth. He breathed heavily and braced his hands on his hips and the long one-piece suit tightened across his stomach. His hardened body thrust against the red cloth. His hair stood out in peaks, and his red beard was darkening a jaw locked in anger and thrusting forward. He looked rumpled and warm and nothing like the well-groomed, careless charmer at her ranch. His eyebrows met in a scowl, separated by a deep line. Steam shot from his mouth in rapid bursts. The set of his broad shoulders was taut beneath the red cloth. "You'd dishonor me, would you? Make me break my promise to Koby to keep you safe?" he demanded.

"You dawdle. I can't afford to," she returned slowly, trying to keep her eyes from the bulge above Simon's heavy thighs. Richard had had that problem every morning; she expected every male did. Her gloved fingers tightened on the saddle horn. Simon's body disturbed her—set off little wary tingles that she preferred to ignore.

"I'll dawdle you," he threatened grimly and ran his hand through his rumpled hair, making the peaks stick out like horns. He didn't resemble the spit-and-polish, unflappable, charming ladies' man whom she considered her bad-luck omen. Simon looked like a man at the end of his tether, and Delilah rather liked the thought that she could nettle him for a change. She realized then that Simon Oakes had annoyed her since the day she arrived to pluck him from death. No other man had told her he loved her or dug into her protected emotions and pried out ill temper. The small revenge was heady. She allowed herself to enjoy his dark mood.

Simon continued to scowl up at her. "You haven't had your breakfast this morning. You've been sick and you need a hot, proper breakfast to start the day. What do you mean packing up in the middle of the night and riding off? Where are your manners?"

Then he turned and strode back to camp. The back flap of his union suit came free at one corner and Delilah glimpsed a pale buttock before Simon jerked it shut. He glared at her over his broad shoulder, the set of his shoulders tense with anger, then continued stalking toward camp. Stunned to find herself smiling, Delilah closed her eyes—then regretted the habit she attributed to her bad-luck piece, Simon. She pressed her heels against Phantom's belly, and the horse eased down the embankment to the road bordering Okanogan Lake. There was only one trail along the lake. Simon could catch up after a session of precise folding and rolling and tucking everything away neatly in its proper place.

She found herself smiling again at deer drinking from the lake. Simon looked outrageously endearing as he stood in the woods in his perfect polished boots and his red full-length union suit.

"Don't try to make up with me," Simon muttered that night when she complimented his stew. They sat at the campfire, dressed in their jackets. Delilah's legs, encased in two pairs of trousers and long flannel drawers, held the aching chill of the long day, and she rubbed her thigh, shielding the movement from Simon. The long hours in the saddle had left her stiff, despite the hours of ranch work. She shifted uncomfortably on the hard log as Simon continued. "I promised Koby to take care of you. You saved my life, you little demon. Your family thinks you're sweet, precious, unsinkable . . . just short of a martyr with angel's wings. I don't. I have my honor at stake here, you know. What if something happens to you? All you've had to eat all day is jerky and bread and coffee from that mining camp."

He glared at the barley-and-elk broth that remained in the bottom of her bowl. "Eat every damn bit. You're far too pale, my girl. I have to take care of your precious little hide, you know. Would you have Koby coming after me with his guns blazing?"

He tossed a buttered roll into her bowl. He swiped the remainder of juices in his bowl with short, efficient strokes. "That farmwife wouldn't like her baking wasted on someone who's determined to kill herself. Eat it."

Delilah pushed the roll through the juices. She didn't want to admit how tired she was, too tired to finish the meal. Once the warm stew filled her stomach, she was sleepy immediately. Simon seemed to have a knack for acquiring food in his cloth sack. He had charmed the farmwife while Delilah was asking questions of her husband. They left the farm with a loaf of freshly baked bread and a sack of vegetables.

Richard would have checked with these farmpeople if he had returned to the territory. They remembered him passing, filled with excitement and laughter. They remembered his horseshoe stickpin and the missing tip of his little finger. "Black crop of hair and blue eyes like yours, miss," the farmer had said, leaning against his prime cow. "Good boy, that. Helped me chop and stack wood for his keep."

Simon stared over the campfire at her. "When you look so sad, so vulnerable, I know you're thinking of your brother. You think of little else but the people you love. Are you afraid of me, Delilah?"

"Of course not." She didn't like Simon popping into her thoughts. She stood and stretched, then bent to wash her dishes in the heated water. Simon could be charming; he crocheted and cooked. She saw little to be afraid of; the wild fear that went sailing through her when he fell on her in the snow was a fluke, taking her back in time to Ezrah. Her stomach twisted as she thought of Ezrah's clumsy attempts while pinning her on her back.

She ignored Simon's stealthy curiosity and concentrated on Richard. He'd be twenty-one now and probably not the gangling boy she'd seen off on his grand adventure. He was being hunted now, a boy with black hair and vivid blue eyes . . . missing the tip of his left finger and wearing a spectacular pearl-handled derringer and a horseshoe stickpin—

"You wouldn't be afraid of anything you should be," Simon remarked darkly. "You're all tied up in your mission, to find Richard. There are men who would—never mind. Go on. . . . Go on to bed. I'll finish up." He handed her the cup of oil and the lighted wick. "Go on, read your mother's journals. That should ease you off to sleep. You look like you need it."

Delilah didn't argue. She managed to pull her boots off and lay down staring at the fire, the journal opened in front of her. Simon moved around the camp, a big man casting shadows on the pines. He tied blankets around the horses, settling them in for the night. He talked quietly to them, and Delilah wondered distantly how a man could take such infinite care of horses— checking on their hooves, quickly fashioning protection from the wind, and covering them against the freezing temperatures—then ride another one into a blizzard and certain death. Even a man who drank would have understood the dangers of riding a horse into a coming blizzard.

Richard . . . Richard . . . keep safe. . . . I'm coming. . . . The flames shot high as Simon added wood. He studied the fire as though seeking answers, just as she was doing. The light outlined his face—glistening on the day's growth of new red beard and on his dark hair. It was curling now, flattened a bit by his hat.

She ran her fingertips over the open book in front of her, wishing desperately that she could read.

Simon turned to look at her. "Not reading tonight?" he asked as he stood and walked to the lean-to.

He slid off his boots and began the brisk, ritual polishing. He nudged her feet with his toe. "Come on, dear heart. Let me read to you. Just to trim your nerves a bit and let you sleep well."

"What? No promises not to leave you? Were you frightened, Simon?" She yawned and stretched, snuggling down in the familiar worn quilt of Tallulah's. She watched the fire drowsily and thought of Richard, of her mother. . . . How could a lone woman travel from the Oregon Trail at the southern part of Washington Territory, cross an entire land, and enter Canada? How could she bear three children, each to a different man? Had she been afraid? Didn't she want to marry and stay in one place?

What had driven her mother? A pine knot caught fire and blazed. The mule brayed suddenly as a wolf howled.

"Marry a good man, Delilah. . . ." Yet her mother had never married.

Delilah smoothed the ink on the pages. How her mother had begged to teach her to read—but Delilah had been too furious then, a child carrying burdens too large for her shoulders, and angry at a parent for leaving her. "Well?" Simon questioned. "What is it? Take your choice. I can crochet or I can read to you."

Delilah gathered the sweater Artissima had knitted closer. Her breasts ached uncomfortably beneath their tight binding. "Simon, have you ever thought how ridiculous you look sitting and crocheting night after night?"

"Busy hands, dear heart. If I had anything to read, I would. But I don't. So that leaves crocheting."

Delilah held the book tightly. She desperately needed to know what her mother had written. "Here. Read this."

Simon took the journal carefully. He propped it on his knees and began to read slowly. . . . " 'I know I'm dying and there is so much to say to my precious daughter, Delilah. How angry she is with me—' " Simon looked at Delilah, who gripped the quilt tightly. Through all the years and the pain, her mother was there.

She'd looked so small, so pale; her black hair had turned white soon after Richard was born.

Simon closed his hand over Delilah's gently. "Do you want me to go on?" She nodded and he spoke softly, a man's deep voice speaking her mother's thoughts. She clung to his hand, felt the warm, strong safety of it.

" 'Some day, Delilah, you'll understand. Tallulah has promised to keep my journals for you until you're ready. You see, a woman has to make choices to survive and I made them. I have three lovely children, and I ached for Koby every day since he's been taken. I pray you'll understand, my poor sweet Delilah. I want you to know what is in my heart. How I love you, my only daughter. . . . I'm lying here day after day and filling my waking hours with the hope that someday you will understand. . . . How do I begin? . . . At the beginning, I suppose. My daddy's name was Jacob and Mama's name was Margaret. They were God-fearing people. I knew I couldn't go back to them after the buffalo hunters took me. We were going to Oregon country, and I shouldn't have been picking flowers away from camp. They were so pretty. Yellow flowers sweeping across a mound of green hills. I wanted them for Mama. She was always tired, having one baby after the next. There were ten children in our family, and Daddy didn't like girls. I don't think he missed me. I was just twelve.' "

Simon's large fingers slid between Delilah's, and she couldn't find the strength to push them away. "Dear heart, are you certain you want me to read this?"

She swallowed, slashing the back of her hand across her eyes. She hadn't known her mother had been stolen from her people, taken and hurt in the coarsest of ways. She wouldn't cry, wouldn't give into the burning behind her lids. "Go on."

The firelight twisted in the branches over the lean-to as Simon continued. The buffalo hunters used her mother roughly, taking her northward along the Columbia River into Canada. She'd tried to run away, only to be punished savagely.

Simon snapped the journal closed; his expression was grim. "That's enough for tonight, dear heart. We need to rest." Then he leaned over and kissed her cheek. It was a brother's kiss, and Delilah allowed the trespass, clinging to the comfort in a realm of loneliness. "Go to sleep, Delilah."

He pulled the quilt up to her chin and the buffalo robe over them, settling down by her side. She lay there watching the firelight flicker on the pine boughs of the lean-to and thinking of her mother. Hours later she realized drowsily that Simon still held her hand. His fingers tightened gently when she tried to ease away. "Shhh, dear heart," he whispered sleepily. "We'll find Richard. Don't worry."

For a long time Delilah lay still, absorbing Simon's warmth. She wasn't used to sharing her life or her thoughts, and Simon had shared them both. She eased her head slightly to one side and looked at him. She'd looked at Ezrah in the same way, trying to find the strength that was now in Simon's face. In sleep Simon's face was rugged, angular, and his mouth softer and curving. He'd kissed her cheek—just a brush of his lips against her skin. As though he were kissing away a child's bruise.

Delilah turned away and forced herself to sleep.

She awoke to Simon tugging her braid. Fully dressed, he sat on his heels in front of her. "You won't be abandoning me this morning, dear heart. Wake up, I've got your morning wash water and a good hot meal waiting."

He smelled like soap and leather, smoke and a tangy male scent she recognized as his own. She yawned and snuggled down in the warm pallet, looking up at him. Simon's smile was quiet and slow. He touched her braid with a lingering, gentle fingertip that trailed to her flushed cheek and down to her mouth. "You look more like a child, Delilah, than a woman."

The remark shouldn't have nettled her. It did. "You would know all about women, wouldn't you?"

One dark brow arced high. "A bit, dear heart."

"I can travel just fine without you," she said, disturbed by the green gaze that slowly strolled down her body, then met her eyes. She swallowed, trying to breathe as Simon's gaze held hers for a heartbeat. She was surprised to find herself asking, "Why haven't you married Amelia?"

The lines deepened beside his eyes. "Because, dear heart, I have just discovered the reason myself. I won't settle for anything less than love like my parents share, and it hasn't come around yet. I want lightning and heat when I touch my woman. Amelia and I are childhood friends and that heat has not entered our relationship."

Delilah thought about the heat that had ached in her breasts, causing them to feel swollen and heavy when Simon's back brushed her in the night. "But you would marry her."

"Love could come in time."

"Love?" Delilah asked. "Or a woman with enough money to keep you? What will poor Amelia do then?"

Simon's fingertips slid slowly across her lips and his eyes darkened. "I'd want everything and more from the woman I marry, and I'd give her back the same," he said firmly. "Have you ever been in love, dear heart?"

She frowned, uneasy with the shifting, intimate play. "I've never thought about it."

"What about babies?" he pushed, the air between them crackling with tension Delilah did not understand.

"No. Not since before I was married," she answered honestly, remembering that wistful girl filled with dreams years ago.

"You might start," he said lightly before tugging her braid again and standing. "I want to see you eat a good breakfast. By the way, did I tell you we're stopping at the first lodging we come to tonight?"

Delilah jammed on her boots and began folding the quilt. If Simon thought he could start taking over now, he was mistaken. "I can't afford it. You can stay there if you want."

Later in the day, he insisted she join him in singing a French tune, "Frère Jacques." His brothers and sisters had sung the song in turns. When he was ready, Simon said, he wanted a houseful of scamps just like his family and a woman to love until he was a hundred and twenty. When Delilah declared romance and love as "cobwebs and dreams," Simon had launched into a round of poetry that turned to naughty limericks, and she had found herself turning away to smile. Simon challenged, teased, and pried the "Frère Jacques" song from her. He looked delighted when she sang. "You have a beautiful voice, my dear," he said formally, guiding his horse close enough to capture her hand and press it.

"Hand-holding, Simon," she muttered, trying to draw away. "You're wasting your charms on me. I'm not susceptible."

"Think nothing of it. Just a way to keep warm, dear heart,"

he returned easily, watching a hunting party of Okanogan Indians ease into the thick trees bordering a tumbling creek.

It was dark when Simon opened the door to the hired man's log cabin. He glimpsed Delilah's furious expression soon shielded by the muddy boot flying toward him. He closed the door, pushed a smile on his face, and waved at the farmer who was entering his log home. The boot thumped heavily against the door. Simon inhaled and pushed open the door a few inches to find a second boot sailing at him. This time he caught it and stepped inside. He dropped the boot and slid the saddlebags from his shoulder. "Shut that door," Delilah ordered, crossing her arms in front of her.

Dressed in Mrs. Yancy's soft flannel gown and a towel turbaned around her hair, Delilah stood near the big fireplace. The heavy woman's gown draped around Delilah's slender body and pooled at her feet. The flames outlined the spread of her long legs, and Simon's mouth went dry. "I take it you're not happy, dear heart?" he ventured, taking off his coat and hanging it on the peg. He yanked off his boots and placed them neatly by the door.

"I was just asking questions about Richard until you had to interfere—'Honeymooners,' you said. 'Need a place to wash and sleep.' You're underhanded, Simon. I thought we settled the matter this morning—I don't have funds for this."

"They wanted us to stay, dear heart. They wouldn't hear of us leaving tonight."

Glaring at him, Delilah picked up the front of the gown to pace back and forth in front of the fireplace. The voluminous folds of the nightgown swirled around her ankles when she lifted it with her hands, and the back hem trailed behind her. It outlined her body from the taut uplift of her breasts down her flat stomach to her legs. She stopped and placed her hands on her waist and the nightgown tightened; two dark nubs thrust at the worn material. " 'My bride would love a bath. . . . Our clothes washed? My eternal gratitude from my bride and myself. . . .' Simon, that woman and her three huge daughters literally stripped me. They had the fire blazing and had me in the bath within fifteen minutes. They giggled, Simon, and took every stitch of my clothing with them. They're in their house now, washing and giggling and hanging my clothes up to dry. Simon, they brought you a nightshirt, and they think we're . . . we're . . ."

Simon would remember Delilah's outraged blush for the rest of his life.

"That we're . . ."

"Yes?" he invited softly. Simon raised an eyebrow and deeply, fervently wished they would eventually do what the farmers thought they would be doing. He glanced at the turned-down bed and fought the image of Delilah tangled and flushed in the blankets. "From the look in his eye, the farmer couldn't wait to bed his wife."

" . . . *And it's your fault,*" Delilah finished, pivoting toward him. "Don't say things like that. You kissed me, Simon. Full on the mouth and wrapped your arm around me as though you—You behaved indecently. . . . 'We need a wash,' you said. . . . 'Could my bride wash our clothes here?' As if I would! My clothes are not that bad. Of course I'm not Mr. Soap and Fold . . . Mr. Spit and Polish. You kissed me!" she repeated indignantly.

Simon thought about that kiss. The soft, surprised part of her lips; the sweet, hot taste; the sudden darkening of those brilliant blue eyes; and that innocent, enticing blush.

His mouth dried as the folds settled between her legs and a dark triangle shadowed the cloth. He was tired and cold . . . and erect and hard. The gown's folds shifted, and Delilah's toes appeared and wiggled; Simon stared at them, entranced. They were pale and slender and very feminine. He realized as his body surged against his trousers that he'd only seen Delilah's hands and that every muscle in his body wanted to explore her. The voluminous gown enticed; Simon had a quick image of pulling it from her, and the sound of thunder began beating in his pulse.

She jerked away the towel as Simon slid his suspenders off and began unbuttoning his trousers. She stared at him as he began opening his shirt. "What do you think you're doing?"

Simon bent and drew his soiled clothing from his case. He dropped his shirt and trousers on top of it and began to unbutton his union suit while Delilah continued staring at him.

"Farmer Yancy didn't want his wife or daughters to collect my clothing. He'll be knocking at the door in minutes. Hand them out, will you?"

"Me?" Delilah ran for the bed, slid into the thick quilts, and drew them to her chin. "No!"

A rap sounded on the door. Her eyes widened as he stripped away his stockings and eased off the union suit. He handed it around the door to the beaming farmer.

"Simon!" Delilah exclaimed when she could speak.

Simon pushed down the rage that another man—her husband—had seen her in bed, her damp hair tangled around her flushed face, her eyes fastened to his body. He eased into the large, scarred tub, and plunged his head beneath the hot, steaming water. Her eyes were still on him when he emerged and began soaping his hair. He rinsed it and leaned back against the high back of the tub, closing his eyes and extending his feet over the edge to luxuriate in the water. "You've seen other men, dear heart."

"Well . . . Richard and Ezrah," she conceded in an unsteady whisper, peering at him. "Simon, are you feeling all right? I mean . . . I can't afford to pay for the cabin, but if you're not feeling well . . . you can stay here while I go on."

He turned his head toward her and opened one eye. "And have Koby shoot my brains out? You can't run off in the morning, dear heart. You don't have any clothes until the farmer brings them with our breakfast. Neither do I."

"Amelia will hear of this if it's the last thing I do. She'll come after you."

"If you're done threatening me, dear heart, would you mind scrubbing my back? Amelia never got around to it." Amelia never got around to kissing him as if she were trembling with desire, either, Simon added mentally. "I haven't seen Amelia for over a year."

"Mmm," Delilah returned archly. "No doubt she's worried about the begetting business."

"You're shocking." Simon chuckled and relaxed deeper into the tub. He dozed and opened his eyes to find her sitting on a small stool in front of the fire and brushing her hair. The strands had dampened her gown and when she turned to him, he caught a delicate nub thrusting at the material. "Dinner was good," he said conversationally and thought of what he'd like to have for dessert.

"Yes." She swept back a heavy swath of gleaming hair as the fire crackled, firelight flickering at the log beams of the cabin. She stared into the flames and brushed her hair slowly, sensuously. She seemed so innocent, so unaware, that Simon wanted to take her in one hot stroke.

He forced himself to relax on the promise that before they left the cabin, he would kiss her. He caught the lift of her eyebrow, the slant of her cheek, and the long line of her throat where the nightgown had lost a button. He hadn't wanted a woman in years, and since he'd met Delilah, he could think of nothing but. If he moved too quickly, he would frighten her, and he suspected that Delilah had had enough of poor treatment to last a lifetime. He wanted to show her the tenderness he felt, smooth away her fears.

Simon sighed and plopped a wet washcloth over his face. If ever he desired to make love to a woman, that woman was Delilah . . . the sister of the man who had probably killed Rand. With the warm fire blazing, and Delilah's body outlined against the flames, he'd be lucky if he could sleep, let alone ride the next day.

She'd fight to protect Richard, and nothing could come of wanting her—

After a time Simon left the tub and dried, slipping on the farmer's clean, worn nightshirt. It was tight and short, reaching his knees. He moved his shoulders against the confining fit and a seam split. Delilah looked up at him, her eyes widened, and she began to laugh. "Your legs are hairy, Simon . . . and white."

The nightshirt sleeve split open as he sat beside her, exposing part of his chest. He watched, fascinated by the play of emotions across Delilah's face. Slowly her fingertip rose to lightly touch the hair on his chest. Simon barely breathed, fearing that he would frighten her as her finger slid slowly along his chest. Then her eyes lifted to his, and Simon found himself leaning down to brush a kiss across her parted lips. "I won't hurt you, dear Delilah," he whispered, laying his cheek along hers.

She rested against him for just a moment, then eased to her feet and looked down at him. "No, you won't. I won't let you."

Simon rose to his feet and stroked away a long, silky strand. The texture clung to his fingers, glazed blue-black by the firelight. "I'm not Ezrah, dear heart."

She sighed tiredly and plucked at the brush in her hand. Shadows circled her dark blue eyes. "Richard is just a boy, Simon. Just a boy on an adventure. When he didn't come back that first year, I should have gone after him."

"We'll find him," Simon whispered, fighting the need to draw her against him, to comfort her, this valiant woman who had tended the needs of others before her own. Instead he picked her up in his arms, ignored her clout to his jaw, and carried her to the bed. "None of that fancy chop-and-kick business now, Delilah. I'm too old and tired right now to play games. In the bed you go. I'll sleep on the floor in front of the fire."

He didn't want to let her go as he lowered her into the bed and pulled the blankets up to her chin. His hand brushed her breast, it quivered, and Delilah inhaled sharply. "Bloody hell," Simon cursed beneath his breath as her eyes widened and, off balance, he fell onto the bed.

It crashed to the floor beneath them. His nightshirt split down the back and Delilah grinned up at him. "You should see your face, Simon. You look embarrassed and dismayed."

"Embarrassed and dismayed, am I?" he asked, easing himself from the bed to stand, holding the back of the nightshirt with one hand. "Drafty in here, isn't it?"

She skimmed out of the bed, and Simon glimpsed a length of long, curving leg. She dragged a blanket in front of the fireplace, slid into it, and tugged the corner over her. "There. You paid for the cabin. You get the bed. It will keep your backside warm."

Simon thought of how he wanted to keep his backside and every other part of him warm. There were times when a man had to take a stand. "Letting a woman sleep on the floor isn't my idea of a gentlemanly act," he said stiffly.

The shoulder seam split wider as he inhaled. A button popped from his chest and rolled toward Delilah. She picked it up and studied it. "You've been pushing me all day, Simon. I sang your song, not once but twice. If you're in a bad mood, don't take it out on me. After all, I am not Amelia."

He lifted his eyebrows. "Me? Moody? You, Delilah dear, would test the patience of a saint. And leave Amelia out of this." He began putting the slats back in the bed and lifted the feather tick and blankets up. He placed his hands on his hips and ignored the ruined nightshirt draped around him. Delilah's widened eyes fell away from his backside as he turned. He watched, fascinated by her blush. "Tell you what. You hop into bed and under the covers like a good little girl, and I'll read to you. Maybe that will settle us down, then we can get a good night's sleep."

"You don't need to read to me, Simon." She yawned and curled into a ball facing the fireplace.

Simon had reached the end of his leash. Delilah dismissed him as easily as a child when every bone, every muscle in his body desired her. He picked her up and eased her into the bed. "Stay."

"You can't keep handling me and giving me orders like a child, Simon. I can manage by myself."

"Where are the bloody books?" he asked tautly, walking to the saddlebags and jerking one out. He walked back to the bed and sat down carefully, his back to her. Eons ago he was in control of his temper and his need for women. He had dreams of a sensible marriage with children. Delilah had changed that. She was no more aware of him than she was Koby. Simon snorted in disgust. If Delilah practiced, she could not succeed any better in cutting down his pride as a man. In his experience he had never met such a maddening, enchanting woman. He thought he heard a muffled giggle, and when he turned to frown at her, Delilah's expression was pure innocence.

"If you could just see your face. You're scowling, looking as dark as Koby does when Artissima teases him. I don't know why you are so . . . so . . ."

"Frustrated, dear heart? Now, why would I be frustrated?" Simon muttered as he propped his back against the bed and drew up a feather pillow, ignoring the sound of tearing cloth at his shoulder. Damn. He was hard and aching. Delilah's freshly bathed and soaped womanly scent caused the blood to pound in his head and every other part of him. "Just lie down and listen."

"Yes, Simon," she said too meekly, eyeing the ruined nightshirt as he found where he had left her mother's story. Usually immaculate, the image of Simon's brown shoulders bursting through the small nightshirt was a humorous sight.

Simon crossed his legs and settled the book on his lap. "Let's see . . . yes, here it is." He quickly scanned the neat feminine script and glanced down at Delilah. "Perhaps we should just go to sleep."

She frowned, looking up at him. "Read it."

Simon eased away a black strand clinging to her cheek. It was warm beneath his touch. He reached out and placed his arm around Delilah, drawing her head down to rest on his shoulder. He liked the feel of her against him, the soft womanly scent rising to tantalize his senses. He nuzzled her damp hair, inhaling the fragrance. "You rest while I read. She's been captured by buffalo hunters, remember?"

"Yes. I've thought about her all day. She never told me anything about it. She felt so dirty and used," Delilah whispered softly. "She had no choice. I know—go on, read."

Simon could guess how Delilah knew about her mother's emotions. Delilah's husband had left his mark.

"Shhh. Close your eyes." When she lay against him, Simon began to read her mother's story. " 'I ran away and they followed, more animals than men, hunting for their property. When I could run no more, I fell and prayed for death. I lay and waited, knowing that I had sinned, that man after man had taken me. I was dirty in body and soul and wanted the freedom of death. Then gentle arms were lifting me, and I looked into a handsome Indian's face. His companions, a large hunting band, faced the buffalo hunters, who left, riding away and cursing. Brave Bear let the others go on because winter was coming and I was too weak. He was a Blackfoot warrior and eventually Koby's father. It was so long ago and yet yesterday, dear daughter. Brave Bear cared for me and I came to love him. For the first time in my life, I was loved deeply and tenderly. We were married in our hearts.' "

Delilah jerked a pillow in front of her and held it tightly. "She believed she was married to Koby's father," she whispered in a sound so soft the crackling fire almost swallowed it. Because she looked so alone, so fragile, Simon leaned over to kiss her lips and found them damp from tears.

Delilah stared blankly at him for a heartbeat. "I know you're short of women, but don't play with me," she said carefully before she tried to push him out of bed. "Dream of Amelia."

Simon quickly caught her hands and pinned them beside her head as he leaned over her. A muscle tensed in his jaw as his gaze flicked down her body as it arched and buckled beneath the quilt. The quilt slid down to her waist and Simon stared at the two dark nubs thrusting at the nightgown's cloth.

Nothing could have stopped him from taking Delilah's breast in his mouth. His mouth caught the tremor that ran through her; her sudden indrawn breath slid by his head.

Simon lifted and searched the darkened depths of Delilah's eyes before lowering his mouth to her other breast. It quivered and leaped to a hard nub that he worried with his teeth. He heard her heels drumming against the bed, or was blood pulsing through his body? She whimpered and arched against his mouth and writhed on the featherbed, then Simon kissed her lips quickly. "Think about that tonight. Sleep well," he whispered.

After an hour of listening to Delilah toss and turn on the bed and his body jerking to attention with each sound, Simon snapped, "What's wrong?"

"What you did," she whispered back darkly. "Like a baby nursing. It isn't right."

"It's very right. I'd like to suckle and tease and nibble on you until I explode . . . and it had better damn well be in a hot, wet tight place," he answered heavily and knew it was the truth.

There was silence with only the fire crackling before Delilah whispered, "Simon? Explode? What do you mean? Where?"

He groaned and threw back the quilt; he walked out into the cold night with his torn nightshirt flapping around his hardened body. He compared it to his shredded nerves. With luck and a good icy wind up his backside, he hoped to reclaim a measure of control before he returned to the cabin.

Chapter Nine

———◆———

Delilah ate the roast partridge and stared at the campfire. Kamloops lay behind them, and in four more days they would be at Clinton. From there they would take the old Cariboo Wagon Road and traveling would be easier. She chewed methodically and counted the number of stones around the campfire. Each night Simon used precisely the same arrangement and number of stones, adding or subtracting one or two according to size. Everything Simon did was precise, studied, and for a reason. Sparks soared into the mountain pines and night sky; around the camp, the firelight danced off the icicles formed from melting snow. Ever since they'd left the cabin before dawn, Simon had been grim.

His green eyes had lashed at her throughout the day. She glanced at him across the campfire. He was sipping his tea and looking into the fire as if it held the answers to whatever troubled him.

Delilah shifted on the log. She had liked singing children's songs with him and sharing the wild beauty of the soaring, majestic mountains. But then Simon knew how to entice women; Delilah had seen him swoop into Artissima's and Tallulah's hearts and endear himself.

Then there was that suckling her breasts through the nightgown as hungrily as a baby needing nursing. She'd ached for hours, and each bounce of Phantom jolted breasts that seemed heavy and swollen.

Delilah didn't have time for endearments, wondering about Simon's mouth suckling at her breast and the heat racing through her, nor for Simon's dark mood. She was tired, weary in her heart and her body. Her mother's journals told of loving her Blackfoot husband; she had been happy. Brave Bear had performed a small ceremony and had said he was her husband. So in her heart Delilah's mother had married Koby's father. She'd had a dark, painful time before he rescued her and after his death. She'd come this same route, fighting to keep her son safe and well. Now they were tracing her mother's journey—the Hudson's Bay Trail to the Cariboo Wagon Road, then on to Barkerville.

Simon's rumbling voice had read her mother's story. She had loved Koby's father desperately, passionately, fighting at his side. She was just fourteen when she saw Brave Bear killed by white men. The Blackfoot warrior had defended her to his death, then the white men had taken the girl to a farm that catered to passing miners. She earned her keep working in the kitchen and cleaning after the endless stream of miners to the gold country. Koby was born three months after Brave Bear's death, and her mother had been delighted by her strong son. " 'I had been loved and had given love. I tasted the first sunshine of my life. Brave Bear was my heart and I was his. We were united in marriage, body and soul, as certain as a minister had said words over us. This is the love that I wish for you, my sweet Delilah.

" 'Then, as soon as I healed, the life of my son was threatened if I did not keep company with the owner. You were born three years later, and I loved you just as much as Koby.' "

Delilah closed her eyes and shivered. Her mother did not say where the farm was or give the man's name. That man was Delilah's father, she was certain of it. She'd been spawned to save Koby's life.

She was the price—the bastard child—and somewhere she had half brothers or sisters who didn't know she existed. Delilah shivered against the cold fist slamming into her heart. The farmer had probably found more than one helpless woman trying to survive, to keep her child safe.

Delilah forced herself to swallow and brush away a tear. Her mother had loved Brave Bear deeply; the words were tender, those of a woman remembering with joy, then tasting sorrow when her happiness was severed from her. Delilah placed her plate aside and tucked her chin over her knees, rocking on the big log and thinking of her mother.

She'd met her trials as best she could; in her place Delilah might have done the same to save her child. A taut, painful cord eased within her. It was an old wound, and the knowledge of her mother's desperate trials eased the ache.

Delilah slanted a glance at Simon's dark scowl. The firelight threw shadows on his face, sweeping over the angles of his brows and jutting cheekbones. There was nothing soft or playful about his expression—rather a hard man, set upon his course.

What was Simon's course?

Why did he look disgusted one moment, then look as though he'd like to feast upon her?

He wanted marriage and babies, he'd said. No doubt he would begin his begats quickly with Amelia.

Sitting opposite her, Simon didn't look like a potential husband, nor a father. He looked like a seasoned frontiersman.

She pushed a rock out of the exact campfire circle with her boot, and Simon scowled at her as if she'd hidden his embroidered suspenders. She turned the thought. What man, other than a useless dandy, would wear embroidered suspenders? He was a drunk, a drifter, a man who cooked, crocheted, and who polished and folded and packed.

"A petunia," she muttered. With luck she could lose him at one of the mile-houses along the way.

The campfire smoke layered the small clearing away from the road. The mule brayed; Phantom and Lasway moved uneasily, nickering softly. Wolves howled in the distance, a spine-chilling, ghostly song.

She had two brothers. Koby was keeping the ranch safe. Richard was out there somewhere. Was he safe? Was he warm? Was he alive? He was; she would have sensed if he weren't alive. Delilah rocked her body and found Simon's hand weighting her shoulder. "Dear heart, we have visitors. They've been circling us for the last half hour. Five men . . . three to the north, one south, and one west."

Simon cursed darkly. Fifteen minutes ago he'd told Delilah to act normal, drawing the men's attention, while he retired and pulled down the tarp in front of the lean-to. He planned to circle and capture the men easily. They would be watching Delilah as Simon eased through the cut striplings on the other side of the shelter.

Now he stood watching the men's shadows follow Delilah away from the horses. He cursed again. Moonlight slid through the lofty pines and skimmed patterns across the snow. Four men closed in on Delilah like wolves circling prey before Simon could get to her. She looked very small pressed back against a tree, her face pale as a blossom in the shadows. One man was missing. . . . Simon realized he had stopped breathing and inhaled slowly just as a rifle butt swung past his head. He hit the man's soft belly, satisfied with the blow and the flattened sound of air pushed from lungs. He caught the man, easing him to the mud and snow so as not to make a sound.

There was a pistol shot, and Simon glimpsed Delilah's white face as one man held her and another ripped away her coat and shirt. She was furious, her head held high, her expression disdaining. A cold fist closed around Simon's heart, and he realized it was racing wildly from fear. Another man filled his hands with her hair, crooning softly. Simon moved closer, sliding from tree to tree. The men were too close; they could hurt her. They were laughing now, and one man's big hand reached out to paw at her breast.

She struck at him, an efficient chop to his encroaching hand, and kicked him in the groin. "Bitch!" he yelled, doubling over.

The other men roared with coarse laughter. Then Simon was there, throwing one man against a tree trunk and leveling his carbine at the other three. He placed Delilah at his back. "Stay put."

A bullet hissed by him, and Simon fired toward the flash of fire in the night. The men slid behind trees, and he pushed Delilah behind a big pine and followed her. Bullets shattered the bark, and Simon took a deep breath. "Exactly what were you doing?" he whispered roughly before stepping from the protection of the tree and returning the gunfire.

"Saving you." Delilah clutched her torn clothing to her. He noted with satisfaction that the bows of her camisole were still intact. The low neckline revealed twin mounds caressed by the moonlight. They surged, pressed tightly by the binding cloth beneath her camisole.

Simon blinked; Delilah's breasts were meant for kissing.

His kiss alone, Simon decided firmly, scowling as another blast splintered the tree over his head. He thought of suckling her breasts, taking those sweet dark nubs one at a time into his mouth and—another bullet broke a tiny branch from the tree. It fell to rest in Simon's hair.

Delilah brushed it away and grabbed his jacket with her fists. "You're a . . . a petunia," she whispered sympathetically. "I thought I would draw them away from you and take care of them before you got hurt."

"My heroine rescuing me again?" Simon glanced down at her, then nothing could stop him taking the kiss he wanted. It was hot and hard and fast. He pushed his tongue into her mouth and played with hers. Simon watched with delight as she gasped, leaned back, and blinked twice. Then she frowned up at him, the tip of her tongue touching her lips. She wasn't frightened now, and as her eyes darkened, he kissed her again, a hunger sliding over her expression. "Now you're aware of me . . . and you do have quite nice breasts," Simon muttered as he thrust his carbine into her hands.

He reached to pat her bottom and found the warmth between her thighs. She was very soft. He pressed his fingers gently into her, cupping her possessively. "This time, do what I tell you."

"Not yet," she said firmly and drew his head down for her kiss. Her mouth at first mashed against his, then she hesitated, took a deep breath, and with the air of one diving into a cold stream tried again. Simon braced himself for another onslaught of firm and determined lips. Her untutored lips stirred seductively beneath his, cut short by another round of gunfire. Delilah looked up at him; her hand smoothed his hair and slid to cradle his jaw. "Thank you. . . . Be careful, Simon."

"You've picked a fine time, my precious," Simon muttered unevenly, then shoved away from the tree. The gunfire followed him, and he thought he heard Delilah whisper something about a drunken, petunia drifter.

Simon circled the beefy man and destroyed him with his fists. Another man surged toward Simon and met a series of deadly, efficient jabs. A third man met the same fate.

Delilah inhaled slowly, her fingers tight on Simon's revolver. Simon knew how to handle himself in a brawl and with a gun. He was deadly.

She shivered, the hair on the back of her neck rising as she realized that Simon could be a professional gunman . . . *or a bounty hunter.* She touched her lips with her fingers— his burning kiss remained. . . . *"You do have quite nice breasts. . . ."*

He hauled one man to his feet, pulled him close, and said something dark and fierce that caused the man to shake his head violently. Steam from their breaths swirled in the

layers of campfire smoke. When Simon released him, the
man stumbled off into the night. The other men scrambled
to their feet and followed. Simon ran the back of his hand
across his mouth as if ridding himself of a bad taste, and
sought her instantly. Their eyes locked, despite the shadowy
night. He walked back to her. "You'd damn well better be
staying put, dear heart. You've cost me a good scare. Koby
would have my ears if anything happened to you."

Delilah gripped her torn shirt tight as Simon drew away
the revolver and placed it in his holster. He ran his hand
down her hair, smoothing its wild disarray. "Good girl,"
he said quietly, drawing her into his arms and placing
his chin over her head. It was like being enfolded in a
hard, warm, and very safe wall. His heart raced beneath
her cheek. "Shhh, precious. You're doing fine."

"Fine?" she managed in a husky voice she didn't recognize. Simon had stared at her breasts as if he'd like
to devour them. His tongue had foraged for hers, teasing
it, and he'd placed his fingers . . . She swallowed. He had
placed his fingers between her legs and rubbed her gently,
a caress that left her slightly damp.

Delilah remembered the firelight stroking Simon's hard,
erect member, which jutted away from his flat stomach. She
remembered how Ezrah had tried to push himself into her,
and she shivered.

He peered down at her with a look of fear. "You won't
faint now, will you?"

She gripped his shirt tightly and realized she'd started
trembling, her usual late reaction to violent fear. She'd
shielded her rage and terror from the men, just as she had
concealed her emotions all her life. Simon didn't seem to
mind, gathering her closer and stroking her back. The pulse
running along his throat pounded against her forehead, and
a whorl of hair tickled her nose. She realized Simon was
rocking her gently, and she was clinging to him, unable
to step away from his strength. "You're good with guns,
Simon. You can fight."

She didn't understand what was happening to her now,
she just knew that her breasts ached terribly, feeling very

heavy and full . . . and deep inside her body tiny little aches surprised her. She thought of Simon's thrusting, lightly furred, beautiful body, and her legs went weak.

He lifted his eyebrows, then spoke in a dark, husky voice that caused something to quiver and heat inside her. "You have very nice round breasts and you kiss like a furnace. Want to try that part again?"

"Those men didn't touch you. You're not even bloody," she stated, amazed that in the flurry of punches Simon hadn't been injured. He'd been methodical and neat, easily sidestepping the men's clumsy advances. She drew away slightly to touch his cheek. It was sweaty and rough with the day's growth of stubble, and very endearing. Simon kissed the center of her palm, once, then again. He nuzzled her hand and she curled it into a fist, restraining the wild urge to wrap her arms around him . . . and her legs around him, if she were honest about her wants.

She gathered her shirt closer, remembering the men's expressions, like hungry, salivating wolves. Simon's eyes were tender and teasing as he kissed the corner of her mouth. The warm spot tingled. "You're not disappointed that I'm not a bruised, beaten man, are you, dear heart?" he teased.

She remembered the methodical, precise blows and Simon's grim expression. "You're very thorough, aren't you?" she asked in an uneven voice.

"Yes, you could say that. I finish what I begin, dear Delilah." Then he kissed the other corner of her mouth. "Good. You've stopped shaking. We should retire for the evening. The men won't be back."

"What did you tell them?"

"I asked if they'd heard of Richard. They hadn't. Then I said that I took offense to them pawing my wife and that if they returned, they would die. The other options were to shoot them on the spot or to keep them tied and fuss with them for the next sixty or so miles. But then you might not be likely to smash those lips of yours against mine, and that would be a pity." Simon took her hand as casually as if they were out for a Sunday stroll. He tucked it through

his arm. "Come along now, Delilah. Time for bed," he said
pleasantly, as though they'd been married for years.

While Simon checked on the horses, Delilah changed
her torn shirt. She touched her breasts and wished the ache
would fly away. Simon returned to the lean-to and began
polishing his boots as if nothing had happened. He stood
them neatly to one side and looked at her as she huddled
beneath the quilt. "You're safe," he said simply, then lay
down beside her. "You won't injure me with one of those
fancy hand blows if I hold you, will you? No little kick to
my manhood?"

She laughed outright—a nervous release more than
humor—partly because she remembered the fevered look
in the men's eyes, and just a little because she realized
how much she enjoyed Simon's kiss. She tingled when
she thought of his expression as he looked at the moonlight
flowing across the tops of her breasts. He braced on one
elbow and grinned down at her. He looked rumpled and
very safe.

"Don't ever be afraid of me, dear heart," he said gently, then gathered her against him and placed his hand
firmly on her breast. Her body seemed to surge to meet
the heavy, warm weight, and the gentle mound above her
thighs tingled, as though remembering how he had cupped
her intimately. "Good," he murmured with satisfaction and
ran his thumb across the aching tip. "I wasn't dreaming."

His mouth coaxed and brushed and asked temptingly.
Delilah found herself seeking his kisses, lifting her mouth
for the tender enticements. She'd never experimented with
kissing, and now slanted her mouth against Simon's firm
one. He lay on his back and her hair spilled around him as
she leaned over him. "You are a very warm man, Simon,"
she whispered and noted that his hands were open and holding her breasts as though they pleased him immensely. She
arched against his cupping hands, and he groaned shakily.

"Hot, dear Delilah. Right now I am very hot," he corrected unevenly.

She fell asleep with Simon's warm hard body against hers
and the safe, slow beat of his heart. His slightly rough palms

felt just right as they continued cupping her breasts.

Simon awoke an hour before dawn and realized that very little kept him from making love to Delilah. He lay curled to her back. Her soft hips, though sheathed in trousers, were nestling over his aroused manhood. His heart was hammering, running with the shreds of the dream that clung to him like spiderwebs. In his dream Delilah lay tangled with him, warm and flushed and very hungry—and she did have very soft, very hot thighs. . . . She was damp—

In the next instant Simon jerked on his boots and strode down to the tumbling creek to splash his face with icy water. He scanned the lofty, snow-covered mountains and cursed. He should have taken time to deliver the men to the law, but he didn't want to arouse attention, nor leave Delilah.

One man in the gang had recognized him as a Mountie, another reason for keeping them from Delilah.

"Koby, keeping your mouth shut only goes so far. You've got something to say—spit it out," Artissima snapped as she whipped the cake batter with her wooden spoon. She frowned, concentrating on the quick, angry movements. "Don't blame me if you're stuck here. Don't take it out on me. I've always thought you were mulish, Koby. Pure country mule, through and through."

She poured the batter into a pan, plopped it into the oven, and rounded on him. She placed her hands on her waist. "Don't you go getting all dark and sulky with me, Mr. Koby Smith. I'm not afraid of you. Now, I want to measure the shirt I'm making you. I won't have poor sweet Delilah and your brother coming home to their brother dressed like some hombre ready for a shoot-out. I've just got time before I feed the chickens."

Artissima loved the calves and the colts and the baby chicks, exclaiming with delight as she watched them. Koby knew that she had clawed her way out of the stricken South and that she loved mothering anything. While a baby straddling her hip might soothe her need to coddle, he didn't intend to act as a substitute.

When a baby nestled in Artissima's round, soft body, her breasts would fill—Koby frowned darkly, pressing his lips together. His fever for Artissima shocked him.

Koby glanced outside to Moose and Tallulah planting seeds in the morning sun. In the three weeks since Simon and Delilah had gone, Artissima had him under fire, running and fetching for her and repairing the barn and the roof. His patience was wearing thin. If he could just get outside . . . He stood slowly and took a step.

"Koby, you scoundrel, don't you dare move," Artissima said slowly, biting off each word.

Koby closed his eyes as Artissima began unbuttoning his faded, torn shirt. He caught her busy fingers and brushed them away. "You cantankerous mule. I was just helping," Artissima began heatedly, glaring at him.

She was flushed from the oven, her blond curls spilling to her shoulders. The sunlight from the window gleamed like a halo around her head. She placed her hands on her waist, and the movement pulled her blouse tight against her breasts. From his height Koby could see the crevice between her white breasts where a button had come undone. He saw the froth of lace on her camisole.

He wanted Artissima badly and had from the moment he first saw her.

Her head went up, her brown eyes dark with anger. "Koby Smith. You just take off that shirt. I want to check the sleeve lengths."

"You want plenty," he said tightly, aware that no woman had ever managed to ignite him like Artissima. "You're bossy, missy. No wonder you're not packing a baby on your hip. You probably chased off any takers."

Her eyebrows shot high. "Me? Bossy? Baby?" Then she frowned and leveled a shaking finger at him. Just as her mouth parted to sass him, Koby bent his head and kissed her softly.

He smelled the scents of spring flowers and newly cut hay and babies fresh from their baths. He smelled feminine, intimate scents, vanilla, and cake and sunlight dancing on rain.

Artissima held still a moment, her eyes staring straight
into his. Then she stepped back, her hand to her throat, her
color high. "Mr. Koby Smith. I do declare," she whispered
breathlessly.

Later Artissima served the dinner and gave the blessing
without looking or speaking to Koby. She lifted her chin
and her curls bobbed as she came close to him in the small
cabin. As she reached past him, her breast touched his arm
and Koby inhaled. Artissima exhaled in a soft explosion.
She whipped her napkin over her skirt, glanced at Koby
coolly, and asked, "Tallulah, please pass the gravy."

When dinner was finished, Koby stood to leave. Artissima
did not look up when she said firmly, "I'm expecting you
to try on your shirt tomorrow, Koby Smith. We have some
unfinished business."

Koby didn't sleep that night. Artissima came from a
gentle life. Her family had been wealthy until the War Between
the States. She made tea cookies and read and knew how to
make people feel good. She had been raised to be a wife for
a wealthy man, and knew her lineage. Koby had nothing to
offer her.

The next day he touched the embroidered initials on his
pocket; they gleamed in the late afternoon sun. Artissima
jerked down his arm, tugging at the cuffless sleeve and
pinning it. She whipped a string around his wrist, measuring
it. Koby caught the fragrance of her hair, like flowers on the
high meadows. "Lordy, Koby. You're going to need another
button on the shirt."

Artissima began to unbuckle his belt, and when his hands
stopped her, she glared up at him. "That mean old thing
ruins the line of the shirt. I can't measure where to put the
buttonhole, you arrogant, kiss-stealing sidewinder."

Koby didn't like being reminded that he had kissed her.
He should apologize . . . but he wouldn't. He ripped off
the bullet-studded belt, wrapped it around the holster, and
placed it on the table. "Lift," Artissima ordered around the
pins pressed between her lips. She pushed his arms out
level to his shoulders and began fussing with the front of
his shirt.

Her touch on his belly caused Koby to react. He gritted his teeth against the hard tug of his body. Her fingers fluttered downward, measuring the buttonhole from the last one. He inhaled sharply as her touch brushed him. "That's enough."

"Mmm?" She concentrated on pressing a pin through the place she selected.

"Don't," he managed unevenly through his teeth.

"Mmm?" she asked absently, her blond curls fragrant and tantalizing beneath his face as she tended her task.

Koby realized with horror that he was sweating despite the cool room. Artissima continued to work around him, her hands fluttering across his shoulders and tugging on the sleeves. "You're coming to church with me next Sunday, Koby. I'll have to hurry to get this shirt ready. You could do with a pair of Sunday pants the next time we get to the emporium."

"I don't go to church and I don't need any fancy shirt." The shirt belonged to a man who suited Artissima, a well-bred, cultured, wealthy man who could give her a nice home and children. Koby fought the rage rising inside him at the thought of another man touching Artissima.

She slid under his arm and began lifting and smoothing the collar. "I say you're going, you polecat. I want you sitting next to me on that church pew," she stated around the pins. "You're my best friend's brother—the closest thing to a sister I've ever had—and you will sit in church and be as downright respectable as any other rancher hereabouts. Hold still, Koby, and don't you go flashing those hot eyes at me. You don't scare me one little bit."

Koby gritted his teeth. He wouldn't . . . yes, he would. . . . He gripped her upper arm, jerked her to him in one arm, and plucked the pins from her lips with his free hand, tossing them to the table. He cupped the back of her head in his palm, turning her head up to him. Her lips tasted sweet and hot and sassy.

He tried to free her, to free himself, and lost. Artissima arched up to him, locked her arms around his neck, and held on tightly.

The kiss was the sweetest journey Koby had ever taken. He was trembling slightly when he put her away, his hands caressing her upper arms. Artissima took a deep unsteady breath, parted her lips once, then closed them. She inhaled and opened them again. She blinked and tears came to her eyes. Koby's stomach turned, a cold fist slamming into him.

What had he done? What right did he have to touch her? To kiss her?

"I . . . I'm—" he began before Artissima's pale fingers fluttered over his mouth.

"If you say you're sorry, Mr. Koby Smith, I swear I'll hit you over the head with a skillet," she whispered adamantly. "Don't you dare."

He shook his head. "I know better than to touch you."

"Do you, Koby?" she asked softly, tilting her head. He noted the sunlight tangling in the blond sausage curls and wondered if the same shade nested between her legs. He forced the thought away, just as Artissima said huskily, "I've been waiting for you. By the way, I'll want your son. Reckon you'll have to touch me good, once or twice, before we make a baby. . . . And if you're touching me plenty, reckon you might as well take your place in the pew beside me. . . ."

Koby shook his head and tried to think why everything she just said wasn't logical. Then Artissima hugged him tightly and whispered, "So, see? You did need a good shirt, didn't you, Koby?"

He looked down into Artissima's beaming smile, tried to remember something, and failed. He found himself grinning widely. Artissima stared at him critically, tilting her head one way, then another. She ran her fingertip across his lips. "My, you will make me a fine son, Koby Smith. It's time for me to be a mother. I've decided not to waste time, now, since you're so willing and all. It has occurred to me lately that if anybody puts a baby on my hip, I want it to be you."

Koby left the house minutes later in a daze and feeling that his knees would crumble with the next step he took.

Chapter Ten

———⟡———

At Clinton they met the Cariboo
Wagon Road, which began further south in Lillooet, Mile
Zero. The road had taken thousands of miners north to the
gold country in the 1860s. Prospectors from the South, from
China, England, San Francisco, and the world poured into the
wild, new country filled with soaring mountains, rocky gorges,
and fierce, raging rivers. They came for the gold lying in the
gravel bars and the mines, and some of them went to die.
Great cattle drives had passed this same route, taking beef
to the north gold fields, where the winters were too severe to
raise livestock. Roadhouses occurred frequently, named for the
miles on the northbound trail. The Canadian Royal Engineers
designed impossible feats of daring, bridges crossing chasms
and roads huddling along the soaring Rocky Mountains.

"Clinton is at least two weeks from Barkerville by horse-
back," Simon stated firmly as they walked their horses into
the town. He glanced at a broken two-wheel, Red River cart

used by the "Overlanders"—men who pushed through into the interior from the Pacific Coast.

"*Less* than two weeks and we'll be in Barkerville," Delilah corrected. "Traveling will be easier now. Because of the snow and mud and your eternal fold-and-pack camping, we've only been averaging eighteen miles a day. We can do twenty or thirty now, even with the mud."

Simon noted how Delilah calculated numbers, tossing them out easily without concentrating. She had an easy knack for numbers, if not for relaxing. She was as taut as a bowstring now, leaning forward, scanning the muddy streets of Junction as though she might spot Richard coming out of the barbershop. He patted Lasway's muscled neck and watched the stagecoach pass emblazoned with the company's famous BX trademark, followed by a team of mules pulling three wagons. Mud sucked at the stagecoach's wheels, and the half-broken horses struggled to lift each hoof. On the sides of the wagons the jacks were coated with mud. Simon leveled a dark look at Delilah from beneath his hat. Rain spilled from the brim. He looked at the gray curtain of rain and knew that Delilah wanted to push on despite the late-afternoon hour. "We're staying here tonight. There hasn't been a word of your precious baby brother since Kamloops, and I want to ask around."

"Richard," she threw at him sullenly and blew away the raindrop clinging to the tip of her nose. "My brother, Richard . . . and I can ask around myself."

"You mean you'd swagger into a saloon or a bawdy house, have a whiskey, spit tobacco, and ask, 'Has anyone seen my little brother, Richard Smith? I've come to take him home.' "

Her magnificent eyes caught blue fire, then darkened and she lifted her head. "Richard wouldn't visit back rooms or drink whiskey," she said tightly.

"Young men do," Simon gritted through his teeth with finality. Delilah's obsession with her younger brother was understandable, yet it rankled, and he admitted a spark of jealousy. "They go to men's places and do men's things. There's only one way a man would tell a woman anything in those places."

Her eyebrows shot up. "Oh? So you spend a lot of time in those places, do you?" she asked archly.

"We're putting up here for the night, dear girl," Simon stated flatly. He didn't want to explore with Delilah the youthful hours he and Rand and Thane had spent in just such places. Those hours had taught him how to get information without causing notice.

"Petunia," she muttered beneath her breath and sniffed. Tucked into his collar, his jaw was rigid and dark with the red stubble that was beginning to grow. Since their set-to with thieves in the forest, Simon had seemed wary and stiff. He also seemed disgusted, his movements while making camp brisk. Once, he stood and studied the pallet for no reason, as if committing it to his permanent memory. Then his gaze swung to her, pinning and burning her as if she'd committed a treasonable crime.

The hairs on the nape of her neck had raised, and peculiar little tingles echoed low in her belly. In the firelight his crochet needle had slashed through the red thread in an angry, quick silver line. If anyone had a right to be angry, it was she. She hadn't invited him along. "Petunia," she repeated darkly.

He reined Lasway to a stop and glared at her. "What?"

"I said, 'Pretty soon you'll give up.' I'll make better time without your eternal camping early to cook and make a proper shelter. Now that there will be roadhouses every so many miles, you'll want to stop and crochet by a warm fire at noon."

"Crocheting keeps my hands busy. There are times when I want to throttle you. You can be single-minded and as obstinate as those mules." He smiled nastily and nodded to the six-mule team that stood packed and waiting beside a store. When she glared at him, he adjusted the drape of the long rain slicker he'd forced her to wear around her throat. "You won't have to worry about me fussing tonight. We're staying at a proper hotel."

He looked at her warily as if expecting a heated argument. She refused to comply and continued to glare at him. She would have managed just fine without him. She hadn't been sleeping at all at night, and it was his fault.

She shot a dark look at him. She wished she hadn't turned to his arms when he'd read that the farmer was her father. He'd rocked her and held her; he'd whispered, "Shh, dear heart. Your mother loved you very much. She named you for her, didn't she? It was the best gift she could give you when she had nothing to give."

Delilah stared through the gray rain to the backside of a passing miner's mule. She'd given Simon pieces of her life from the day she'd pulled him from death. She'd never fought so hard with anyone, nor let anyone else see so deeply inside her. She'd controlled her life and trials with a grim determination to succeed. Simon was peeling off layers of control she'd carefully forged and unraveling her. The mule swished his tail and stopped, his hooves sunken in the deep mud.

That damnable kiss. Simon's tongue had nudged her own, startling her, then there was that low, hungry growl deep in his throat and the press of his big warm hand on her bare breast. She sensed he had locked onto her and that nothing could take her away if he wished to hold her. Her flesh had seemed to spring into the palm of his hand.

That kiss had poured into her like sunlit honey and set off warming tingles that unbalanced her nerves. She hadn't been able to shed it, tuck it away, or control it. She felt taut and warm and sweet and hot every time she thought about Simon's lips pressed against her own. She couldn't sleep or relax. And when she thought of Simon's hand pressing between her legs, her body tightened and moistened against the constant caress of the saddle. She resented the intimate moistening of her drawers and resented Simon's ability to be sweet and hungry. Delilah rubbed her glove-clad hand against her thigh. She was a little past her time to be curious about men's bodies, Simon's in particular. She rubbed her palm again, and a vision of Simon's manhood, hard and erect, shot behind her lids. Every night she felt like a coiled spring, and the morning found her mood worsening. She didn't understand why, but Simon was at the bottom of it and thoughts of what had happened couldn't be pushed away even by worries for Richard. She continued to frown as they stabled the horses behind the hotel and climbed the stairs to their room.

Simon closed the door with a kick of his boot, dropped his valise, and ordered, "Undress. Strip down and get in bed. You're exhausted."

"I'm not taking orders from you anymore." Delilah tossed her bedroll to a chair. She ached with cold, she was deadly tired, and in no mood for Simon's bullying or orders. She'd lost control of her life, and nothing was going according to her plan.

Simon glanced at the pitcher filled with fresh water and poured a measure of it into a large wash bowl. He stripped off his coat, then washed his hands briskly and thoroughly with the bar of soap. He dried them precisely and concentrated on the task, as she had once seen a riveting piano player do before a performance, without looking at her. He folded the towel with one expert snap, then hung it precisely over its rack. He turned to her and lifted a challenging eyebrow. "Well?"

"Simon," she began reasonably and found the tattered tarp she'd been wearing for a raincoat whisked away from her.

Simon arranged it over the back of a chair with an air of disgust. "You look like a shabby young girl—an orphan who's never had a bit of care," he muttered, looking down at her darkly. "Do you ever think of yourself?" he asked under his breath in a tone that resembled a growl.

He was wading into her thoughts, demanding that she spread them out for him. Well, she wouldn't. "Of course. I think how much I'd like to find Richard and be shed of you."

Simon's jaw hardened, thrusting out that bit that told her he was going to be difficult. Delilah raised her head. Fine. She felt like a good argument—she felt like ripping Simon's carefully packed valise apart and messing his neatly packed camp goods. Delilah shivered; no one had ever disrupted her control like Simon. He was too big, too controlled, and she wanted to—

He began grimly unbuttoning her coat. "I won't be responsible for you collapsing and getting sick. You're having a good, hot bath and hot soup and a good night's rest."

She swatted at his hands and found her wrists caught firmly and held behind her back. She blinked and decided to give him one warning before she raised her knee to his impressive body part that was now pressed hard against her stomach. When she opened her mouth, Simon's lips closed over it. He kissed her slowly, gently, enfolding her in emotions that swirled and washed over her like warm silk. Simon's beard chaffed her skin, exciting her as his lips pressed gently, firmly against hers. She wasn't cold any longer, drawn closer and closer to the fire that was Simon. "I'm not Ezrah, dear heart. Remember that," he whispered against the ear he'd been seducing with nibbles and the tip of his tongue.

Her coat was on the floor now, peeled away methodically with the other layers of her clothing until Simon's fingers were pressing against her breast, seeking it. One by one the bows of her camisole came apart, his fingers trembling as though he were unwrapping a present he had anticipated and wanted desperately.

Simon stared at her freed breasts and swallowed heavily. She was uncertain then, glaring up at him and yet caught by the look of wonder on his face. His eyes closed as his hands fitted gently over her softness, and he kissed her lips very softly, very tenderly.

Delilah could not move away from his mouth, returning his kiss in the slanting, teasing way he had taught her. Simon breathed unevenly, his hands caressing her breasts, exploring the shape of them. When she was trembling and aching, quivering with emotions that ran hotly through her veins and pulsed low in her stomach, Simon leaned back to look down at her tenderly and eased away the camisole.

She watched, fascinated by the tender yet hot way his eyes devoured her breasts. "Lovely," his whispered roughly. He breathed unevenly, cherishing her tender weight with his fingertips. He bent slowly and kissed the budding tip. She inhaled as he opened his mouth and began to suckle her. She bolted, pressing her hands against his head for just a heartbeat, then her fingers locked to him and she dissolved, giving herself to the hot, moist tugging of Simon's mouth. She heard a whimper from a distance and realized that it was her own.

Delilah's knees gave way just as Simon sat on the bed and spread her legs apart to straddle him. He whispered sweet words, telling how he wanted to touch her, how he wanted to kiss every part of her and taste her and fill her with himself. He spoke in French and very proper crisp English, and then soothingly and desperately. Delilah shook as Simon slid his hand into her layers of trousers and drawers and pressed his palm over her soft mound, gently massaging it.

Her thighs pressed together, quivered, then opened to his gentle seeking. His fingers traced the soft opening, and Delilah gasped as she realized how slick, how damp she'd become.

She wanted to move away, to pull back into herself and control what was happening to her as she had learned to do so well. She realized with distress that she had locked her fingers to Simon's taut shoulders, digging in as though she would never let go. She could not force her hands to release him, to push him away.

She held her breath and fought the waves of pleasure washing over her. He suckled her breasts, kissing them gently, and tiny cords tightened within her feminine place. His teeth bit the tender nubs of her breasts, and she cried out, lost to the pleasure storming her. Simon's long finger teased her gently and her body loosened, warmed, opened for him.

"Sweet Delilah," he whispered unevenly against her breasts and then his finger slid deeper.

Bells and fireworks shot through her. Her body tightened into one taut knot, tightened again until she couldn't stand more, then burst gloriously, pooling sunlight and honey and flower petals through her. The sensations defeated, elated, and poured through her as she sagged against Simon, burying her face in his taut throat. She couldn't move, weighted by soft, enveloping sleep.

Then he was rocking and kissing her. Tiny little soothing kisses taking away the tears on her lashes. Just before she allowed herself to fall into the sleep that had been tugging at her, she managed unevenly, "Simon . . ."

She thought she felt his smile against her throat and with the last bit of her strength tightened her arms around his neck and arched luxuriously against him.

The street was dark and muddy when Simon left the emporium. He regretted the hard ache lodged in his body. He was a

North West Mounted Policeman, trained to find criminals, not to seduce unsuspecting, innocent women and tuck them into the top of his pajamas.

The pajama top shrouded Delilah's body, but left her long legs bare.

He'd never forget the quiver that sailed across her soft thighs just before she sighed sleepily, and he forced himself to cover her.

He nodded to a hard-eyed woman who bared her huge breasts from beneath her coat. An odor of unwashed flesh drowned in heavy sweet scents enveloped him, and he thought of Delilah's fresh scents. Simon gritted his back teeth, a habit he seemed to do constantly since he'd met one Delilah Smith.

Stepping on the wide boards trailing to the blacksmith, Simon thought about Delilah's drowsy frown as he'd undressed her, easing her into the pajama top and placing her between the bed's warm, flannel sheets. Her hand had gripped his collar tightly just once before he took it away and pulled the blankets up to her chin. Whatever had happened in her marriage, Delilah had had her first sexual experience.

He'd acted grimly, determined to hear those sweet hungry sounds she'd made at his side every night. Determined to place her mind on him and no one else.

Simon glanced at the hotel room they shared, which overlooked the street. The window was dark. The hotel clerk had said they would keep hot soup in the warming oven for Simon's "wife." They would have hot water for bathing, to be used any time of night, though the charge was extra, and after a hearty breakfast, they would pack a large meal fit for traveling.

Simon pulled his collar high against the cold rain and gripped the cloth bag of purchases in his fist. Delilah was a woman of deep passion. She'd been taut and snapping, and Simon had acted instinctively to release the tension radiating from her like lightning. While she slept deeply, her ultimate beautiful release had left him hard and aching and dazed and humbled.

His pajama top swallowed her and enticed him more than any fancy gown. He liked her wearing his clothing, his mark, and frowned when he thought that another man had touched her.

From her shocked response, Delilah's husband had not handled her well.

Simon visited the constable first, who had news of Mordacai Wells's claim-jumping near Quesnelmouth. He was a dangerous man, adept at blackmail and thievery, and he matched Richard's description except for "hard, glittering eyes of a killer." Simon wired his location and destination to his superior officer and requested that any information on Wells or one Richard Smith be forwarded to the Quesnelmouth law.

Simon made his purchases and queries in different stores, at the blacksmith's, then in the back rooms, lounging and playing cards. A woman slid into his lap, her garters showing on white fleshy thighs when she crossed her legs. "Richard Smith? No, can't say—did you say missing the tip of his little finger—a pretty boy with black hair and eyes the shade of whiskey? A pretty little pistol and a horseshoe stickpin? That's Mordacai Wells. Heard he went to north to Quesnelmouth. A bad one, eh? Gypped a miner at cards and shot an old Chinaman working a worthless mine. Cut off his pigtail . . . that's their honor, you know. Scattered the old man's wife's bones that were packed for shipment back to China. Mean thing to do."

The woman slid away, and a younger, prettier one took her place. She nestled down in his lap invitingly. "My name is Candy. Don't you think I'm sweet? I've got a room upstairs," she whispered into his ear and proceeded to tell him the things that she would like to do to him without a fee. She cuddled and whispered and settled her lush hips more deeply on his burgeoning manhood, which was now thrusting against the buttons of his trousers. Candy informed him how she'd once licked and sucked a man into insanity, and that she was looking for another candidate. From the looks of Simon, Candy thought he might last a while longer than the last man she'd found appealing. "How about it, handsome?" she purred, placing her hand on him and squeezing gently.

Hard in her practiced hand, Simon wanted to take her offer, to shed the need humming through him like lightning waiting to strike. Delilah had caused his need; she deserved to pay for his torture, and she wouldn't get off easily. The punishment would fit the crime. While Candy purred and stroked him, Simon sweated and promised himself that Delilah deserved every whimper he took from her. If ever a woman deserved to need him, it was Delilah Smith, a woman who considered him a petunia, he decided grimly. He wanted her committed, dedicated to making long, sweet love with him. Along the way there were a lot of other things he wanted from Delilah Smith. Like a home and babies and making love in front of their own hearth.

He tossed down the small glass of whiskey. Candy almost tumbled from him as he stood abruptly. "You are sweet, Candy," he said, dropping coins into her trembling bosom to soften her loss. "But I'm tied to a mean cuss, who needs me more than you."

He nodded to a gnarled old miner. "Try that."

Candy patted his backside and grinned cheekily. "Honey, he was just twenty last night before I had my way with him."

Later, Simon unlocked the hotel room. Mordacai Wells had left a high, wide trail and no one had heard of Richard Smith. *". . . Cold eyes the shade of whiskey . . . hard, glittering eyes of a killer."* Simon concentrated on the woman's description. Richard had startling, sky-blue eyes like his sister, yet Wells had "whiskey"-brown eyes. The clerk followed him into the room with buckets of water and glanced curiously at the sleeping woman on the bed before Simon moved in front of him. "Dinner will be up in a minute . . . I'll knock soft. You can hand out your things then. My missus has some other travelers' wash to do," the clerk whispered on his way out.

Simon bathed quietly, fitting himself into the tiny tub and considering the woman sleeping soundly on the bed.

He should have more sense than to get involved with the sister of the man he was hunting. He ate the hearty soup while sitting in the tub and placed the empty bowl on the floor. Delilah's tiny muscles circling his fingers would probably haunt him forever. Her soft gasp was almost a scream. She lay there now, curled beneath the layers of quilts like a child. Only an unfeeling brute would want to stretch himself out on her and—Simon poured the pitcher of cold water over his head.

He awoke before dawn, resenting the sleep he wasn't able to take. The soft tangle of Delilah's arms and legs, her breasts nuzzling close against his bare chest, did little to trim a desire that rode him throughout the night. She wiggled against him, her hands spearing through the hair on his chest as though it was Blue Boy's pelt. Her hand rested on the flat of his stomach, just over the knot of his pajama bottoms. A plump nipple pleasantly scraped along his ribs, and a soft thigh bumped his hard one. Delilah sighed, the motion raising her breasts against his side as she rolled on her side.

Simon swallowed hard, folded his hands behind his head, and thought of his reputed discipline with his career and with women. The woman beside him severely tested both. He'd had two relationships in his life and had wanted to marry both women. He wanted children and a home; the instinct was bred into him and ran deep. Amelia had been a sensible choice— before he met Delilah. The thought of another man holding her, drawing those sweet cries from her, caused his fist to clench the quilt.

Delilah's soft backside nestled comfortably against him. Then she turned, her breasts quivered against his ribs for an instant before she turned again and backed her bare bottom against his thigh. Simon ground his back teeth and slipped from bed. He dropped the pajama pants to the floor and stood rigidly. He let the room's chill swirl around his aroused body before he stepped out of the pajamas wadded at his ankles. Delilah sighed in her sleep and nestled on the bed and Simon tensed. He forced himself to the washstand, poured icy water into the basin, and splashed it on his face and chest. Delilah sighed again, and he turned to see her slide her arm around a feather pillow and draw it into the curve of her body. He groaned, dressed quickly, and went down to the kitchen where the Chinese cook was preparing breakfast for early travelers.

"Mmm?" Delilah asked sleepily as Simon shook her shoulder.

She awoke to him grimly studying her, his jaw covered with early morning beard. He looked fierce and disgusted as he placed the breakfast tray over her lap with a jolt that made the dishes clatter. "Are you going to sleep the day away?" he demanded roughly.

The blankets spilled to her waist, and before Delilah could pull them up, Simon caught her hand. The buttons had opened and when she looked down, her breasts lay exposed to Simon. In a heartbeat his expression changed from irritation and disgust to hunger. He stared at her breasts as if he were desperate for them, then closed his eyes, cursed, and slowly lowered his mouth to suckle one, then the other. When she ached and shuddered, he raised his head, scowled down at her, and said between his teeth, "Your bath is waiting, Your Highness."

As they left the hotel, Delilah bumped into a woman sliding from a room and closing the door quietly. She glanced down Delilah's slender body, dressed in a hat, coat, and trousers. "See me when you start shaving," the woman rapped out before her eyes raised to Simon. She smiled and snuggled close to him, lifting a hand to smooth his chest. "So you couldn't leave your son last night, eh? If you stayed at Mable's house last night, we could have sent one or two of the girls over here for your boy."

Simon smiled tightly and nodded as he moved away. "My wife"—he glanced at Delilah and leered cockily—"needed my attention."

The hard eyes of the woman strolled down Delilah from her hat to her jacket and down her trousers to her muddy, worn boots. Simon apologized, "She's seen better days. I clean her up now and then."

The woman laughed coarsely and leered at him. "I'll just bet you do. A big chap like yourself needs a proper woman who knows what to do with what's in her hand, eh?"

Simon chuckled, bent, and kissed Delilah's hot cheek. He lifted the hand she'd raised to slap him and kissed her palm. "She's a poor bit, but she suits me."

" 'A poor bit,' " Delilah muttered when she placed her foot in her stirrup.

Simon chuckled aloud and bent to nuzzle the side of her throat, then lifted her onto Phantom's saddle. "You went drinking and carousing last night, Simon. Don't deny it," she thrust at him as he mounted. "You're lucky you're not in the hoosegow, drunk as a skunk. You know your weakness is drink."

"Yes, worthless lout that I am," he said simply, raising his hand to the brim of his hat in a salute to a passing lawman. "I sacrificed for you and stopped my thirst quickly. All in the job. A necessity when investigating your brother's whereabouts."

"Hah! I just bet. And what of information of your brother's murderer?"

"I'm working on that."

After two hours of solidly ignoring Simon's comments on the majestic Rocky Mountain scenery, Delilah turned to face him. "I don't want to talk with you."

"Hmmm," he said in a satisfied tone. "You can turn your neck. I thought it would be permanently stiff."

"You . . . you know what you did . . . when you . . . you know what you did," she repeated hotly, color rising in her cheeks despite her efforts to control her frustration.

"Yes, I do," he agreed, his eyes twinkling.

She shifted uncomfortably on the saddle. "You are improper, Simon. What would Amelia say? No gentleman would touch a lady like that."

"Oh? How would he touch her?" he asked with interest and began to grin as Delilah floundered.

Delilah flushed as she remembered how Ezrah had touched her. Ezrah had fallen on her, pushing himself at her coarsely. He'd attacked her the moment they closed the bedroom door.

"However he did, I'm certain it wouldn't be like you . . . like you attempted to touch me," she stated heatedly.

"Hmm. Now, why would I get the idea that you liked me touching you? Kissing you?" he asked curiously. "Could it have been when you held my head to your bosom and cried out?"

"Shut up. You're about as useful to me as a . . . a petunia."

"Rash, damning words, my dear. Who would do your foraging for word of Richard in sporting houses and back rooms if not myself?" he asked, reaching out a finger to stroke her hot cheek.

Delilah refused to look at him when they stopped and quickly ate the hotel's packed lunch. She didn't understand her body's reaction to Simon's intimate caress, nor the way he cherished her breasts as though she were the sweetest thing he had ever tasted. She glanced at him—his jaw was clean shaven, and he sat straight in the saddle as if nothing had happened last night or this morning when he'd stopped shaving to study her soaking in the tub.

Lather had streaked along his jaw and along his throat as he kneeled by the tub. His big dark hand spread across her breast, despite her efforts to push him away. He handled her gently, caressingly, and she watched horrified as his hand slipped downward to ease between her clamped thighs.

Delilah closed her eyes and fought remembering her heated reaction, the response that his fingers drew from her until she felt herself opening to his touch. She shook, holding her breath as the contractions gripped her, and dug her fingers into his shoulders for a lifeline. His damnable sweet kiss later drained and soothed. She hated him for that kiss.

She glared at him, shivered, and found herself saying, "It won't happen again."

He looked at her blandly and moved Lasway closer. "You're a very responsive woman, Delilah. You go up in flames."

She thought of Ezrah's taunts, his bumbling, hurting hands.

Simon studied her, then said quietly, "You know that it will happen between us."

"No. I don't," she tried valiantly and hated his chuckle. "You did that deliberately. You calmly washed your hands and proceeded to . . . to . . ." She was horrified as her blush rose.

"Feast upon you? That's what men want to do to desirable women unless they're dead. You needed sleep, dear heart. Are you going to relive the whole damned incident through the entire day?" he returned grimly.

Delilah avoided looking at him. "You deliberately set out to—"

"Yes?" he asked with interest as her cheeks turned rosy.

"It won't happen again," she repeated, and dismissed the uncertainty within her. Simon's chuckle caused the hair on the nape of her neck to rise.

That afternoon they stopped near a deserted cabin to rest the horses. Before she could dismount, Simon plucked her from the saddle, carried her to the cabin, and pinned her against the wall with almost rough, tantalizing kisses. She found herself shaking. "Kiss me," he ordered tightly in a deep, husky voice and placed his mouth down on hers before she could move away.

His kiss was soft and sweet, and his knee moved between her legs, lifting and bumping the softness between her legs with a rhythm his tongue repeated in her mouth. Delilah fought the flames starting low in her stomach, then followed his lead and locked her arms around his waist. He opened her jacket and jerked up her shirt and camisole, finding her breasts. His mouth was open now, and hungry, heating her. She arched toward him, needing the hunger and the warmth. Bits and pieces of her were slipping away, and Simon was replacing them with something she needed desperately. She sank into the emotions, wallowed in them, clinging to Simon, and realized that he was trembling as he stood back and whispered reverently, "Look at you. You're beautiful."

She followed his gaze down to her breasts, peaking against his caressing hand. Simon's look was tender before he slowly tucked her camisole and shirt down and buttoned her coat. He lifted her gently and placed her on Phantom. "We'd better go, dearest," he said softly. "Or I won't be responsible."

For the next hour Delilah dealt with her emotions. Ezrah had never been gentle, nor playful—Simon was both.

But then Ezrah did not have the methodical determination that marked Simon's every move.

That night Delilah lay fully dressed in the blankets while Simon read from her mother's journals. When he was finished, he lay down beside her just as though he'd done it every night for years. "She did what she had to do to protect you and Koby. She stayed with an old voyager, caring for him until he died. It gave her a measure of safety, and Louis enjoyed having children around him."

Delilah found Simon's fingers laced with hers. She enjoyed the comforting touch, though she had been very aware of Simon's dark looks through the day. He'd made camp and cooked with the same precise methods that marked everything he did. There was a comfort in that sameness.

There was no comfort in the desire to rip away Simon's clothes and explore him. Ladies did not pursue men in that manner. Simon didn't seem to notice what Ezrah called her "deficiency." He turned on his side and stroked her hair. "Your mother loved you and Koby very much, and she was married to Brave Bear in her heart, if not by the church."

Delilah turned away only to be brought back by Simon's hand cupping her chin. "Did you want children with Ezrah?"

She flushed, avoiding his gaze.

Simon kissed her lips gently. "It's a natural thing to want children with the man you love."

She shrugged slightly. "I've never thought of myself as a mother."

He smiled tenderly and bent to kiss the side of her throat. "Dear Delilah, you've been too busy surviving. You nurture and protect everyone near you. Perhaps it's time you thought of what you want from life." Then he bent to kiss her again, this time parting her lips with his and slipping his tongue inside.

When he lifted his head, Delilah found her fingers gripping his shoulders. "No more of that," she managed huskily, unevenly as she began to tremble.

"Oh, no?" he asked with a boyish grin that caught her breath.

"No." She tried for a firm note and a whisper came out. "You went to the saloons and the bawdy houses last night, Simon. It was on your mind when we arrived to deliberately— you set out to . . . when you—"

His eyebrow lifted. "Yes?" he prompted with interest.

"Because you've attached yourself to me for the trip doesn't mean anything else comes with it," she said primly as his lips dipped for a quick, hard kiss.

"Mmm?" he questioned. "Such as?" She pressed her hands over his wandering fingers, which had been unbuttoning her clothing.

"You know what, Simon Oakes!" she shot back heatedly. "You're demented."

"Hot," he corrected in a dark tone as if he had reached the end of whatever tether bound him. "You explode when I touch you, dear heart. You give everything when you kiss. You flame. You tremble and every part of you strains toward me. You melt beautifully."

"Melt?"

He slowly tugged open the bows on her camisole as her hands rested on his wrists. "I'm going to make love to you soon, Delilah," he said slowly. Then, watching her, he lowered his mouth to open over the peaked tip of her breast. His lips tugged gently, and the melting she found she'd been waiting for began. Her body convulsed when his fingers first found her, and Simon's mouth caught her cry as she soared.

Simon shuddered and kissed her again, very gently, then drew her to his side and rocked her until she fell asleep.

Chapter Eleven

—⟡—

"Seventy-Mile House is just ahead. I have a friend who lives not far from there. Richard may have stopped in as he passed," Delilah said, scanning the heavy timber as they waited for a heavily loaded wagon to labor through the mud. The BX stagecoach driver behind them cursed and yelled for the wagons to let him pass. A blond woman with her curls spilling down to her bosom hung over the window and called to Simon. The invitation was lusty, and he grinned back while she swatted mosquitoes away from her bouncing breasts propped on the open window.

Delilah frowned at Simon. He looked rakish and boyish as he blew the woman a kiss and took off his hat to swing it in a gallant bow. She shook her head and closed her eyes when he turned to blow her one.

"Child," she muttered, drawing her collar up against the hail and guiding Phantom back onto the muddy road.

Simon's grin widened. "What?"

"I said, 'Chicken would be nice.' "

"Breast? Or thigh?" Simon asked too pleasantly.

Delilah ignored him. When he wasn't giving orders, or flirting with women, he reveled in teasing her to the limits. She'd had enough for the entire trip. They plodded through the mud behind the slow-moving stage and double wagon teams. Late in the afternoon Delilah recognized the narrow, almost concealed trail leading toward a log cabin. Smoke hovered over the snow-covered meadow and swirled around the small cabin. Traps hung from the big gray log walls, and a wolfish-looking dog howled. Bones and litter, cans and bottles lay spread over the yard. A beast craned its craggy head around the corner of the house to peer at them down its large muzzle.

"Hello, pretty boy. Hello, Claude!" Delilah exclaimed with delight, and the camel seemed to leer at her through his long, sweeping lashes. He swung toward Simon and shook the shaggy hair on his neck with the air of immediate dislike.

She dismounted just as the dog howled mournfully again, and the cabin's wooden door creaked open. The barrel of a buffalo gun emerged to point at them. "Why for you here, eh?" a man asked in a cracking French accent.

"François, it's Delilah."

"Eh? What you say?" The door opened wider, and Simon's hand rested on his revolver as he stood slightly in front of Delilah.

Simon's broad back looked like a protective wall. She hadn't asked for his protection, nor his company along the trip. Nor his kisses or his soul-reaching hands.

She elbowed by him and took one step toward the door before Simon's fist locked to the back of her collar. He dragged her back like a child about to step into danger. The barrel of the gun lifted and disappeared inside the cabin. A bent, aged man dressed in sagging, dirty leathers eased from the shadowy depths, blinking in the dim light. A strong odor of smoke and unwashed human flesh boiled out into the clean fresh air. He pushed back the grimy hair from his eyes and stroked a grimier gray beard with a dark streak from spitting tobacco. He reached out a gnarled hand that trembled as it touched

Delilah's shoulder. "My sweet little girl," he crooned. "My little *bébé*, Delilah, come to see me."

He turned to the camel peering around the corner of the cabin. "Claude, Delilah's here. Come on now, you come say hello."

The camel remained where he was. A breeze washed his overpowering scent to Simon. The ancient trapper grinned happily, exposing gums with one remaining blackened tooth. "My little girl," he repeated warmly. "Come inside. Bring your man. We eat."

Delilah looked warily at Simon. She pressed her lips closed before informing François that Simon had no claim on her. The small victory pleased Simon immensely.

The cabin was dirty and foul smelling, coated with smoke and grime, yet Delilah took off her hat and entered as though it were a grand palace. "François," she said warmly. "How are you?"

He swept aside the cluttered table and pushed cans from a chair. "*Magnifique*, now that you come. Sit."

He frowned at Simon, who bent to enter the cabin. "What you do with my fine pretty girl, eh? Look how poor she dress, *n'est-ce pas*? She your woman, you dress her warm, hear, boy?"

While Simon clamped his pride, Delilah held the old man's hand. "I'm fine, François. I am trailing Richard. He's headed north, maybe to Barkerville. I have to find him. Has he passed through here?"

The old man nodded, then shuffled to the stove and started the fire that billowed out at him. He swatted the flames and the smoke away. "Richard come here. *Oui*. He say he go back to Barkerville, no? He have your mama's fancy gun."

He held up two fingers, then three. "Three, maybe four year ago. All the same to an old man."

"They say he's changed his name, and now it's Mordacai Wells. He's wanted for gypping and killing prospectors and for jumping claims. I don't believe the stories for a minute, but I must find Richard."

The old man turned to her. "Richard is good boy. But I hear about Wells. He's a bad one. You stay, talk with François a bit, and count my money for me, yes? You see if store men cheat old François, eh?"

She laughed aloud, the sound rich with pleasure. "Yes. And I'll cook for you, too."

The old man raised his head regally. "I am French-Canadian. Voyagers cook good food. Me, my papa, and my brothers come to this big country to make friends with the Indians, get furs, and we know how to cook good. So you come back to old François, eh?" he repeated as though Christmas had come to him in May.

Simon peered into the cluttered, dirty corners and wondered what vermin might be nesting for the night. "I believe I'll set up camp, dear heart. Come along when you're ready."

"She stay with me," François said darkly. "When I have woman, my Secwepemc wives, I dress them both and all my children damn fine. What no pride you got, man, eh?" he asked with a scowl. "Look this poor pretty woman, dressed like boy, eh? Go. Shame. I got no use for you in that warm coat, while she have rags and poor boy pants. Shame. Don't talk to Claude. My camel has pride. Go."

Simon backed up a step at the fierce attack. His expression darkened, and the day's dark red beard gleamed as he locked his jaw in place. He shot an accusing glance at Delilah and took a step toward her as if to claim her. The old trapper lifted a steel-tipped, four-foot spear threateningly. Tapered at both ends, the one-and-a-half-inch-wide shaft of wood, the "Lahausse" of the Dene Indians, was light and deadly. Simon nodded stiffly to Delilah, who had just ducked her head to shield a smile. He didn't like retreating before the tiny trapper, who looked like an enraged father protecting his daughter from a lecher. "Will you be all right?"

"Yes. Thank you," she returned too politely.

"I'll make camp. You are welcome to share my humble cooking, François. Though I doubt it will be up to your fine palate. I insist," Simon offered stiffly. He nodded once to Delilah, then retreated with his nicked pride. Claude issued a sound that was either a snarl or a belch. François spat on the ground, regarding Simon with furious small, beady eyes. Simon leveled a look at Delilah and sensed that François wanted to set Claude on his heels. "I'll expect you when you're finished visiting."

"Yes, Simon," she said patronizingly. "You may go along now."

Delilah slid into the light of the campfire three hours later. She looked tired, but pleased. She bent and lifted the lid of the covered pot. She sniffed the simmering meat mixture. "François will be along later. He's enraged that you insisted on cooking."

She glanced at Simon, who was lounging on the pallet and crocheting, his hook flashing in the firelight. "Put that away," she ordered just as François walked into camp carrying a pottery jug. "François, Simon must not drink," she said adamantly, then lowered her voice. "He has a problem."

She nudged Simon with her boot, her eyes ordering him to put aside his crocheting. He leisurely placed it in his saddlebags. Delilah bent and quickly tucked away a condemning red corner that escaped, and Simon sighed. "I must stop at the next store for more thread."

Delilah frowned at him warningly.

François studied Simon darkly. "He beat you when he drink? I get my bullwhip now. He be good boy then."

"He won't raise a hand to me," Delilah said heatedly and settled on the pallet Simon had vacated to finish dinner. Simon flicked her body a look that said where he wanted to place his hands, and she flushed.

François sat on a stump, pulled the cork from the jug, braced it over his shoulder, and gulped deeply. He wiped the back of his hand across his mouth and studied Simon as he began ladling out dinner. "When I found him, he was drunk and hanging from a tree," Delilah said clearly, and began unbraiding her hair. It rippled in the firelight, pouring down her shoulders and over the front of her coat. She sat, legs crossed, looking like a child.

"Waugh." François nodded and sipped again as if he understood Simon's completely worthless life. "Maybe that why there are no *bébés* in your belly." He shook his head sadly. "Sometimes whiskey take man's power away."

Simon inhaled slowly, his eyes narrowed at Delilah. "Yes,

sometimes a man's power can be sorely tested."

Claude's odor preceded him. His bulging eyes stared at Simon steadily. "The Dromedary Express?" Simon asked, referring to the introduction of two-humped camels as transport animals to the gold fields. Claude's appearance transferred the topic from Simon's slandered manhood.

Though each two-humped animal could carry eight hundred pounds and could survive the dry hot and cold temperatures, they were famed for biting and kicking whatever was nearest. Packers and freighters hated them. The venture was a failure; the camels' hooves were adapted to sand, not the rocks of the Cariboo country.

"*Oui,*" François agreed sadly, looking at Claude as he would a brother whose time had passed. "So, boy. You do not beat this pretty little girl, eh? What you do? Marry her? Make babies?"

Delilah's gasp caused Simon to grin. He handed François the plate of food. The old man inspected it warily, then he beamed with delight. "Fresh venison soup," he crooned, pushing the small meat cubes through the rice and tomatoes. "I hear no shot."

"I used the spear. I felt like a little exercise." Simon nodded to the carcass hanging high in an aspen tree.

"You ran down a deer?" Delilah asked in a disbelieving tone.

"It didn't run to me."

Simon lifted a cloth from a pan and held it out to François, whose layers of grimy wrinkles shifted into pleasure. "Stick bread." He murmured the word like a lover's endearment.

"Nothing like a good hunt before eating, right, François?" Simon asked as he gave Delilah her plate and sat by her. She noted that he smelled like soap and his hair was damp. His cleanly shaven jaw gleamed in the campfire. The look of the hunter remained; his green eyes darkened when he glanced at her mouth. He pressed his fingertip to a crumb by her mouth and took it to his lips. "So you think you have a champion tonight, do you?" he murmured quietly.

"Blancmange!" François exclaimed later when Simon gave him a cup of white pudding.

"A little preserved eggs and evaporated milk. Nothing special, I'm afraid."

François's beady eyes were dreamy, filling with tears. "We cook like this in those days. We had big canoes, trading with the Indians. I married many times, had many children. They are gone now. Dead. So is Louie. Louie keep Delilah's mama and *bébés* for years. When he die, he give her money and send her to me. She want to go to gold fields to open boardinghouse for miners. This sweet girl here maybe nine . . . ten years old."

The little man shrugged. "I send her north to Gregor, my brother. He help her go to the gold fields, but he want to keep her as his wife pretty damn much."

Delilah pushed the meat bits through the rice and tomatoes. She'd met Gregor, a big bear of a man, again at the Mortons' store. He recognized her mother's features in Delilah's face. Gregor cried when told of her death, then told her what he knew about her mother's trip north. Louie had taken care of her after running from the farmer, then François, and last was Gregor. All three men had loved Delilah's mother, though she was kind in denying their offers of marriage. The three brothers loved children and had wanted to adopt Koby and Delilah. Their mother wanted a life she could control, and she did not want a husband. She said she had loved too hard, and her heart was buried. The voyager brothers met every spring and mourned their loss, though they had married and had many children. Gregor decreed that if Delilah needed help, she should come to him. Gregor was the first person she had sought when she decided to leave the gold fields.

Delilah rocked and stared at the fire, remembering the hardships as she, Richard, and Tallulah traveled southward to find the Millennium mine. She'd clenched Ben's deed to Delilah Smith—her mother—tight in her fist, holding on to a dream of making a home and a new life in the Washington Territory. She'd desperately wanted a fresh life away from the dark memories.

Simon sat next to Delilah, his body touching hers. He stroked her loosened hair once, his hand passing over it soothingly before he offered to spend the day hunting and cooking voyager foods with François.

The little trapper's eyes watered, and Delilah touched his hand. "You do this for me . . . spend time with old François? Jerk meat? Cook beaver tail, maybe? Liver and lights?" he asked, referring to the butchered animal's lungs.

He beamed like a boy anticipating his first camping trip. "We go fish old way, with nets. We start early in morning while this child sleeps. François smoke meat to last long time. We stuff guts. I be fat next time you see me, eh?"

Delilah shot Simon a dark look. "You're deliberately trying to—to woo him," she whispered in an aside. "You'll be hurt, and I can't afford to lose the time looking after you. Whatever happens is your own fault. I don't believe you got that deer with the spear. Not at all. You're not the sort."

He turned to her and pressed her thigh through the layers of clothing. His kiss was brief and hungry, and Delilah's body started heating. "I do try, dear heart," he murmured humbly, his eyes sparkling.

"If I didn't agree that he needed help, I would leave you before dawn," she whispered.

"I can always count on you to take care of those who need you," he returned intimately, his eyes darkening.

François chuckled as she flushed. "Delilah have bath in my house, then we talk, no? I have water ready on stove. All time, her mama like bath," he added softly a moment later, then chuckled. "Koby, he wear a voyager medal, but he did not like bath. We hide from her. He was a good boy."

"He found us last November, François," Delilah said, rising to her feet.

"That's good. He stopped by here, too. We hunt and fish, just like tomorrow with your man. All your mama's children come here . . . see François. She teach you good—respect for old man. . . . Good food," François said between ravenous bites.

"Why don't you run along, dear heart?" Simon asked, his teeth flashing against his dark skin as he rose to place his warm coat around her shoulders. He handed her the pajamas, soap, and a small but clean towel. "Wear my pajamas when you come back to camp. I don't want you catching cold."

Delilah walked toward François's cabin, badly needing her privacy to sulk. She'd taken care of herself and everyone around her for years, and now suddenly Simon had appeared to interfere and manage her life. François's beaming smile of approval of Simon's care followed her.

"Petunia," she muttered, and held on to the hope that tomorrow would find Simon awakening to the fact that he should have stayed out of her life. François would surely hunt for bear, his favorite food.

"Shhh," François whispered as he eased into the cabin two hours later. "Wait until it is safe, my good friend."

When he motioned, Simon followed him past the pile of unwashed, smelly clothing that Delilah had tossed outside the cabin. Claude stood guard over the nearby discarded piles of cans and bottles as though he were looking for a delicacy. Delilah had tossed everything but François's rope cot outside. She lay sleeping on it, dressed in Simon's too-large pajamas and wrapped in his warm jacket. Jars of coins stood on the table.

"Her mama clean like this for me, count my money, write letters to the old country. Everything shoo-bye-go, she throw outside at first. Tomorrow she scrub soap, wash."

His layers of wrinkles shifted into something like fear. "Me, too," he added in a tone of pure dread. "Bath." François spat the word into the hushed cabin with disgust.

Simon tugged away Delilah's dirtied stockings. Her face was very pale in the mass of gleaming black hair, her lashes laying shadows on her cheeks. Taking care, he eased her from the cot and nodded to François. The old man brushed a tear from his eye. "Take care this little one. She have much trouble in her life. Now she lose another brother. You must help her find him. She have great heart. Good heart. All the time, take care of her family."

Simon gathered her closer, tucking her face into the warmth of his throat. "I will take care of her, François."

Delilah curled against Simon as he carried her to their camp. She grumbled when he slid away the coat and eased her into the pallet.

Delilah lay tucked against him. Her nipple pushed through a gap in the pajama buttons to gently bump his side as she breathed. Simon fought down the desire riding him, making him ache from eyebrows to toe and lodging painfully in his lower body. He waited for each delicious little thrust of that plump nipple and fought remembering how it had hardened in his mouth. Delilah stirred and yawned and the perfume of her skin swirled around him tantalizingly.

Delilah awoke to Simon's uneven breathing, his body stretched out taut beside her. With each breath her breasts nudged the hair on his chest. The slightly rough, warm sensation reminded her of his mouth, drawing emotions from her that she had never experienced. She eased away slightly, looking up at him. His arms were behind his head and he was staring up at the tarp over their heads. He was probably wishing for his friends of the previous night—the friendly woman in the hallway, who'd thought Delilah was a boy. Or the woman with her white breasts spilling over the stagecoach window. Delilah wondered darkly if he'd touched the woman's breasts, caressed and laved them with his tongue as he had done with her body.

She shifted on the pallet and found Simon looming over her, his arms braced beside her head. "Stop moving," he ordered hoarsely.

She couldn't. Her hips bumped his angular ones as she settled more comfortably into the pallet. Simon's hand found her breast beneath the quilt. Her hips flexed again, and he groaned unevenly. "Dear Delilah," he murmured reluctantly, lowering his face to the curve of her throat.

His skin was rough and hot, and he trembled against her. "Dear Delilah," he repeated in a softer tone; the tip of his tongue touched her ear.

She shivered, her fingers gripping his taut shoulders. The thought sprung to her mind, then to her lips. "I'm not my mother, Simon."

His teeth stopped their gentle nibbling on her lobe, and he stroked her hair in a caress. "What do you mean?" he asked very carefully.

"She . . . I . . . we're different . . . as women . . . with men," she managed shakily.

Simon's lips curved in a smile against her throat. "Yes?" he asked in a tone that invited her to explain.

She cleared her throat. It was very important that Simon understand that she . . . His mouth was tugging on the flannel pajama top, easing the buttons open to find her breast. "I know what you are, sweetheart," he murmured gently. "You're beautiful and you're sweet and you take care of everyone around you. Someday you'll see that you have needs, too."

"Simon." Her breath slid out on a sigh.

He drew her on her side, sliding his hand beneath the flannel shirt to caress her breast. "I wanted you from the first moment I saw you—I haven't wanted another woman as badly as I want you."

The reluctant, raspy statement delighted her. Simon's eyes were warm and tender as he unbuttoned the pajama top and tugged the knot free on the bottoms. She couldn't unlock her fingers from his shoulders as he bent to kiss her breast. "I've dreamed of these all day. So sweet . . ." His lips swept across to suckle her other breast, his hands caressing them until she gasped.

"You can touch me," he whispered against her stomach as she gripped his hair, tugging him away.

She was frightened by his mouth trailing lower to kiss the curls between her legs. "Simon!"

He nuzzled her and she cried out, fighting the heat and the desire racing through her.

"What do you want to tell me?" he asked roughly as she wrapped her arms around him and held on tight. She wanted his touch, the heat and magic to go on forever, but she couldn't tell him anything. His chest pushed against her softness, the hair rough and crisp against her nipples. She moved tentatively, experimenting, and Simon chuckled, a deep rich sound.

He raised over her, settling on her very carefully. "Simon, you don't want me," she managed, afraid to move her fingers away from his shoulder. It wasn't possible—Ezrah had said that no man would want her. The firelight danced on Simon's expression—the narrowed, tender look of his eyes, and the bold lock of his jaw—which said that nothing could keep him from her. That every particle of his soul and body wanted to lock his body with hers.

"I don't?" He rocked his hips against her, edging one leg between her own. The length of his desire thrust between them, heating her stomach. Delilah closed her eyes and shivered. "If you're going to tell me to stop, dear heart, do it now," Simon whispered rawly in a sound that tore from him. "But make no mistake. I want you very, very much."

He waited a moment, studying her tightly closed lids carefully. "It isn't bad to want to make love, Delilah," he whispered as he smoothed away the pajamas, his rough legs tangling with hers. He kissed the skin he had revealed, his big hands trembling as they caressed her. Hunger and excitement raced through his gaze as it swept over her. "Sweet," he said, lifting her chin with his finger. "You're very sweet and very, very warm."

"Simon," she whispered, desperately wanting him. She had to tell him that she wasn't the woman he thought, that Ezrah had cursed her for unmanning him. Her hips lifted and she shuddered, trying to lay still as Ezrah had said men wanted. Her traitorous hips moved again, and Simon smoothed them, his hand sliding up and along her ribs until he found her breasts. Then they slid down again, caressing her thighs and the backs of her knees, gently arranging her legs over his.

He was heavy and solid, bracing his weight away from her. She lifted her mouth for the sweet, seeking, hungry kisses. When Simon trembled, she sensed that Simon leashed himself tightly.

"You can move your hands," he offered with a gentle, teasing smile. "Preferably on some part of my skin."

"Where?" She wanted to touch him, anywhere, skimming the hard muscles and cords, delighting in the rough warm skin against hers, but she didn't want to frighten him away.

Simon laughed outright and Delilah found herself grinning. "There is a lot of skin on you, Simon. You are not a small man."

He chuckled pleasantly. "Well, let's see. How about here?" he asked, placing her hand on his chest. His eyes darkened when she smoothed his hard nipple. "See how my heart races for you, Delilah. You have that effect on me."

They lay still for a time while Delilah smoothed Simon's chest, his legs cradled between hers. She was warm and safe, wrapped in the old soft quilt with him. "This is nice," she whispered finally, with the sense that Simon would wait forever to please her. Her hips lifted again, and the tip of Simon's manhood found her moist, heated opening.

He cleared his throat and shuddered. "Yes," he agreed rawly. "Very nice."

She should tell him that she would be inadequate. That he would be unmanned—but she couldn't. Poor Simon—if he didn't stop, he would be doomed. She pressed against him gently, tightening her thighs, and wished they would stop quivering. She ached so deep in her body that only his touch could unlock the pain. "Simon, help me. . . ."

His hand cupped her bottom and lifted her gently, deepening the intimacy with a rhythm that his mouth continued as he bent to take her breast in his mouth. She arched against him, clasping him tightly to her, desperate for the sweet warmth that Simon offered her. Her legs began to thrash, and Simon's mouth tugged harder, his body pushing against hers.

"Simon!" Delilah tightened her legs and arms around him, and he tensed, resisting, waiting—

Simon's hot face lay against her breast, his bold strength pushed down into her, and stopped. He breathed raggedly as Delilah squirmed beneath him, trying to get closer to the ultimate tightening she'd experienced with his hand. He tested her with a gentle thrust and retreated to rest just within her. "So," he whispered raggedly between breaths, his great body trembling. A fine sheen of sweat gleamed on his forehead, and a muscle clenched in his jaw. "You are a woman of surprises, my dear."

"Oh, Simon . . ." Now he'd leave her—just as Ezrah did—swearing and damning her for shrinking his manhood. She couldn't let that happen to Simon. She found and took him in her hand, exploring his heavy jutting length with trembling fingers. He seemed intact, like hot silky steel, and there was nothing unmanly about the shape and size of him. She fluttered her fingers over his entire length, testing him delicately. He remained heavy and solid, and Delilah bit her lip, wondering desperately how she could manage to sheath him to the hilt. He inhaled sharply, his manhood springing into her hand. She pulled him gently, and Simon groaned loudly, a desperate, hungry sound that Claude answered from a distance. "Am I hurting you?" she asked against his lips, for he had begun kissing her feverishly.

"My dear, if this is hurting me—" he began roughly as she placed the tip of him slightly within her aching warmth. He raised slightly, brushing her swollen lips with his. "This will hurt, dear Delilah. But the pleasure later—"

"Oh, Simon, I'm aching," she whispered desperately, locking her arms around him. He was safe, she thought fleetingly, large and safe just as he had been lying at her side every night. Though tonight, hunger and heat vibrated from him, this was the same man who had rocked her to sleep and who had treated her gently when he touched her intimately. Even in this desperate moment he had left the choice to her. She wanted him to trust her with himself, to give his body to her care.

More. She wanted more—she wanted Simon locked deep within her to complete what he had started—

He caught her cry in his mouth as he thrust through the tight barrier. Filled with Simon, adjusting to his strength and size, she quivered, holding on to the safety of his shoulders. He moved gently, tugging her breasts at the same rhythm, and the sensations gripping Delilah stirred, soared, and tightened. She arched back her throat and let herself burst through the flames to the startling, flying pleasure.

Simon thrust down into her deepest passage, raising her hips with his hands, and cried out. His body poured into hers, the magnificent pulsing adding to her pleasure as she tightened on him once more. Trembling, soothing Simon's taut, damp shoulders, Delilah found herself tightening again, the heating starting again, pounding, flying at her with pleasure that she never wanted to end.

Simon stiffened again, then slumped in her arms. "Oh, God," he said shakily, as if devastated.

She stroked his hair as his head lay on her breast. "I hope

I didn't frighten you," she whispered, kissing his damp forehead. He seemed to need soothing, as if he'd flung himself against the hardest task of his life and was just resting—

"Oh, God," he repeated in that same, shattered deep tone of a man who had been purely, completely devastated.

She cleared her throat, aware that his heart was still racing as if he'd run for miles. "I . . . I hope I didn't frighten you too much, Simon," she whispered. "I . . . I'm sorry I moved. . . . I know ladies shouldn't, but I just couldn't stop."

"Mmm." The ragged, deep sound that seemed to come from his soul was all he managed after a long, deep sigh. Delilah bit her lip. She'd destroyed him. She hadn't meant to, but a ravenous, hot hunger swelled out of her, and she'd needed him deep inside her. She hoped she hadn't hurt him too badly; her own pain was a slight wound to what Simon must have suffered. . . .

Delilah lay beneath his sprawling weight. He showed no inclination to move away from her, his hands leisurely caressing her hips as if he would continue until the world spun away. After a time he shifted to take her breast in his mouth.

The poignant pleasure speared through her instantly, and her fingers tightened hard on his hair urging him nearer. "My, my," he said in a deep rumbling tone of pleasure as he moved to nibble on her other breast.

When Simon's hand touched her, Delilah's hips jerked immediately. He smiled against her breast, nuzzled it, and murmured, "My sweet Delilah."

"Oh, I'm so sorry, Simon," she whispered as he slid into her again.

"Shut up, dear heart. Nothing can protect you now. Not now that I know what you want. I want everything you have . . . don't hold back," Simon whispered against her lips.

She tightened around him immediately, stunned by the swirling heating sensations as he eased deeper, then stilled, filling her. "I'm afraid you'll ache in the morning, dear heart," he whispered unevenly and shuddered. "We should wait—"

She reveled in the strength and heat that was Simon, and he looked down at her tenderly. " 'Don't hold back'?" she repeated tentatively.

"I can stand the onslaught. Do your best," he challenged unevenly as she eased back a wave from his damp brow.

"Poor, poor Simon," she whispered with a grin, then she let her hips writhe up against him, gloving him completely. He'd have to fight his own battles, because she certainly had her own and wouldn't show him a drop of mercy.

Chapter
Twelve

"What are you doing?" Delilah
demanded, horrified to find Simon placing the bucket of warm
water beside her legs. She'd drifted into sleep the moment
Simon had cuddled her in his arms after making love a second
time. He'd acted as devastated, delighted, and surprised as
the first time. As though the world could shatter apart and
nothing could make him leave their intimacy. She'd gone to
sleep instantly to the sound of his racing heart, his trembling
caressing hands moving up and down her back. Now the air
was cold as Simon pressed one hand against her inner thighs,
preventing her from closing them.

Delilah sat up, grabbing the quilt to her chest, only to
have Simon's open hand push her down. "Stay there," Simon
ordered roughly, looking very rumpled in the firelight with a
quilt wrapped around him. She'd done that, Delilah thought
proudly. She'd ruffled his groomed, shaven image and his
easy, leisurely manner. She'd arched and writhed and torn

it from him. Simon had been desperate for her, gentle yet firmly, undeniably hungry. That Simon—methodical, deliberate Simon—had been so shaken that he'd needed her stroking and cuddling to recover sufficiently, pleased her immensely.

"You're looking smug." He scowled at her, but his hands gently cleansed her with the wet cloth. She shivered as his fingers glided intimately over her, and she caught the quilt up to her chin. The intimate task caused her to unravel, her uncertainty tangling with the desire to lift up and kiss his swollen mouth. She lay quietly watching his mouth, the lips that he had placed on her so deliberately, finding the heated cords and suckling them to life. Her thighs quivered as his fingertip touched her delicately, circling and toying with a tiny concealed nub. She released the breath she had been holding as he smiled tenderly, then placed the bucket aside and slipped beneath the quilt with her.

Simon held her hand on his stomach. His desire bobbed pleasantly against her wrist with every breath. He lifted her hand to kiss it, then replaced it firmly around himself. He held her hand there with his own. She shivered, remembering his dazed expression when he had poured himself into her, then the long, slow grin moving along her throat and the playful nipping of his teeth. "My dear, how were you married for three years and still remained a virgin?" he asked gently, inviting her hand to move smoothly up and down his silky manhood. The play fascinated her.

He seemed just as heavy and strong and thrusting as before they'd made love. She frowned, debating the term, "making love." She didn't expect love, but at least she'd tasted the grand sweetness of Simon's body locking with hers and climbing to the summit. "I'm so glad you weren't unmanned or frightened, Simon."

He chuckled and kissed her hair, nuzzling it away until his lips rested on her damp temple. "You little terror. Of course, I was frightened for you."

"Simon, do you think this was right? I mean you weren't angry when I didn't lie still?" Her hands found the gentle softness between his legs, seeking the shape.

"Bloody hell, no," he returned immediately. He jerked to one elbow and pulled the quilt up to her throat, then his hand slid to her breast, fondling it in a motion that was soothing and sensual. "No wonder. I suppose your dear husband told you that. That it was your fault he couldn't perform. Now it all makes sense—the loose, dull clothes, the way you pull your hair back. The bastard did that to you, didn't he? I should have known."

She blushed, fully aware that she was lying naked beside a man who was naked, too. His rough thigh caressed hers soothingly. He took her chin in his hand and lifted her mouth to his. "This was a very special gift, my love. I will cherish it," he whispered between kisses. He made the words sound like a promise he would keep forever.

Nothing lasts forever. Time had a way of reaching out and snagging what little pleasure she had found in life. She frowned. With Simon she had found more than a little pleasure.

She turned to him, placing her hand on his chest. "Do you mean that, Simon? You didn't mind that I moved?"

"With all my heart, dear," he said formally, though his breath had become a little ragged and he pressed his hand against hers, signaling her to stop stroking him intimately. Because she believed that Simon needed someone to challenge him, she continued. "You moved me very much," he said, sighing unsteadily against her hair.

The question that had been swirling in her mind leaped across her lips. "You know who I am, that my father forced my mother . . . that I—"

He stopped smoothing her hair, then continued, gathering her closer as if she were his to protect. Delilah gave herself to the luxury of Simon's safety as he rocked her gently. "Shhh. Don't say that. You are wonderful, clean and sweet and perfect, in everything you do. Go to sleep now. We'll talk about this tomorrow."

She sighed tiredly and nuzzled his chest. It smelled comfortingly of soap, sweat, and Simon's clean scent. Beneath her cheek his heart began pounding faster. "Delilah, dear. Perhaps you should sleep now," he offered unevenly in a deep, ragged voice. "You need to rest."

"Mmm, yes." She nuzzled his chest and continued the motion of her hand. She marveled at his strength, relieved that she had not unmanned him. In fact, he seemed even more powerful.

Simon groaned hugely, then flipped aside the blanket to kneel between her legs. He placed them over his shoulders and cupped her bottom in his palms, lifting her. His mouth found her instantly. "Simon!"

Delilah braced her hands back, her fists gathering the quilt as the sensations dived into her, flooded her, and took her. The knot built deep within her each time his mouth moved over her, then it tightened and drew her into fire. When he eased away, Delilah lay trembling in the aftermath of the fire and fell asleep to Simon gathering her close.

"There. Well done, sweetheart," he murmured into her hair as she fell into the warm tide of sleep.

Simon concentrated on the winter-thin caribou buck that François had flushed into the clearing. He sighted a clean shot, and the buck fell heavily into the snow.

François scampered from the woods, jerked out his huge hunting knife, and slit the buck's throat. Simon nodded to the old man's victorious wave, his thoughts locked on Delilah. Her husband had abused her cruelly, demeaning her as a woman. "Good thing he's met his Maker already, or when I met him, he surely would," he muttered, watching a bear lumber into the thicket and geese fly through the bright, crisp May day.

Simon sheathed his Winchester. Was he any better? Rand's murderer could prove to be Delilah's brother, and he would have to be brought to justice. He caught a scent lurking on his skin and closed his eyes. Delilah. Sweet Delilah, who desperately wanted her brother enough to return to the pain of her childhood and marriage. She'd wade through hell for her loved ones. She firmly believed Richard was innocent, that he could not have committed a wounding of another person, or a theft that would create hardship. Was it possible that Wells and Richard were not the same man?

She'd moved so sweetly in his arms. . . . A fierce need to protect her swept through him. He wanted to protect her

from pain—she'd had her share already. Yet he would claim
Richard, retrieve him to the Queen's law, as he was bound to
do.

Delilah. How she would hate him. . . .

Simon cherished her scents swirling on his skin in the early
morning air. If there was the slightest chance that Richard and
Wells were not the same man . . .

Loving Delilah was not a light passion. She enchanted him,
his discovery of her purity had stunned him, and a sweet, fierce
joy rose in him. Simon realized that he would have been deeply
affected even if her blackguard of a husband had taken her
virginity.

She was a fearsome woman, his Delilah. Clasping him
tightly and taking him with a desperation that stunned him.
That sweet maelstrom had reached into his primordal essence
and drawn the soul from him as no other woman had done.
Delilah had bonded him to her and Simon frowned, momentarily resenting her power over him and the lack of a clear
path when on the hunt for the suspected murderer of Rand.

He followed François through a thicket, the old man bent,
stalking his prey with the old spear and making noises to quiet
the deer. Delilah loved deeply, caring for those who were dear
to her and protecting them fiercely.

Simon smiled and realized that this morning he was a wee
bit light-headed, having supped upon his Delilah.

His Delilah. Simon turned the thought, enchanted by it. How
she'd rant at him if he tossed it at her.

"Waugh," François said as they walked, leading Claude
back into camp, the pack on his back filled with the morning's trapping and hunting. "That sweet girl, she washing and
cleaning. Poor old François. It is the bathtime."

The dust clouds shot from Delilah's broom. Washed clothing hung on the rope strung between several trees. Her hair
hung loose, gleaming blue-black in the shadows as she carried
a bucket out and dumped it. She wore Simon's shirt, belted
at the waist, and his pajama bottoms tucked into her boots.
Claude roared and she pivoted, her hair fanning out around
her like black silk. She lifted her hand to shield her eyes, and
the material covering her breasts tightened.

Her unwelcoming scowl challenged Simon as they began to unpack Claude. François hummed merrily as they hung the caribou beside the deer Simon had killed the night before. "Get me some coffee, will you, dear heart?" Simon asked lightly as he bent to kiss her lips.

She wiped his kiss away with the back of her hand, her eyes blazing up at him. He ran a testing finger across her flushed cheeks, and she jerked away. Simon grinned, picking up her challenge instantly. "You haven't shaved," Delilah stated, eyeing him. "Simon, you look like a pirate . . . all puffed up from killing and swaggering back here to order me around. Well, it won't work."

"Won't it? And how many pirates have you met, anyway?" Simon let his laughter escape. He felt young and certain. He leaned closer and nuzzled her ear. Delilah slapped him away. "You've missed me, is that it?"

"It won't happen again," she stated beneath her breath, and glanced at François, who was happily chopping and cutting and tossing fish onto his smoking rack. "You're a methodical man, Simon Oakes. You found that you were running short of . . ." Her flush deepened. "And you deliberately— Oh!"

Simon patted the rounded, feminine backside he had just tossed over his shoulder. "François, it looks as if you can manage without us. Delilah needs a nap."

Delilah struggled against him, and Simon clamped her thrashing legs still as he walked into the forest. He placed her on her feet and blocked the flying hands and feet as she attacked him. "This is how you did it, isn't it, my sweet little Delilah?" he asked with disgust, sidestepping a kick to his groin and letting his forearm take the brunt of a quick, efficient chop of her hand. "This is how you kept that bastard from you. . . . I'm not your departed husband, dear heart, and I want everything you have to give. You keep yourself from me, and I'll come after you. That's a promise."

He caught a flying kick and held her leg, drawing it around his hips and forcing her against his thrusting desire. He wanted her to know that whatever he felt for her, it wasn't sympathy or mechanical needs of the body. He wanted more from her— he wanted every drop of savagery, every sweet nuance that lay hidden within her, buried by her life's pain. Simon jerked away the knotted pajamas, ripped open the shirt, and lifted her bottom in his hands. He tore open his trousers and eased her down upon him. He saw Delilah's anger change to indecision, then awareness. She closed her eyes and shuddered as she eased deeper into intimacy with him. The hot, moist warmth enveloped him like a homecoming, tightening as she cried out. "I want you, Delilah," he whispered rawly against her breast, taking it in his mouth. When he stopped to kiss her, he whispered, "You're exactly what I want. Perfect."

She blinked, her body held him tightly, and she cried out, arching as he took her breasts, tugging on them. She cried out, a long, high keening sound that soared past the aspens. The contractions pulled Simon, and leaning against a tree, he thrust higher into her. The world spun and glittered and blazed before Delilah went limp in his arms. She stroked the damp nape of his neck and nestled her face against his throat.

"Better?" he asked, kissing her damp cheek.

"It hurts, the pain—" she whispered shakily, and when he cursed and straightened, she clung tighter. "Don't go, you feel so solid, so safe. . . . Oh, Simon, this isn't very ladylike."

"I never wanted to hurt you," he whispered, shaken by her admission of pain. When he moved to let her down, her legs tightened on his hips, and her arms locked around his neck.

"Before, Simon. It hurts before you . . ."

He understood, drawing her closer. "Before?"

She cursed, a very ladylike flurry of indignation, against his throat. "Before you . . . fill me. . . . I'm not certain this is proper, Simon. Not even married people take these liberties."

"I'd expect them in my marriage," he returned roughly. "I've never been one to hold to protocol," he admitted as he began to fill her once more. He wanted to wipe away any memories of another man's touch.

François beamed at them over the campfire dinner of roast caribou. "You take care of this little girl's sweet skin, boy," he said around his pipe. "Maybe put a little kiss on those scrape marks on her neck, eh?"

Sitting on the log by Simon's side, Delilah flushed wildly and studied her worn boots. She whispered to him in a tone François could not hear. "You're an animal, Simon, for all your fancy manners."

He placed his arm around her to gather her against him and whispered in her ear, "Only with you, my dear heart. Only with you. I've never met another woman as lusty as you."

"Hah. Don't tell me you act like a gentleman with other women. Especially the sort you seem to attract in hotels and from stagecoaches." Delilah tried to ignore the pain spearing through her at the thought of Simon making such exquisite love to another woman.

Simon whispered back, "I prefer the nymphs that hunt me in the woods. That lock their legs onto me and cry out as if they've been wounded in some delicate, soft, hot, moist place," he teased and caught her flying hand, wrestling her to the pallet as François watched and grinned.

Simon rested over Delilah, pinning her hands above her head and looked over his shoulder to the old man as he was leaving. "We're expecting you for breakfast. I'll make an extra pot of blancmange and bannock bread to last you awhile."

François chuckled. "Maybe you don't have time, eh?"

"François!" Delilah cried out before Simon began in earnest to show her how perfectly ladylike she was in every way.

Richard huddled by the blazing fire in the old miner's cabin not far from Barkerville. He pushed back a long strand of hair and smoothed the beard that now covered his jaw. His back ached from digging with a pick in One Tooth Annie's mine. A former Hurdy Gurdy girl, One Tooth now worked the mine left to her by her deceased Chinese husband, Chen-Yu.

The only women he'd seen, other than One Tooth, was her daughter, Fritzi. One Tooth depended on Fritzi, a poker dealer and a prostitute at a Barkerville saloon. Sloe-eyed Fritzi brought groceries and news.

Richard looked into the flames and saw Mordacai Wells's eyes leering at him. Two years ago he'd stopped at a miner's shanty and asked if he could stay the night. The miner had glanced fearfully back at the open door of the shanty and whispered, "Boy, if you want to live . . . git."

The miner's head had snapped back when the shot fired, then he crumpled at Richard's feet. Blood spread from the gaping wound in his back. A fancy-dressed young man leveled a Colt .45 at Richard's chest and stepped over the body. Three rough-looking men came out of the shanty. Despite his struggles, a man held each of Richard's arms, and he saw two more bodies piled against the shack, half hidden by brush.

"We're the same age and build. Same coloring," Wells had said thoughtfully in a soothing, hypnotic voice. He used the tip of the .45 to raise Richard's face up to the fading sunlight. "Boy, we could be the same man," he mused softly after close inspection of Richard's features.

Wells had glanced at Richard's hand, held by a burly thug. "You're missing the tip of your finger. Left hand. Reckon I can take care of mine." He had jerked the stickpin from Richard's coat and tucked it in his own expensive, well-tailored dress jacket. Wells went for the derringer in Richard's belt as though he were magnetized to it. He turned the silver etching to the light and smoothed the pearl handle like a man about to make love with a woman. "Pretty. Too pretty for a farm boy."

Richard studied the flames and thought about a man making love with a woman. That had been his top priority when he began the trip. At twenty-one he had yet to sample a woman's body. There wasn't much chance while he was at home with Delilah. She wouldn't understand and he didn't want her shocked.

His need to take what Fritzi offered him regularly felt like a molten volcano about to explode. But One Tooth doted on her daughter, though she deplored prostitutes. Fritzi had been seduced by a passing tin peddler, and One Tooth loved and mourned her daughter. Taking Fritzi would betray her mother, and Richard couldn't add to One Tooth's grief.

He glanced slyly at the object of his concern—his benefactress, One Tooth. Worse than working in the mines from dawn until dusk and hiding like a rat was the fact that fate had trapped him with the female prospector. Not that he wasn't grateful for her protection and care. But if God had to jail him with a woman, why couldn't it have been with a woman about two centuries younger, a hundred pounds lighter, and one who knew how to use a bar of soap? "I can't stay here forever," Richard muttered.

One Tooth smoked her pipe and rocked by the fire. "The whole countryside is looking for a man meeting your description. Soon as Wells stops rousing and murdering everyone he meets, the fuss will die down and you can move on. I'm mighty glad for your help in the meanwhile."

"I've got a sister at home who needs me," Richard muttered and wished he could say he had a girl waiting for him, too.

"Delilah," One Tooth murmured in her heavy German accent. "She wasn't a Hurdy Gurdy dancer brought in from San Francisco—I mean your mama, Lady Delilah. Just showed up with a half-breed boy and a sweet little girl with big blue eyes, same as yours. Tallulah got Lady Delilah work at the Hurdys and no one noticed. Lady Delilah wore a red dress and a feather on her head just like the rest of us. We helped her when we could. Those miners loved to hold us up off the floor and dance to the music. Not a one of them fell down when they danced with Lady Delilah."

One Tooth puffed on her pipe and hitched up her suspenders. "Now, me. Any man who held me off the floor for an entire dance was some dancer."

"Those must have been exciting times," Richard said and wished he'd had a chance to hold a Hurdy Gurdy girl in the air and dance around the room.

"What about your sister Delilah? Think she'll send someone after you?"

Richard shook his head, and ice slid around his heart. "She doesn't have the money."

One Tooth puffed for a while, then said, "Could be she'll be coming herself. If I remember right, she always took care of her family and Tallulah, though can't say I liked the husband she picked—Ezrah Morton wasn't worth spit."

"I think she did it because she thought it would make things easier on us." Richard's throat closed when he thought of Ezrah pushing the tip of a knife into his throat and threatening him. "She was always quiet, but after she married him, she was just plain grim. I think if ever a man might be afraid of a woman, though, I'd have to say that it was Ezrah."

"He took it out on the whores. There was something between those two. He loved Delilah, I'm sure of it. But I could tell she didn't like to come within two feet of the bastard. Did he beat her?"

Richard shook his head. "No, but he liked to take out his moods on other people. He caught me once at their house and proceeded to . . . demean me." What Ezrah started to do was even too evil for One Tooth's seasoned ears.

"That so?" She rocked more quickly. "What happened?"

Richard's smile touched his lips, then his eyes, lighting them. "Delilah happened to come home. I've never seen a woman do those fancy Chinese kicks and chops and throws before or since. She was beautiful, hair flying around her, and glorious in her anger. Ezrah didn't have a chance. She was all over him. After he apologized—Delilah ordered him to— he picked himself up off the floor and ran. Delilah made me promise not to tell anyone, and I haven't until now."

"Makes sense. I'd say Delilah would take better care of those around her than herself, poor thing. She was a tiger— a regular hellcat—when Koby needed her, and the same with you. She kept a lot inside, like the way she loved her mother."

Delilah stood in the saddle, easing the slight twinges that had been protesting in her muscles since Simon's lovemaking. She glanced at him and at the packages fastened on the back of his saddle.

"I won't wear them," she promised herself, remembering the way he held the store's dress up to her, and the divided skirt and polished boots. The colorful selection of hair ribbons and camisoles, petticoats and drawers had cost a fortune.

She eyed Simon's broad back, the straight way he sat in the saddle, his head lifted and eyes following any movement along the wagon road. His head turned and he looked at her, the air heating between them. She tightened her lips and followed the passing band of Secwepemc Indians. She'd given herself just as her mother had. Her mother had loved Brave Bear deeply, then had allowed the farmer—Delilah's father—to take her to protect Koby. Delilah tightened her grip on the saddlehorn. Now she knew the desperation of making love. She wanted him now and resented his hold over her.

Simon's large hand rested on her knee. "You're thinking too hard, sweetheart. You've done nothing wrong."

"Haven't I?" She wouldn't tell him how making love to him was like coming home. Simon was a drifter who could tangle a woman's senses, a ladies' man—and he crocheted. His hunger for her seemed unnatural. Delilah glanced down at the strong, dark fingers clamped to her leg. They rested there possessively, yet she knew his strength. Just looking at his hands made her body butter-soft. She lifted her chin, and Simon's green eyes darkened. He eased Lasway closer, nudging Phantom off from the road into a thicket.

Delilah frowned as Simon lifted her down, wrapped her in his arms, and kissed her hungrily. His breath struck her cheek unevenly as he eased his hand beneath her coat and camisole to take her breast. Delilah locked her arms around his neck, unable to stop her hunger as Simon's hand caressed her breasts. "You're so—" he muttered unevenly.

Delilah allowed her hands to slide down and touch him, and Simon went rigid, groaning like a wounded man. She moved her hand and he shuddered, his smooth steely manhood spilling into her hand and reassuring her that she had not unmanned him. Delilah took a fierce pride in the way Simon responded, as if he could not get enough of her. She wanted his mouth on her and ripped away the buttons of her coat and shirt, plucking free the camisole and freeing her breasts to him. A flush rode his cheeks, and Simon placed his mouth on her and began suckling.

Delilah's knees gave way under the onslaught, and Simon caught her. He eased open her trousers and lifted her hips to spread her legs around his hips. She cried out the moment he impaled her, tightening around him instantly and shuddering with the fiery emotions. Simon's shout followed hers into the thick forest. He trembled as she smoothed his hair, cuddling him and whispering into his throat. "Witch," he muttered as though devastated, then added, "My witch."

He slowly lowered her feet to the earth and bent to take her breast again, heating and laving it with moisture. Delilah allowed herself to be held and stroked until the wild trembling slowed. She cleared her throat. "This is very unusual, Simon. It's not right," she muttered when she could draw herself back into reality.

"It's perfect."

"You'll be unmanned." She stroked his still rigid manhood, and it lifted to her touch.

He roared with laughter, his eyes sparkling with it as she blushed. "My dear, you unman me perfectly," he whispered, gathering her against him again and rocking her. "Sweet, sweet Delilah."

Then he looked down at her tenderly and smoothed the hair that she hadn't had time to braid. He wrapped a strand around his finger and brought it to his lips. Heat passed between them again, and Delilah reeled with confusion. He pressed against her, just as hungry as before. "Simon?"

"Again," he said roughly, his eyes dark with passion.

She slowly opened her clothing, watching the hungry expression cross his rigid face. "You know what I want," he said with just a touch of arrogance to challenge her.

"Yes," she whispered, easing aside the camisole to reveal her breasts, which were heavy and aching for his mouth. He tugged harder this time, his hand reaching between her legs to part her intimately. He filled her magnificently, and she closed her eyes, sealing in the pleasure. She threw herself into the fire, treating Simon to the savagery boiling within her and nipping the side of his neck as he thrust into her again and again.

The second time she cried out louder than the first, and the horses whinnied and the mule brayed.

By the time they made camp that night, Delilah had decided that making love with Simon couldn't go on. Nothing that gave her so much pleasure could be honest. When Simon kicked aside his boots carelessly and gave her that hot, hungry look, she found herself opening her camisole for him.

"You're going to die . . . waste away from all this . . . this . . ." she murmured helplessly minutes later when Simon's head lay on her breast and he smoothed her bottom that he had just raised to receive his thrusts. He hadn't been gentle, and she hadn't wanted him to.

Simon nibbled on her throat and grinned. "We're lucky you didn't frighten away the stock from the cries you made." He shifted on her luxuriously. "Lie here while I cook supper."

That night he cleansed her intimately as before, taking care to nourish the tiny nub hidden within her intimate folds. "I'm certain this is ungodly," Delilah managed much later when she slid back into herself after soaring into the fiery universe. She noted that Simon's boots, which were usually neatly polished and placed together, had been carelessly pushed aside. In his hunger for her, he hadn't neatened up, washed, packed, and folded, nor polished his boots. The thought that she could distract Simon from his precise schedule caused her to smile.

They passed 150-Mile House, then Williams Lake. Simon lifted Delilah down from Phantom despite her look of distaste. He allowed her to slide down his body just to watch the quick heat splinter in her sky-blue eyes. He wanted to take care of her, despite her protests that she could manage by herself. He turned to the farmer who had stopped tilling the field with his oxen and now leveled a Winchester at them.

They walked toward the farmer, leaving the horses and the mule to graze near the woods. Deer ran along the forest, slipping into it, and a fat groundhog stood on a tree stump to watch them. Beyond the field lay the cliffs leading to the mighty Fraser River. Paddleboats would be making their way from Soda Creek to Quesnelmouth, and Fort Alexandria could be seen in the distance. The farmer sighted the Winchester on them as they walked toward him.

"We're looking for a boy," Simon said. "About as tall as me, blue eyes and black hair. He's missing the tip of his little finger, left hand."

The farmer spat a stream of tobacco and glanced at his house, a big square gray log cabin. "Mordacai Wells. The constable told me to watch out for him. He's a mean one."

"What color are his eyes?"

The farmer stared at him blankly.

"Do you know a Richard Smith?" Simon pushed, locking his hand over Delilah's cold one and tucking it in his pocket.

"No. But Wells jumped some prospectors a while back near Quesnelmouth and took their grubstake. Has a fancy derringer he's fond of using and a horseshoe-shaped diamond stickpin. Killed four Chinese working a mine not far from here. Cut their pigtails off to dishonor them. He's a mean one. He's round this country somewhere. Murdered a North West Mountie's brother and now the Mountie is out to get him. They're deadly, those North West Mounted Police. He'll find Wells. Until then, better take good care."

That night Delilah sat with her chin tucked on her knees and watched the campfire. "Richard would never dishonor a Chinese. He knows how much store they place in their braids, and they helped us survive. I can't imagine Richard being hunted by the law. He's just a boy."

Simon placed aside his crocheting and drew her head to his shoulder. Worried for her brother, Delilah was too quiet. Simon stroked her sleek hair, which she had been wearing tied at the back of her neck. He pulled the leather thong away gently and eased his fingers through the strands. The evidence against her brother was convincing. She would hate Simon when she discovered his purpose—to bring Wells to justice.

Simon stroked her hair. Delilah treasured her family and she would fight for Richard. She was more mother than sister to the boy.

Later, Simon read some more to her from her mother's diaries. "Koby was stolen?" she asked in disbelief. "Mama was told that he would be killed if she searched for him? Oh, Simon . . . all these years I thought she didn't . . . that she didn't miss him. She said that she felt part of her heart was taken away. . . . She kept her secret even from Tallulah . . . and me. . . ." Delilah turned to Simon, kneeling on their pallet. "She loved him. Koby thinks she wanted free of him because of his mixed blood. Oh, no . . ."

Delilah rocked on her heels, her hair spilling down around the pajama top. Tears trailed down her cheeks, and she dashed them away until Simon drew her down into his arms. "We'll find Richard, dear heart," he whispered against her temple. "We'll find him, and then we'll tell Koby."

"She was so frightened that mad Russian would kill Koby if she searched for him. I was so furious with her for not searching. Oh, Simon . . ." He held her as she cried, battling the years of desperation and anger. Then he made love to her sweetly, reverently, trying to ease her pain for a time.

In the morning Delilah pushed the journals into her saddlebags after looking at them closely. She turned and faced Simon, her fists tight against her thighs. "You know, don't you? That I can't read."

The admission had cost her, and there was a flickering wariness as though she expected him to—to what? To hurt her, to shame her? Because Simon was furious with her husband, he gripped her upper arms and pulled her against him hard. "I'm not Ezrah, sweetheart. I won't blame you if I'm unmanned, though around you, I am permanently hard . . . and I've known you can't read for some time. I've also known that you're the one woman who can drive me to distraction," he muttered before kissing her with devastating thoroughness.

When Delilah could barely stand, Simon lifted her and plopped her unceremoniously on Phantom. "Someday you'll realize that Ezrah was a dim-witted fool and that you've carried too much unwarranted guilt for too long. You were a child when your mother died, and yet you managed to take care of your loved ones. She was proud of you and loved you, just as you loved her. It's time you realized that you're a beautiful person, who has given more than anyone could ask of you," he stated grimly. "Now chew on that for a while."

Chapter Thirteen

———⊷———

"*Koby Smith!*" Artissima exclaimed, pushing her hands against Koby's chest and forcing him to lean against the wall. She slid her palm into his shirt and over his heart. "I said kiss me. . . . That's an order. Give me one of those long, slow, sweet kisses that drive me wild. Then lay me down and make love to me. Right here, right now, while Moose and Tallulah are in Loomis getting supplies."

She closed her eyes and lifted her puckered lips to his. Koby pressed back against the wall just as Artissima's breasts pressed into his stomach. She reached up and locked her arms around his neck, laying her weight against him. He began to sweat, and if ever a man was wrapped in fear, it was Koby Smith. Artissima opened her eyes and watched him closely. "Well?" she demanded, peering up at him.

"Kisses don't mean that a woman can stand up to a man and just take him," Koby grumbled, a hot flush moving beneath his dark skin. Artissima squirmed closer, aware that his hand had slid to her hips and his fingers were clenching and unclenching.

"Oh, no? Kissing you makes me feel all hot and bubbly, like a volcano in Hawaii where the women bare their bosoms to the sun. I can't breathe and my skin gets too tight and starts burning. Part of me wants to fly and the other part wants to see just what all the commotion is about—why my legs start trembling until they can't hold me, and why deep, low inside me feels like hot, melted butter. I feel like a steam kettle ready to boil when you look at me with those sinful, black eyes— like liquid ebony fire that plain old curls my toes."

She took a breath, pushed a kiss against his closed lips, and continued, "I start thinking about black-haired babies nursing at my breast and you cuddling them just like you do the calves and the colts. I think about gettin' all warm in the winter beneath the blankets with you and waking up to you each morning. I think about Delilah and Richard coming home, maybe Simon, too, from the way he looked at Delilah, and all of us being a family."

"They'll be coming home. But you don't want me," he said between his teeth after an uneven swallow. "I've got nothing to offer you but hard times."

"Hard times," she repeated, wrapping her fingers in his hair and tugging him down to her face. "You think I haven't seen hard times, Koby Smith? You think all I ever missed in this life was a few good messes of collard greens and fatback?"

She spread her hands and studied them, as if looking into the past. "You think I don't know what I want? Let me tell you something, sugar pie—I've fought off carpetbaggers, scalawags and no-goods most of my life. I fought for food for my family, and yes, I begged, too. The war left girls like me to fend for themselves and for their kinfolk. I've come from Georgia by my wits alone, and I'm still—"

Artissima cleared her throat. ". . . I'm thirty-three, same age as you, and I know how low people can get. But you aren't one of them, Koby Smith. You're a no-talking, eye-flashing, lean piece of muscle and bone, and there's not a bad spot in your whole heart. You're kind and gentle and sweet and a pretty man to boot. You'll make beautiful babies. . . . I've been saving myself"—she flushed deeply, gritted her

teeth, and tightened her fingers possessively in his hair—
"just for you."

She stroked his hair, following the coarse black strands
down to his nape. "Lord, you are a pretty man, Koby," she
breathed.

He snorted as her fingertips caught the heat from his cheeks.
"Pretty. Now, there's a word for a man."

"Sugar pie, you are pretty, pretty, pretty," Artissima whispered teasingly, her finger stroking the curve of his lips.

Koby placed his hands on her waist, easing her away slightly. He was trembling, fighting himself and his desire for her.
Artissima didn't intend to spare him any mercy this time.
She'd tossed invitations at him like pebbles in a pond, and
they'd sunk unnoticed. He was edgy, but this time she had
him cornered. "I live by my gun hand, missy. Men like me
don't live long," Koby rasped unevenly, and in a rare show
of emotion, he shuddered, fighting the dream she held out to
him. It wasn't possible.

Artissima leaned her hips against his and reveled in the
thrusting hardness, proof of his desire for her. But there were
other things, like the sweet way he held her hand when he
wasn't edgy about being faced with his immortality—the sons
and daughters she wanted from him.

"Horsefeathers . . . Men like you were meant to live long
and make plenty of babies. I want a whole passel of them
from you, Koby. I'll take care of you. Don't try to crawdad
out of this, Koby. You're the one man I want. Love me now,"
she demanded, stepping on the tops of his boots and tightening
her grasp. "And give me my baby."

"The child of a métis?" Koby asked in disgust.

"You aristocratic snob," Artissima returned heatedly. "You
think you're so high and mighty. I'll have you know that I
come from some pretty high bloodlines myself."

"A métis is not a bluestocking. It is a war to grow up
between the bloods."

Artissima shook her curls and frowned up at him. "I know
about wars. I grew up in one. Are you saying, Koby Smith . . .
that I can't take care of my babies? Well, we won't know, if I
don't have any, will we? 'Cause I've made up my mind. It's

your black-haired babies I want, Koby."

She stood back and placed her hands on her hips. "Well? What do you have to say for yourself? And I don't want any hogwash, either, Koby Smith."

Koby took one look at her full breasts straining beneath the dress's bodice and closed his eyes against the desire singing through him. He inhaled, looked at her set face, and said tightly, "You talk too much, woman."

Her smile was bright and victorious. "Well, then. I guess you'll just have to work on keeping my mouth busy, won't you? By the way, my father's name was Xanthus. He fell before the Yanks on our front steps, a fighter until his last breath. He was a fine gentleman, a warrior who held his honor dear, just like you."

A spear of pain skimmed through her brown eyes, and Artissima cleared her throat. "We'll name our first boy Xanthus, and if it's a girl, Susannah, after my mother . . . Susannah Delilah, then we'll have both of our mothers remembered and your sister, too."

Koby shook his head and, in his pain, met Artissima's darkened gaze. "Lordy, you've got soulful, sweet eyes. . . . I'm set on your babies, Koby Smith," she muttered. "And you. I've lived through a war and lost my entire family. I've lived by my wits and not much else, crossed this great land to make my fortune, and now I've got you. I'm claiming you as mine. Now kiss me and stop wasting time," she ordered, stepping into the waiting circle of his arms.

"Are you asking for stud?" Koby asked unsteadily, afraid to hold her tightly, to take the dream she offered.

"I'll take whatever I can have of you, Koby Smith, and that's the Lord's simple truth," she answered reverently. "I've seen a nation of men, looked down into the blackness of their souls, and prayed every minute that somewhere I'd find a man like you to father my babies. A man who held honor high, who was kind and fair and loving. Who would cleave to me and no other woman, and in my heart, Koby Smith, I know you are that man. 'Course I wanted a wedding band along the way, but I know that no other man will have my heart after you, so I reckon jewelry isn't a necessity."

She reached her fingertip up to trace the curved line of his upper lip, then the fuller bottom one. "I truly hope our babies have your mouth, honey."

Koby held her against him, smoothing the taut line of her back and luxuriating in the feminine softness and scents enveloping him. He knew that he could resist her as much as he could refuse air. He nuzzled her hair. "Are you certain, little one?"

Artissima took his shirt in her fists as though she'd never let go. Her eyes filled with him. "Yes. With all my heart and soul—yes. . . . Oh, Koby . . . don't you want me, just a little bit?"

He closed his eyes and saw the babies nursing at her breasts. "Yes, more than I want to see tomorrow," he whispered, bending to kiss her with all the tenderness filling his heart.

He bent to swing her up in his arms, and Artissima wrapped her arms around him tightly. She nibbled on his ear, and his knees almost buckled. "Hurry, Koby, sugar pie . . . just hurry and show me what to do. Oh, Lordy, I've been wanting you so bad it hurts. . . ."

Artissima kissed him hard as he bent to lower her into the feather-tick bed. Off balance, Koby fell on top of her. He started to push away to begin making love to her slowly, but Artissima rolled over him in a flurry of skirts and petticoats and locked her arms around his neck. "Hurry, Koby," she pleaded, pressing tiny kisses around his face and clinging to him. "Hurry."

"Little one, I would like to make love with you without my boots," Koby murmured unevenly against her ear.

She frowned down at him, the sunlight from the window spreading a halo around her blond curls. "I don't have time for dillydallying, sugar pie. Women who talk about this sort of thing say a man's . . . a man's need can go down powerful fast, and I don't want to lose what time we have before that happens, you hear?"

Koby laughed outright, letting happiness fill him before he whispered against her lips, "I think we can manage."

Artissima considered that, batted her lashes, and sent him her best, simmering Southern belle smile. "Anything you say,

Koby honey. Maybe I'll just take my shoes off, too. My toes are fairly curling."

In a cabin overlooking Quesnel Lake, Mordacai Wells preened in front of a standing oval mirror. He smoothed the stickpin on his lapel and studied the missing tip of his little finger. "Simon Oakes. That bastard scarlet coat. He's left a wide trail, asking about me, rousing people up. He's setting a noose around my neck—I can't move for hearing about the constables, deputies, and Oakes."

"He's a North West Mountie," Bones Morris rumbled. "He wants his brother's killer. He's got the law stirred up here. Maybe it's time to move on. A freighter said he saw a man like Oakes traveling with a woman, headed this way. One of the boys talked to a man buying goods to head to the Yukon. He said they'd tried to jump Oakes and the woman. She's a pretty bitch, they said, and Oakes swore he'd have their hides if they came near her. She's a fighter, too. Does those fancy Chinese kicks."

Mordacai studied his new shave in the mirror. "If we could find that damned boy, we could serve him up to Oakes. Where is he, Bones?" He lifted the derringer to the beefy man's chin and watched him in the mirror.

Bones arched his neck away from the small barrel. "That was over two years ago, boss. Haven't heard of him. He's either dead or gone."

"That's what you are going to be. Dead," Mordacai hissed, pushing the barrel higher into the layers of Bones's jowls. "All you had to do was plug the boy and lay him out where the law could find him."

"You weren't ready to give up the stickpin or that fancy palm-squeezer, boss," Bones whined, using the term for the derringer. "People recognize them things right away. That and your missing little fingertip. We'd needed the palm-squeezer and the stickpin to pin the murders on that boy."

Mordacai hit him on the side of the head, leaving a bloody gash. "No, I wasn't ready to give them away. They're mine," he said calmly, wiping the silver etching on the derringer. I'm heading south. Where that damned Mountie hasn't stirred up the law. There will be plenty of fresh pickings down in the new silver fields in Washington Territory. Bones, you take the men. Oakes will probably contact the law in Quesnel. He'll probably be on his way to Barkerville by way of Cottonwood House. The grades just past that will be perfect to pick him off. Find that scarlet-coat bastard and kill him. I'll have the pickings laid out when you get there."

Simon braced his arms beside Delilah's head, his face stark with passion as he thrust deeply into her. Delilah arched her throat against his mouth, locking him to her and whimpering her needs—she tightened around Simon, convulsed, and soared with a tight, high cry. He tensed and cursed in a dark swift blend of several languages, and she forced her lids open to see him scanning the evening shadows. He looked down at her, frowned, and let out a shuddering groan as he reluctantly pulled himself away. "We've got visitors."

Ten horsemen rode through the trees, coming into the camp from different angles, winding around the trees, their horses blowing steam in the cold night air. Simon dressed quickly, and Delilah tugged on her trousers and quickly buttoned her shirt without retying her camisole that Simon had eased open with his teeth. She ached desperately, her hands trembling as she jerked on her boots, wrapped the quilt around her, and stood at Simon's side as the men approached. He was dressed, his hand resting casually on his revolver. He eased Delilah behind him when she would have stood at his side, holding the rifle. "You stay put, or I'll paddle that pretty backside of yours," he ordered curtly.

He looked down at her, the remnants of desire still clinging to his eyes. One hand reached to smooth her tangled hair and touch her shoulder, then he looked at the approaching men.

"Ho, there!" a man's rough voice called as the horses drew into the small clearing. "You're on my land, boy."

The ten horsemen surrounded the camp, leather creaked, and horses nickered to Lasway and Phantom. A big man with a barrel chest and spindly legs swung down from the riders. He doffed his hat to Delilah and squatted to warm his hands at the campfire. "You burned supper, missus," he noted, tearing away a blackened bit of the partridge.

Delilah inhaled. Simon had taken one look at her and forgotten about basting the partridges roasting over the fire. She slowly pushed the air from her lungs, startled now that he could be distracted by her simply brushing her hair. Cooking was a serious matter with Simon, a methodical event. The burned partridge seemed impossible.

The big man angled his broad face up to Simon and took off his worn slouch hat. "I'm Rufus Gilchrist. Most folks just pass by on their way to Quesnelmouth, then they spend the night there in comfort. When we have visitors out here, we want to know their business."

Delilah blushed and hoped it wouldn't show in the light of the campfire. Her legs trembled, her body feeling cold and empty without Simon's.

Rufus studied her slowly, then Simon's hair, peaked by her fingers grasping it as he had moved his mouth on her. Delilah's flush deepened, and she couldn't meet the intense level stare of the big man.

"Hmm. She's blushing like an unwedded girl, man. Are you certain you're married?" Rufus asked, nibbling on the partridge and studying the camp and the mule. "You're traveling. Won't have unmarried folk sinning on my property, I won't. Strapped the last pair of sinners we caught. They were married to others. Now if you're willing to make an honest woman of her, if you're wanting to wed, my brother stays with us now. He's a minister, and we hold services at my house every Sunday. He can marry you right quick." Rufus glowered at them. "Unless you're married to others. Lusting and sinning is the devil's work, and I won't have it go unpaid on my property."

Simon reached out, gathered Delilah to him, and said, "Simon Oakes at your service, sir. We've heard of your brother's weddings. My girl said it was romantic, and since neither one of us is a youngster, we didn't want a church wedding—in a regular church. We were just headed to find you, and she took a chill, so we thought we'd better stop and get a good fire going, since we didn't know the exact location of your house. I've got a special license right here in my pocket."

Delilah stared at Simon. He'd just made love to her desperately, and now she didn't trust him. "Simon," she warned firmly.

"I have everything under control, dear heart," he whispered back, then he took Delilah's hand. "Could your brother marry us?"

Rufus beamed and stood up to shake Simon's hand. In a fatherly gesture, he gathered Delilah against him and kissed her forehead. "Well, now. That's good, real fine, my lad. Come on, lads, help pack these two to my place. My missus loves brides and weddings. A wedding will be just the thing to cheer her up. Her time is any day."

"Simon, could I *please* talk with you in private?"

"We'll have all the privacy you want later, sweetheart," Simon returned soothingly. "Rufus's brother will perform the ceremony and we'll be on our way."

"I want to talk with you *now*," she ordered between her teeth. "I'm not marrying you."

"But I'm willing to make the sacrifice," he explained in a logical tone. "I promised Koby I'd take care of you, and I do owe you for saving my life," Simon returned a bit too smugly.

"I won't marry again, and *what about Amelia* and her creaking bed?" she forced her rising tone into a hushed whisper.

Simon smiled blandly and lifted one eyebrow. "If I'm ready to sacrifice for you, the least you could do is oblige. We could have started the begetting already."

"Simon!"

With the feeling that she had been sucked into a fast-moving river, Delilah opened her mouth to protest, then Simon ducked his head quickly and kissed her. Rufus roared with laughter. Delilah tugged away from Rufus's bearlike grasp. "I . . . we can't get married—"

"Uh?" Rufus grunted, scowling down at her.

"Tonight, sir," Simon added. "My girl says she wants to get married in the morning. First thing, before we move on."

Delilah raised the Winchester tip slightly, daring Simon to make matters worse. Rufus studied her closely while his men packed away camp and saddled the horses. "She's pale, boy."

Simon chuckled. "Bridal nerves. I've been courting her for a long time. Not until she heard of your brother would she agree to marry me."

"Heard of my dear brother, Rob, has she?" Rufus beamed and wrapped a big arm around Delilah, nearly smothering her as he drew her to his chest. "He married all my own daughters, all five of them. Each one was squeamish, though the lads they married almost all got sick before the ceremony. Not to worry, my girl. My Nora will settle you down tonight in a proper bed for a good night's sleep. She'll talk to you like your own mum, while I have a bit of a talk with the lad here. If you've been feeling badly, my dear, having a good night's rest in a good bed will make you feel better."

Simon grinned widely, and Delilah thought he looked wicked to the core. "Yes, sir. We knew you'd be like our own dear folks, who aren't here anymore. That's why we sought you out."

Delilah stared at him. For very little she would raise the Winchester and— Simon took the rifle from her hand and placed it in its sheath. "It's too heavy for a lady like you, sweetheart."

"I've changed my mind," Delilah said, smiling up at Rufus. "I don't want to get married after all."

The farmer scowled down at her. "Eh?"

"Bridal nerves—she means not right now . . . tomorrow morning is fine," Simon said, holding her hand. "We just had a tiff before we set up camp, Rufus. She didn't want to stop, but the way she was pale and all, I thought it was best. We don't want to lose the baby—"

"Simon!" Delilah protested as he fondly patted her stomach.

"Baby?" Rufus roared. "Strap that sinner to the tree, boys, and make him pay for his soul's redemption!" He strode to his horse and jerked a wicked-looking quirt from his saddle. "Strap him up."

Two big men grabbed Simon's arms and began dragging him to a tree. He hung there limply like an empty sack, like a man condemned to death who had no more battle in him. Like a man who knew he deserved his punishment. . . . Rufus strode toward Simon, tapping the wicked quirt on his broad palm.

Delilah pressed her hands to her stomach. Rufus looked as though he could laugh while peeling away a man's back, reveling in punishing a sinner on his land. She had to protect Simon.

"I'll marry him," Delilah whispered bleakly, aware that her heart had stopped beneath her hands. Rufus pivoted to her like a hound on the scent of his prey.

"Eh?"

"I said I'll marry him," she said louder, not bothering to conceal her disgusted tone. She frowned when she saw Simon's wide grin as he stepped away from the men and briskly straightened his clothes.

Rufus looked from her to Simon, who had tucked her against him protectively despite her stiff resistance. "That's what I thought you said."

"My heroine," Simon said grandly as he grinned and swept his hand in front of him in a gallant bow.

Delilah did not feel like curtsying.

The Gilchrist house was big and warm, and Nora reached for Delilah like a broody hen needing to cuddle her last chick. Though her five daughters were grown and married, Nora was heavy with child and excited about the new baby. Rufus beamed while Nora reheated dinner and hustled Delilah into a waiting bedroom with the new clothing Simon had purchased for her. "Oh, I just love weddings and brides," Nora cooed, placing a cup of tea on the night table and sitting on the bed beside Delilah, who was dressed in a new long nightgown with a high ruffled collar and long sleeves.

Nora brushed Delilah's freshly washed hair. "My Rufus is giving Simon a lecture downstairs on how to be a proper husband. They're probably having a bit of brandy."

She inhaled quickly and placed her hand on her distended belly beneath the nightgown. She closed her eyes, then released the breath she had been holding. "I'm certain that this one is the son Rufus has always wanted. It's lonesome out here on the farm. How I miss chatting over tea in the afternoon. Before

the baby, Rufus took me to Quesnelmouth—sometimes on a
sleigh in the winter—and my friends and I had a grand old
time, quilting and chatting for at least two days." She frowned
and looked away into the night past the window.

Delilah touched her shoulder, and Nora swung worried eyes
to her. "The baby will be fine, Nora. And you will be, too."

Nora grasped her shoulders and sat heavily on the bed. Her
open hand rested low on the baby and pain clouded her eyes.
"Poor Rufus. He's so excited about marrying you that I didn't
have the heart to tell him that the baby is coming."

"Nora, we must tell him." Delilah put her arm around the
older woman and rocked her, just as Simon had rocked her.
Then she stood and held out her hands to Nora. "Come on.
We'll put you to bed. I'll stay through the birthing."

Nora brightened, and for a moment her faded beauty returned.
"Oh, would you, would you really?"

"Nothing could tear me away."

"Don't you touch me," Delilah hissed at Simon as he pulled
her into the pantry and closed the door. Despite her struggles,
Simon trapped her in his arms and kissed her face all over,
ending with nuzzling her nose with his. In the shadows his
laughing green eyes stared down into hers.

"Go find yourself some pots and pans and cook the night
away. It's going to be a long one," she muttered as she found
herself smiling up at him. Simon wrapped his arms around
her and lifted her even with his face. "So you have a special
license. When did you get that?"

Simon's large hands cupped her bottom, caressing it luxuriously. "I decided about the instant I poured myself into you.
You were purring so loudly that I couldn't think straight.
I've spoiled you, sweetheart. The least you can do is let me
marry you."

She hoped the dim light hid her blush, but Simon's rough
cheek rested along her hot one. She smoothed his collar, then
the hair at the nape of his neck. It was crisp and felt warm and
soothing to her touch. "I've been married. It wasn't good."

"You were married to a jackass," Simon said pleasantly. "It

didn't qualify as a real marriage. . . . I haven't been married. Don't shatter my dreams." He nibbled her ear and rocked her gently.

"Why are you always rocking me?" she whispered as Simon tucked his face against her throat.

"Because you haven't had enough of it, and I like you cuddling against me," he answered a little roughly, gathering her closer. He tucked her face into his throat and stroked her back soothingly. "And I like thinking that maybe I'm rocking my baby in you, too."

"Simon!" When Simon eased her to her feet, Delilah found herself stunned and shaking.

Nora's baby took his time coming after hours of hard labor. Nora had exiled Rufus for the duration. During those hours Simon was always nearby, and once he sat holding Delilah on his lap while Nora rested. Simon was there with tea and clean wash water, lifting Nora when Delilah cleaned her bedding and settled her into a warm, flannel nest to give birth. The scents of bread and cake swirled around the room, and Simon winked at Nora. "Rufus is peeling potatoes now to go with the roast. He's peeled a tub already, and one of the workhands has kneaded the bread until I'm sure it won't rise."

But Nora was locked in her own painful world and squeezed Simon's hand, paling the dark flesh. It was Simon who braced Nora against him and encouraged her, while Delilah examined her beneath the sheet.

"You've done this before, dear heart," he'd whispered as she smoothed Nora's stomach with warm oil. Delilah thought of Richard's birth and her mother's hands guiding hers over the taut distended stomach. *"I'm so sorry, my love. . . . You're doing fine. . . . When the baby comes, do as I told you. . . . I love you, Delilah. . . ."*

She'd delivered more babies after that, and each time, Delilah fought the sad, lost dreams of children of her own. The baby slid into her hands just before dawn, a strong son. She looked up and saw something so fiercely gentle in Simon's eyes that it stunned her for half a heartbeat. "That's my girl," he said softly. "There, there, sweetheart, you're magnificent," he soothed, and she realized he was speaking to her, rather than Nora. Tears burned at her eyes as she cleaned the baby and settled it in Rufus's large trembling hands.

"She's a fine one you picked, Simon," Rufus said softly as he examined his first son and chuckled at the tiny fist soaring in the air. "Thank you, Delilah," he murmured, delighted with the baby's huge yawn. "Sorry to interrupt your wedding day."

Standing behind Delilah, Simon wrapped his arms around her. Exhausted, Delilah allowed herself to rest against him. They had shared a miracle, and the magic still twined around her. She lifted her hand and rested it on the strength of his. Simon's fingers laced with hers slowly, as if nothing could keep him from her. "People love you for yourself, dear heart," he whispered, setting his chin over her hair. "For what you are . . . good and strong and kind."

"I have an idea," Nora said tiredly, holding her husband's hand. "We'll have the wedding right now—here in my room where a new life has just begun and so should a marriage. Simon, poor dear, has run up and down stairs all night, cooking and tending me. He kissed Delilah a few times, too, if you must know, Rufus. Just little caring kisses that a man gives the woman he loves when she is needing. He has baked a lovely cake and marvelous wedding dinner. Rob can marry Delilah and Simon, then we can all have a rest."

Simon drew Delilah against him, despite her resistance. "If you'll just change into your new dress, sweetheart. . . . We shouldn't keep Nora up too long, should we?" he asked with a tender smile. "I could help you dress—"

Rufus bristled and glared at Simon. "None of that."

Nora, though obviously exhausted, smiled serenely. "Rufus, go get my wedding dress down. I was about Delilah's size when I was a bride. She'll look lovely in it. It will be wrinkled, but hang it up and set a kettle of steaming water beneath it. Then place it over the stove to dry. I've done the girls' dresses like that enough times in a pinch."

"You're still my bride," Rufus rumbled gallantly, peering at Simon over his new son. "Keep that in mind, boy. Treat your wife like a bride."

"Oh, I intend to, sir." Simon's green gaze darkened, and tiny sensual ripples washed over Delilah's skin and lodged deep in her belly.

"Since her kinsmen aren't here, I'm asking you for your promise that you'll treat this woman well."

"Very well," Simon said huskily.

Delilah moved away from him. She was barely standing on her feet, yet she knew in that instant that Simon was determined to marry her.

To escape Rufus's strap, he had little choice. Nor had she. She couldn't stand the thought of Simon's pain, no matter that he was a drifter, a drunk, and a ladies' man who cooked and crocheted. "Yes," she murmured, not disguising her doomed tone. "If we must."

Chapter Fourteen

***

Delilah stood by Simon during the ceremony and tried to catch her breath. Her stockinged toes—Simon had removed her worn boots and refused to let her wear them—flexed against the braided rug, and Delilah's mind searched for reality. Nora's rose-scented toilet water clung to Delilah's flowing hair, which Simon had insisted hang free. Loosened from her braids, it rippled over her shoulders and the bodice of Nora's wedding gown—an elegant ruffled affair of muslin and lace, scented of lavender. The gown had a high ruffled collar and muttonchop sleeves, a bodice filled with tucks and pearl buttons flowing down into a tight waist, then a long three-tiered skirt with layers of petticoats. It was soft with time and care, though Nora regretted it wasn't as white as the day she married Rufus.

Nora's blue satin garter fit beautifully, a whimsy that delighted Delilah from the first moment Nora drew it from the folds of the long wedding gown.

The gown was the most beautiful creation Delilah had ever seen. Hopes and dreams and happiness clung to each soft fold and played around the lace that nuzzled Delilah's chin. When Simon saw her coming into the room, he had stopped talking to Rufus and his eyes had burned her, devoured her, until she thought she'd burst into flame and crumble into ashes at his feet.

Dressed in the black suit from his valise, Simon had shaved and his hair was wet, the marks of a comb grooving his dark hair. She noted that an irrepressible little wave near his ear remained uncontrolled, just like her tumbling emotions for Simon. His big hand trembled slightly as it wrapped around hers, and he repeated his vows firmly after clearing his throat. When it was her turn, Simon looked down at her tenderly.

Sunlight tangled around them, wrapping them in a warm, sweet cloak as the others in the room faded away.

He wrapped her in his arms while Nora, Rufus, and Rob watched, and kissed her slowly, thoroughly, leisurely, as if he intended to bed her right there. When Rufus finally cleared his throat, Simon reluctantly lifted his head, and Delilah felt that in another minute she would collapse to the floor. Simon ran the tip of his finger across her swollen, sensitive lips and whispered in a low, dark voice that curled inside her and set her trembling, "There, take that, Mrs. Oakes, and see what you can make of it."

She blinked, aware that she was flushing wildly as Simon slowly gathered her against him. He stroked her hair and pushed her face gently against his throat. He'd fared no better than she, Delilah thought as his heavy pulse beat against her cheek. "You are shameless. What will they think?"

"That I'm a bridegroom, well warmed for his wedding night," he whispered against her temple, which he had just kissed.

"Hush. Let me go." In another minute Nora and Rufus would know everything—that Simon and she had . . . It was surely written on her face with big fiery letters. Delilah tried to pull away, only to have Simon pick her up and carry her from the room.

"We want a few private words.... Rufus ... Rob ... Nora.... My new wife wants me alone for just a few minutes."

"Not long, boy," Rufus said in the tone of a man trying to smother laughter and failing. "Nora needs her sleep, and we've got the hands waiting downstairs for that fancy wedding dinner you cooked last night."

"Be right back."

Rufus guffawed and Nora tried to shush him, though she was beaming drowsily—no easy matter—as Simon carried Delilah through the hall and into the next bedroom. She shook free of him the moment he kicked the door shut with the heel of his boot. "Yes, Mrs. Oakes?" Simon invited, stripping off the jacket and tossing it to the bed. He rolled up his cuffs as a man would do before he undertook a great task.

"Why?" she asked simply, fearing that her soul would step free from her body at any minute. She tried on the new emotion swirling in her, lifting her heart, and decided she was happy. She'd had little experience with sheer delight, and she settled into it with a determination to make it last at least until they finished Simon's wedding dinner, which would be eaten for breakfast. She wanted to roll in her joy like field clover, swallow it like warm honey, and strip herself to the golden beams of sunshine tingling inside her. Delight bubbled within her, simmering and waiting to erupt in a burst of laughter. In another minute she'd be floating off the floor and walking on the ceiling.

Delilah trembled and locked her stockinged toes to the oriental rug. Surely it was unhealthy or immoral or sinful to feel the way she felt just now. Her toes uncurled and the garter around her thigh slid lower. She loved that silly little bit of blue satin and lace, which was totally useless. But Nora had given it to her for a wedding gift, and Delilah knew she would always cherish it. She ran her hand over her hair, pushing it back from her flushed cheek. She tried to pull the smile from her lips and failed. Of course, her notions were silly and unreal, but they were hers and she'd hoard them away forever. She desperately wanted just these few hours or minutes of happiness.

Simon sauntered toward her with a determined look in his eyes. His jaw locked into place as she had seen it do when he made up his mind. "Because I want my babies born on the right side of the blanket, Mrs. Oakes." He flung the name at her. "And I want you badly enough to forget what I am bound to do."

His finger strolled down the strand of hair that skimmed along the multiple tucks in the bodice and swirled across the tip of her breast, causing it to bud instantly. His eyebrow lifted as she backed away. "Simon—" she began, then stopped as he jerked her to him.

He flattened her body to his as if he'd never let anything or anyone come between them. "I'm not Ezrah," he said between his teeth. "Did you ever love him?"

She could barely breathe, her heart racing against his chest violently. No one had ever cared about her feelings for Ezrah, at least enough to ask. She should have been frightened by his fierce demand, but she wasn't—Simon's dark skin was flushed, and there was a brightness in his eyes that said how she answered mattered a great deal. She lifted her head proudly, and at that moment realized that Simon held her tightly, but without the pain that Ezrah had caused. The desperation driving him made her ache; she could give him no less than the truth. "No. I didn't love him. Not for a second."

Simon's hard mouth curved smugly. "Good. That's what I thought. But make no mistake, this will be a real marriage in every way. I intend to keep you and care for you like a proper wife. I will honor you and hold you above all others. I expect you to welcome me in your bed and your life. Because you're what I want for a wife and the mother of my wild brats, Delilah . . . Oakes."

His hand flattened over the layers of material to press against her lower belly. "If you're carrying my child, it will have my name and my protection. I made up my mind that first time I gave you my seed. . . . There's no escaping me now, dear heart. Because as soon as your brother is found and cleared, we're starting our life together."

She pushed at his chest and found his heart racing beneath her palm. He lifted her hand and pressed a kiss into the exact center of her palm, looking at her over it.

Delilah would wonder later why she lifted her lips to his gentle seeking kiss. She would wonder why she rested her head on his shoulder and wrapped her arms around him as if she'd never let him go.

He rocked her in that familiar, tender way, and she sighed deeply. "You must know that I'm tired from staying up with Nora and not thinking clearly. It seems a poor time for making decisions, and I'm certain that it's not sporting or gentlemanly to run a woman to the ground and then marry her."

His smile slid along her cheek, and he nibbled on her earlobe causing her flesh to jump and heat. "When the stakes are high, winning is sometimes more important, dear Delilah."

Delilah traced his rugged features, his soaring cheekbones and strong jaw. In that slice of golden morning sunlight drifting into the window to lock Simon with her, she wanted a baby desperately. She gripped his arms and found them trembling, and an endearing slice of uncertainty slid through his eyes.

"I'll make you a good husband, dear heart," he promised rawly.

Then he kissed her as though all the tomorrows depended on her response. She found herself arching up, wrapping her arms around him, and giving back everything.

"I know little about you," she whispered against his lips.

"You know enough and you'll know more as we go along. Meanwhile I ask that you trust me. I ask that you remember that I will cherish you and hold what you hold dear . . . that you remember I want to keep you and what you love safe," he said roughly and kissed her as if he were desperate for the taste of her. She sensed his hesitation, as if he wanted to say something more, and she didn't want a moment of the dream ruined.

"I'll make you pay for this," she promised, meaning it, and lightly placed her hand over the buttons on his trousers.

Simon's eyes widened with surprise, then he pressed her hand against him and groaned deeply. "Nothing can save you now. We've got the important parts right, dear heart. Beware, Mrs. Oakes. Because I am about to burst for the need of you."

Delilah laughed outright and sniffed. The long searching look Simon gave her tangled and warmed her senses as though time had stopped and locked her with him in that gentle sweetness. Simon's jade-green eyes held promises and tenderness and something that frightened her and set her heart jumping in her breast. She realized that tears filled her eyes when Simon bent to kiss them away and rock her once more.

She could have stayed forever, resting against him and listening to the safe beat of his heart.

"We'll find Richard," he whispered against her hair and held her tighter. "And when we do, we'll clear him and begin our life, dear heart."

"Wells is young, but he's as rotten as they come," said the constable near Quesnelmouth. "After you left and the thaw set in, a few more bodies turned up. Two bachelors . . . old Overlanders farming not far from here. Wells is laying low now, but he'll turn up, and when he does, there will be more killing. Meantime, that fancy horseshoe stickpin is keeping his luck."

Through the office window Simon watched Delilah move from store to store down the other side of the street. Dressed in her riding clothes, a tattered coat and trousers, she didn't look like a blushing bride.

Her hair swirled around her shoulders, the sunlight catching the glistening tips, and she dashed a clinging strand away from her strained, pale face.

Simon gave the constable a sealed envelope. "If anything happens to me, or you don't hear from me in three months, have this posted, will you?"

The envelope contained a short letter to Delilah, listing his accounts, which were now hers, and the names and whereabouts of his parents and brothers and sisters.

They were both tired after a night spent delivering Nora's baby. Though Simon wanted to spend the next week in bed with Delilah, he knew she was too tired and too desperate to reach Barkerville. He breathed slowly as she leaned her forehead against the arm braced on Phantom's saddle. She was running on nerves now, but when they were rested that night, he would explain everything. He wanted their marriage to start out on truthful grounds.

Rufus's threat of a beating had swept away the courtship Simon had planned after explaining his reason for hunting Richard. The opportunity to marry Delilah fell into his reach, and he grasped it with both fists.

He'd do it again in less than a heartbeat.

What had she done? Delilah glanced at Simon from beneath the brim of her hat as she guided Phantom around a freighter's double wagon and mule team.

She'd married Simon. She'd gotten tangled in the birth of the baby, Rufus and Nora's loving marriage, and against her better judgment she had stepped into the ceremony just the way he wanted her—without shoes and with her hair tangled around her. There was no denying the way Simon could tangle her emotions and muddle her thinking just by staring at her as if she were everything he'd ever wanted from the Tooth Fairy and from Santa Claus. There was an eagerness in him to have children that frightened her. Delilah touched her flat stomach and doubted that Simon had begun a life there. No sweet child's life could spring from the passionate storms Simon aroused in her, as if she'd fight and hurl herself at him into the flames. She was strong and certain, as if she'd take flight and soar safely through lightning-filled skies, then drift slowly, like a gloriously spent, golden autumn leaf into his warm, comforting arms.

Delilah shivered despite the warm spring day. If she were truthful now, she would admit she wanted him straining full and hard in her and whispering his wicked intentions.

He had the folded marriage certificate in his pocket. He had the right to take her when he wanted. Why hadn't he?

What had changed?

Delilah shivered again, remembering how Ezrah had changed. A cold ball of doom rolled down her spine. She'd married Ezrah because he came from solid people, because he was a "good" man.

She shook her head. There was not one reason to marry Simon, other than to save his dark, scarred hide.

The idea that she wanted to kiss every scar stunned her.

"Worthless as spit," she muttered, fighting the drain of the long night spent birthing Rufus's son. She'd just fallen asleep in the saddle and resented Simon's straight back. It looked broad and strong, as if he could ride forever. Then she knew he'd set his course and would see it through to the end and nothing could keep him from what he sought.

This time she'd taken her mother's advice to marry a good man and flung it to the wind. Simon was a drifter who crocheted and cooked and wore embroidered suspenders, and who didn't offer an ounce of the security her mother had asked that she find.

A strand of hair blew across her cheek, and Delilah brushed it back. Then she whipped off her hat, draped it on her saddlehorn, and braided her hair in brisk, angry movements. She ripped away a slender length of cloth from her coat and tied her braid, allowing it to dangle down her back.

Her new husband had the right to make decisions for her now. To wrest away the life she had carved for herself and her family. He could sell her property or her stock—she closed her eyes, shook her head, and plopped her hat back onto her head. Simon knew about as much about ranching as she knew about reading. He'd been trouble from the moment she met him. Just looking at him angered and heated her in a way that was wicked even for a married woman.

The indecent craving to drag Simon from his horse and throw him on the ground couldn't be explained reasonably.

She sensed he wanted to tell her something, the same way she had sensed disaster when Richard decided to fly away. Simon had been grim throughout the day, but no more than she when there was no word of Richard. Several people remembered a lanky, pleasant blue-eyed boy passing through on his way to Barkerville, but he hadn't been back. They also remembered the horseshoe stickpin and the derringer and noted that the boy was wanted for killings.

The young desperado was wanted for killing a Mountie's brother; the rumor was that the Mountie was on Wells's heels and would just as soon have him dead as alive. The man hunting Wells was one of the best fighting men in the Queen's service. He was deadly and big and more likely to succeed in bringing the murderer to justice than any other lawman. Though North West Mounties were not seen this far west, this one would cross through hell to avenge his brother's murder.

Delilah saw a blaze of sunlight hitting metal in the lofty forest, then a shot shattered the early afternoon quiet. Lasway reared, then he and Simon tumbled down an embankment.

Taking the mule with her, Delilah rode Phantom into the trees on the opposite side of the road and swung to the ground. She slid her Winchester from its sheath and ran to the embankment, peering over it as a second shot rang out and the fiery heat of a bullet grazed her thigh, tearing the cloth and staining it with her blood.

Fearing for Simon, Delilah pressed her hand to the pain and ran to the shelter of a stand of aspens. "Simon?" she called as Lasway struggled to rise to his feet.

"Delilah, stay where you are." Simon's voice was cut by two more shots hitting the white bark of the aspens in front of her. The echoes in the small canyon were carried off into the shadowy pines and the clean spring air.

Simon's rifle answered, and a man's high cry of pain sailed over the small meadow. "You got me, Mountie. I'm dying. Don't shoot—have mercy, Mountie," he begged.

Delilah's gloved hands tightened on her rifle as Simon bent to the wounded man, his rifle barrel tracing the movements of five other men riding away in the forest. Then he was running after them and more shots rang out.

Lasway struggled, then managed to stand, favoring one leg. Delilah checked the slight wound on his flanks and decided that he had injured his leg in the fall. She knelt by the man, and one look at the gaping hole in his chest told her he was dying. "Don't let that Mountie get me," he begged.

"What Mountie?"

The man labored for breath, blood staining his chest. "It's Simon Oakes, North West redcoat, what did me in. I'd recognize him anywhere. . . . He was in the constable's office while I was back in the jail—that was last spring. He's sworn to bring his brother's murderer in or kill him on the spot."

He coughed and a dark red ribbon bubbled from his mouth and trailed down his chin. Delilah tugged off her coat, rolled it into a pillow, and carefully placed it under the man's head. "You are an angel. . . . Oakes looked right at me with those cold green eyes of his and told me to spread the word around that he wouldn't hesitate to kill Wells on the spot. He was looking for a trail to Wells, and he swore to find it. He said that Wells better turn himself in—I told Wells that, but he laughed at me and threatened to shoot me with all four slugs in that fancy little palm-squeezer."

"Have you heard of Richard Smith?" Delilah pressed automatically, stunned as she realized the identity of the man she had just married hours ago. "Are you certain he's a North West Mountie? Is Simon Oakes a Mountie?" she demanded with fear throbbing in her throat, closing it until she had to force a swallow.

"I swear he is. Don't let him at me—" The man's eyes glazed, then he shuddered and died.

There were more shots, and more than a mile away Simon loped over the crest of a hill, coming toward her with the long easy strides of a hunter. *". . . I want you badly enough to forget what I am bound to do. . . ."*

Delilah stood slowly, her blood chilling.

The wind lifted the tendrils at the back of her neck and sailed through her heart, freezing it.

Simon had found his trail to the boy he believed had killed his brother, Rand. She had to find Richard and escape Simon's noose.

Delilah turned, grabbed Lasway's reins, and began easing him up the embankment. "Come on, boy . . . come on," she urged desperately, bracing her shoulder against his injured leg. "Oh, I'm so sorry, Lasway. I know it hurts, but please, please move faster."

She mounted Phantom, tied the mule's rope to her saddlehorn, and stood in the stirrups, scanning the woods for Simon. Two shots rang out, then again, and Delilah knew he was ordering her to stop. She couldn't—she had to find Richard before Simon arrested him. Limping slightly,

Lasway followed as she began hurrying the animals down the road toward Barkerville.

Almost five miles later Delilah drew the animals off the road and let them drink from a small rippling stream. She stripped away her coat and shirt, then soaked the shirt in the cold water and washed the graze across the gelding's haunch. Then she bent to wrap the area above his hoof and tie it securely. Her leg ached and Delilah stared at the wound she had forgotten, her trousers marking it in blood. She opened her belt with trembling fingers—small wounds could become infected and cost her time. Or her life.

The slight graze across her thigh burned when she cleaned it, but it was not deep. She hugged the gelding and soothed him and ignored the tears streaming down her cheeks. "We have to go, boy. We have to find Richard."

"*. . . I ask that you trust me. . . .*" Simon had said. "*. . . that I will cherish you and hold what you hold dear safe. . . .*"

Lasway nickered and nuzzled her as though he understood that she was suffering, too.

Delilah jerked on her coat and led the horses out into the late-afternoon sunlight.

Simon stood in the middle of the road. He was breathing heavily, his bare stomach sucking in and releasing air; sweat glistened on his bare shoulders and chest.

Beneath the sweaty bandanna tied across his forehead, his dark fierce scowl lashed at her. He looked more like a raiding Comanche warrior than a North West Mountie. "I thought you'd be past the nervous bride stage by this time," he said tightly, walking to crouch beside Lasway's injured leg. "Having second thoughts, love?" he asked in that same tight tone. "For you or for someone else?"

He stripped away her wet shirt, which covered the gelding's leg. His experienced hands ran over the sprain, concentrating on his task before rewrapping the injury. He stood, slid his rifle into its sheath with a quick, angry shove, then turned to her.

She came at him with raw fury in every blow, her heart tearing within her. "You want Richard. . . . You're the Mountie everyone is talking about. . . . You . . . You—"

Simon simply stepped into her arms and clamped his over hers. He shifted his manhood away from her threshing legs and simply held her immobile while she glared up at him. "Let me go," she ordered, struggling against him.

There wasn't an ounce of giving in Simon's granitelike expression. "You're mine, dear heart. You wear my name, and nothing can keep me from having you now. If you think that my search for Rand's killer has anything to do with my unreasonable hunger for you and a future with you, you are mistaken. Shall we be on our way or do you want to camp here?"

"Ohh! I should never have—"

Delilah's protest was sealed by Simon's rough, hungry kiss forcing her lips apart. Because she was angry and frightened for Richard, Delilah refused to be intimidated and returned the kiss with a desperation to prove she could meet Simon on any ground and hold her own.

When he lifted his head, Simon's expression shifted from startling desire to pure delight.

"If I could get free of you . . ." She breathed heavily, straining away from the jutting proof of his desire and fighting her own needs to throw him to the ground. "I would like just one good shot at you . . . just one."

His grin widened, dazzling her as she panted against him and he began to stroke her back slowly. "Gun or fist?" he asked, then began chuckling.

"Both," she snapped. "And then I'd like to scalp you."

"I'm tired, love. Perhaps we could try something a little more horizontal," he offered, reaching down to fill his palms with her bottom and lifting her to his long, sweet kiss.

"Traitor. You married me to get at Richard," she said as his forehead rested against hers. "You would do well to worry about your own murder."

"Yes, well, I'm not exactly happy, either," he said, lifting her into Phantom's saddle and dismissing her charge. He placed a possessive hand on her thigh and inspected the graze with a dark frown. "Did you wash it?"

"Of course."

Simon's finger traced Nora's garter beneath the homespun trousers. His eyes darkened stonily, then he grimly swung up behind her. "You're my wife because I want you and you want me, if you'll be truthful about the matter. Nothing can keep me from you tonight, dear heart. I intend to have my bride," he said grimly.

"Hah! There's little chance of that happening—Richard didn't kill anyone," she stated darkly, and sat very straight as Simon nudged Phantom into a slow walk.

"I don't think he did, either. But if you keep wasting my energy running after you—and I will keep you, dear heart— we won't be able to prove it."

She clung to the "we" and decided that when the first opportunity arose, she was leaving Simon.

"I've just run over five miles to catch a woman—my wife— who tried to disable my manhood. I'm not in a generous mood. Tears won't work. Try something else," he said impatiently when she sniffed. Then he pushed a handkerchief against her nose, and she blew into it like a child, which grated on her pride. Simon sighed tiredly. "We'll talk it out when we're both rested."

Delilah pushed her shoulders back and ignored him. She would ignore him all the way to hell and back for deceiving her.

For giving her a glimpse of a dream, a taste of happiness, and then ripping it away.

She dashed away a stream of tears, clamped her lips against a sob, and promised herself that if she had a way to torture Simon Oakes until he begged her for mercy, she'd do it without regret.

Behind her he shifted uncomfortably and cursed. "Here," he muttered, and placed the handkerchief to her nose again. "Blow."

Simon looked down at his sleeping bride, curled in the bed and dressed in her camisole and drawers. Nora's beguiling garter circled Delilah's long, slender thigh. Upon entering their room at the Cottonwood House, Delilah had sent him one seething, threatening scowl. Then she had stripped away her coat, boots, and trousers on the way to the bed. She fell, sprawled on her stomach, instantly asleep.

Beneath their room at the mile house, which had been used since 1864, the owner and his family settled in for the night. Throughout the meal set with blue-willow patterned plates, the man and his wife had wanted news, and Simon had given them enough to satisfy their curiosity. "He's a North West Mountie," Delilah had muttered around a large piece of dried-apple pie. She'd taken a sharp knife and studied the blade until Simon had placed it away from her. "Hunting a killer."

The man had puffed on his pipe and poured a measure of whiskey into Simon's empty teacup. "Bad luck about the horse, but he'll heal with a night's rest. . . . Unusual to take along the wife, isn't it, mate? Eh?"

"Honeymoon and business," Simon replied as Delilah pushed back her chair and stood. "I couldn't leave my bride alone on our first night."

The owner's wife brightened. "Oh, my dear. Congratulations."

"Yes. Thank you," Delilah said tightly, formally, as if she'd held on to the words until the last moment, then they had been torn from her.

"My bride is tired," Simon said, placing a warning hand on her shoulder. She looked just short of telling the well-wishers that she was being held captive against her wishes. Delilah shrugged off his hand, nodded to the family, and made her excuses before retiring upstairs. "Don't drink too much, dear heart," she had murmured at the bottom of the stairs. "You know how you act when you drink."

She lowered her voice and confided to the owners, "It could take him days to sober up. I had to rescue him once when he was drunk in a blizzard. He was hanging from a tree."

The owner's wife frowned disapprovingly at Simon. Her husband's eyebrows shot up. "A Mountie?"

"I've reformed," Simon had stated curtly.

Upstairs, after pouring water into the bedroom's basin, Simon soaped and washed his naked body thoroughly, then sat the basin on the floor. He pulled up a chair, sat in it, and soaked his feet while studying Delilah.

She had every right to be angry and hurt.

Simon placed the towel over his jutting manhood and set his back teeth. If he came close to Delilah now, he couldn't trust himself to be gentle. He ripped open his saddlebags and jerked out the ball of red thread, his hook and his latest project, and began to count and crochet as if he were racing the devil for his soul.

Chapter Fifteen

Delilah dreamed of Simon's long hard body over hers, pressing her warmly, gently into the soft, fluffy feather tick beneath her. She dreamed of his lips, pressuring hers, nibbling at the corners. She floated along pleasurably, the slightly rough scrape of his beard teasing her. She sighed and nestled her hips down into the feathers, making a comfortable nest to welcome Simon within her. She arched against him, rippling luxuriously from her chest down to her toes. She thrust her breasts against the hair on his chest, rubbing and caressing the steely, slightly damp skin and reveling in the hard muscles tensing over her taut nipples.

She sighed, sliding her hand to rest on his rapidly pounding heart, then upward until she locked her arms around his neck.

Simon groaned longingly, his sweet nibbling kisses tormenting her lids, her cheeks, the tip of her nose, and always returning to her lips.

Delilah rubbed her arches against Simon's hard calves, allowing him to settle within her thighs. She undulated in the feather tick, rolling her hips and breasts as though she were a wave catching Simon and flowing beneath him, carrying him where he wanted to go.

Something troubled her, something dark and ominous and ugly, and she pushed it away, clinging tighter to Simon and the delicious dream punctuated delicately by a gentle *creak-creak* sound beneath her.

Simon's mouth slid over her skin, his beard slightly chafing her, exciting her as he caressed her breast, slightly squeezing the delicate nipple until a beautiful ache radiated down deep in Delilah's womb.

She stroked his trembling, taut shoulders, easing him, soothing him. Then his mouth opened on her breast, drawing her higher, and the tiny muscles within her body contracted, hungry for him to fill her. She trusted him to complete her, to cuddle and kiss and make her feel as if she could fly. As if she were new and clean and strong and she was meant for him as he was fashioned for her. . . .

The poignant pain caused her to open her eyes, and there in the night Simon was poised over her. "You're mine, dear heart," he whispered with the same driving desperation that heated his gaze. She knew that she was his in this terrifying, happy moment. But did he know that he was as much hers? She wondered when he said in a low, dark tone, "You know what I want."

She did, she thought proudly, gloriously, she really did—reveling in her power to disturb and heat him. He looked desperately wild, hungry for her, his breath brushing her cheek unevenly. His eyes were brilliant in the shadows, searing her, his face hot against her throat. His hands found her breasts, drawing them to him as he nuzzled one, then the other, taking nibbling kisses that plucked at her swollen, aching flesh.

He shuddered and groaned and spread himself upon her as if making her a part of him, his hands flowing over her and leaving her skin burning where they passed and lingered and caressed.

Then his fingers slid under her bottom, cupping it, rubbing the cloth between her thighs until she dampened and cried out, holding him tightly.

His heart thudded against her breast, damp hot flesh against hers. Unable to bear the slightest cloth between them, Delilah found the tie to her drawers and ripped it away. Simon completed the task, tearing the flannel cloth from her in a frenzy that delighted her. He lowered himself into her intimately, his hands cupping her hips to lift her higher.

She smoothed her hand down his rippling, hard, flat stomach to find him. He cried out softly and shuddered as her fingers closed slowly around him, her thumb brushing his smooth tip back and forth with featherlight strokes.

Oh, how she wanted him buried deep inside her, finding the very spot at the end of his search, nudging, laving the delicate bud as she harbored his desire.

Delilah shivered and sought the soft underneath of Simon, his most vulnerable endowment. She cradled and warmed and traced, and when he shivered and groaned helplessly, she knew she had him in her power. Nothing could save Simon from her now. She had full right to his glory and heat, and before they slept, he would fall before her.

Simon's long fingers found her soft, moist folds, delving into them, and Delilah gasped with pleasure, her body arching up to his in a sensuous, luxurious undulation. She burst when he touched her, crying out with pleasure. Her nails dug into his shoulders, so great was her flight. Then, in pieces, she began to fall like petals from a summer rose kissed by warm golden sun.

The bed creaked magnificently as Simon knelt and lifted her knees over his shoulders, taking her in his mouth to carry her higher into the flames. Delilah clenched the bars at the top of the bed as he spared her no mercy, tantalizing her until she exploded softly, crying out her need. Her thighs quivered as Simon kissed the soft inner skin, his face rough and hot against her.

She gasped with the outrageous need of it, speared her fingers through his hair, and squirmed down beneath his trembling body. When they lay pressed deep within the fluffy feathers, she took him in her hand and eased him within her.

"So tight . . ." he muttered between lips swollen from her kiss. "Like a silk glove."

They rested, panting, staring at each other like two combatants pausing before one led the battle again. Then Delilah pulled her body tight, pitting her tiny muscles against his hard steely length, and Simon's eyes widened just once before he thrust, his seed pulsing deeply into her. He braced his hands beside her head and gave a muffled, strangled shout before he slowly lowered his head to her breasts.

"Vixen," he muttered, kissing and nuzzling the soft, slightly damp flesh luxuriously . . . as if he could settle on her for a lifetime. "Wildcat."

Delilah allowed herself a victorious smile into his hair.

She'd vanquished him, loved him until he didn't have the strength to leave her. She'd tamed him, gotten revenge for some dark, evil deed, and sapped him until he could fight no more. She arched slightly, wickedly reveling in the heavy weight, in her trophy, this warrior she had conquered.

Delilah closed her eyes and stroked Simon's hard, rippling muscles with a curious soft, warm, happy, fuzzy emotion. She placed her open hands over the hollows in his buttocks, then marveled at the hard mounds that tightened and thrust him gently deeper in her. She drifted along, pinned to the soft feather tick by Simon's great trembling body, still joined to her. There was a quiet settling within her, an easing, as if the world had suddenly righted and whatever happened in the new day, she would have this from Simon.

As if together they were one perfect whole, one heart, one life, strong and sure and forever.

He stroked her hip, gliding over it to test her waist and then down to her thigh. It was a gentling stroke, easing her as she gave to him.

Her hands flowed over his taut back, traced the rigid muscles and cords and smoothed his arms. His smile slid along her breast. "So that's the way it is, is it?" he murmured teasingly. "You think you've had me—fought me, brought me down to my knees and conquered me, don't you, dear heart?" he asked before flipping her over and lifting her hips.

"Simon!" Delilah cried out as he spread her knees and thrust deeply into her feminine heat.

"You're not getting away with that, dear heart," he whispered, easing out until he was barely touching her, then the long, slow passage back to spread and fill her aching body completely.

"Simon, this isn't—" she began, then cried out as he withdrew, leaving her poised and empty.

Delilah held her breath, fearing that the new ache would go on forever, her breath coming in sobs as Simon boldly filled her to the hilt, his hands anchoring her waist, then glided up to cup and caress her breasts. Delilah cried out again, grabbing the pillows and holding them tightly. Then she reached out and latched her fists to the bars over the bed as Simon began in earnest and the bed creaked in his rhythm. Each thrust took her higher, catching and holding her until she could stand no more— "Simon, please . . . Simon—"

The shattering, brilliant pleasure burst, her body tightening, clenching him gently, and Simon groaned almost as if in pain, pulsing deep within her.

Delilah collapsed on the bed, careless of the squeaking sound as Simon settled by her side. He drew her into his arms and smoothed away the dark tendrils clinging to her cheek. "Thank you, Mrs. Oakes," he murmured, grinning wickedly down at her.

She couldn't manage enough strength for a reply. "I'm certain that none of this is legal," she heard herself whisper in the near distance.

Simon's deep, rumbling laughter filled the room. Delilah listened closely to the sound and decided she loved it. The smile that curled and lingered on her lips seeped into her heart, and she curled against him, fitting herself close and holding him tight. Then she didn't care about anything as she drifted into sleep, just as long as Simon held her close, smoothed her with his large, safe hands, and whispered sweet, dark things to her.

Simon studied Delilah's proudly lifted head, the stiff set of her shoulders as they rode side by side toward Barkerville.

He held a chuckle as she turned to him, her mouth parted. It clamped shut and a marvelous blush began to rise from her collar to stain her cheeks for the tenth time that morning. "Yes?" he asked invitingly as she whipped her head away to concentrate on the road.

"You know what they thought," Delilah said tightly, carefully guiding Phantom away from Lasway and Simon.

"I'm certain your cries of pleasure stirred their own longings, dear heart," Simon returned in a soothing tone.

"How . . . sinful. The whole event was . . . sinful. Kissing that scratch on my leg and cleaning it and kissing it again. One would think I'm a baby—then what happened before and later—"

"Yes?" he asked, encouraging her to go on. When she refused his bait, Simon pressed, "You know, the way we left this morning, sliding out of the house like we'd created a crime, wasn't polite."

Delilah closed her eyes, another blush rising up her cheek. "I didn't want to sit there at the breakfast table as if nothing had happened. You didn't have to pick me up and carry me back to the house when they called breakfast. You could have told them we needed to be on our way."

"Dear heart, you needed a nourishing breakfast."

"Posh," she answered flatly. "I was mortified. If you had any conscience, you would have been, too."

"We're married now," Simon returned piously and tried to not to laugh outright. "You looked as if you'd crawl under the table."

"Huh. If you had good sense, you would have wanted to crawl under there with me."

"Oh, I wanted to. You jumped out of bed this morning and dressed so quickly, that I didn't have time to linger in my new role as your loving husband. For a time last night—or was it this morning?—I had the impression you were trying to savage me in some delightful way . . . to make me pay by way of sheer exhaustion . . . to wring me—"

Delilah's head whipped toward him and she glared at him. "Just what do you want from me?"

"I want you to trust me, dear heart," Simon said slowly,

meaning it. Now was not the time to tease her. Her trust was very important to him.

Delilah's deep blue eyes cut through the shadows to him. "You? A man who deliberately sought out the home of the man he thought killed his brother? Me, trust you? Ask for the moon," she finished heavily, looking away at some deer sliding through the pines.

"I don't think Richard is Rand's killer," Simon said slowly, watching her.

She turned to him slowly. Her brilliant blue eyes staked him in the sunlight. "What?"

"I've questioned several victims along the way—a Secwepemc family, when we watered our horses before Rufus captured us, and others. Victims note that the suspect had brown eyes, Delilah."

"Richard has very blue eyes, like mine." She leaned toward him, her expression intense, sliding from concern into excitement and sheer joy. "Oh, Simon, do you mean it? Something like that could prove Richard to be innocent, couldn't it?"

"Proof, dear heart. That is the heart of the matter. To prove that Richard is innocent, another man must be proven guilty. If there is a Mordacai Wells, we must find him, too."

"I detest that name. Tell me what you know, Simon," Delilah asked, easing Phantom closer to his horse. Simon talked quietly and, from his inside pocket, took the small slug which had caused Rand's fatal wound.

The lead rolled in his palm as he held it out to her. "Note the two scratches. Notice anything familiar?"

She studied the slug intently and gave it back to him. "Yes. Ben's gun had two burrs in the barrel. He said it fell on a pointed rock once and scarred the metal. He said that it would make marks on the lead . . . those same marks. Later on, when I told Richard about Ben, we checked the marks."

"Whoever has Ben's derringer now is pinning his crimes on Richard," Simon stated.

"Yes." Delilah's single word rang with deep emotion.

Simon took her hand. "Richard will be hunted until he is found."

Pain shadowed Delilah's dark blue eyes. "I am so sorry

about your brother, Simon. But Richard couldn't have—have murdered him. If we find him in Barkerville, please don't—"

"I'm willing to hunt for the other man, dear heart, to prove Richard's innocence. But first we must find him. If he's with us or in custody, he can't be suspected of crimes committed at that time."

"You're a Mountie. Surely that will account for something. The law will listen to you. Richard could be hanged if he's declared guilty." Delilah's beautiful eyes pleaded with him. "He's just a boy, Simon."

"I'm married to his sister. The best proof is the appearance of a man looking like Richard who has brown eyes, the derringer, and is missing the tip of his little finger. Wells is a well-known whiskey trader. He should be easily identified."

Delilah's hand pressed his, and she closed her eyes. "Richard must be safe. He must be safe," she repeated like a litany.

"He will be, dear heart," Simon said grimly. "But he's probably scared and hiding. I would be, in his place."

"William's Creek," Delilah said, nodding her head toward a fast, tumbling creek in the rocky valley of two soaring pine-studded mountains. Smaller creeks, dashing down the mountains, fed it. Portions of the mountains had been ripped away by hydraulic water blasting.

"Richfield . . . cemeteries . . . Twelve-Foot Davis Claim . . . Dutch Bill's Claim is over there. . . . Slaughterhouse Road, where they took the cattle from the drives. . . . Black Jack Hill . . . Gopher Hole . . ." she noted as they followed the Cariboo Wagon Road, which ran along William's Creek, flowing down into Barkerville.

William's Creek was lined with Cornish waterwheels— giant, creaking wooden wheels, fed by flumes and ditches. The waterwheels powered the winches that raised the heavy masses of mined earth and splashed water into it, separating the gold from the dirt. In the late afternoon miners trudged along the streets, many with damp trousers and boots that never seemed to dry. Smoke curled over the town set into the steep mountain, and layered across to William's Creek to another mountain soaring high against the sky.

Delilah kept her eyes straight ahead as they passed through the dark gray board buildings. Flags of Scotland, England, Wales, Spain, and more, sailed in the spring wind. The flags represented the miners who had come from all over the world; people called this the Valley of the Flags. The old Chinatown, with bold slashing characters marking the meeting house, lay on Barkerville's Main Street, and Billy Barker's legendary big-strike mine lay near William's Creek. Terraced gardens, vegetables and herbs, separated the row of shops built into the mountain's sharp incline. Flowers and forgotten Chinese rhubarb struggled to push their broad leaves into the sun. There was Sing Kee's store, where many miners came to find Chinese herbs to cure them. "There is Wa Lee's," Delilah said, pointing. "He's expanded his laundry into a goods store. The town burned once, and they started rebuilding within the hour. . . ."

Beyond Chinatown, Barkerville curled down the single, boardwalk-lined street lined with shops, saloons, the old *Cariboo Sentinel* newspaper office and the Theatre Royal building, flaunting its posters. Hotels and breweries and woodlots stood along the street, crossed by tired, dirty miners. St. Savior's Anglican Church with its jutting, angled roof dominated the street, and Simon noted shingles for a doctor and a dentist. The faint, grim lines appeared beside Delilah's mouth as she nodded to a shop. "The Mortons' Emporium was over there. Ezrah squandered what was left of the trade in the two years he had charge of it. . . . The Mortons had worked their entire lives for that store and Ezrah gambled most of it away after they died. There's where the Hurdy Gurdy girls danced, day and night—ladies practicing their 'Terpsichorean Arts.' They were good to Mother, though she wasn't one of them. She wore a red costume and a plume and she was the most beautiful lady anyone ever saw—my mother, Lady Delilah. The Theatre Royal wanted her to try acting, but Mother wanted to stay with the Hurdys, whom she loved."

"She loved you, Delilah," Simon said, glancing at the shredded canvas pipes running over the streets.

"I'm beginning to understand," Delilah murmured softly, memories leaping at her. She spoke more to herself now than to Simon, and was surprised to hear her voice. "It was a hard time. The cemeteries are filled with people who died of snow avalanches, mine cave-ins, or fighting. Then there was, and probably still is, typhoid—mountain fever caused by bad water—so they brought drinking water down from the mountain by hollowed trees running over the buildings. The Mortons' house is over there. Ezrah and I lived in it after his folks died. They're buried in the cemetery with Mother and Ben. . . . Ezrah is there, too."

She dismounted slowly, looking at the rugged mountain so steep that its creeks—fed by snow or rain—could sweep through the town and tear away foundations. The buildings were built on high foundations to allow the water to flow past easily, and occasionally store owners added more boards for more height. During rains or when the snow melted, an unexpected wall of water could come rushing down Barkerville's Main Street.

Two old miners passed by the blacksmith's, one man in front and the other behind, balancing the cart set upon one central wheel. "Over there," she said, following a pathway through the growth to an old cemetery.

Simon tethered the horses and followed. Delilah bent to tear weeds away from a grave and smooth the small weathered stone with one word: DELILAH. Simon watched her for a moment, then bent to help her neaten the two graves. When they were finished, Delilah stood in front of her mother's stone for a long time, resting back against Simon's strength as his arms enclosed her. "People cared for her, I suppose. The Hurdys did, and her stone was carved by a man who gave headstones instead of flowers. Mrs. Morton liked her because Mother told her she had a beauty that came from her soul. . . ."

Her breath caught, hurting her throat. "She said things like that . . . good things to make people feel better. Mrs. Morton's heart was soft and big, but she was horribly marked by a large birthmark and a bent back."

She looked at another stone—Ezrah Morton—and Simon asked gently, "How did he die?"

"When . . . I told him I was leaving him—I'd found Ben's

deed to the Millennium mine made out to Delilah Smith by then, and I intended to claim it for my own. Before I could stop him, he mounted a horse, poor Bianca. . . ."

Delilah swallowed, and Simon wrapped his arm around her. "She killed him?"

She rested against Simon for a moment, her whisper barely heard above the breeze sliding through the pines. "Bianca was a gentle horse, but Ezrah frightened her so badly she reared and lost her footing. They went over the cliff together. Ezrah's neck was broken and poor Bianca . . . I shot her."

"Delilah, you did what you had to do," Simon murmured, kissing her temple and rocking her for a moment. "It's late. We'll come back tomorrow," Simon urged, taking her hand in his and leading her back to the horses.

Tucked into the mountain, the Mortons' house had been boarded shut . . . a promise kept by the miner whom Delilah had allowed to live there with his family. Despite the overgrown brush and weather damage, it still held the old-fashioned charm that Delilah remembered as the Mortons'. It was small, two-story, and elegant in comparison to the gray board buildings that lined Barkerville's Main Street.

Chilling memories swirled around Delilah as she brushed aside the cobwebs and walked through the empty rooms. She'd told the miner to give away everything to those who needed it, and now only a table and chairs remained.

Delilah moved her toe on the old boards. They were narrow and elegant, and once she'd spent hours cleaning them with lye only to have Ezrah stride across them with muddy boots. Simon checked the massive cookstove and the ornate smaller one in the sitting room and noted that the pipes needed cleaning before use. "We may as well be comfortable while we're looking for Richard," he said, finding a ladder and climbing up on the roof, leaving Delilah with the stifling, cold past.

The heavy cookstove had become her nemesis. Working long hours at the Morton store didn't leave time for the beautiful dinners Mrs. Morton had cooked. Delilah swallowed, aware of Simon's footsteps on the roof, the quick gush of bird's nests and leaves which he'd dislodged falling into the stoves.

"You're a failure as a woman!" Ezrah's screams echoed off

each papered wall. *"As a woman, you're about as exciting as that floor."*

Delilah smoothed her painfully tightened stomach as Simon's footsteps sounded on the old roof. She thought of Simon luxuriating beneath her, his new beard covering his jaw and his hair riffled by her clinging fingers. His expression had been pure, wicked satisfaction. At least she had that, because in Simon's arms she hungered and fed and loved with a desperation that he returned. He stripped away her walls and demanded everything. "You were wrong, Ezrah," Delilah whispered against the echoes. "Very wrong."

She pressed her hand against her stomach and kept it there, her body tingling with small aches that Simon had caused in his desire. She needed that knowledge—that he had found her womanly and warm . . . that she could laugh with him and speak aloud her arguments and yell them at him and toss away her control, freeing herself.

There was the small room that had served as Richard's bedroom and another that was the Mortons'. In those three years of her marriage, Tallulah had stayed apart, living in a storeroom. Delilah had missed her terribly and had helped her in every way she could.

She walked up the narrow stairs to the bedroom, time weighting each step, and barely noticed Simon as he stepped through a broken window to stand beside her. A small wind caught the leaves in the room, hurling them at her feet, and Delilah slowly forced her fists to uncurl.

She tested a board with her foot and it creaked. "Here," she said quietly, her heart beating rapidly. She tore off her gloves and kneeled to tug at the board, which would not move. "If Richard was here, the box will be gone."

Simon knelt and pulled the board free to reveal an empty cavern. "Oh, Simon," Delilah murmured as he stood to his feet. "He came this far at least."

Simon poked a pencil into the dust, stirring the layers, then replaced the board and stood. "That was some time ago. Let's unpack, then go into town for groceries and start asking questions. You need a hot dinner in you and a good hot cup of tea. We could stay at the hotel tonight."

"One of us could," she returned archly, looking at the space where the bed had stood. "If Richard comes back, I won't miss him for staying at a hotel. You go."

"Ah, dear heart, how you try." Then Simon wrapped her in his arms and kissed her until she was dizzy and warm and arching up to him, answering the hunger on his lips. "Concentrate on that for the time, Mrs. Oakes. Because nothing is coming between me and my bride—especially not memories of her first, dear departed husband. Time to put this behind you, sweetheart," he said gently as he stroked her back and rocked her.

Delilah settled against him and rested for a moment. "I'm too tired to think this out."

His smile curved against her forehead. "Wonderful. Then I've got the meantime to take advantage of you, my love."

She tightened her arms around him, grateful for the safe, sturdy warmth. He had deceived her, tormented her, and hung heavily in the men's hands when they would have strapped him by Rufus's orders. Delilah closed her eyes and remembered how he had fought when they were attacked by the gang. Rufus's men wouldn't have stood a chance if Simon had wanted to fight. "You're a villain, Simon Oakes."

"I know," he returned, unbothered. "I'm hoping to prove that tonight. Shall we unpack and unsaddle, then have our tea, beloved? I could do with a stroll down the street, showing off my new wife. You can introduce me to old friends."

She closed her eyes and shook her head. "We're only married because Rufus would have strapped you. Have you no conscience?"

His great body tensed and his arms tightened around her. "Not a bit where having you is concerned. Let's get out of this place. The first thing I'm doing is renting the biggest, softest, squeakiest bed in town and installing it in this room."

"Simon," she said, pushing away from him and turning her head to shield her blush. "There will be no more of that."

"Oh, won't there?" he asked, reaching to fondly pat her bottom. "You'll want your revenge, dear heart. You're a savage little beast once you're set on your course, crying out your victory—"

He glanced at the broken window. "I'll nail that shut. I don't want your cries frightening the whole town."

"Simon!"

After they had placed the horses and mule in the livery, they ate at the hotel. Simon insisted on a leisurely dinner and a visit to the kitchen, and managed to dredge up an entire crowd of Delilah's friends. With a wistful expression, Simon had told them how they were honeymooning and Delilah wanted to stay in the old house; however, the house needed cleaning and a few household goods to make it livable for their visit.

The Hurdys, many of them married now, and an entire parade of friends in Barkerville hurried home. By the time Delilah and Simon returned to the house, miners and shopkeepers and entire families were sitting on the porch with goods to be loaned and buckets and rags for cleaning. "There must be seventy people here," Delilah whispered as Simon began shaking hands and drawing her after him.

Simon rolled up his sleeves, tugged up one embroidered suspender that had slipped, kissed Delilah's forehead, and told her to sit and visit with her friends. He took charge with an air of a general commanding an army. Delilah watched him intently. He knew how to get his way—to tell the men stories and charm the ladies—and make the giver be glad, she thought just as Mary Perkins declared what a good match Delilah had made for her second marriage.

Then, when the house was swept and washed and a few borrowed household goods stood in their places, Simon tucked her beneath his arm and rocked her once more. "Mrs. Oakes has had a busy day," he murmured, and the entire legion of men and women wished them well as they passed out the newly hinged door. "We need a day to rest, then I'll be over, Giles, to help lay tin on your roof. We need a day to rest and catch up. . . . Marsh, I'd enjoy a good game of billiards. . . . Etta, I must have your recipe for that gingerbread."

He bent and captured a toddler and held the sleepy boy against him while his mother drew on her coat. Delilah's heart leaped as Simon rubbed the boy's back and rocked him, just as he had rocked her. Simon knew how to handle grumpy, sleepy children well, as though he'd made a lifetime practice of it. "*. . . I want a houseful of wild Oakes brats. . . . I want a marriage just as strong and happy as my parents' and the rest of my brothers and sisters. . . .*" he had said once, and looking at him now, she knew that he'd make a wonderful father.

Delilah's hand rose protectively to her throat. She shook her head slightly, trying to clear it. Simon was deceptive, and he wouldn't stop until he had Richard in hand.

As the tired but happy group filed past, Simon placed Delilah's hand on his arm in an elegant, old-fashioned gesture, but she caught the challenge in his emerald eyes. These people had left their warm homes to help. She smiled, letting the warmth in her heart show through, and said to each person, "We'll be here for a time. Come back and visit, won't you?"

She meant the invitation; each friend had greeted her warmly and wished her well. They'd spared their evening and energy and would have to rise early in the morning to work. There had been little visiting since the Mortons had passed away within months of each other. Ezrah wanted to rule his house without visitors.

"I'll let you know about the party," Simon said to Mrs. Givens. "We're counting on you to help."

Delilah glanced at him before Dennis Moriarty bent his ninety-year-old body and grandly kissed her hand. Between Mrs. Freemont and Jonas Welch, she asked, "What party?"

"One high hell of a social. I want this town to remember you as a happy, proud woman, who married a man who doted on her." Simon smiled to Mrs. Flannery, a round cherub of a woman who snorted her wild, excited laughter.

"Why?" Delilah asked baldly.

"It's important, that's why," he said gruffly. "And tonight you're going to tell me just how and why you left before. Don't try to distract me—I will not have people whispering like they did tonight about how my wife ran from town. Do you know that there is some gossip that you may have caused dear Ezrah's death? Not these dear people, but apparently when you left suddenly, there were those—Ezrah's friends—who pointed a finger of guilt at you."

Simon's eyes darkened and his jaw locked into place as he nodded to Aneirin Culhwch, an old Welsh miner. "I will not have gossip about my wife. There will be no doubt in anyone's mind that you have a good future in front of you and that you are loved and held in respect."

"Simon—" she began, uncomfortable with Simon's declaration; then John Simmons's toothless, shy grin caused her to stop. "John, you'll come back, won't you?" she asked the man who had stopped Koby's tormentors by dragging them by the scruff of their necks back to their mothers.

How could she have forgotten all these dear people who had filled her life? These were the good people who had helped when they could, sparing kindness in a hard, rugged land that swept away life on a whim. John Simmons had carved Koby a feather once, and later he'd fashioned a wooden sleigh for Richard. He'd given her a doll, and apologized in his stuttering, shy way, saying that he didn't know much about little girls and their toys. Delilah bit her lip and forced away the hot tears burning her lids and allowed Simon to draw her close against his familiar safety.

Fifteen minutes later Delilah crossed her arms and looked at the brass bed that filled the entire room and had taken four men to get up the stairs; it was the ornate match to the bathing tub Simon had installed in a corner of the kitchen. Simon fluffed the giant pillows and smoothed the bed's red satin quilt. His polished boots slid in and out of the dangling black fringe, reminding her of the many boots that probably had been tucked beneath this—"Acre of pure sin." Delilah realized she had spoken aloud, and that her cheeks were flushed just thinking about the escapades performed on that same bed. They couldn't be worse than Simon's lifting her to her knees and— She flushed deeply. "That bed belongs in a sporting house."

"That it does, my love. That it does." She caught Simon's wide grin the minute before he leaned back his head and roared with laughter.

Then he picked her up and tossed her on the bed, following her down to kiss her with nibbling, sweet, hungry brushes of his lips on hers. "Hello, Mrs. Oakes," he whispered unevenly, rubbing his nose playfully against hers. "Would you mind, dear heart, if I undress you for the night?" he asked very politely.

Despite the draining miles and emotion weighing her, Delilah could not help smiling up at him and stroking that beguiling wave away from his ear. Her hands stayed to frame his jaw, riding the hard angles and prickled by his new red beard. She found the cord that tightened when he was angry and soothed it with her fingertips, then she tilted her head and studied his face near hers in the dim light. He looked too familiar, too dear, his eyes shadowed and gleaming down at her and his mouth softened and mobile beneath her trailing, seeking fingers.

Could she trust him? Her heart leaped with each dark, hungry look now, waiting for the moment when he turned a certain way or gazed at her in a way that filled her with joy.

When they found Richard—oh, how she prayed they would—would Simon give him to the Irish constable who had been searching the mountains after the crimes? Would Simon protect Richard, knowing how dear her brother was to her?

She smoothed that untamed wave and wondered how it would all end. She did not doubt that beneath Simon's charms ran a wild streak that he controlled—she'd touched the edge of it and pried beneath; the idea that she could so unravel his composure tantalized her, though she was glad for the quiet moment of understanding passing between them.

The moment shimmered and tangled in the darkness, wrapping them in tenderness. There was comfort in Simon's tall body heating hers, a safety and a warmth that soothed her soul, she thought drowsily.

"Have a care, Delilah Oakes, because I'm after you and I intend to keep you," he whispered softly, looking down into her eyes.

"We'll see," she returned, because she couldn't let his challenge slide by unnoted. She found she enjoyed sparring with Simon and relished his quick burst of delighted laughter when she did. Then as his fingers began to slowly unravel her braid and spread her hair over the huge, fluffy pillows, the magical moment drifted, tangling around her heart and easing it.

She closed her eyes and yawned, suddenly very safe and warm beneath Simon's body, though he held his weight from her. She squirmed her backside into the bed, heard the slight *whoosh* and stirring of the feather tick as it billowed up and around her. In this moment, just now, with Simon so close, she sensed a homecoming, and her tense emotions melted out of her like warm butter.

She yawned again and stroked the wave just at the nape of Simon's neck. It was an endearing little wave, an unlikely, whimsical softening to be found on Simon's great hard body. The boyish wave curled up and fitted her fingers just as Simon's slow heartbeat fitted over hers. She sighed and arched and placed her arms around his neck.

"That's my girl, sweetheart," Simon whispered unevenly as he opened the first button on her blouse. "Go to sleep."

"I should undress—"

"My dear, what are husbands for?" Simon asked tenderly.

Chapter Sixteen

———❧———

"This is indecent, Simon," De-
lilah said, drawing up the red satin quilt to her chin with both
fists as Simon entered the bedroom. He carried a tray filled
with coffee cups and laden breakfast plates—and the bacon she
had smelled when she awoke. Bright daylight knifed through
the slats in the boards Simon had used to cover the two
windows. She blew the clinging black fringe from her chin.
"What time is it?"

"Hmm?" he asked, concentrating on balancing the tray as
he stepped over their tangled clothing. "Around noon."

"Noon?" Delilah whirled to the window and blinked.
"Noon?" she asked again in a voice laced with panic. She
sensed her life had flip-flopped into another person's, one who
had snuggled in bed with Simon all night. She either awoke
to have his arm dragging her back to him, or awoke missing
his warmth and curled against his back. Though they hadn't
made love, there was a sense of completeness in their tangled

limbs. Delilah had found peace in the slow, unerring way
Simon's hand had found her breasts. He smoothed them before
moving on to her hip, the slight pressure of his tightening
fingers claiming her; his weight tugging down the bed beside her.

Delilah flushed and shivered. She'd slept deeply, her back
warmed by his chest, his thighs hard against her bottom.

She blinked again and swallowed, then wished that her blush
would fade into the shadows. The bacon and eggs stared up
at her, and Delilah's stomach contracted uneasily. Simon had
stoked the stove and cooked breakfast, and she had slept
through everything. "I've never slept until noon in my life."

"Well, now you have. I have big plans for the day—spe-
cifically eating this breakfast, letting you lather my back in
a long bath, then taking an afternoon nap." Simon carefully
sat on the bed, balancing the tray in his lap. Dressed in his
flannel pajamas, he acted as if he were in his own home of
many years. He leaned back against the headboard and slid
his bare feet under the quilt to touch hers. He placed a fork in
Delilah's hand and a plate of bacon, eggs, fried potatoes, and
buttered biscuits on her lap as though he'd being performing
the same routine for twenty years.

She looked down at the massive breakfast, swallowed, then
shook her head. Her hair spilled over her shoulders, and Simon
placed his open hand on her bare back, causing her to start. He
rubbed the tense muscles and whispered, "You need to rest,
sweetheart. You haven't had enough of it."

"Your feet are cold," she noted, distracted as she tried to
adjust to sleeping through an entire morning and Simon's
pampering. She drew her toes away from his wiggling, playful
ones. "No doubt all this sleeping is due to this pagan bed—
this red satin quilt with black fringe. I'll never find Richard
if I sleep all day."

She started to push the quilt away, then remembered that
Simon had thoroughly undressed her. His pajamas showed no
wrinkles, and she decided he had just drawn them on to cook
breakfast. Her flush deepened as she thought of Simon's hard,
naked body cozied close to hers in the sinful bed, where
more than one miner had sought release. How many shouts
of male pleasure had swirled over this bed? She blinked again

at Simon, whose shouts bordered on pain as though his very soul had been taken from him and she was guilty of the crime. Delilah swallowed, remembering her own cries. "This is your fault."

"Get used to it," he said flatly, then nuzzled her bare shoulder with his rough chin and nibbled it. He grinned widely, looking like a pirate when she began to smile. "No doubt you're counting how many women have experienced their ultimate joy in this same bed. . . . Give me my morning kiss, wench."

"What will people think?" she mumbled, distracted by Simon's bold leer at the quilt slipping a little on her breast. She shivered, uncomfortable with Simon's uncanny tiptoeing through her most intimate thoughts. She studied him intently and decided his prowling through her thoughts was an accident and that his leer was friendly—if such a thing were possible.

Friends. Delilah's thoughts stopped when Simon bent to kiss and nuzzle the crevice between her breasts. Her hand—poised to urge his face against her—stopped just inches from the back of his head. "What will people think?" she repeated, foraging for answers to her unsteady emotions.

"Mmm. That I am a very lucky . . . very hungry man on his honeymoon," he stated flatly, and gently pushed a slice of bacon between her teeth.

"Honeymoon. We're here to find Richard. I can't have you waiting on me, Simon." Delilah chewed the next bite, followed by a fluffy biscuit. After years of taking care of herself and others, Simon's care caused her to be uneasy. She licked a buttery crumb from her lips and savored it. She would find a way to repay him.

He raised his eyebrows in a full-fledged lecher's leer. "I have my reasons, dear heart."

She wouldn't let him distract her. "You can't always have the upper hand, you know," she noted primly after Simon fed her another bite of bacon. She took one of the cups of coffee, closed her eyes, and inhaled luxuriously. Then she said in her most proper voice, because Simon had gotten chilled feet and because he had cooked a mouthwatering breakfast, "Thank you, Simon. This is very nice. But I refuse to be pampered and leched after."

Then she slid him a look under her lashes and added, "I don't want to be responsible for unmanning you, after all."

"I shall try to survive, my dear," he returned gallantly, and tucked her butter-slick finger into his mouth, sucking it.

There was no denying the hungry little *whang*s zinging through her body, nor the lazy, hungry look in Simon's green eyes. She shivered, still unused to his blatant pursuit, yet it filled her with an excitement too rich to ignore.

Taking care not to upset her plate, Delilah rubbed her finger across the buttery biscuit. She held Simon's gaze as she trailed that same finger down his chest to his navel. His indrawn breath, the muscles tightening beneath her touch, told her what she wanted to know—that Simon welcomed her play, reacted to it in a very satisfactory way. To slide beneath his control was more exciting than anything she'd experienced in her life. She wondered when she had been so excited, feeling very smug and warm and happy.

"You know," he said unsteadily as her finger continued beneath the tray he held. "Last night you were tired—"

His eyebrows shot up in surprise as her fingers closed around him. "Delilah, that is mine." Then in a deeper, raw tone—"Oh, you think you're funny, do you?" he said unsteadily as he placed her plate and the tray to the floor.

Delilah let her giggle escape as Simon rolled over on her, then burrowed under the quilt to nuzzle her stomach with his morning beard. When Simon caught her squirming hips in both hands, kneaded them gently, then lifted her to his mouth, Delilah caught her breath and let the tropical heat that Simon alone had caused in her life to flood over her.

That was before the stars burst and she slid into a million golden pieces.

Simon chuckled and nuzzled his way up to suckle on her breast, teasing it with his teeth and lips until she arched against him again. "Oh, yes, dear heart . . . oh, yes," he whispered unevenly, tenderly, as he thrust deeply into her.

In the kitchen Simon soaked in his bath and thought of the woman who slept soundly upstairs. At four o'clock in the morning, the open oven door to the cookstove provided a measure of heat in the kitchen. After three days of visiting with the townspeople and enjoying life with Delilah, who was definitely and enchantingly uncomfortable with their everyday roles, Simon was no closer to finding Richard than when they arrived. It was now the first week of June; if Richard wasn't found before fall, the old house would have to be made ready for the severe winter. With snows as deep as fifty feet, winter travel was extremely dangerous and nearly impossible. Most of the town would be migrating to the coast—Vancouver, Seattle, or San Francisco—to wait out the winter and return in the early spring.

He sucked on the nugget of rock candy, a gift from one of the Hurdys who had remained in Barkerville to raise a family. The sisterhood had remained close and was respected; they remembered Lady Delilah and her children and welcomed Delilah with open arms. As her husband, Simon reaped certain benefits, like the homemade taffy and rock candy.

The previous evening the livery boy had asked Simon what time Delilah would be by for her horse, though his wife hadn't mentioned that she was riding out in the morning to the mines.

Simon sluiced the hot, steamy water over his chest in brisk movements. While Delilah yielded and gave to him in bed, she kept her secrets. She planned to rise from their warm, marital nest and leave without mentioning her plans—the thought annoyed him and had kept him from sleeping.

He took his small revenge in seeing that Delilah also had a restless, exhausting night. Simon's lips tightened as he generously scrubbed soap over his morning beard. He had succeeded in kissing and branding every inch of her delectable body down one side and up the other. He particularly liked the sensitive backs of her knees.

Delilah was preparing to ride out to the mines, searching for Richard, but Simon believed that Richard would come to them, given the chance. While Delilah had walked to the closest mines, Simon visited the saloons, and it was only a matter of time before she discovered where he spent his afternoons. If the jewels were missing, Richard had arrived and someone would have recognized him. "How is Richard?" was a common question, but others did not ask . . . probably because they knew something concerning Richard's arrival—like Fritzi Chen-Yu, the Oriental-white poker dealer at the Mayson Saloon—there was a cautious shifting of her eyes. Fritzi concealed some secret that touched Richard, and Simon had deliberately sought her out at the saloon as she served watered drinks. Fritzi knew Richard from their childhood, she had said cautiously.

Delilah's allegiance just now was to Richard, and that knowledge chafed. Simon sipped the glass of locally brewed ale, which he had placed on a handy chair, then shook his head. "A sergeant in the North West Mounted Police and on a manhunt—let alone a honeymoon—and I have finally yielded to the need of alcohol at four o'clock in the morning."

He lifted the ale to the lantern light and studied the rich color. "She's driven me to drink," he muttered finally, downing the rest of the glass's ale.

Once his loving wife found that he had visited the saloons—searching out word of Richard—any measure of trust between them would be tested. Simon did not doubt that she would scurry her little brother to safety and away from the law and her new husband.

If she brought Koby into the matter, Simon's life would be a short piece from hell. He poured another ration of ale from the small bottle given to him by Cyrus Pennington, a miner who treasured the lore of alcohol like most people treasured life.

Simon leaned his head against the high back of the borrowed tub, an ornate claw-footed copper affair. He needed the time away from Delilah to think straight, because when he was near her, he was distracted by the delicious welcoming little purrs she had begun to make when sleeping, and the sensuous arching and stretching of her body next to his on that grand old bed.

There was no word of Richard after three days of asking questions, though someone had noted there was a light in the bedroom window one night almost two years ago. They thought it was one of a constantly flowing stream of miners, needing shelter for the night.

Fritzi Chen-Yu would have to yield her secret, Simon decided, as Delilah, dressed in his too-large union suit, his shirt, and thick stockings, padded sleepily into the kitchen. She would have dressed quickly in the chilled room, and Simon was pleased that she was comfortable in choosing his clothes, fresh from the Chinese laundry. Entranced by her sleep-flushed face, the long sleek hair that he had gloried in when they made love just an hour ago, Simon observed her quietly. He could spend a lifetime—and he planned to do just that once Rand's murder was resolved—watching Delilah stir from their morning bed. Unaware that she was being watched, Delilah closed the open oven door, peered under the cloth which Simon had covered his rising bread dough with, shook her head slowly, then reached for the freshly perked coffee. After pouring a cup, she went to the window and leaned her head against the pane. She opened and spread her free hand on the glass, staring out into the cold darkness with a sorrow that clenched Simon's heart. "Delilah . . ." he said softly, unable to bear watching her grieve for Richard.

Startled that she was not alone, Delilah whirled to face him, her color high with anger. "Spying on me is not polite, Simon," she said tightly.

"Obviously, I was here first, waiting to ambush you," he stated cheerfully, deciding to push away his dark doubts and enjoy his wife. "There's room in this bath for two. Come scrub my back, like a good wife."

Fascinated by the small tremor that swept up Delilah's body beneath the layers of his clothing, Simon grinned. She stared at him blankly, then shook her head and sipped her coffee as if it could awaken her from a bad dream and will him away. Simon settled down in the tub. He wouldn't be pushed away from her that easily. He ached for the day that Delilah would reach out for him of her own will. He wanted Richard found and Delilah's thoughts occupied with their marriage. Though Simon understood, he disliked the flicker of jealousy as he thought of Delilah's determination to find her brother. Simon inhaled sharply. If Richard was innocent, their marriage stood a chance. If he was guilty, he would be brought to trial, and their future together would be left in Delilah's hands.

She looked up at the ceiling as if dredging her patience, then leveled a steamy blue gaze at him over the rim of her coffee cup. She placed it on the table very precisely and placed her hand on her hip. Dressed in his too-large clothing, she looked very irritated, very soft and cuddly, and very young. Simon realized with a smile that if their daughters were half as fetching, he wouldn't be able to hold his own. He'd enjoy spoiling them and toting his grandchildren on his shoulders. Delilah caused him to think like that—like a man who wanted to live his life with this one special, determined woman. "Simon, you seem to forget why I'm here . . . to find Richard."

She flung her distaste at the bottle of ale standing on the chair next to him, then seared him with another dark look. "And you forget that we are in a temporary situation for convenience . . . and you forget that *dear Amelia* needs you," Delilah threw at him, placing another hand on her hip as she stood near him.

"And a good morning to you, too, dear heart. I realize I'm keeping you from your morning ride, scouring the countryside for Richard, but I insist," Simon returned as he reached out to wrap his fingers around her wrist. Then, taking care not to hurt Delilah while she protested, pulling away, he drew her into the tub to sit on his lap.

"Damnation!" Delilah sputtered, too stunned to move as she watched Simon draw off the wet stockings. They plopped soggily to the floor, followed by his shirt. "Simon!"

When she sat perched on his lap, the union suit pressing damply against her breasts, Simon leaned back and placed his arms on the sides of the tub to wait for her reaction.

It was not long in coming. With her fingertips Delilah held the damp cloth away from her breasts and glared at him. Her eyes were brilliant, flashing sky-blue. "It's just morning and you smell like a brewery, you low, misbegotten son of—"

"My parents were happily married when I was conceived, thank you. They still are," Simon returned, tamping down the fine anger that Delilah had caused by taking their marriage lightly. He tightened his fingers around her wrist. "The same as you and I will be when our first baby arrives. There's no turning back, my girl. Our vows were as real as any said in church, as lasting and as binding."

"Your jaw is sticking out so far, someone could lay a brick on it," Delilah noted darkly.

Simon shook his head, trying to clear it. With great effort he tried not to tighten his maligned jawline. "What's that got to do with anything?"

"You do that when you've got your mind set to something. Like a lock that is being turned inside your mind. You know that I can't trust you with Richard . . . you set out to arrest him for your brother's murder. How do you think I feel . . . married to the man hunting my brother? Once Richard is found—oh!" Delilah slid off Simon's lap and under the water as he stood up and stepped from the tub.

Water splashed over onto the floor as Simon stood in front of the cookstove and briskly toweled himself dry. He slammed the towel aside and found Delilah's gaze locked to his aroused body. Because he was angry—wanting more now than she was ready to give—Simon reached down, cupped her jaw in his hands and held her for his long, hungry kiss. "Yes, you little disaster," he muttered against her lips. "I desire you and for the whole of our time together, I've not had proof you care enough to lock on to me for life. If just one time you showed some—"

Delilah's eyes widened and Simon fell into the clear blue depths for a heartbeat. Then he stood, reached for his control, and resisted stepping back into the tub with her. Her power over him nettled. He clamped his lips shut. No other woman had cost him the measure of pride that Delilah had taken. "Richard or not, you could be carrying my baby. What's between us is apart from Rand or Richard," he stated tightly.

"What are you asking?" Her whisper was raw, uneven, seeping down into Simon's stomach and hitting him like a butting ram.

"What I want is for you to want something desperately for yourself—yourself, Delilah, dear heart, sweetheart, my love. I want you to want that something so badly that you'd snip every thread of your martyrdom to get that certain something. God forbid, you might even forsake your trousers, put on a dress, and act like my wife. You'd be greedy to a point of forgetting the needs of those you have fostered and protected—at least for a moment. And damn it, I want that something to be me. I dream of you sliding on that silly, little blue garter and setting your mind to having me as though I were a bowl of berries that you couldn't wait to devour. Selfish, aren't I? And don't bring Amelia into this." Simon regretted his quiet, tight roar.

He reached for the bottle of ale, hesitated, then closed his hand into a fist. To drink—which he seemed to need when he thought of Delilah and marriage—would only reinforce her first low opinion of him.

After a hesitation in which Delilah's dark brows locked together, she said two damning, challenging words, "We'll see."

Then she threw the bar of soap at him. Simon watched lazily as the misfired missile hit the stove and skimmed across the iron surface to bubble on the iron griddle. Simon jabbed a fork into the soggy mess and briskly placed it on a plate in the warming oven. He left the battlefield with Delilah's shocked, disbelieving expression as she stared at her guilty, soapy palm.

Only when Simon entered the cold dawn did he discover the lather, which had hardened on his beard. Standing nearby, a wrinkled, ancient Chinese man laughed outright as Simon bent to the creek to rinse his beard in the freezing water.

Dressed in her trousers and a shirt, Delilah planned to ride to the outlying mines at daybreak. Yet the journals on the small parlor table caused her to pause and run her palm over them to the small, new primer Simon had given her. She touched the sheets of letters she had practiced with Simon's hand guiding her own. They had eaten breakfast in stony silence before Simon announced that he was helping Ole cut logs for a new cabin. He'd jerked up his embroidered suspenders with the air of a knight preparing to ride off into battle, glared at her, and walked out the door, leaving her to the quiet house.

The echoes clawed at her, steeped in the aroma of freshly perked coffee and newly baked bread. Simon's bread dough had risen, crawled over the sides of the giant pottery bowl, and had started plopping onto the stove's griddle. She'd had little choice but to stuff it into pans and bake it.

She'd sipped the rest of his bottle of ale and checked the bread as it frothed over the top of the pans.

Delilah sniffed the odor of burned bread. It clung to the house despite her opening the doors and waving it away with a towel. Simon was like that, leaving her few choices and causing emotions that clung to her just as sturdily as the odor of burned bread.

She rubbed her temples, which felt as though a herd of buffaloes was thundering between them.

Just once—after Richard was safe—she'd like to take her choices in hand and wrap Simon from head to foot in them. She'd like to spread them across that jutting, locked jaw and widen those I-know-so-much eyes.

She'd like to shock him into as base a reaction as he grabbed from her. "Throwing soap . . . I have never done such a thing in my life."

She'd never done several things until she'd met Simon Oakes, including whimpering and crying out her need of him. Delilah rubbed her tight, upset stomach, uneasy with her careening emotions. She'd placed one foot in front of the other, doing what she must do throughout her entire life.

Delilah closed her eyes, her fingers gripping her mother's journals. Her mother had been loved and had given love. She'd seen beauty in love and hope and dreams, despite her poor times.

Was this how her mother had felt? Like warm butter when the man she loved looked at her? As if tiny little flowers within her had opened to the sunlight with each touch? As if she wanted to wrap her arms around him and hold him tight and never let him go? As if she were strong and certain about everything when he held her, and cold when they were apart?

Beneath the journals, paper shifted and Delilah slid them free. She traced the row of large slanted A's, which Simon had helped her make, his large hand guiding hers as she sat on his lap.

She thought of Simon's frown as he concentrated on helping her form the letters. He was determined to teach her to read as soon as possible. Simon had locked his hands to her face, nuzzled her nose, and against her lips whispered, "The only shame is in not trying, my love. And I'm here to help you."

At that moment, with Simon's hand guiding hers, something within her softened tenderly, and she'd reached to smooth that impetuous, boyish wave at the nape of his neck. She'd shocked herself with thoughts of trimming his hair, tending him and loving him for a lifetime. "Mama," she said to the shadowy echoes. "Oh, Mama, is this how you felt? As if when he touched you, you would burst for the sheer joy of living?"

Delilah wiped her forearm across her damp eyes.

If ever there was a man who could cause her trouble, it was Simon Oakes.

She sniffed just once, smelling the burned loaves and salty tears. She fought a second sniff, because she wouldn't allow Simon's ill temper to ruin her day. Then she walked out the door to find Richard.

The sunlight blinded her eyes and set her head aching more fiercely than before, and it was all Simon's fault.

No doubt Amelia was brainless.

As Delilah rode out of town, she passed Simon at Ole's new log cabin. She held her head high and refused to look at the man who had stared brazenly and darkly at her, his fists clenching on his ax.

Delilah tightened her fingers on the reins, trying to ignore the invisible tug that Simon caused within her. The fancy suspenders ran down his broad sweaty chest. With his hair riffled by the spring wind and his legs taut and wide apart, he looked delicious.

As if he needed to be thrown to the ground and devoured—Delilah straightened her shoulders and forced her thoughts to Richard.

She rode to the mines, walking her horse down the steep inclines to visit the miners, and half expected to see Simon looming at her back.

She returned just after dark, weary in every bone as she brushed down Phantom in the livery, then dragged herself up the front porch to the Morton house.

The door jerked open and Simon stood there, filling the lighted doorway. "You burned my bread," he accused in a tone that she did not consider welcoming.

He took her upper arm in a painless, firm grip to jerk her into the house. He smelled of soap and was dressed in his laundried, ruffled shirt and dress trousers. His tense jawline gleamed with freshly shaven skin. "Where have you been?" he demanded in a tone that said he had every right to know.

Delilah straightened her tired shoulders. She refused to be intimidated. "Out."

"Out? As in trudging up and down mountains, fording streams, just waiting for an accident *out*?" he demanded, lowering his face to hers. His hand fastened to her other arm, locking her in front of him. "Has it occurred to you, dear wife, that I might worry about you?"

Delilah hesitated. No one had ever demanded her whereabouts with such shimmering frustration; no one had ever acted that worried. She just hadn't thought about accounting to Simon, and now the guilt of her wrongdoing swamped her. Because she didn't know how to answer, she asked a question which seemed logical. "What time is it?"

"Time you discovered that there are two of us now," he returned flatly, then added, "Or three."

He released her arms to draw off her shabby coat and hurl it at a chair. Then he framed her jaw with his hands and lifted her face to the light, studying her. With his hair standing out in peaks as though he'd run his hands through it many times, Simon acted so anxious, so harried, that her guilt rose like a huge wave and she wanted to comfort him. She cleared her throat and decided not to mention the short nap she'd taken in the morning and again in the afternoon. "Simon, you saw me ride out this morning."

"This morning," he repeated flatly, running his hands through his hair once more, then shoving them deep in his trouser pockets. "I expected you to be gone a short time. If you hadn't returned within the hour, there would have been a search party scouring the mountains and no doubt someone would have been injured because of you, my sweet little wife."

Chapter Seventeen

———◦◦◦———

        Delilah smoothed the red velvet dress that caused her breasts to push up and shimmer in the candlelight. She tugged the bodice higher; it wouldn't budge, the off-the-shoulder cut flowing into long tight sleeves. She stared down at the deep crevice between her breasts and took a deep breath. The soft, pale flesh bulged over the constricting bodice that flowed into a narrow waist and a short skirt held out by starched black petticoats. The black fishnet stockings, supported by gaudy straps, covered her legs down to the red, gleaming shoes. She refused to think of the red satin drawers with the black bowstring, just asking to be plucked and loosened. "I'll catch cold," she muttered to the other woman beaming in the shadows of the bedroom.

    She crossed her arms to cover her chest. The movement only served to thrust the damning pale evidence up at her.

    "It's almost June. I'm sweating," Cold Heart Bathilda Claas said, though she never took off her long handles, summer or winter. A lady miner, a "sourdough," Cold Heart hitched up her trousers, hooked her thumbs in her suspenders, and strolled around Delilah, inspecting her. "I've been waiting to repay your mama, child. She nursed me back to health after someone beat me and took my poke. She died before I could hit paydirt. . . . You'll need a dress like that to claim back your man."

Delilah pushed her hands down against her thighs. Simon had left her with one tight explanation: "I'm going out, dear wife."

"I don't know about this." Delilah wasn't certain about anything once she saw Simon dressed in his suit and a shirt with ruffles. Though his eyes lashed at her and his scowl was set firmly between his brows, he was the prettiest thing she had ever seen, big and tall and broad across the shoulders.

Delilah thought about those shoulders—taut and powerful and trembling as Simon poised over her—and she went weak all over, her throat drying.

Just the sight of him caused her stomach to lurch and her bosom to tingle, her heart to race and her skin to tighten until she thought it would burst.

He looked so angry, like a steam engine puffing and heading for a destination that nothing could stop. Delilah had felt like throwing herself at him just to see if he'd catch her.

Cold Heart chewed her tobacco cud, her layers of wrinkles shifting on her face. "I never liked One Tooth sayin' she was the best lady sourdough—the one with the biggest, warmest heart. This gives me a chance to do something good, as I see it. Her daughter, Fritzi Chen-Yu, is probably entertaining your man right now. He's spent a couple afternoons at the Mayson Saloon, and I saw him strolling down there just as I came up the street. Fritzi is a pretty little thing—a celestial flower—not at all like One Tooth. You'll need a getup like that to lasso your husband from his dallying. The dress was give to me by another pretty little thing down on her luck. I had a few extra grains in my pan, so I staked her to a ticket out on the BX stage."

Delilah crushed the red velvet. She'd like to do the same thing to Simon's windpipe. He'd acted so distraught that she'd set her mind to soothe him when he returned from his walk.

She had fried chicken and mashed potatoes. She had scrubbed and soaked her aching body. She had washed and brushed her hair until it gleamed. She had practiced draping herself on the sprawling bed and fluttering her eyelashes beguilingly as she unbuttoned the top button of his flannel pajamas.

She'd noted that Simon seemed distracted when she moistened her lips . . . as though he were fascinated, his hunger stirred by the movement . . . so she had practiced running the tip of her tongue across her lips until they were slightly chapped.

But Simon never returned, and she knew why—Fritzi Chen-Yu, a delicious and available celestial flower, was occupying his time.

At ten o'clock in the evening any respectable husband should be in bed with his wife. Simon wasn't, and he would pay.

He'd walked out—" . . . *Out* . . . "—tiptoeing around celestial flowers, when he'd dared to insinuate that now there were three of them to consider.

Delilah ran her hand over the velvet covering her uneasy stomach. "No. It couldn't be," Delilah muttered, jerking up the slipping bodice impatiently. She straightened her shoulders, which only made her bosom more startling and prominent.

She wiggled down into the dress and tried slumping, but Cold Heart shook her head. "They're yours. Stick 'em out proud. Men like that. Swish those hips."

Delilah slowly straightened again and decided Simon did seem to like them and that her breasts could not possibly be larger than when she had met him. She'd never studied her body before, and just the thought of what she was doing caused her to flush. Her breasts ached slightly and felt heavier—probably due to the way he—Delilah didn't want to think about the way Simon touched or placed his mouth on her. Or where he did. Or that when he did, he could draw her very soul flying to that exact spot.

If Simon was dallying at the saloon—right next to a known sporting house—Delilah decided she could try to find word of Richard in the same place. At least *she* would have an honorable purpose for visiting the rowdy saloon.

Delilah yanked the red plumed headdress from the bed and shot the acre of pure sin a dark, condemning look. Simon clearly loved frolicking in the bed, though now he was gone in pursuit of other activities—other than wedded bliss. *How could he?*

She plopped the headdress on her head and let Cold Heart adjust the red plumes, then smooth the long length of her unbound hair until it touched her waist. "You got to walk like this, Delilah," Cold Heart said, sashaying her three-hundred-pound bulk around the small section of the room that the bed did not occupy. "Like you're bouncing a ball on one hip, then the other. Only do it slow, like a snake gliding through grass. Try it."

Delilah walked back and forth stiffly, then, challenged by Cold Heart's disapproving frown, she allowed her hips to sway just a bit to make the black starched petticoats bounce side to side. "I'm only doing this to see if anyone has seen Richard," she stated archly, and dismissed Cold Heart's disbelieving wink.

Delilah turned and the short skirt flared around her thighs. "Doing a thing like this could make me seem like a—"

Cold Heart guffawed and swallowed her tobacco cud. When she stopped sputtering and coughing, she wiped away her tears and crooned, "Nothing could make you look like a sporting lady. You're too elegant. You're not spending your life in Barkerville or hereabouts, so what difference does a few hours make, honey?"

Delilah blew the tip of a red plume away from her nose, adjusted the headpiece, and said, "I could do a lot of good in this outfit. I'll listen to men's life stories—they talk while under the influence, you know—and maybe someone has word of Richard."

"Yes," Cold Heart agreed sweetly and stuck another wad of tobacco under her bottom lip. "I'll just walk you down to the Mayson. Wouldn't miss seeing the boys spilling their guts to you for anything."

Simon stood at the bar and studied the filled whiskey glass in front of him on the polished elaborate bar. Someone with the initials *I.P.* had probably paid dearly for marring the walnut finish.

Fritzi was busy playing poker and couldn't leave her table. But according to her sly glances, she would, and Simon would be waiting for her. He was certain that Fritzi knew something about Richard's whereabouts.

The drunken Welsh miners in the corner lit into a ribald verse, and an Irishman at the bar challenged another to Indian wrestling, hand to hand. A dandy dressed like Simon, but sporting a cane—which probably had a poisoned knife or a sleeping potion hidden in it—leaned against the upright piano. A bare-knuckle fighter-turned-miner nursed his lonely drink at a table, and a couple of the girls of the line worked the customers in the smoke-filled room.

Fritzi's youth and pale, elegant beauty was framed in the rough elements. The sensuous, slender saloon girl was dressed in a glove-tight long dress that covered her front and draped to a sinful low in the back.

Simon studied the dregs of the drink he had just tossed down and lifted the glass for a refill. The burly bartender sloshed through a row of waiting glasses down to Simon, then back up the row again. The time alone let him wallow in his thoughts about Delilah. He didn't like the way she had disappeared for hours without a thought that he might be worried.

So much for sharing each other's problems. Delilah had one goal—to rescue her brother, accused of killing several people, including Rand.

Simon tried to concentrate on Mordacai Wells, on Richard, and on Rand, and Delilah—missing for hours during the day. She walked slowly toward him like a downcast child whose very dreams had been torn away. She'd come out of the shadows of the street on her way from the livery, dragging one muddy boot after the other, looking as if her heart had dripped out of her.

Rage had ripped out of Simon when he saw her pale, haunted face looking up at him. He wanted to say, "Have a care for yourself, dear heart." Or at the very least, "Have a good day, dear? Was it pleasant—scouring the countryside and forgetting that you have someone who would dearly like to be a part of your life?"

Instead, he'd lashed at her about the burned bread.

Simon swirled the glass's amber liquid. He was thirty-six and a sergeant in the North West Mounted Police, although on a special mission. Yet for all his control, he'd derailed from his course this morning and earlier this evening, and now he was licking his wounds like a half-grown, bleeding-heart boy.

The alternative was bringing Delilah to heel. Only a brute would have staked her out and wrung her dry of pleasure, loved her until she begged for more. Only a brute would have demanded and soothed his own torn passions on Delilah's poor, tired mind and body. If he had stayed at the house, that's exactly what he would have done, and so he had left, a martyr to injustice, trudging out to seek the solid, base company of men.

Of course he was guilty of misleading her at first.

But now they were wrapped in an honest marriage, and circumstances were different. Or should be.

Simon ignored the nudging elbow of an Irishman next to him and moved farther down the bar. His personal needs were no different from when he had started out to find Rand's killer. He had wanted, eventually, to find a woman whom he could love—maybe. But good marriages thrived when children were added, and a gentle love could grow.

He inhaled wistfully. Delilah's heart was taken, wrapped tightly in her family and the search for her youngest brother.

He pushed the glass around the wet spot on the bar and ignored the second nudge of the Irishman's elbow. The room stirred like a hot wind had just swept through it, no doubt due to more miners entering the saloon, which adjoined the sporting house next door. Simon looked idly over his shoulder to Fritzi, who was just dealing another round, her black hair gleaming under the swaying lantern.

Fritzi lacked Delilah's passion—he could read it in the studied sweep of her sloe eyes—and at once thought of blue ones angrily flashing at him or drowsy after making love. He contemplated making love to Fritzi to ease the frustrated passion running through him. He tried to picture her slender body undulating beneath his like a hot tropical wave and failed.

He tried to imagine her cries of almost painful joy sweeping into his ear and the taut, contractions imprisoning him deep inside. He shook his head slightly. Delilah had ruined him with her anxious, hungry body and the soft screams that he had caught in his mouth, reveling in them like fine, rich wine harvested by his efforts.

If he battled another man for a slice of her affections, he could fight that—but stealing a piece of her heart from her family . . . The room stirred again with a rash of deep, rumbling excitement, and Simon dismissed the fever that gold could raise. He had more important things to do, like mourning his manhood, his husbandly rights to his wife's affections.

He tapped his fingers on the bar, turning back to the newly filled glass of whiskey. This morning it had been ale and now whiskey. By the time his wife was finished with him, he'd be a soul-searching, wound-licking sot—not a credit to the force, to the Oakes name, or to himself.

Delilah had reduced him to a brooding, self-centered, sniveling husband.

She'd ruined him.

He sighed wistfully as an Australian miner stepped up to the bar on the other side of him. "Eh? What about that female lode just newly arrived, mate?"

Simon nodded dully to appease the Australian and hunched over his drink. He thought of all the men felled by their wives, and silently toasted them with a lift of his glass.

"A bona fide female lode," the seven-foot, brawny Irishman rumbled. "Nice tits."

"Uh-huh," Simon agreed to quiet the two men.

"Now, that's one fine sporting lady," drawled the Australian. "And she's coming after me, mate. Reckon I'll empty my poke a few times this night, eh? And I won't mind paying good dust for that fancy piece, I won't."

The Irishman straightened away from the bar; Simon supposed dully that he was flexing his muscles. The Australian turned away, too, and Simon was left again to his sorrows and his contemplation of his role as a ruined husband.

The woman's hand curved over his shoulder. "Not interested," he said hollowly. He didn't relish creeping back into

Delilah's bed like a chastened boy—he had his honor, too.

"Simon," Delilah's husky voice whispered close to his ear.

He straightened and turned so quickly that the Australian's poke spilled to the sawdust floor, and there was an instant scramble by the saloon girls. They fell to their knees, slashing and yelling and trying to sweep the gold dust into their handkerchiefs.

Simon stared at the jaunty tall plume and followed it down to the long, shining raven hair and blue eyes of his wife. The beautiful apparition licked her lips with the tip of her tongue and edged away from a girl crawling through one miner's legs. He slowly took in the gleaming, alabaster shoulders above the low bodice that pushed her breasts together and raised them like a shimmering confection for tasting. "Go home," he said when he could speak.

The high red plume quivered when Delilah shook her head. "Sorry," she said lightly, cheerfully.

Then she smiled slowly and gloriously, wetting her lips with the tip of her tongue as though sifting through and enjoying each heartbeat of his outrage and mortification.

He glanced at the other men, who were bug-eyed and salivating as Delilah sashayed her long, black-net-covered legs away from him. Not even the saloon girls, scrambling for the gold dust, had distracted the men's eyes from Delilah. The Irishman licked his lips, expanded his massive chest, which burst a button of his shirt, then began to saunter toward Delilah, who was just taking a glass of whiskey from a grime-covered miner. She leaned a hip against the piano, draped an arm over the flamboyant shawl on top, and sampled the drink. Then she licked her full ruby-red lips with the tip of her tongue and surveyed the room as though she were selecting her prey.

Simon could feel the sensuous, lusty punch in his loins just as he suspected every male drooling over his wife was experiencing. He jammed his hat over his head and knew what he had to do.

"Hell," Simon bit out before he punched the Irishman in the jaw and ducked when the injured man retaliated. The Australian caught the Irishman's punch, and a brawl ignited like a fast-moving forest fire, catching everything in its path.

Little Ass Rosy jumped on the back of a burly Welshman, who
was ready to punch her "dandy of a little sweetheart." Fritzi
calmly stopped shuffling cards, gathered them into a neat deck,
and slid through a side door to the sporting house's parlor.

Simon latched his fingers to Delilah's upper arm and hurried
her up the stairs to the rooms over the sporting house. She
swatted at his hand and tried to arch away from him. "Simon,
what are you doing?"

"Getting you the bloody hell out of here—using the back
stairs," he stated between his teeth, and feared that his raging
anger at the moment would permanently lock his jaw.

"I'm sure you are familiar with the back stairs, Simon. . . .
I have just as much right to be here as you do," Delilah threw
back, trying to draw back from him and digging her heels into
the tattered carpet every few steps.

He stopped in the hallway just as on the other side of a
bedroom door, a woman screamed out a rhythmical simile of
pleasure. Delilah's blue eyes swerved to stare at the bright
red roses on the wallpaper as though she could see the event.
Another, a masculine edition of the same incident sounded,
and from another room a man joined in the symphony. Simon
didn't try to push the smirk away from his lips. "This is not
the place wives should be. They should be home waiting for
their husbands," he stated in a righteous singsong.

Delilah's eyebrows raised and a wild flush moved upward
from her white shoulders to stain her cheeks as another woman's voice chanted an urgent, "Yes . . . yes . . . yes . . ."

Because the object of his misery was just inches from him,
Simon braced his hands on either side of her head. She watched
him warily as the red plume trembled in front of his nose. He
yanked it away and shoved it into his pocket.

"You look like—" she began warily. "Don't even threaten
to spank me, Simon," she muttered, backing up against the
wall. "I'm a woman, not a child."

Delilah closed her eyes as the bed on the other side of the
wall began to thump in a telling rhythm. Then she angled
her face up at Simon and straightened her shoulders, which
caused her breasts to push higher. Simon glared at them, then
at her frosty, dark blue gaze. "What do you mean, dressing like

this . . . coming into a place like this, dear heart?" he asked
acidly.

"The other women are dressed far worse. You can see right
through that one's dress to her . . . her . . . the dark spots on her
person."

"Imagine that." Simon caught the intimate perfume of
Delilah's body and the thrust of her nipples against the
tight velvet. He placed a finger in the crevice between
her breasts and tugged at the soft material. "Of course,
you, *Mrs. Oakes,* my darling bride, are dressed much more
demurely."

"I'm on a mission. I've come to find word of Richard," she
exploded valiantly, squirming away from his finger. "You said
men talk when they drink, and I'll listen."

"That's your plan, is it?" he demanded, not trying to shield
his temper. "Go home and let me do the thinking. Yours
appears muddled. What if that were you in there on your
back and howling while some bastard sweats over you?" he
muttered in a gravelly explosion of male indignity.

She smiled bravely, though Simon had the satisfaction of
seeing her lower lip tremble, just once. "But I'm not, am I?
I've been taking care of myself and my family for a long time,
Simon."

"Uh-huh," he returned in a disbelieving tone, just as Delilah's
eyes flickered past his arm. Her hand reached for his lapel to
crush and hold it tightly.

Fritzi leaned against the vivid cabbage-rose wallpaper. She
looked slender and elegant as she blew a smoke ring into the
air and idly watched it float, then dissolve into the stale air.
She lifted her long cigarette holder to her lush, glossy lips and
inhaled while she watched Simon and Delilah from beneath her
lashes.

She shifted slowly, restlessly, against the garnish roses as
though aligning her lithe body on a bed. Simon smiled tightly
and nodded. "Fritzi. This is my wife, Delilah."

Fritzi smiled as though amused and arched sensuously, rolling one slender shoulder, then the other against the wall,
then showed perfect, small teeth. "Charmed, I'm sure. Why,
Simon . . ."

She pushed away from the wall to glide to Simon, placing her small, well-manicured hand on his shoulder. Her eyes glided down, then up Delilah's body. "How nice. You didn't tell me she was a working girl. But then, I hear her mother was quite the charmer. She's inherited a certain measure of—"

"That's enough, Fritzi. I was just taking Delilah home."

Fritzi lifted a thin eyebrow to the straight cut of her glossy bangs. She blew smoke toward Delilah. "Come back anytime, Simon. I enjoy our little . . . chats."

Simon shifted his neck within the suddenly tight starched confines of his collar, then returned Delilah's dark scowl.

Fritzi flicked her elegant cigarette holder. "Problems at home?" she cooed, her hand caressing his shoulder.

"I'm going downstairs to finish my mission," Delilah said between her teeth, and slid under the arm Simon had braced against the wall.

"The hell you are," he returned, taking one step before Fritzi gripped his arm.

"I think I can help you," she offered after a husky laugh. She pressed her body against his. "I know what you want. We can trade."

Simon fought the flush rising up his throat to his cheeks as Delilah slashed a look of blue fire at him, then at Fritzi and back again. "Simon?" she asked softly.

A come-along-now demand rode through the one, soft word. Simon searched Delilah's set, pale face as an idea swished gloriously around his brain.

Finding clues about Richard wasn't the only reason Delilah had appeared.

She'd come to claim her husband—that was himself.

To drag him back to her lair.

A heady sense of excitement and pride wafted over Simon, stronger than anything he'd ever known. He wallowed in it, poured it through his senses and took his fill. His slow, knowing smile caused her to flush, but the battle-light skimming her dark blue eyes lingered as she watched Fritzi.

The poker dealer smiled with catlike grace and blew smoke into Delilah's face. "Stay," Fritzi ordered tautly.

Her beautiful face contorted with surprise and pain as Delilah gripped the hand on Simon's shoulder and twisted it expertly. In the next instant she had brought Fritzi down to her knees. Releasing the grip before Simon could act, Delilah shot him a damning look, stepped around Fritzi, and began walking down the stairs to the saloon.

The Oriental girl snarled a guttural German curse and threw herself at Delilah, who reacted instantly. She gave the side of the girl's neck one swift, light chop, felling her.

Simon bent to check Fritzi on his way to Delilah and found the fallen girl coming to her senses. Three more steps brought him to Delilah.

"Enough, Mrs. Oakes. You've won the battle," Simon muttered as he lifted Delilah over his shoulder and strolled down the hallway to the back stairs, claiming what was his.

"Stop—" she began breathlessly. "My dress is slipping!"

"Pull it up. That will give those fast little hands something to do so you won't injure me," Simon returned cheerfully. He placed his hand on the bouncing petticoats and pushed them down as he tipped his hat to the men coming up the stairs. "The little woman wants me at home," he said, and the lusty guffaws began, following them out of the saloon and into the night.

Minutes later Simon opened the door to the house, carried Delilah through, and kicked it shut.

"Put me down," Delilah ordered for the fifth time, squirming over Simon's hard shoulder.

"Certainly. When I'm ready," he said, sliding his hand beneath the black petticoats to her bottom as he began up the stairs.

He squeezed her buttocks gently, stopped, and backed downstairs, still holding her. "Down," she insisted once more as he walked into the kitchen.

He placed her to her feet and shackled one wrist while he jerked open the door to the warming oven. "I thought I smelled fried chicken . . . mashed potatoes . . . biscuits . . . gravy. . . . Mmm . . . fried-apple pie dusted with sugar—my, my."

Delilah didn't trust the happy gleam in Simon's dark emerald eyes, nor the pleased curve of his lips. "You care, Delilah. Admit it. You may even go so far as to love me."

"You're a brick shy of a full load," she shot back, though her body trembled with the urge to fly into Simon's arms.

He grinned—a magical, boyish, wicked, delighted, endearing grin that caught her heart on the stark tip of a flashing sunlit sword and held it—while Delilah wished she could fly anywhere but under Simon's close inspection. "It's about time, Mrs. Oakes. You were jealous tonight and so you came to claim me. Tell me, did you ever go after dear Ezrah like that?"

"I was hunting word of Richard," she stated righteously.

His eyes skimmed down her body, warming it. "Of course you were. Well, I'm home now, dear heart."

Delilah cleared her throat and locked her hands behind her back, which caused her bounty to thrust higher. She felt awkward and young and uncertain as Simon stripped away his coat and flung it to a chair. He watched her intently as he flicked open the collar of his ruffled shirt.

Just the sight of the hair curling at his throat caused her to tremble and boil and soften. She shivered and gripped her pride in a stranglehold. Simon's finger prowling across the low cut of the dress did little to help her control. He wanted everything—she read it in his gleaming green eyes and the set of his jawline. Because her heart answered wildly, happily, Delilah wrapped her arms around his neck and placed her cheek to his chest.

His heart beat like a wild creature, running toward its goal. "Is it so bad, Delilah?" he asked in a deep, raw tone as he gathered her into his arms and rocked her gently.

"Yes," she answered quietly, locking her arms around him. "It is."

"Then we'll have to make it better, won't we?" he said unsteadily as he lowered his mouth for a long, sweet kiss.

Chapter Eighteen

———————————————

Simon patted the napkin against his lips and loosened another button on his shirt until it draped open to his waist. "You haven't eaten a bit of this wonderful meal, dear heart," he said, reaching for another fried pie.

Delilah pressed her lips together, refusing to say anything. For the past hour Simon had thoroughly enjoyed the meal she had cooked, commenting on the beautifully browned chicken, the lumpless mashed potatoes, and the light and fluffy biscuits.

He had talked about the Anglican church, weather, the silver boom near Loomis, whaling, and the matriarchal Secwepemc Indian culture. He noted the pies' flaky crusts and was certain that Delilah could learn the alphabet and write very quickly.

She pushed at the fried pie he had placed in front of her. He didn't seem like a man anxious to make love to his wife.

Delilah refused to look at his gaping frilled shirt. Her heart had stopped every time Simon had leisurely opened another button. She refused to admit her hunger for every dark, hairy inch of his chest.

He sat there, looking rakish and delectable, and yawned. He yawned again and stretched his arms out, rolling one heavily padded shoulder, then the other. Delilah forgot her promise not to look at his chest and found her eyes locked to the dark expanse glistening in the lantern light. The frilled shirt only set off the dark masculine angles and planes beneath it, and Delilah's throat went dry.

Simon yawned and stood. He stripped away his shirt and began stacking dishes with a sigh of regret. "I'd better do these now. If I go to sleep now, I'll never get these done."

Delilah gripped her fork just the way she'd like to throttle his thick, muscled neck. She wanted that dark excitement flickering in his green eyes, the heady knowledge that she'd stirred him as when he first saw her at the saloon. As if he could devour her and ask for second helpings. She watched the lantern light catch red tints from the hair lightly covering the back of his hands.

She wanted those hands on her.

She wanted him relishing her with as much intensity as he'd given the meal.

Delilah straightened her shoulders and scowled at Simon's dark, rippling back as he began to dip water from the cookstove's reserve into the granite washing basin, humming as if he had all the time in the world and enjoyed the task.

". . . You'll have to ask," he was saying as he dried his hands and placed his hands on his hips. The movement caused his trousers to sag lower, and Delilah's mouth went dry.

She stood and braced her hand on the back of the chair, gripping it. "What?"

He loomed over her. "Ask me to make love to you, Delilah. You came after me tonight, rigged out in this—" His eyes swept down her bare shoulders and the short red dress to her black net stockings and red shoes. "Rigged out to do battle . . . to drag me back into your lair and have your way with me. From the way you looked at Fritzi, I imagined you'd probably chain me to the bed until you'd exhausted my husbandly reserves."

"That wouldn't be proper." She blushed, thinking of his power throbbing within her. That was just what she wanted now, but she wouldn't satisfy his ego by telling him. She wanted that fierce joining of their bodies, the hunger and the completion . . . and she doubted that Simon's "husbandly reserves" could be depleted for more time than it took her to slide back into her skin after the pleasuring.

"No doubt you're caught up in the sounds of the . . . the sporting house. . . . The echoes of pure sin are probably unbalancing your brain. You're complimenting yourself, Simon," she muttered as he bent to brush his lips against hers.

"Am I?" he asked, sprawling in a chair and drawing her to straddle him. He pushed the bodice of the dress down, the sleeves trapping her arms when she would have shielded her breasts.

He gazed so long and so hungrily that Delilah shivered, aware that over his hardened body she had dampened the satin drawers. She shifted restlessly over him, pressing her hips down, and Simon's expression tightened. He covered her softness with his hands, kneading them gently and brushing his thumbs across the tips. He bent to tease the tight, aching bud of her breast with his tongue, then treasured the other until she arched to him and a long, shuddering groan escaped her lips.

The nibbles at the very tips of her softness didn't deepen. They tormented and shifted from one to the other, his lips and teeth playing, driving her hunger higher. The velvet seam confining her breasts ripped as Delilah inhaled and pushed her body toward the torment. She fought the frustrated wail, her hands digging into his taut thighs as she strained toward his mouth. "Simon . . ."

"No," he said rawly, his face hot and damp against her flesh, his great body lifting her feet from the floor. He shuddered, his hand sliding up the satin drawers to caress the damp, hungry feminine folds. "Say it."

"Do it." The words flowed between her teeth, despite Delilah's resolve. "Take me."

With a groan Simon swept away the remaining dishes from

the table, lifted her, and placed her on it. Delilah lifted her
skirts, cried out in frustration when she couldn't find the knot
of her drawers. Simon opened her legs, stepped between them;
his hands foraged through the black petticoats, found her satin
drawers and ripped them open. Delilah tugged apart his trouser
buttons, found him, magnificent and waiting, spilling heavily
into her waiting hands.

"Now," she said, feeling as if she would die without his
bounty filling her to the hilt. "Love me."

"Dear heart," he whispered rawly, thrusting into her, finding
her safe and true until she could hold no more.

Delilah cried out her joy, wrapping him tightly in her body
and her love. The table creaked beneath their weight, and
Delilah squeezed her eyes shut, taking in the pleasure and
the pain as he lifted her knees, spreading them wider. Simon
shouted, his body thudding into hers, pouring his essence deep
into her, and she rejoiced in the taking, her harvest, before she
threw herself into bright, dazzling heat.

"Damn," Simon muttered against her ear an eon later. He
raised slightly and looked so vulnerable and rumpled that
Delilah laughed with the joy humming through her. For all
his promises, Simon could no more control his hunger than she
could contain hers. She thought about the bar of soap skidding
across the hot burner to sizzle and foam softly before Simon
put it into the warming oven. She felt slightly soft and bubbly
and scorched herself.

The table creaked gently as Simon shifted, unwilling to
leave her just yet and gathering her closer like a greedy little
boy hoarding his most precious toy and not wanting to put
it away.

Delilah allowed herself to smile. If the truth were uttered
at the moment, Simon made a delicious, vast toy that seemed
newer and better each time he made shattering love to her.

"I think you broke a borrowed dish or two," she whispered
against his ear and bit it gently.

He shook his head as if clearing it and glanced at the dishes
on the floor. He frowned and closed his eyes, disbelieving
the event, which only endeared him more to her. "You're a
disaster, Mrs. Oakes."

"Come upstairs and I'll show you a disaster," she invited saucily, bending to nibble on his flat nipples. "I want to deplete your husbandly reserves."

Simon's wicked grin said he had a disaster planned for her as he finished ripping away her dress. She mourned its passing and delighted in her victory when Simon eased away from her, then bent to draw off his boots and shuck his trousers.

He cleansed her gently, taking care to smooth the sensitive swollen flesh, then together they walked upstairs to the grand old bed.

This time Delilah took her time, exploring his angles and his softness and spreading herself over him until he cried out, his body arching high up into hers and the bed squeaking magnificently with her efforts.

When Delilah returned to herself, she was draped over Simon and doubted that she had an unmelted bone in her body. She rubbed Simon's hairy ankle with her toes and luxuriated upon her captive's damp body, stroking the muscles and cords of his chest and shoulders. She moved restlessly, unwilling to let the pleasure slide totally away, and over her head Simon chuckled softly. "Dear heart, the conquered must rest before arising."

"Mmm." Delilah smoothed his arms, nuzzling his damp throat and reveling in the slowing beat she found there.

She closed her eyes as Simon was easing her down gently into the big soft bed and curling around her. "Simon?" she whispered drowsily, needing to tell him how he had filled her heart.

How she loved him.

She dozed, nestling her hips back into the aroused length of Simon's hard lap. He groaned, smoothed her breasts in his hands luxuriously, then entered her femininity from behind.

They made love again—slowly, eloquently, with the grand bed creaking in comfortable harmony—and before Delilah fell deeply asleep, she told Simon she loved him.

There was a quiet rendering of her soul just then, as if something dark and ugly had been torn away, leaving a bright new life ahead of her.

Just before dawn Simon slept heavily, sprawled across the wide bed, capturing Delilah beneath his arm and his thigh as if he would never let her go. She smoothed his back, comforted by his weight and warmth beneath the red satin quilt. The wind howled around the house, which creaked in protest.

Delilah listened closely, then frowned. She eased away from Simon to slip on his shirt and button it. Taking his pistol, Delilah slowly, quietly, descended the stairs.

In the dark shadows a tall, thin man hovered near the stove, greedily grabbing food and pushing it into his mouth. His slouch hat covered his face, and from the dirt caked onto his clothing, he'd mined a thousand feet of dirt and kept most of it on his person. His greasy hair hung lankily around his face as he jammed a cold pie into his mouth.

"That would be much better hot," Delilah said quietly as she leveled the pistol at him.

The man rounded on her, his eyes shadowed beneath the broad brim of the hat. Fear clawed at his dirty face like a wild animal and from the mouth filled with food and enclosed in a thick black beard, the youth cried, "Great Molly's tits—Delilah!"

He swept off his hat and gripped it in his fists in front of him as she came nearer, the pistol lifted to his face. Through the shadows the slashing angular brows and high cheekbones caught the faint light and Delilah recognized a younger version of Koby—"Richard?"

Her hand covered the wild, joyous pulse at her throat. Then with a cry, she threw herself at her younger brother. "Richard! Oh, thank God . . . thank God . . ."

His thin, broad shoulders shuddered in her arms. "You came," he repeated like a litany. "When Fritzi told us—One Tooth Annie, that's her mother, and me—that a woman with eyes like mine was asking about me, I prayed . . . oh, God, how I prayed. . . ."

Then he was stiffening, drawing away from her, and standing straight. Delilah clung tighter, crying and shaking, her heart overflowing with happiness.

"Sis . . ." Richard said in a deep, wary voice, placing his hands on her arms to ease her away slightly and look over her head. "We've got a visitor."

"Delilah, it won't do to welcome your brother at gunpoint," Simon said mildly as he walked from the shadows to take the gun and place it on a shelf. He lit the lantern and placed it in its curved iron holder.

Richard, just an inch shorter than Simon, straightened his thin shoulders with the air of a hunted man, trying for dignity. His eyes followed Simon as he asked cautiously, "Delilah?"

She clung to Richard's hand and stepped in front of him when Simon came closer. "You won't hurt him," she said quietly.

Richard's hand tightened on hers. "Who is he?" he asked in a strangled, coarse tone.

"My husband," Delilah said after a moment's hesitation. "And a North West Mounted Policeman."

Simon nodded slightly, acknowledging the introduction, though his expression was grim. "My dear, perhaps you should have told me that you suspected we had an uninvited guest," he said formally, his jawline tightening rhythmically beneath the dark red stubble. "Husbands do take care of this sort of thing—danger to the little woman, you know."

Richard trembled, his gaze running down Simon's bare chest, trousers, and bare feet. "They don't come this far west. . . . There's just been one through here, hunting for his brother's killer . . . Oakes was the name. It isn't possible that . . . He isn't Simon Oakes, is he?"

"I'm afraid I am," Simon said gently.

"Good God," Richard muttered forlornly, and sank into a chair. He stared at his hat, rolled in his hands. "I didn't do it. I didn't do anything."

Delilah placed her hand on his thin shoulder and met Simon's steady gaze. "I know you didn't."

"You're coming back with me, Richard."

"Simon, you can't—"

"I'm on special leave, dear heart. Rand was my brother and respected in the force. If I don't bring Richard in, another man will take my place. When we left Quesnelmouth, I telegraphed the commissioner of the force, informing him of our marriage and that I had my doubts as to Richard's guilt. I will not betray the trust of the force by shielding Richard."

"How could you? He did not do it!" Delilah cried, drawing her fist over her heart. She ignored the tears, which mixed fear and joy, running down her face. "I swear it."

Richard shook his head, his greasy black hair gleaming in the lantern light and lying over the shoulders of his dirty coat. "I didn't. One Tooth hid me. I was with her, but she lies so bad that no one would believe her. They're not bad lies, but—" His head came up. "I know the man you want, Mordacai Wells. I saw him cut off the tip of his little finger just before I escaped his gang. First he drank a big glass of whiskey while his knife was heating—white-hot. Then he looked at his left hand, took off the big diamond ring on his little finger, and put it on his other hand. Then he slashed off his finger—slashed it off—just like that so it would look like mine. He cauterized it himself—wanted to see that the job was done right, he said. He wanted to hold me until he had his fill of thieving and killing, then let the law hang me in his place. He'd be free then. He went on a murdering rampage just after the gang caught me at a . . . visiting a lady. I got away, but he's got Ben's—my father's—stickpin and derringer."

Richard shuddered as though reliving his terror. "I saw him let a man die once—the man was ice-fishing with his partner. Mordacai shot him with my gun and let him bleed to death while he and the gang played cards in the cabin. Mordacai seemed—"

He swallowed and leaned his head back, closing his eyes. In the lantern light Richard looked like a tired, old man. "He enjoys timing things like that . . . marking the changes when a man dies by his hand. I saw him stand and smoke a cigarette while the man died on the lake's ice. I begged him to let me help the man—let me take his place—but Wells wanted me alive. . . . 'That bugger's one of the Mounties who ran me out of the whiskey-trading business in Whoop-Up country,' he said. 'Those scarlet-coats rode high and mighty, worrying about the métis and the Indians, making it hard for honest folks to earn a living.' "

Delilah ached for Simon, his fists pressed against his thighs. Rage paled his face and lit his eyes into a fiery green, consuming Richard. Because Simon was hurting badly, Delilah moved into his arms, holding him and resting her cheek upon his heart.

He held her just as tightly, and over her head said softly, "We'll find Mordacai, son. He'll stand for the crimes he committed. That man's name was Rand . . . Randall Angus Oakes . . . former North West Mountie and my brother. I believe Wells would like to see me meet the same fate."

Richard's head came up, hope leaping in his startlingly blue gaze. "You believe me?"

Simon's jawline contracted. "What color are Wells's eyes?"

"Murderous brown. Black when he's in a temper," Richard shot back, confused by the question.

"Yes," Delilah answered slowly, looking up into Simon's too-brilliant eyes. She stroked his taut jawline and ached for his loss. "He will help you."

Simon's big body trembled against hers, and he cleared his throat. "Yes. I'm afraid Mordacai lost that tip of his finger in vain. We're leaving in the morning, all three of us. Wells is headed for silver pickings—"

"Loomis? Washington Territory?" Delilah leaned back in his arms. "How do you know? Why did you come here first? Why didn't you—?"

Simon's big hand cupped her shoulder, drawing her back to him. "You, my love, you are the reason. You wanted your brother." He grinned at Richard. "I had to run five miles to track her down when she ran to save you. Damned near unmanned me. That's hard on an old man."

Delilah laughed outright, the sound filling her heart with warmth and joy. "Old?"

"I was a pup when we married less than two weeks ago. By the way, Richard . . . I arrest you in the name of the Queen."

"Simon!" Delilah wasn't allowed to move from him.

"He'll be safer that way, dear heart," Simon said quietly, firmly, smoothing her waist with his hand. "In my custody, any man trying to do him in will have to deal with not only me, but the force."

"Isn't there another way?"

"He'll be safer this way, my love," he returned, rocking her against him. "I'll do everything I can to keep him safe. Wouldn't do to have another brother murdered."

Their kiss was long and tender, and when it slowly ended, Simon kissed away her tears. "He'll be safe. You have my word. . . ." he repeated, rocking her.

Richard looked at them for a long time—his sister tucked against Simon, her arms looped around him. "She's happy," he stated quietly. "Good. You're married and happy," he repeated, nodding with satisfaction.

"It was the least I could do. She saved me from a certain death—I told her I loved her on the spot . . . my heroine and all," Simon said with a wicked grin.

Richard drew himself up, his face proud beneath the full beard. "You take care of her, or you'll answer to me, sir," he said firmly and waited for Simon to reply.

"By my honor, I will," Simon returned, extending his hand to Richard's.

The younger man took his hand. "Good enough."

Delilah blinked, disbelieving the sight of the two men shaking hands. "I'm not a child or family heirloom to be turned over from one male to another," she stated heatedly.

Richard slowly scanned the kitchen floor, littered with dirty broken plates, her red velvet dress, the red satin drawers, Simon's boots and shirt. Richard stared baldly at the black net stockings she still wore and at the blue garter that Simon had found with his teeth. His gaze rose to the shirt she wore, which was fresh from the laundry and unwrinkled. "Ah . . . what happened?"

When Simon chuckled, Delilah flushed, turning to start warming food on the stove. She glanced over her shoulder to the table, which had creaked beneath the fury and magnificence of their lovemaking. In a grand, gallant sweep Simon plucked away the tablecloth to replace it with a clean sheet.

Mortified by her needs, which Simon had satisfied quite thoroughly several times, Delilah turned back to the stove.

"Here, my love," Simon said as he bent to lift her foot and place the red slipper on it, then the other. He patted her bottom affectionately and kissed her cheek, nuzzling her teasingly with his stubble. "You'll catch cold."

"Holy Jes—" Richard began to exclaim, cut short by Delilah's scowl. "Uh . . . what's to eat, Sis?"

The cold white gravy stared up at her, and her stomach lurched to her throat. Cold chills ran down her too-hot flesh, and she shivered as Simon lifted her and sat down, cuddling her on his lap. She turned her face to the safe harbor of his throat, locked her arms around his strong shoulders, and willed her stomach to return to its proper place. "Afraid you'll have to heat your meal yourself, Richard. Mrs. Oakes has had a long day. It's the excitement of your reunion and her escapades as a saloon girl."

"Delilah? My sister . . . wearing red satin bloomers and . . ." Richard lifted the torn dress, which Delilah ripped away from him and threw beneath the table. "A saloon girl?" Richard asked incredulously.

"I had to retrieve my wandering husband," Delilah admitted truthfully. "Don't move," she gritted against his throat as Simon began rocking her and the lump in her throat began to rise again. "Just don't you move."

"Anything you wish, sweetheart of mine," he whispered in a deep tone threaded with humor. Over her head he said, "Your sister is a greedy woman. She wants me all to herself."

She sensed his slow, pleased smile and damned it.

"Petunia," she threw at him weakly to avenge her lost pride.

"My heroine," he returned with a lilt of laughter as he cuddled her closer.

Drained by two weeks of traveling hard—Richard had pushed down his fears of traveling by the stern-wheelers, and Simon had grimly insisted on that mode of travel whenever safe—Delilah tried to keep herself in Phantom's saddle as they descended the slight embankment to the Canadian homestead north of the border.

Mrs. Morton's jewels were left to the people of Barkerville and their kind hearts; Simon pinned a note to the door of the house, thanking them and asking that One Tooth Annie receive the delicate filigree pin with a hundred red rubies. Because Richard thought that Fritzi Chen-Yu was sweet and innocent at heart, needing a grubstake to take her away from her ill fortune, he asked that she receive one small Italian cameo and a gaudy diamond necklace.

Delilah's mother's grave had been quiet in the light gray before dawn. Birds began to call, and the mountain wind rushing through the pines soared up and away into the waiting day. Peace settled in the small, fenced cemetery as Delilah smoothed her mother's stone, tracing the letters as Simon whispered them to her. Then Delilah and Simon stood by the grave, each in their own thoughts. "Mother, I love you," Delilah whispered, then lifted her face to the new pink dawn.

She touched Richard's cheek. "She loved all of us. When you meet Koby, you'll know how wonderful she was. He's a fierce, loving man, keeping to himself a bit, but tender in his heart and proud. That's how Mama was—a tender woman who loved us fiercely. I know that now. I never heard her say an unkind word about anyone, and she worried so about all of us. She wanted me to marry well, and now I know she meant it for the best—someone to take care of me. We couldn't be here . . . now . . . fighting this together if she weren't still living in us, Richard. She was strong in her way . . . giving and loving. . . ."

"I see you and I know what she was . . . what I am because of her," Richard returned unevenly. Though clean and shining now, Richard's hair was tied at the nape of his neck. For his safety, his face was shaved and stained dark as an Indian's. His resemblance to Koby caught Delilah each time she looked at him.

They'd talked for hours along the trail and on the rest stops Simon regulated like clockwork. He'd pampered and cuddled and walked her when she was stiff. The two men shared a secret; she caught it in their eyes when Simon cautioned her to rest or sit or walk or eat. He'd raged at her when in her happiness, she'd raced them for the top of a knoll, and Richard had looked sheepish as Simon sent him a fiery, condemning glance.

Delilah tightened her lips. If she weren't so tired, she'd forage for that secret.

She'd pluck it out with her two hands and spread it before them. At times she decided the two males shared a private joke, and at other times she sensed a grimness between them that concerned her. Richard's agreement to ride on the river's stern-wheelers was not a light matter. When he'd first objected, Simon had pulled him aside, and the two men had talked earnestly, glancing at Delilah. Then Richard had chosen the river travel because of a desperation that she supposed was to catch Mordacai Wells.

Delilah feared for Artissima and for Koby and the rest; Wells would not hesitate to harm them, but Koby would protect what was dear to her with his life.

But within her, other secrets had been opened by her mother's journals, and the past had settled peacefully in her heart.

She knew now how her mother had loved both men—Brave Bear and Ben, Richard's father—each in different ways.

She knew how her mother had loved her, apart and very special, and had given her the richest gifts possible—her name and the ability to love and care for those she held dear.

Now she was too tired to think, grimly following Simon's Lasway toward the ranch settling into the shadows of the early July evening. She glanced southward and noted that they were somewhere near Osooyos and the Canada–Washington Territory border; they had passed legions of miners anxious to get to the silver boom in the Territory's Similkameen region.

Five children, ranging from ten to two, churned out of the house and came running toward them like hurricanes bound on a straight course. Phantom sidestepped and Simon's hand shot out to capture his bridle as the hellions ran toward them, tripping and falling and scrambling to their feet.

A tall man with broad shoulders and a build heavier than Simon's stopped walking through the cattle grazing in the shadowed lush green field, and a small woman came to place her hand on his arm. She shielded her eyes against the dying sun, looking at the three riders.

"Uncle Simon . . . Uncle Simon . . . Uncle Simon," the wild

band of children called, each hurrying to outdo the other, with
the two-year-old girl crying because she couldn't keep up. The
ten-year-old girl scowled impatiently at her, then ran back to
carry her on her hip. Three boys, one running with a squirming
puppy in his arms, ran to them.

"Simon?" Delilah asked, not taking her eyes from the
marauding band hurling toward them. "Uncle Simon?"

He grinned and sailed his hat at the boys. There was a scuffle
before the largest one jammed it on his head. Simon swung to
the ground, stretched out his arms, and let the mob fell him to
the lush grass of the field.

They squirmed over him, giggling and shouting, and his
laughter filled the air.

Then the man and the small woman were standing beside
him, and he lay still, grinning up at them. "Delilah, this is my
brother Thane and his wife, Peggy. Thane . . . Peggy . . . this
lad is Richard, Delilah's brother."

He paused, then tickled whatever childish ribs he could find.
"And this is their wild Oakes gang."

Thane grinned at her, and Delilah caught the same line of
brow and jaw, the fiercely green eyes and reddish-brown hair.
Then Simon was reaching for her, lifting her down to stand
beside him. Thane bent to whisper in his eldest son's ear;
both their expressions were serious before the boy ran to the
house.

Side by side, the adult brothers grinned boyishly, clapping
each other on the back and playfully punching each other on
the arms. There was a brief, good-natured skirmish of swinging
fists and ducking and boasting who won what fight.

Then the little girl cried because she didn't know that huge
men played like boys, and Thane plucked her up high in the
air. When she stopped giggling, she sucked her thumb and
shyly held out the wilted flower to Simon, who allowed her
to tuck it behind his ear. She demanded a kiss, then the boys
groaned, and the other girl tugged at Simon's trousers until he
bent to kiss her, too.

With that Thane reached out, snagged Delilah to him, and
kissed her cheek. Peggy reached to hug Delilah and tearfully
whisper, "I'm so glad . . . so very glad Simon found you."

When Delilah found her senses after a round of hugs and kisses from the "wild bunch," she stood there, dressed in her wrinkled dirty trousers and Simon's too-large shirt over her own, and her wish to kill Simon. The two remaining boys inspected her closely until Peggy told him it wasn't polite. With a trembling hand Delilah pushed back the hair that was snarled by the wind and scented of smoke from the last roadhouse. Her trousers were torn, and she smelled of horse and sweat.

She looked down at Thane's polished boots and knew that her own were past redemption. Dust layered her from head to foot. She looked like a shabby orphan asking for a handout . . . or a camp woman. She did not feel like a presentable bride.

Thane's open face smiled down at her, and Peggy clasped her hands in front of her dreamily while the rapscallions danced around them, tugging Richard off to see a new calf.

The oldest boy walked proudly from the house, carrying a great gun and a powder horn. With a wink, Thane took the buffalo gun, prepared the load, and shot it into the evening sky. "There, that's done," was all he said.

Delilah stood close to Simon, afraid of what his family would think. Then his arm was around her and his fingers tickled her ribs for an instant, prompting her to say something. She nodded to Thane and to Peggy, liking them both instantly. She was afraid to speak; they looked too nice to hear what she wanted to say to Simon.

Her nails dug into her palms. Only a very bad sinner would say what she wanted to say to Simon.

"We've got a room ready," Peggy said, her eyes shining at her husband, then at Simon. "Oh, Simon, we're so happy for you."

Delilah edged a little closer to Simon, fearing that he would leave her to his family and wander away with his brother as men did sometimes, leaving the women to fend for themselves.

"We'll try to keep the wild ruffians off you, Delilah," Thane offered in a kindly tone as the little girl lurched from her mother's arms into Delilah's. She puckered her lips for a kiss, momentarily distracting Delilah, who was enchanted as the girl snuggled close to her and smoothed her hair with one chubby hand.

"Come here now, you little darling." Peggy took the child, who sucked her thumb and stared at Delilah with sleepy green eyes.

In the dying light of the field the Oakes family—except Peggy, who was small and red-haired—looked as if they had been cut from the same mold, all reddish-brown hair, riffled by the play, and devilment gleaming in their green eyes.

She saw Simon in her mind's eye, playing with his own "wild bunch," and the thought twined around her heart until she cleared her throat and ventured, "Umm . . . how did you know we were arriving?"

At her side Simon tensed, and Thane's guffaws shot out into the field's crisp air, startling the grazing cows. "Why, he telegraphed, of course. The first message said he'd found the mother of his band of ruffians, and the second one, about two weeks ago said he was bringing his wife to meet us and the wild gang."

"Oh, he did, did he?" Delilah asked sweetly as Simon lifted his eyebrows in an outrageously innocent expression.

Then he swung her up against his chest, kissed her forehead tenderly, and carried her to the house, all the while carrying on a conversation with the beaming Thane and Peggy and the scrambling, happy Oakes children as if the scene happened every day.

Chapter Nineteen

———◆———

Simon carried the bucket of hot water up the stairs to the room Peggy had prepared. Because Delilah might be sleeping after her bath, he opened the door stealthily an inch, and it stopped, blocked by something on the other side. He placed his shoulder against it and pushed and something tumbled, clattering to the floor on the other side. "Delilah?"

"Shhh," she whispered through the open inch of the doorway. "You're not sleeping in here tonight, Simon. You've embarrassed me all you're going to for one day. Go away."

He placed the bucket on the floor. Delilah had seemed uncomfortable when he'd introduced her to Thane's family, but she seemed to relax—laughing outright when Mattie, the two-year-old girl, piled on top of the four children already on top of him.

Simon frowned, remembering the way Delilah had withdrawn her hand from his at the dinner table. He had plans for that hand when she was rested. He intended to wake her up and wallow in her surprised cries and purrs and`. . . "Delilah, open this door," he ordered, not bothering to keep the impatience from his tone.

Thane's rumbling chuckle sounded from his bedroom, soon hushed by Peggy's urgent murmur.

"Go away, Mr. Oakes," Delilah whispered. "I will not spend the night with the man who has mortified me beyond redemption."

He tried to be kind, pushing back the taut anger racing through him that only Delilah could raise. "You're tired, dear heart."

"Of you . . . yes," came back the firm, arched reply. "I have had quite enough."

She'd had enough? He was the one well warmed and barred from his wife's bed! "Exactly enough of what?" he bit out.

"This mighty lord and master role of yours, Simon Oakes—"

"Delilah!" Simon butted his shoulder against the unrelenting solid door, then rubbed the bruise. "Open this door!"

Minutes later, outside the house, Thane's brisk order cut into the night, stopping Simon's foot as he raised it to the ladder's next rung. "You might want to come down off there. Or I can shoot you with this buffalo gun—never liked thieves. Take your pick. . . . Good God, Simon . . . what are you doing up there?" he asked when Simon turned to the lantern light. Then Thane began to laugh. He stopped a moment when the hot water from the bucket spilled over him, then his laughter rang louder. "Peggy. Come out here. You've got to see this—"

Peggy appeared, drawing a shawl over her long nightgown, and laughing at Simon first, then at Thane. "It's your fault, Simon. You've got a thing or two to learn about marriage," she said between giggles as Simon swung the empty bucket into the night.

Delilah jerked open the window and scowled down at him as he edged upward on the wooden shingles. "I'm not claiming him, Thane. You can have him back," she stated, which set off another round of giggles and guffaws.

"What's Uncle Simon doing?" several childish voices asked as the children came to stand around their parents. "Uncle

Simon, what are you doing? Is the roof leaking? Did you find a baby bird who can't fly yet? Can I come up?"

While Thane and Peggy hushed their brood, Simon lay down on his back and crossed his arms behind his head. He looked up at Delilah. "If I fall asleep and roll off here, I'll be a broken, bloody pulp and it will be your fault."

To the children he called, "I'm looking for the Big Dipper," which was answered by several choruses of "Can I come up?" before their parents shooed them away.

"Why am I exiled?" Simon asked Delilah bluntly.

"You didn't tell me you had family in the area. You brought me here, plunked me down looking like a dirty, shabby ne'er-do-well looking for a handout. . . . That's why. *You should have told me,*" she repeated in a whispered scream.

Simon inched closer to the window. "I am your husband," he pointed out, straining to keep the riveting anger from his tone.

"You presented me in a horrible way. You should have let me know. Or stopped and told me that there was someone you wanted me to meet—I'd have cleaned up," her voice rose indignantly in the night. In the moonlight her eyes widened with horror before she clapped her hand over her mouth. "You . . . you make me so mad. I've never yelled at anyone in my life until you came along."

Simon had other plans for the sound of Delilah's voice—cries of delight and pleasure was one of them. He dismissed the niggling thought that her point had validity. He'd been too anxious to see that she was rested, well fed, in a warm, safe house. If ever he'd been frightened, it was when he noticed the dark circles under Delilah's eyes; and two mornings ago she had retched dryly before breakfast. She'd been pale and grim, the strain tugging at her, and with Richard sleeping nearby, Simon had pushed away the desire that was now straining at him.

"My clothes were dirty and torn . . . and my hair, Simon. It was matted like sheep's wool. It's a wonder Peggy let me sit at the table . . . and you're no better, nor Richard. What must she think of me? That I can't care for myself, let alone my family?" she asked in a hushed, outraged tone.

Peggy's nightgown tightened over Delilah's breasts as she leaned out of the window, and the moonlight caught them like two beautiful globes. In a few months his baby would be nursing there, though Delilah seemed unaware of the event, just as she seemed unaware of *his husbandly rights*. This he discovered he'd muttered aloud, a sign that he had lost whatever grip on reality that Delilah allowed him.

"I'll just be reclaiming this now," Thane said from the ground, and the ladder slid away from the house.

"I'll jump and break both my legs and you'll both have to wait on me," Simon said loudly as a pillow came whizzing from the open window toward him. He caught and strangled it. He'd had plans for something soft and cuddly, but not stuffed with feathers.

"You know how to milk cows—I saw you. You know how to help a cow when she's in trouble calving, I saw you do that, too . . . just tonight out in Thane's barn. And all the while you were at my ranch, you just cooked and crocheted."

"He makes lovely booties and baby shawls," Peggy offered sincerely from another window.

In his own defense Simon muttered, "I do it to keep my hands busy. Almost froze them off one winter and the only thing that kept my fingers was crocheting."

"Thane knits," Peggy stated. "The Oakes men are a busy bunch."

Simon thought of how he wanted his hands and everything else on his body busy with Delilah. He closed his eyes, seeking the last memory of what had occurred seemingly two centuries ago—the red velvet dress wadded below Delilah's beautiful white breasts and the satin bloomers tearing in his hands. The locked bedroom offered their first privacy in centuries; Simon groaned aloud, mourning that magnificent big bed in Barkerville with its gaudy satin cover, fringed in black.

"What were you crocheting with that red thread?" Delilah asked suspiciously. "It wasn't a doily. It was too big. You worked at it like a man in a fever."

"That project is still unfinished, my dear. I won't reveal it until it's ready."

"It doesn't matter anyway. I really didn't want to know."

Thane's bawdy laughter ripped through the night. "Brother, you'd better apologize. Whatever she wants said, say it. I don't relish picking you up off the ground in the morning," Thane warned before he entered the house and slammed the door loudly for effect.

Simon chewed on that small, hard, tasteless morsel of pride. Then he said to the woman waiting at the window. "It's cool out here. A blanket would be nice."

"What? You'd actually sleep out there and embarrass me again?" she whispered angrily. "Oh, well. . . . Oh, well. . . . It's not like your brother and Peggy haven't seen me at my worst. You would have them think I'm a harridan, too. You deserve to spend the night out there."

"We think you're perfect, dear," Peggy consoled from her window. "Simon doesn't deserve such a sweet wife. He and Thane may be in their waning adult years, but they are still just wild Oakes boys at heart. They need taming. It's a task that their wives must constantly bear. They're just big scamps."

"Give up," Thane sagely advised Simon.

Just then a flat wagon clattered down the moonlit road, filled with several children screaming at the top of their lungs, and a man and a woman sitting on the front seat. Thane and Peggy appeared in the ranch yard and their children began running for the wagon. Thane looked up to the roof. "Looks like Suzette heard the shot."

"Suzette?" Delilah asked from her window, and Peggy's knowing laughter echoed in the night.

"Our sister," Simon said, not shielding his gloom. Without Suzette and her brood on Thane's doorstep, Simon had just a wee-chance of getting in Delilah's good favor.

Simon gazed up at the stars, counting the moments before his sister called up to him, *"See, Simon? Not every woman is as tolerant as your sisters. What have you done now? I haven't even met your wife and you're losing her. You're not that young, you know. Now I'll never get any nieces and nephews out of you. You'll be one of those old bachelors who smells and talks to his dog. You'll end up in an old men's home, lamenting your life and the evil ways that brought you to where you are—childless . . . alone . . . without a dear loving child to cut food for your toothless old gums or to pat your poor bald head."*

He sighed and thought of the dying plans he'd had for cherishing Delilah and making love to her, once she was rested. He rolled his head to Delilah. "Rescue me?"

"Fend for yourself," she returned flatly and closed the window.

"Don't you move that heavy furniture again!" Simon shouted, working his way up to the window and knocking on it. Fear curled around his heart as he thought of Delilah pitting herself against Thane's massive furniture. "Open this, or I'll smash it in."

She peered out at him. "You wouldn't."

"Try me."

She chewed on the look of him, peering at him uncertainly. "I don't doubt that you would do anything to achieve your small-minded goals. . . . Bully."

Simon smiled coldly, acknowledging the title. Where the life and health of Delilah and his child were concerned, he'd fight anyone, including her.

Later that night Simon closed the bedroom door firmly behind him. Delilah smoothed the new woolen shawl that Suzette had given her and the lovely muslin nightgown with tatted lace on the collar and cuffs. She spread out her spoils on the bed and admired the embroidered aprons and pillowcases and doilies. Suzette had gifted her with a framed photograph of their parents, who were still deeply in love in their eighties.

"You can get your booty off my bed," Simon said, allowing his chafed mood to show through. He'd been teased to the raw nub by his family, who'd loved Delilah at first sight.

Delilah lifted Peggy's embroidered pillowcases to the lamplight, stroking the fine stitches. "Isn't it lovely? Oh, and Simon, did you see the beautiful shawl Suzette made especially for me?" She wrapped it around her shoulders and twirled until the fringes flew out. "Isn't it grand?"

"Grand," Simon returned flatly.

"Richard and the boys are telling ghost stories in the barn. He missed so much of that."

Simon thought glumly of what he was missing. "Uh-huh."

Delilah turned on him as he pushed aside the stacks of linens and hand-stitched quilts. She jerked away an elegant knitted shawl from beneath him as he sat to take off his boots. Thane knocked on the door, offering a new bucket of hot bathwater with a loud, knowing chuckle. Simon jerked open the door, retrieved the water, then kicked the door shut. He poured the hot water into Delilah's cooled bath and stripped away his clothes.

Delilah studied him, carefully keeping her eyes from dropping below his shoulders. "You're in an evil mood for someone whose whole family is glad to see him. You don't deserve them. They've been waiting to see you."

"Uh-huh," Simon said as he bathed quickly, briskly toweled himself dry, and slid naked into bed, turning his back to Delilah.

She was quiet for a moment, then blew out the light and slid down into bed next to him. "I suppose you're tired. Good night."

Simon allowed himself to wallow in her slightly disappointed tone before he flipped over, pinning her beneath him. "I've got you now."

"Shhh." She arched up into him, locking her arms around his neck. "I'd let you take me, but we are just next door to your family," she whispered too sweetly, kissing the side of his throat, then dropping tantalizing nibbles across his lips.

Simon fastened his mouth to hers and took what he had wanted for hours. "There's the floor," he offered grimly, straining not to enter the heat that had dampened at his first touch. "Oh, hell," he muttered as her hand wrapped around him and the gentle up-and-down caress threatened to cause him to explode.

They tumbled to the floor in a mass of blankets and Simon turned to catch Delilah's body over his own. In the dark her eyes shone down at him. "Oh, Simon . . . I've never been hugged and kissed so much in all my life—they're like the family I've always wanted. All ten of the children are a delight."

"They are? That gang of savages? What about me? Am I going to be included in this hugging-kissing business, and soon?" he asked grimly, trying to find her in the swathing nightgown and the wadding of the blankets.

"Oh, you . . ." Delilah whispered casually as he found her. "You're mine, dear heart."

She took him sweet and hard and fast, and when Simon lay winded beneath her, Delilah sighed contentedly, brushed a damp tendril from her cheek, kissed his chest, and snuggled sleepily down for the night.

"Not so fast, dear heart," Simon whispered in her ear before he lifted her to suckle on her breasts. He plied the delicate buds with his lips and teeth, taking the taste deeper into his mouth until her hips bucked against his.

She cried out softly, desperately, her damp hot muscles contracting, sheathing him tightly. Simon took her cry in his mouth and gloried in the shattering heat as his body pulsed into hers once more.

Hours later Simon eased her up to the bed and curved his body to her back. He placed his hand on her soft stomach and smoothed the child he hoped she'd love.

"Simon . . . I'm glad . . ." Delilah murmured drowsily, then placed her hand over his own.

Simon awoke to a rooster crowing and a warm damp drop sliding down his cheek. He opened his eyes and saw Delilah raised over him, her hair spilling around him, her eyes bright with tears. "Oh, Simon, are you certain that we can't take Richard with us? Are you certain that he will be safe here? Why can't we take him with us?" she whispered as he smoothed her back and kissed another tear that clung to her cheek.

"He'll be safe here, sweetheart," Simon returned in a whisper and wished he could say more to stay the fear in her brilliant blue eyes. In the shadows they filled her pale face.

This valiant woman—his wife, his love—had come so far, keeping her family close to her and fearing for each one. "Thane knows how to protect his home and family. It's better that Richard is nowhere in the vicinity of Wells. Thane can witness that Richard was here all the time—his word is good with the law . . . he's helped them out."

"Do you really think the rumors that Thane and Suzette's husband, Girard, heard about Mordacai Wells—a young man

with a derringer and a horseshoe stickpin in the Loomis area—
are true?"

"Yes . . . the missing fingertip was noted when two miners
were killed for their poker winnings." Simon stroked her long
hair and brought a fragrant strand to his lips. "I'll do my best,
Delilah."

She gripped his shoulders, her blue eyes fierce. "You're not
leaving me here, you . . . you pirate. . . . And you . . . you must
keep safe, too . . . dear."

"Yes," he answered simply, then drew her down for his kiss.
When the long, sweet promise of their hearts and lips was
finished, Delilah snuggled against him, sliding into a badly
needed sleep. He lay for an hour, holding her and praying
that he could keep Richard from hanging in Mordacai Wells's
place. Simon did not doubt that if put to the test, Delilah would
risk her life and her happiness—their marriage—to save her
brother. Simon prayed that moment would never come.

For the moment, sleeping quietly in his arms, she trusted
him, and that was enough.

Two days later Delilah looked down at the ranch house and
the people standing and waving to Simon and herself. Thane's
left hand rested on Richard's shoulder, just as his right one
rested on his son. He was a fair man, who loved his family and
had promised quietly that he would keep Richard safe. Girard's
promise followed, while Peggy and Suzette only promised to
spoil him. Delilah waved once more, and Simon drew Lasway
close to her, placing his hand on her shoulder. "He'll be fine,
if he can survive the Oakes gangs. It may ruin him for having
sons of his own."

Then he pulled her close for a brief kiss, which she returned.
"Thank you, Simon," she whispered as the horses moved apart.
"For keeping Richard safe . . . or trying to."

"He's in custody, dear heart," he reminded her. "Thane is
as good as any jailer, though he's probably twice as big."

"But Richard isn't in jail or in a courtroom for sentencing . . .
and you've given us that."

"I'd like to give you more," he whispered huskily, then
plucked a piece of straw away from the shirt covering her

breasts. His hand wandered and caressed wickedly, until she flushed and swatted it away.

"That is another matter," she stated hotly. "Imagine. Just picture in your mind what you did not half an hour ago."

He wiggled his eyebrows lecherously. "Liked it, did you?"

She rounded on him, blue eyes flashing. "You . . . you . . ."

"Yes?" he asked innocently.

"You know what you did. You bent me over the hay, jerked down my trousers and drawers, and . . ."

"Yes?" he drawled.

While they had been packing their horses and the rest of the family was in the house, he'd kissed her breathless until she ached for him. His fingers tortured her warmth, sliding up and down the folds until she'd grasped his jutting, swollen pride in both hands and returned the play. He raised the challenge, jerking open her shirt to take her breast and suckle it hungrily, sending fiery jerks of pleasure zooming down her body. She'd gripped his head and took him to feast upon her other breast, crying out softly with the tender pain. "Hurry," she'd whispered, desperate for him as her body throbbed and ached for him.

Then Simon had whispered back what he wanted to do to her and bent her forward, over a feeder of hay. He'd stepped behind her and eased between her knees to enter her waiting, damp body.

Of course she'd wanted him; he'd just dried another round of tears, and the kiss had deepened in a heartbeat into sheer, raw need. She didn't want him to be careful, nor was he, taking her boldly, and at the last, when she could stand no more, crying out for her release, he'd lifted her knees and his seed had shot high and strong in her.

Simon had cursed when the wild gang came running from the house, calling, "Uncle Simon . . . Aunt Delilah . . . Mama says we're going to have a cousin out of you." Then, chants of "I want a boy," "I want a girl, boys are awful. . . ." "Girls are sissies. . . ."

He had jerked up her trousers and tucked in her blouse, because she was trembling too badly, her knees threatening to buckle. She hid her face against his chest while Simon ordered the wild gang to behave and that he would consider the matter of providing them with a cousin.

His arm had supported her when Thane, Suzette, Peggy, and Girard circled around them. She squirmed as he caressed her bottom out of sight.

"A bit mussed, aren't you, lad?" Thane had asked, plucking a bit of straw from Simon's cuff.

" 'Mussed,' " Delilah repeated darkly now, looking at Simon's wicked grin. "I'll show you mussed."

"Dear heart, you may muss me all you wish."

She arched her head and shot him a sidelong glance. "Cocky, aren't you?"

"At the moment I believe I'm unmanned."

The rocks tumbled down from the mountain cradling the Okanogan Valley. The landslide swept tall trees before tons of rock like toothpicks. Lasway reared, soon brought under control by Simon, who turned to grip Phantom's bridle. He jerked it, tugging Phantom down the narrow riding path, then slapped the horse's strong rump. "Go."

"Simon!" The crashing sounds buried Delilah's urgent cry.

A falling tree swept him from Lasway and landed on him as the boulders rumbled past, dirt flying in the summer air, rocks bouncing and rolling the tree. Simon tried to breathe, the limb keeping him pinned beneath it. The pine needles quivered as the rocks rolled by, the bulk of the tree providing protection as the worst of the landslide passed to the deep ravine, spilling over it. He jerked up the neckerchief as dust boiled over him. He struggled against the weight of the limb, and though he wasn't injured, he couldn't move.

Simon's hands shook as he tested the weight again; he feared for Delilah, images of her fear flying by him— Phantom's ghostlike color shimmering in the dust, rearing as Delilah tried to keep her seat. The horses nickered loudly and Simon's stomach lurched. He prayed that Delilah was uninjured, that their baby— A drop of cold sweat ran from his forehead, then another, and Simon tried desperately to see past the pine needles and the dust. *Was she safe?*

He swallowed, forcing moisture down his tight, dry throat. Delilah was more precious to him than his life, and if she died—

A tree limb broke, the sound shooting through Simon like a bullet. The horses nickered loudly and Delilah's voice soothed them. A rock rolled past as he tried the weight of the tree again. "Delilah!" he called, pushing with all his strength.

The tree held, and over him two very blue eyes looked down into his own, Delilah's black hair gleaming in the sun. "Are you hurt? Can you move your legs?"

"No, I'm not hurt . . . just trapped. My legs are fine," he whispered unevenly, lying back, sickened by fear. He gripped her wrist, capturing her racing pulse, and letting the beat soothe his terror. "Are you?"

"I'm the one up and walking around," she stated flatly, her hands foraging through the pine needles.

"Watch that, dear heart," Simon ordered as her touch brushed him intimately.

She frowned impatiently and continued to work down his legs, searching for injuries. "You've got other things to think about, don't you?"

"Like what?"

Delilah stood slowly and dusted her gloves. Her blue eyes were shadowed as she quietly studied him.

"Don't even think it, Mrs. Oakes," Simon said slowly.

"You're wagering your honor on Richard's innocence, aren't you? Thane said you and Rand had received citations for outstanding service to the force. That the Indian nations held you in high respect as an honest man and that the whiskey traders and criminals shook when they knew you were after them."

A shadow of pain slid through Simon. "Rand was outstanding. The bullet that shattered his shoulder was meant for me."

"But you would have done the same for him," Delilah stated softly as she continued to study him. "You are a man who holds his honor and justice as dearly as his life, Simon Oakes."

"We'll get Wells," Simon returned.

"You'll turn him over to the authorities when another man would have killed him, won't you, Simon?"

When he nodded once, Delilah shook her head slowly. "You're infuriating, you know. Peggy was right. There isn't anything tamed about you. Do you know that I've never yelled at anyone in my life until I met you?"

She sat a distance away and began braiding her hair, which she hadn't done earlier because he'd relished filling his hands with the sun-warmed silky texture. "This would be twice I've saved you, if you don't count Fritzi Chen-Yu. At least this time you're not drunk, so you won't be blathering your love for me."

"Blathering?" he repeated indignantly, and plucked a pine needle from his cheek.

She replaced her hat, pushing it back on her head and lying down with her hands behind her head. She looked up at the clear blue sky and watched a lined chipmunk scamper up the red bark of a pine tree.

"Delilah?"

"Hush. I'm thinking of leaving you, you know. I could leave you here, without a horse, and make my way back to Richard. . . . Make no mistake, Simon. I will protect my brother with my life. I could leave food and water within your reach . . . and your guns. Eventually a poor unsuspecting traveler would come along, and you could bully him. . . . By that time, Richard would be safe."

Simon tapped his fingers on the limb pinning him to the ground. "You do, and I'll remove those trousers and paddle your pretty backside when I catch you."

She sighed and sucked on a stalk of grass. "But Richard would be safe."

"He'd be a hunted man. I haven't lost a man in my custody yet."

"Do you really think my backside is pretty, Simon?" she asked idly, ignoring his threat.

"Bloody hell," he exploded, uncertain if Delilah would actually try to save Richard. She'd have a time of it with Thane nearby, and it would make the boy's chances worse if he came to trial. "Get the horses and get this tree off me, then—"

She lifted a lazy eyebrow at him. "I really don't like orders, Mr. Oakes—Mr. North West Mounted Policeman. You would do well to note that fact."

"Delilah, hitch the horses and drag this thing off me!" Simon yelled, then clamped his lips closed when he realized he had risen to her bait.

"Hush. Do you want to start the landslide all over?" She looked at him speculatively. "Is it true, all those things you said you'd like to do to me?"

"Yes, damn it. Are you satisfied?"

"Huh." She shrugged and rolled over on her side, looking at him. "Really can't move your legs? They're not hurt, are they? Or . . . anything else?"

Simon inhaled just once, watching Delilah rise to her feet and stand over him.

"You're mussed, dear heart," she noted in a thoughtful tone. "You look as if you're having a bad day. As if things have gotten to you—"

Simon refused to answer and continued to glare at her as she kneeled to his side, just out of reach, and stroked his thigh lightly. Her hand rose to cup him gently, and he shuddered. "Now isn't the time for games, dear heart."

"Who's playing?" she asked huskily as she began to unbutton his trousers.

Perspiration cooled on his upper lip as Delilah concentrated on her task of examining him boldly. Her expression filled with wonder and pleasure as he boldly grew in her hands. A strand of her hair tickled his bare stomach as she bent to kiss him. "You're beautiful, my dear," she whispered, pleasuring him until he groaned and shuddered.

"Move this damn tree, sweetheart," Simon managed unevenly, and slashed away a trail of sweat on his temple. He shuddered, gripping a branch and snapping it. "Please?"

"That's better," she said in a satisfied tone as she tucked him inside and buttoned his trousers.

Once the horses pulled the limb slightly away, Simon leaped to his feet. He jerked down one suspender on his way to where Delilah stood, then the other, and began unbuttoning his trousers. Delilah lifted her chin, tossed her shirt to a bush, her camisole sailing through the air to join it.

Simon had never seen anything so beautiful as Delilah's breasts tilted to the sunshine and waiting for his mouth. The dark rose centers were larger now, a fullness to the soft underside that beckoned his lips to kiss it. She trembled as she watched him approach, her blue eyes darkening as she unbuttoned her trousers and loosened the knot of her drawers.

"Is this what you want?" he asked against her mouth.

Her arms curled around his neck, her fingers finding a wave by his ear and smoothing it. She tilted her head, looking up at him saucily. "Maybe."

He laughed as she grinned wickedly up at him. Then her eyes were shining, her mouth parting for his kiss. "Oh, Simon . . . I'm so glad you weren't hurt," she whispered as he lifted and entered her in one sure stroke.

"This is where you were meant to be, sweetheart," he said, meaning it.

They made love quickly, desperately, celebrating their lives and safety. They flew and touched each other's hearts, soothing the fear that had passed only moments ago. When Simon lowered Delilah to her feet, she clung to him, leaning against him as he rocked her. "I'm so glad you weren't hurt," she whispered raggedly against his chest. "So glad you're alive, my dear."

Simon cherished the endearment, wrapping himself in it like a tender caress, for Delilah Smith-Oakes wasn't a woman to give herself easily, and he prayed that a bit of her heart belonged to him and the baby she was carrying.

Chapter Twenty

~~❦~~

On the dusty, bustling street of Loomis, Artissima eased away from the youth whose bold, hot stare spoke his needs. Gold and silver mining drew men like this, but settlers were arriving in Okanogan country every day. They found a wild land; the temporary county seat in Ruby was filled with saloons and gambling halls.

Miners talked of pay dirt, hard-rock drilling contests, placer mining, and the Chinese who slipped into the country. Bawdy houses sprang up on isolated mountains, keeping their trade close to the paying miners.

Dust boiled from the hooves of freighting mules and horses. Talk of getting the railroad lay on the dry, sage-scented wind. The original town, Loomiston, was begun by Guy Waring, a straitlaced New Englander, and J. A. Loomis, who ran the trading post. Those names mixed with Phelps and Wadleigh, the first big ranching outfit, and the tribal names of Columbias, Wenatchees, Okanogans, Yakimas, Spokanes and more.

On a whim the hard new land could take or give dreams. Now the wagons of silver ore headed for the smelters stirred more dust . . . and men like the one walking toward Artissima.

He stepped nearer to tug the bow of her blue calico bonnet.

"I'll thank you to keep your distance, sir," she ordered, her gloved hands gripping her shopping basket tighter.

The young man's eyes were whiskey-brown, meandering down the plain bodice of her matching dress so slowly and intently that Artissima flushed and tried to step around him. He was dressed in an expensively cut black suit, with a frilled shirt and a string tie. The small diamonds in the horseshoe stickpin on his lapel caught the hot August sun, reflecting myriad colors.

She'd seen men just like this hovering around since the South had suffered its losses. Of any age, these men had a lean, vulture look trimmed in meanness that just waited to burn its way out, hurting anyone in its path. Men sheathed in this look took out their pain on the unprotected. She wasn't frightened of this breed anymore; she despised them. They reveled in the terror they created, in the deliberate breaking of spirits and bodies.

The young man's hand shot out to capture her arm as his friends snickered behind him. "Well, now. Suppose I don't keep my distance, pretty lady," he taunted lazily. "Just what are you going to do about that?"

"She wants you, boss," a fat-bellied, dirty man sneered, and the three other men laughed nastily.

The young man tipped his hat insolently. "Jacob Morely, at your service."

Artissima inhaled sharply as he twirled his finger in the sausage curl at her nape. "Mr. Morely, I assure you, your attentions are unwanted."

His hand edged higher on her arm, his finger caressing the side of her breast. Artissima's gloved hand shot out; her slap snapped the youth's head back.

When he looked at her again, his eyes were cold, black abysses straight into hell. "You just made a bad mistake, bitch," he said between his teeth as he pushed his black hair back from his face.

His hand shot out, opened to return the slap, and she refused to acknowledge the threat with anything but a proud lift of her head. Inches from Artissima's cheek a man's dark hand gripped the youth's wrist, staying it.

"No," Koby ordered quietly.

"No half-breed métis is telling me—" Morely began, his free hand going inside his jacket. Koby's reach was faster, plucking away the small silver-barreled, four-chamber derringer. He clicked the release and let the cartridges fall to the dust, then pushed it in his belt. "Apologize," he said in a too-soft tone.

Artissima stared at Koby. He looked lean and deadly, his expression still but for the gleaming black of his eyes. The coppery tint of his skin caught the unforgiving sun as he tightened his grip to bring Morely down to his knees.

One of Morely's gang moved restlessly, and Koby's cold gaze slid to him. "Don't."

"Look at his shooter," one of the men whispered hoarsely, and for the first time Artissima saw what Koby could be—a killer. He stood, legs apart, lean body taut, his mouth drawn into a thin line with Morely kneeling at his feet.

"I'll get you for this," Morely snarled, grimacing with pain.

Koby's hand raised, and Artissima caught it, horrified by the deadly rage in his expression. "No, Koby. He isn't worth it."

He hesitated, his chest rapidly rising and falling beneath the shirt she had made him, as though drawing himself back from another place. He nodded to the wagon filled with their purchases. "Go."

She stood her ground, her glove locked to his taut forearm. "You come, too."

Koby turned slowly to her, his skin taut across his high cheekbones. Then he looked at the youth, slowly releasing his wrist. "This will not happen again."

"This isn't done, half-breed," Morely returned as he leaped to his feet and rubbed his wrist angrily.

Koby nodded solemnly. "No. You are the kind that will not put aside your hates or wants. But you touch my woman again and you will die."

"That b—" Morely clamped his lips closed, his nostrils flaring with anger as Koby waited, his hand resting on the butt of his gun. Morely breathed hard, chafing his hand and darting furious looks at his men before he walked away.

"Koby, I do declare," Artissima began as he helped her up into the wagon seat. " 'Your woman.' "

"Yes," he said simply, climbing up to sit beside her to take the team's reins.

Artissima opened her beloved tattered parasol and tilted it against the sun as they rode the sandy road out of town. "Well . . . I've thought about it and I like it. I've got you—" she touched the embroidery on his chest—"you're wearing my brand, and I'm keeping you."

Despite the drama that had just passed, Koby's lips gave a tiny upward jerk at one corner. Artissima laughed, threw her arm around his shoulders, angled her ruffled, battered parasol to shield them from town, and kissed that masculine curve. She tilted her head at him. "Papa or Daddy?"

Koby frowned at her. "What?"

"Do you want our baby calling you Papa or Daddy? . . . Oh, Koby, honey. I do love it when you look as if you're about to faint!"

"Mordacai is mean drunk," Haggerty said that night, touching his bruised jaw. He looked through the smoke, up to the room above the saloon where Wells was nursing his temper. "He's gonna kill that métis slow-like and make that pretty woman pay. She'll be working for him soon enough—that or she'll die not-so-pretty."

A placer miner passed by, and a fight started between two hard-rock miners, quickly ended by a burly bartender's stick.

"He's gone over the edge. He don't care about anything but killing that métis shooter and getting that woman beneath him. I've been thinking about California or San Francisco. There's always need for a good man on the Barbary Coast," Mad Dog Wilkes muttered, grabbing a drink from a passing saloon girl and pulling her into his lap.

Haggerty brooded, spat his tobacco wad to the sawdust floor, then sipped his beer. "He'll pay plenty to get his way, Mad Dog. Better stick around. No one can plan gyps like he can, when he's thinking straight. He knew to change his name to keep himself clean, didn't he? Jacob Morely—sounds like some preacher, don't it? There's plenty of pickings here, and not enough law to watch the hills."

Mad Dog buried his face in the jiggling bosom of the heavily painted woman, then came up for air. "Tell him I got such thoughts, and I'll slit your throat."

The other man laughed coarsely. "Tell you what. When Mordacai gets the métis out of his blood, one way or the other, we'll invite him along. He can't go north. The law never caught that boy that looked like him, and until they do, it's just a matter of time until they sic the law here on him. He'd be good on the Barbary Coast . . . one of the best. Let's play along. Mordacai is smart. He'll do in the gun and get the woman—wouldn't mind having that high-and-mighty sassy piece myself. The Barbary would be just the place for a classy sporting woman, once he got her broke in."

Early August spread over the Washington Territory mountains, baking the sagebrush and the small, struggling orchards. Cattle watered at the wandering summer-shallow creeks and quail with top knot-feathers scurried across the sandy road.

The countryside was alive with miners and those who made their living from the men. Simon and Delilah passed hard-rock miners, men who sank shafts into the mountains and supported them by timbers. Along the creeks miners with rock boxes and pans staked out claims, and the bawdy houses in the hills flourished.

Stagecoaches and supply wagons rolled across the mountains, passing footbound miners and settlers. A horse race could spring up in a whirl of dust, and the Indians profited from their fast horses.

Yet the land and the scent of new farms and ranches remained. Simon rode by Delilah's side, adding to her sense of coming home. Sitting straight in his saddle, his strong legs flexing to guide Lasway, he looked like any frontiersman—tough, ready to protect what he claimed, and yet when his emerald-green eyes caught hers, there was a tender closeness that bound them. When the horses stopped on the small hill overlooking her ranch, Delilah inhaled the pine-scented air.

"There it is . . . I've longed for this sight. We've been gone almost four long months," Delilah murmured as they stopped to overlook her ranch. Koby was walking a horse around the corral and Artissima was standing on the fence, watching him. Moose was sitting in the shade of the house, and Tallulah was hanging wash over a line between two quaking aspen trees. New calves played by the creek, the cows lowing to them, while a massive bull lay in the shade, aloof and majestic, ignoring a large raven perched on a log.

Artissima hurried to the small cookstove, stirred the contents in the granite preserving kettle, and hurried back to the fence.

"Home," Delilah stated, her eyes filling with tears.

Artissima turned then, watching the horses and the mule ease down the rocky slope. Then she was running toward them, her skirts lifted and her petticoats flashing white around her black boots. Koby gripped the horse's mane and swung up to its bare back. He galloped to Artissima, then walked the horse beside her. She lifted a wagging finger, and in the distance Koby's teeth flashed white against his dark skin. He bent, holding out his arms to her, and Artissima was lifted in front of him. Koby's arm circled her instantly, and Artissima placed her hands over his, laughing up at him.

"Good," Delilah said, then looked at Simon, who was grinning. "Good," she repeated, her heart lifting with joy.

Later that night as they sat lingering after dinner, Koby smoothed his mother's journals. "I will read them."

Delilah placed her hand over his. Koby would take his time, reading deliberately, looking deep into Lady Delilah's heart for the truth, and he would find that she loved him in a special way . . . just as she loved each of her children. "We must keep them safe for Richard. He must have this much of her at least. I was so wrong, Koby."

"Life was hard then." He swallowed rawly, and Artissima came to stand behind him. She placed her hands on his shoulders and bent to kiss his cheek. Koby stared at the journals, his dark fingers splayed and smoothing the battered covers. "You said she . . . was frightened for me. Afraid that mad Russian would kill me if she hunted for me. I should have come back when I escaped, but I—I didn't think she wanted me—"

His cheeks tightened; a thin vein raised the dark skin on his temple and beat heavily.

"She loved you, Koby," Artissima said, stroking the hair at his temples and smoothing the tiny vein with her fingertip.

"She loved all of us," Delilah said. "When Richard is safe, he'll read for himself how much she loved his father and him. Something went wrong when she had Richard—I know that now. She was too drained and I . . . I was just a girl, dealing with her illness and the new baby. I ache for the things that I said, but I think that—now that Simon has read Mother's journals to me—I think she understood. I'm learning to read, Koby. Simon purchased a primer for me. And some-day I'll read her thoughts myself. It's important to me. She writes lovely things . . . from her heart. And you just know that she was a beautiful person, despite all her hardships . . . and somehow—" Delilah held Simon's hand. "Somehow Simon's voice detracts from her thoughts. Like a bull moose stampeding over sweet little violets."

She smoothed Simon's jawline, which had just tightened with the small slander. " 'Bull moose,' " he muttered in a deep rumbling tone that did resemble the animal's, and Delilah grinned up at Koby.

"When I can read for myself—I'm already picking out small words—it will almost be like having her here again."

Tallulah dabbed her tears, muffling her sobs, and Artissima rubbed the older woman's shoulders. "There, there, honey. She's at peace now, thanks to you. Her children understand who she was—how she loved them and fought to survive because of them. She was a good-hearted woman, and she left three beautiful, wonderful children. What you have to think about is the new baby coming—Koby's and mine—"

Koby flushed, his beautiful eyes shielded by his sweeping eyelashes.

"Isn't he pretty, Tallulah?" Artissima exclaimed. "Koby, honey, I hope our baby has your eyes."

Koby glanced at Delilah, who had begun grinning, delighted by his impatient blush. "She torments me."

Artissima's musical, lilting laughter rippled through the cabin, and Delilah was surprised to find that she was laughing, too.

Surrounded by the people she loved, Delilah's happiness bubbled and warmed her. With Simon's warm, safe hand holding hers, the moment was perfect.

Her family knew about their marriage, Simon's sworn honor, his attempt to protect Richard and prove Wells's guilt.

Koby leveled his dark, steady gaze at Simon. "I understand the honor of finding the murderer of your brother. But I must defend my sister's honor," he said quietly. "To take her—to marry her—while away from the protection of her family is not right. You did not ask my permission."

"Koby!" Delilah and Artissima exclaimed in unison.

He didn't relent, but nodded at Simon. Both men stood, equally tall, though Koby was leaner.

"Outside?" Simon invited with a tilt of his head.

Delilah stepped between them and glared up at Koby. "What are you doing?"

"He must pay. As the elder of this family, I claim the right."

"Dear heart, get out of the way," Simon said quietly.

"No." Over her head the two males continued staring at each other. She looked from Simon to Koby and back. "I don't believe this!"

"He took you when you were unprotected," Koby murmured.

Simon lifted an eyebrow. "And Artissima. I suppose she was protected."

"I was here," Tallulah said.

"Me, too," Moose added. "We're family."

"Koby was the most delicious man I've ever seen. I wasn't about to pass him up," Artissima said in his defense. She placed her hand protectively over her stomach. "I corralled him and he's mine. Wedding or no wedding."

Delilah recognized the stubborn set of Simon's tight jawline, and the sight of him hanging between Rufus's men and waiting for a strapping for sinners flew through her mind. She'd wanted Simon, too, if she scraped away the clutter and admitted to her needs.

"I wanted him then, and I still do," Delilah said quietly, standing in front of Simon. "You'll have to fight me to get him."

Koby's curved mouth moved with a smile he pushed away as he looked over the top of Delilah's head to Simon. "When she left, the door within her was shut . . . now it is open. My little sister has a fierce temper when you are threatened, and she laughs now—the sound is good. This wedding—she made you marry her? Tossed you to the ground and tortured you until you agreed?"

"Koby!" Delilah turned back to see his wide grin.

"Oh, yes. She set her trap for me and I—a helpless innocent—fell into her lair." Simon placed his hand on her waist and scooped her up beside him. Delilah's polished boots dangled inches above the floor, and she was forced to wrap her arms around him. She flushed at the display of affection as he kissed her cheek, and she returned it quickly.

"It was the honorable thing to do. I told her I loved her the first time we met. I had to consider a breach of promise lawsuit if I didn't follow through. She jumped me when I wasn't looking. Broadsided me. . . . Koby, if it's payment you're needing, how about help rounding up wild horses? You can keep my share for payment."

"Trading for me?" Delilah rounded on him, her legs tangling in the new skirt and petticoats which she had worn for Simon's benefit. The pleased expression on his face had been worth the effort. Now his cheeky grin demanded revenge.

Before she could move, Koby looked longingly at Artissima. "I, too, am a tortured man. If a wedding will ease my pain, then perhaps I should fall before Artissima's threats."

"Threats? Me?" Artissima looked stunned, then she caught the glint in Koby's dark eyes. "I'll have you, Koby Smith, vows or no vows. I've staked you out and you're mine."

Koby looked at Simon. "So she keeps telling me. I fear her like a buck stalked by a hunter."

"Ohhh, Koby . . . you'll regret that," Artissima promised before he reached out his arm to bring her against his side.

The demonstration of tenderness was rare for Koby, and when Delilah's feet touched the ground, she looped her arms around Simon's waist and rested her head on his shoulder. He rocked her in his safe way, and she leaned against him, glad for the comfort.

"We will do this wedding soon. I must learn the ceremony," Koby said, his soft voice breaking as he cleared his throat. "I want my son to have my name."

"Koby, I told you, I don't need marriage," Artissima began heatedly, her words halted by his finger lying gently on her lips.

"I am the man, so you—the woman—should obey."

"Hah!" Artissima tossed her curls just once before she caught Koby's laughing gaze. "Oh, you . . . how I love you, Koby."

Koby didn't answer, but his eyes were suspiciously bright.

Later that evening Simon and Koby stood out by the corral. "Morely . . . Jacob Morely?" Simon asked darkly as he inspected the weapon that had murdered Rand. The silver gleamed in the moonlight, and with the tip of his little finger Simon detected the two burrs in the barrel. "I venture a guess that Morely's real name is Wells."

"You think it is the same man?" Koby rested his hand on the butt of his gun.

"Yes. Mordacai Wells." Simon fought the shudder running through him, the memories of Rand's wide grin, then his lifeless body lying on the ice. "He must be taken to court and hanged. A bullet won't do. He's outwitted too many people. . . . They need to know that the Queen's justice will be seen through."

"I will help you," Koby offered, looking at Phantom circle the herd of wild horses he had tamed for sale. "Wells's spirit is black with pain that he seeks to take out on others."

Then he watched Artissima carry blankets into the barn, and Simon said, "We'll talk tomorrow."

Koby nodded at Simon, then followed his love.

Simon stayed in the darkness, watching Phantom's pale body move among the darker ones. Delilah was too tired now; he'd read it in the dark circles beneath her eyes. Nothing could endanger the child she sheltered within her, not even Simon's need to bring Wells to justice quickly. With a sigh

Simon turned and walked to the cabin where he would hold his wife and keep her safe.

Simon lay down on the pallet beside Delilah's cot, thinking of Wells, of how close he was to justice. Yet one wrong move and the criminal would fly—

Delilah's hand reached to smooth his hair. "Simon, move over. I'm coming down."

"Oh, no, you're not. You need a bed, Mrs. Oakes. We've been riding for weeks."

In a flurry of blankets Delilah settled the matter by sliding from the bed to him. "Hold me," she whispered sleepily as he muttered halfheartedly—because he really wanted to hold her—and arranged the blankets around them. "I want to know that you're safe. That you won't go hunting Wells without me. You're such a petunia, you know."

"My heroine," Simon murmured into her silky hair, but for once he was not smiling.

Delilah moved among the cattle, marveling at the new frisky calves playing in the field. Because the creek that meandered through her meadow had mysteriously slowed, Simon and Koby were checking it for a beaver dam. Artissima, Moose, and Tallulah were giving her this time alone with her thoughts and the cattle that were thriving. She smoothed the new skirt and petticoats she'd worn for Simon, and smiled. When Simon found the black net stockings and her blue garter, he'd be shocked.

She traced a sturdy bull calf and marked it for Richard. A century ago she'd had to strip away frozen hides for the price of leather. Now she was certain she carried Simon's child, and she'd put so much pain behind her. Once Richard was returned safely, she could relax and enjoy capturing Simon.

He'd unlocked her selfish greed for him, for a life together, and deserved to pay the price of stirring her needs, of opening her heart.

She let her gloved hand rest on a cow's flank, noting the healthy calf that impatiently sucked the teats. Daisies and yellow sunflowers caught the morning sun and danced across the green meadow. Higher on the mountain, sagebrush blended with bunchgrass. The new flume would run along a high rocky ridge, emptying water into the irrigation ditches of the new apple orchard.

She and the rest had worked for this bit of heaven, payed for it with hours of work and worry. Her hand covered her flat stomach and a lurch of joy rocked her heart. Simon had spawned the first of his wild Oakes brood.

Delilah plucked a bouquet and ignored Phantom's warning nicker. "I don't have a carrot. You'll have to wait until tonight," she said.

"Now, that's an invite if I ever heard one." The nasal male twang skidded along her spine, chilling it as she pivoted only to be lassoed by a tall, scraggly man. "Pretty lady, the boss said to bring him a woman from the Smith spread, and I reckon you'll do. He's already got your menfolk and that sassy high-nose missy."

An expert horseman, the man leered at her, then flipped the rope around her again. "What do you mean?" Delilah asked, frightened by the wild look in the man's eyes.

He reached down and yanked the rope, careless of the rope burning her arms. Then he dismounted and lifted her to his saddle, swinging up behind her. "Bet they thought the water stopped because of natural causes. We just had some Indians saw down a log before we killed them. So I guess it *was* caused by nature."

Delilah fought the fear and the nausea rising in her throat. "What about my . . . my menfolk?"

"Tied the métis to a tree," the man said in a bored tone. "The boss said nobody would believe a half-breed, and living was the best hell he could give him . . . after the boss had his woman. Wells took Oakes. Fancy that, he's a Queen's Mountie, come all the way from Canada to get Wells, and now Mordacai has him. Once Oakes heard we had you tucked away, he stopped fighting—easy as can be. 'Take me,' he said. 'Leave her alone.' "

Delilah shivered, nausea and fear crawling up her throat. If anything happened to Simon, part of her would die. She angled her open hand across her stomach, protecting the new life they had created. "Where is he?"

The man cackled. "Don't you worry. You'll be seeing him soon enough. That fancy lady will be along, too, just as soon as Mort plucks her from the house. We've got a nice little cabin waiting for you. Boss said he wanted a little privacy. Sometimes he don't and sometimes he does."

Chapter
Twenty-One

"Tie her to the bed," Wells hissed as the man carried Delilah, still circled by rope, into the single room of the log cabin. "Where's the other piece?"

"Mort will bring her."

Delilah found Simon bound and sitting in the shadows. One eye was swollen shut, and a trickle of blood gleamed on his jawline. She knew the set of that jaw and the raw anger behind it.

A stark emotion ran through his expression, and she recognized it instantly. Though he was in danger, Simon feared for her.

"I want them both here, and I want that palm-squeezer back—it's mine," Wells snapped. "Tie her to the bed, and we'll go after Mort. I want the ladies broken into work fast, so we can take off for the Barbary. You and the boys can have them, but only when I say so and how I say so. . . . I don't want them spoiled for work. This piece and the other can make enough money to get me started in business there. They've got the high-class look that boys will pay well to get."

"You'll have to help me, boss. This one is tough. She grabbed my thumb and did something fancy with it before I smacked her with my other hand."

"I can do more," she offered darkly.

"Dear heart . . . shut up," Simon said too politely.

Wells glanced at Simon, then at Delilah, and laughed wildly. "Good. It's better when sweet love is at work. My performance is always better."

Simon swallowed and Delilah recognized the slashing green promise as he stared at Wells. "You hurt her and you'll pay."

Haggerty's fist slammed against him, and Simon slumped against the wall.

Wells snorted. "Look who's talking. You came along nicely when you heard we had her, didn't you? I gave you a bit of payment already, didn't I?"

After Wells's kick, Simon's smile was too pleasant, and Haggerty hit him again. The sound of the blow shafted into Delilah's heart. A fresh flow of blood started from Simon's mouth. She wanted that mouth crooning baby lullabies to their son, and she wanted it telling her how much he loved her. She wanted him grinning boyishly at her, or sulking when she tormented him—because she did intend to torment Simon to the limit. Haggerty raised his ham-sized fist, and Delilah shivered. She had to divert their attention.

Delilah's stomach contracted, and she muttered her thoughts: "I'm going to throw up."

Wells looked horrified. "Not on my boots, you're not. They're new."

She glared at him. "Then you'd better stop talking to that man. I can't stand him. Just the thought of him in the same room makes me sick. I've had to save him twice already. He's a petunia."

The two criminals regarded the tall man, unconscious and slumped against the wall.

Haggerty's snorting bawdy guffaws echoed in the cabin until Wells looked at him coolly.

When Delilah lay bound on the bed, Wells bent over her. She continued glaring at Simon's grim, beaten face. The cold light in Simon's single opened eye willed her to be silent as Wells was saying, "Bright blue eyes . . . I knew a boy with eyes like yours once."

He slid the stub of his finger across her lids, and Delilah fought the shudder caused by his touch. "I did this myself, to send the law sniffing after him. But it didn't work out." He smiled, a cold shifting of his expression without warmth. "We'll be back soon with your high-and-mighty friend, and then I'll begin teaching you what I like. The Mountie will see me enjoy you before he dies, sweetheart—Delilah, wasn't it? The name does suit you, my pretty."

Then Wells was gone in a burst of mad laughter. "I've done in two Mounties out of that bunch that ran me off the Whoop-Up. Two!" he crowed, slamming the door behind him.

"Simon?" Delilah whispered after the horses rode away. Her heart started beating again when he slowly lifted his head.

"You," he said quietly, as if the single word explained every dark deed that had come his way. "I thought I told you to be careful . . . to stay close to the house. Koby and I suspected an ambush, not a dammed creek. We weren't prepared for them capturing you."

"I won't be kept from my stock or my land. Perhaps *you* should have stayed near the house. Did they hurt Koby?"

"Badly," he said grimly, "but he's alive."

Simon looked at Delilah stretched out on the bed, her hands tied to the posts. "*Now* you choose to wear your new clothes. Fine time. They'll like tossing up those pretty petticoats."

He fought the fear clawing at him. A tear slid from Delilah's eye into her hair. "Oh, Simon . . . what have they done to you?"

"We had a discussion about water rights before we fell for that business about Wells's gang having you and Artissima. After that it was their game," Simon bit out, ignoring the painful meeting that had occurred after Wells found legal papers in his pocket. While Koby was unconscious, hanging from ropes lashed to a tree, Wells's men had turned their attention to Simon. He ached badly; two ribs were bruised from boot kicks administered while Wells methodically described how he had done the same to Rand.

Simon inhaled, damning his stupidity. He should have known that Wells was baiting a trap when he said he had Delilah.

He tested the practiced knots around his wrists, the rope slick with his blood. Delilah began to rock, side to side, pitting her strength against the bed. Her petticoats and skirts inched higher, revealing her long legs sheathed in black net and the blue garter. "So, you love me, then," he said, dismissing the pain of his swollen lip.

"Mmm?" Delilah was concentrating on freeing her hand, which was tied to the post over her head.

Simon pushed against the wall, inching his way to her on the hard-packed dirt floor. "You love me. You said it once. Say it again."

More than his life, he wanted her safe. Ordering her to say she loved him was a bandage on his fear. Delilah's bright blue eyes flashed with temper and frustration as she tugged at the ropes.

"You tell me what you were crocheting in that awful red thread, and I might consider telling you . . . something."

"I'll tell you when I'm ready. Stop that. You'll hurt yourself," he snapped, raising his mouth to her wrist.

"What are you doing?"

He bit into the rope binding her wrist, tugging at it.

"Why did you stop crocheting?" she asked while he loosened the rope with his teeth.

"Mmm. Do you have to choose now to interrogate me?" Simon asked impatiently. Then he said, "In case you haven't noticed, I've been making love to you in my spare time. My hands have been busy."

She thought about the truth of that and how Simon loved her whenever he could. "That's true. But when we're out of this, I demand to see that red thing."

"Women," he said in a disgusted tone.

"I love you, Simon," Delilah whispered quietly. "We're going to have a baby. We have to get free."

"Yes," he said grimly, spitting out the blood that had sprung into his battered lips.

"You know?" she said indignantly. "I'm telling you I love you and that we have a baby coming, and you know?" she asked in a hushed, furious voice. "How?"

Simon tugged the rope free, and Delilah quickly freed her other hand. "Because I love you. Just like I told you when you saved me that first time. I've never stopped loving you, you maddening little, infuriating—someday you'll learn to listen to me and to trust me. *I told you to stay near the cabin!*"

"Well . . ." She considered his admission while she freed her bound ankles. "How do you know the baby is coming?"

"Experience. Five brothers and sisters in the wild Oakes gang business. Hurry up."

"I had a majestic event planned. A quiet walk after dinner . . . then after you . . . well . . . after you discovered these stockings and the garter you love so much, I wanted to tell you at the right time. I really don't like my schedule disturbed."

Simon laughed outright, despite the pain to his jaw, and Delilah smiled before she offered, "I'll let you rescue me this time."

"That I will, dear heart, my love," he stated firmly. "You're my life, Delilah. Exasperating as you are, you're exactly what I've wanted forever."

The tip of his wife's tongue stopped foraging in his ear. "What about dear Amelia?"

"Who's that?"

Delilah bent to kiss his battered lip gently, her eyes shining. They kissed again, a sweet promise of warmth and joy, then she bent to free him.

Simon stood and reached to draw her to her feet, enclosing her in his arms and rocking her. "My love . . . I treasure you more than my life. . . ." he whispered, and realized that he was shaking badly. Delilah locked her arms around him and buried her damp face in his throat.

"I want our baby," she whispered slowly, unsteadily, quieting his last fear. "I'm so afraid."

She wondered when she had ever admitted the words, her fears, to another person. Simon was a part of her now, and she wanted to keep nothing from him.

"He'll be safe. You'll keep him safe." They kissed slowly, leisurely, then stopped, listening to the approaching horses. "Dear heart, would you mind lying back on the bed? Just for a minute or two, to divert Wells?"

Mordacai Wells's eyes bulged as he stared down at the pit of rattlesnakes. Suspended by a rope tied to his feet and running over the branch of a tree, Wells dangled over the pit while Simon lowered him an inch. "I'll do anything . . . sign anything . . . just let me go!"

Artissima, freed from her bonds, muttered, "Let the buzzard visit those snakes. My pies will be burned by this time, and I want to find Koby," she added, wiping away a tear. "I just wish I had my butcher knife here, Mr. Mordacai Wells. You need lessons in manners."

"He's not hurt!" Wells screamed wildly. "The métis isn't hurt bad!"

"Poor Koby," Artissima whispered, holding Delilah's hand. "I haven't even got him to the altar yet. Oh, I do love that man. Hurry up, Simon. I want to find Koby."

The sumac bushes rustled, and Koby stepped into the sunlight, looking lean and deadly, his hand resting on his gun. His eyes cut to Wells dangling over the snake pit, then to Artissima, raking her from head to toe, then to Simon and Delilah. "I'm late," he noted in his usual terse manner. "Artissima?" he asked, his expression stark with fear.

"They didn't hurt me. Oh, but you . . . Koby, they beat you!" Artissima cried, running into his arms. She started touching his face, inspecting it, and worked her way down to his trousers, where Koby's dark hand restrained her fingers.

"Enough," he said, grinning.

"They hurt you," Artissima said, drawing his face down to hers and kissing each bruise.

Koby grinned sheepishly, his hands on her waist, before he answered, "Yes . . . a little to the right . . . my mouth was hurt."

Artissima had locked her arms around him, and they kissed long and sweetly, ignoring the others.

Delilah leaned against Simon, her arm wrapped around his waist. She kissed the scar on his shoulder, the wound that Artissima had neatly closed. For the rest of her life, Delilah would see Wells's expression of surprise as Simon had descended on him, laying out the five men in a series of methodical blows.

She ran her open hand across her stomach, and Simon's green eyes left Wells to look deeply into hers. "Say it," he demanded arrogantly of her. "Say you love me and that you'll wait for me while I take this filth back for trial."

"I'm going with you."

"Oh, no, you're not. You're carrying our first wild Oakes baby. You'll rest and think about me and Richard coming home safely."

"Or?" She grinned up at him and met his tender kiss.

The rope slipped on the branch, lowering Wells an inch into the rocky pit of rattlesnakes. A hissing, vibrating sound like no other slid into the fresh air, that of giant rattlesnakes warning an intruder. Wells shrieked wildly. "I'll sign anything! Take me back to Canada! Let the judge have me!"

The first of September, Delilah sat in the sunlight, studied her primer, and practiced her letters while Artissima made green-apple pies.

Fall was settling in, the wind tumbling the bright leaves of the aspens and cooling the meadow at night.

She looked at the mountains, the sage and creosote bushes dotting the rocks and sand, and a fierce joy that everything was right poured into her.

Despite his injuries, Simon had left immediately with Mordacai Wells in tow. Soon he'd be coming home with Richard.

Delilah trusted Simon to come back to her. She carried—a baby—who he wanted very much.

Her tongue moistened her lips and tasted the sunshine on them. Simon's last kiss had been meant to last, reminding her of him. He was very thorough, though one eye was swollen shut and his lips were bruised. "I'll be back, dear heart," he'd said rawly, rocking her against him as she cried.

He'd given her that—an open, sunlit heart, ready to love and be loved. "Oh, Mama," Delilah whispered to the gentle wind easing against her clothing like a caress. "I'm so happy."

Artissima smiled at her and brought a freshly baked pie to the outdoor table. "You look pretty," she said, inspecting Delilah's smile, her loose hair, and the blue calico dress. "Any day Simon will bring Richard home, and we'll all be a family."

"Yes," Delilah answered, holding Artissima's hand. "We'll be a family again."

"Your mother must have been a special woman, honey . . . to make such good, sweet-hearted people. When I think of how you were—not that anything was wrong with you before Simon—but to see you with him. The love just shines out of you. That baby you're carrying will be wanted and loved, just like mine and Koby's."

Delilah inhaled, wishing Simon and Richard would ride over the low place in the mountains . . . wishing she could hold Simon and talk to him about their love and the baby. There had been no time before he took Wells to Canada and his justice. "I want him back home so much," she whispered urgently.

Artissima nodded. "When he's home, we'll have a big wedding and invite the countryside. My wedding dress should be finished any day, and when Simon gets back, Moose says we'll start a cabin-raising and everyone will help build it. Koby says we'll get married two ways. One that suits his Indian blood and one that suits me and his white blood. He's a romantic man, my Koby."

Koby rode toward them, coming from Loomis, where he'd just taken his broken wild horses. He swung down and scooped Artissima—who had been running to meet him—into his arms.

He smiled over her blond curls at Delilah, who marveled at the love passing between Koby and Artissima, and the changes in Koby as he prepared to be a husband and a father. His flashing, boyish grin was stunning and filled with delight. When Artissima responded heatedly to his teasing, Koby delighted in sweeping her off to stun her with a kiss. Now he handed Artissima a brown paper parcel, and she stood on tiptoe to kiss him. Her blond curls bounced as she opened the gift, her eyes widening as the paper fell to the ground and a ruffled pink satin parasol emerged. "Oh, Koby, honey—how I love it . . . how I love you!" Artissima cried, propping the parasol open and twirling it saucily as she swished her skirts in a quick dance around Koby's tall body.

Koby glanced shyly at Delilah, and a blush stole quickly up his dark cheeks before Artissima leaped into his arms. "Carry me someplace and kiss me, sugar," she demanded, twirling the parasol as he walked into the pines with her.

Delilah shook her head and turned her face to the sunlight. Aching for Simon, she placed her hand over the baby nestling in her womb and thought of how his green eyes had darkened as he rode away, making promises he would keep. He'd watched her until he'd turned in the saddle, straightened his shoulders, and tugged on the reins of Wells's horse. "Come back to me, my love," Delilah whispered to the sage-scented wind. "Come back safely, Simon."

Chapter
Twenty-Two

Delilah settled against the old rocker, drowsing in the warm sunny afternoon. She sighed, nestling her head back against the pillow Tallulah had placed there. The tickling continued at her nose after she wrinkled it.

She brushed her hand in front of her nose, only to find it caught in a bigger, stronger one. She opened her eyes to find Simon's warm green gaze. He dropped the red plumed headdress she had once worn into her lap, and picked her up in his arms for a long, hungry kiss.

"Simon!" she cried and clung to him, kissing him until his hat fell away, leaving his tousled red-brown curls to her seeking fingers. "Oh, Simon."

"Love," he whispered back, between kisses, and gathered her closer.

"Ah-hem . . ." Another man cleared his throat, and Delilah turned to see Richard—wearing a full black beard and looking like a devilish pirate—grinning at her. She hooked an arm around him and drew him close for a kiss.

Richard allowed the trespass before drawing away and looking embarrassed. "Hey, Sis . . . don't. . . . Simon is wearing his uniform, and it looks strange for men to be too close."

"Oh, come back here," she ordered, drawing him to her for another kiss. "Oh, Richard . . . Simon . . . is it really you? You're here . . . right here where you belong?"

"I certainly hope you don't greet every man this way, dear heart," Simon drawled as he lowered her to her feet and ripped away his gauntlet to place his open hand on her stomach. The sun gleamed on the red stubble covering his jaw as he kissed her nose and stroked her hair, holding her close against him. "How are you feeling, love?"

"Happy. Just happy," she returned, launching herself at him again.

He held her close, rocking her, and whispering what she had wanted to hear for three long, tense weeks. "I love you, dear heart. I do so love you, Delilah."

When she stroked Simon's cheek, she discovered it was damp.

She held him until the fear that he would move away had passed. When at last she stood away, she studied Simon, dressed in his scarlet uniform, trimmed in black and gold, and his black jodhpurs. He still held one gauntlet in his fist, and his new Hambletonian-cross horse bore a uniform saddle and blanket.

"You'd better look well, my love. Because I'm homeless now. I've left the force, my money is gone, and I'm a drifter once more," he stated unevenly, watching her warily.

She caught the gold sergeant's chevrons in her fist and asked huskily. "You spent everything trying to find Richard and save him, didn't you? You paid with your savings."

He tilted his head, and the dying sunlight caught the red in the irresistible wave by his ear and the red in his beard. "Not quite. I ordered that grand bed with the red satin quilt and paid the passage of a friend to come visit us."

Delilah leaned her cheek against his scarlet chest and toyed with the polished gold buttons. "Then if you're a drifter, I guess I'll have to rescue you."

That evening Delilah sat on Simon's lap, refusing to let him leave her as the homecoming spread into the early morning. Sometime in the wee hours she fell asleep, still clutching his chest. When she awoke, Simon was undressing her and the cabin was empty. "They're sleeping in the barn, my dear," he whispered raggedly as he unbuttoned her dress to smooth her stomach.

Simon rested his cheek against the delicate rounded shape. "I do love you," he managed roughly, then kissed his way to her breasts, which he studied just as intently. "Sore?"

"Aching," she said unevenly, wanting him to fill her.

They undressed each other with a sense of homecoming . . . of love and dreams and promises that would grow with each passing hour. They lingered in slow kisses and long, claiming caresses, easing away their clothes until Simon lowered Delilah to the bed. "There now," he said finally, laying his head on her breasts. "There."

She stroked his hair and his bare shoulders, tracing the endearing scars. "Thank you for bringing Richard home to me, Simon."

"Wells was hanged within a week of our arrival. Witnesses poured into the courtroom, and the judge found him guilty within two hours. Richard has been cleared of crimes, though he shouldn't go back for a few years." Then Simon bent to kiss her tender breasts, easing one, then the other deeply into his mouth.

"Now!" she almost cried as his fingers lingered in her damp warmth, stroking her until she tightened.

When he rose over her, solid and tender and loving, Delilah brought him home with a hungry kiss.

Simon placed the picnic basket under the pines and flicked out the blanket. He settled the patchwork quilt under the pines and began recklessly stripping off his boots and clothes.

Delilah ripped off a button as she hurriedly tore away the new dress he'd brought her. She tugged down her petticoats until she stood in the sunlight dressed in the repaired satin drawers, her black net stockings, and the blue wedding garter.

Simon's emerald eyes flashed in the sunlight as he studied her from head to foot. "We'd better be getting more time alone than we have had in the past two days," he threatened grimly, the sunlight stroking the set of his jaw, his tensed neck, and his broad shoulders. Suddenly shy of him, Delilah stepped onto the blanket and forced her eyes to keep above his waist.

"Hmm . . . you act as if you hadn't been welcomed home properly. I seem to remember having my skirts wadded up to my neck when I walked out to check on my cattle," Delilah teased. "I've been shoved into dark corners, lifted into haylofts, and bent over stalls. Although each time was quite gentle, if I must admit the truth of it."

"So you've drawn out your battle garb, have you? Your red drawers and those hideous black stockings." He lifted an eyebrow as his gaze swept down her long legs. "Then that nice little sweet touch, your wedding garter, to remember our vows—though we're going to repeat them next week with Artissima and Koby."

Delilah allowed her fingers to wander down his flat stomach, smoothing the tense muscles until she found him, hard and waiting.

Simon grinned boyishly, and she knew she would have a time controlling his wild brood. "You may have me, wife," Simon offered as his finger reached to trail around her full breasts.

"Really?" Delilah lifted her eyebrows innocently, her body tugging intimately in every place that Simon's finger drifted—to her navel, then to her other breast, and sliding down her ribs to her waist. It glided over the satin to stroke her intimately. Delilah arched against the touch, allowing her breasts to drag along the hair covering his chest. She closed her eyes, reveling in the crisp mat gently abrading her sensitive softness.

She opened her eyes to Simon's heated stare, his hands opening to caress her breasts, to cherish them. "It's true, then," he murmured in a tone filled with awe. "You're having my child."

His big palms cupped and caressed, and Simon's hair brushed her chest as he bent to kiss her body reverently. Delilah arched into his lips, her legs weakening. "Now," she whispered urgently against his ear, and bit it as her nails slowly, gently, scored his back.

The red satin bloomers ripped a second time and were tossed to the sumac bushes, frightening away a watching chipmunk. Simon smoothed her legs as he knelt and drew her down to him. "So you love me, eh?" he asked, grinning at her flushed face. "And as my heroine, you'll keep me—a worthless, penniless petunia—and bear my wild brood."

"Not if you keep talking, I won't," Delilah stated as she lay down on the blanket and drew him over her. When he rested, arms braced by her head, his eyes darkening, she whispered, "Because if you're wanting mercy today, Simon Oakes, you are sadly in the wrong place. Perhaps dear Amelia would listen to you asking for a rest, but I won't."

Simon's lips toyed with her bottom lip, then kissed a slow, tantalizing trail down to her breasts. There he suckled and played until she reached for him, crying out her need.

Passion caught them, thrust them high on a silky, golden pinnacle, before releasing them gently to the ground. Then Delilah lay over Simon, spreading herself on him and taking him again until he crooned with dark, sweet pleasure and gave her what she wanted.

When she slid back into herself, Delilah nuzzled Simon's damp throat and stroked his chest, propping herself on it. "What was that red thing you were crocheting?"

While he reached for his trousers and searched the pocket with one hand, Simon caressed her back and hips with the other. Lying beneath her, his hair tousled by her fingers, he looked like her future, her love, her eternity. Delilah nibbled on his lips until Simon groaned and eased her away. "Here," he said, dangling two tiny, tasseled baby booties in front of her.

"Oh, Simon," she managed unevenly, taking them and sitting up in the sunlight. Though they weren't long, the booties were precious. He stroked her thigh as she wiped away her tears. "It's all true, isn't it? We're a family and there is a baby coming. Oh, it's all too beautiful!"

"Shhh, my dear . . ." He nuzzled her stomach, kissing it. "If you keep after me, I'll be unmanned."

"Hah!" she sniffed, wiping her eyes and disbelieving that Simon could be anything but strong and certain and her beloved.

A year later Simon watched Delilah stroll across the pasture to him. The moonlight touched her hair and full breasts in silver, and her skirts swished around her ankles. He smiled, recognizing the determined lift of her head and that brisk walk.

She'd given the baby to Tallulah's care, and she'd set her mind to claim him, to drag him to her lair, and feast upon him. She'd purr and cry and take him and give him everything.

While he couldn't withstand the big blue eyes of their daughter, Martha Louise—Delilah was another matter. She'd be wearing her red bloomers and her black stockings and her wedding garter, and when she had him under her spell, she'd ask the question that he would answer tonight: "What's the red thing you were crocheting?"

He continued to gaze at the big silver moon rising over the Okanogan Mountains. Richard had set off, seeking his fortune in the whaling industry, and Koby and Artissima were snug in their new cabin.

Simon inhaled the fresh night air and watched a giant horned owl swoop against the moon as Delilah came to stand beside him. "Come along, dear heart," she whispered, sliding her hand through his arm. "You've got work to do tonight, and then you'll tell me what I want to know."

Simon wrapped his arm around her shoulders and drew her against him, rocking her as he loved to do. "Your bloomers won't stand another ripping, my love," he whispered, smiling into her fragrant hair and letting the silky tendrils slide along his freshly shaved jaw. He had learned to prepare for her onslaughts after damning himself for the abrasions to Delilah's creamy skin. "Are you certain you're healed enough for your dark plans?"

Martha Louise's birth had been frightening—so simple and quick that Delilah fretted something was wrong. Simon added to her distress by not shielding his tears. With black hair and blue eyes, Martha was a miniature of her mother and just as beguiling and cuddly.

"Ready? Simon, you've been hedging since Martha's birth. You're mine, Simon Oakes. You're my love and my heart and my life and you've given me a sweet, beautiful, blue-eyed daughter. Suppose we begin?"

This time when they made sweet hungry love, the satin bloomers were shredded beyond repair, but the red crocheted ones served even better. The matching shawl delighted Delilah and she posed provocatively in the moonlight, enchanting Simon. "Fitting garb for my heroine," he said, before she came to him.

In the morning Simon watched Delilah nurse Martha, the most beautiful sight he'd ever seen. His daughter curled her tiny fists into the air, waving them in protest as he lifted her away to rock her as Delilah buttoned her blouse.

His wife was shy of him this morning, and for good reason. He had plans for Delilah because he was certain she would be wearing her red crocheted bloomers. She smoothed her red shawl lovingly and sent him a look that drew him to her. Simon kissed her, savoring the intimate tenderness as Delilah whispered, "I do love you, Mr. Oakes," and he returned the pledge.

Moose wrinkled his nose and Tallulah frowned as a malodor wafted into the house. Delilah's eyebrows lifted, her magnificent blue eyes sparkling. "Claude and François! Oh, Simon, you've gotten them to come here. How wonderful!" she exclaimed, before she kissed him quickly.

He bent to receive her hurried kiss and propped Martha Louise to his shoulder for burping, which she did delicately.

Standing in the doorway to the cabin, he rocked Martha Louise and watched his wife stretch out her arms to hug the grizzled old camel driver. She turned to beam at Simon. "Oh, how I love you, my dear," Delilah whispered across the sage-scented wind.

AUTHOR'S NOTE

My thanks to Mr. Ben Cohls of the Okanogan Historical Society (Washington State), Shirlee Matheson of the Alberta Historical Society (Canada), Mr. John D. Spittle of British Columbia, and the wonderful people at restored Barkerville, British Columbia (Canada). I traveled the sandy, rocky "hills" of Loomis, Ruby, and Conconully. The research for this book entailed driving the entire scenic route. We began at the site of Fort Okanogan on the Columbia River (Washington State) and traveled the Okanogan Trail into Canada, which is the same trail used by Native Americans before the fur traders. This trail intersects in British Columbia with the Cariboo Wagon Road as it continues through soaring, majestic mountains and beautiful, rugged gorges. There are many historical sites and museums along the way and at the end is the wonderfully restored, gold rush–era Barkerville, which I fictionalized.

A surpreme thank-you goes to Rebecca Luft-Meadows, a special person, of KOZI Radio.

To the readers (and my editor, Hillary Cige) who encourage me, who enjoy sharing my love of sensual romance layered over history, and who have made all this possible for me, thank you so much.

C.L.